Cindy poked her head around a corner
— and froze.

Al was stark naked, combing his wet hair
with one hand and eating with the other.
Holding the blow-dryer was a little silver
statue; an odd sort of prop, but if it
worked —

Dear God, he's a hunk. Al still hadn't
noticed her; the noise of the blow-dryer
must have covered the sound of her
entrance. She felt like a peeping Tom.

Caught between embarrassment and an
undeniable attraction, she started to back
out — and ran into the corner of the
cabinet instead. "Excuse me!" she blurted,
as Al suddenly looked up into the mirror
and met her eyes.

She froze like a deer pinned in a car's
headlights. The little silver statue turned to
look calmly at her, still holding the blow-
dryer. The dryer cord dangled straight
down, and though the dryer was running,
it wasn't plugged in.

Unlike the statue's metal ones, the eyes
that met hers in the mirror were emerald
green and slitted like a cat's. The ears,
standing up through the wet hair, were
pointed.

WHEELS OF FIRE

A NOVEL OF THE SERRATED EDGE

MERCEDES LACKEY

MARK SHEPHERD

BAEN FANTASY

A Baen Books Original

Baen Publishing Enterprises
P.O. Box 1403
Riverdale, NY 10471

ISBN: 0-671-72138-0

Cover art by Larry Elmore

First Printing, October 1992

Printed in the United States of America

Distributed by Simon & Schuster
1230 Avenue of the Americas
New York, NY 10020

Dedicated, with love and gratitude to:

Mothers — ours and others —
Who believe, nurture, and forgive just
about anything

• CHAPTER ONE

Streamlined shapes of bright metal hurtled across asphalt, machines that roared, whined and howled, leaving hot air and deafness in their wake. They were without a doubt louder than any dragon Alinor had ever encountered. But instead of scales, these monsters were covered with flashy, bright endorsement decals for Goodyear, Penzoil—

And, since the sport of automotive racing was more expensive with every passing year, such other odd sponsors as pizza and soft drinks.

The cars were no longer just racing machines; now they were, in effect, lightning-fast billboards. While these machines used many of the products they hawked, Alinor could only marvel at some of the strange connections made between the sport of auto racing and the things humans consumed.

The decals flashing under the sun only emphasized the vehicles' speed; they moved too fast to be *seen*, much less read. As car after car flashed by Alinor's vantage point, he was left with a vague impression of shapes and vivid colors. Presumably commercials had imprinted those shapes and colors in the minds of humans vividly enough that there would be instant recognition.

Alinor marveled at the sheer *power* of these metal beasts. The only other creature that could approach those speeds was an elvensteed, and then only if one wore a car's metallic seeming.

Sun beat down upon the track, numbing the brain,

and Alinor yawned, pulling a red SERRA cap tighter over his head. Last night's final preps had taken more out of him than he had anticipated. Even for one of the Folk, two hours of sleep wasn't quite enough. He stretched a little and glanced at his watch; the team had been out here in the pits since just after dawn, and even the workaholics would be wanting to pull the car in and break before too long.

I hope, anyway, he thought, combating the sleepglue that formed on the inside of his eyelids. *That break better happen soon, or I'll fall on my nose.*

In spite of his fatigue, he had to grin a little as he looked around, contrasting himself with his surroundings. *Hallet Motor Speedway is not where you'd expect to find one of the Sidhe hanging out. Not even one who's a founding member of the South Eastern Road Racing Association. Strange days, indeed.*

Not that there weren't more elves and mages in the pits and driver's seats back in SERRA territory than anyone could ever have dreamed. Roughly a third had some connection with magic, and there were a few, like young Tannim, who were known for wandering feet. But for the most part, the elven drivers and mechanics of SERRA never left their home states and tracks, much less traveled to the wilds of Oklahoma.

Quaint little state, he had thought during the trip in, though "little" referred more to the size of the cities, not the square mileage of this new land. In many ways this was refreshing to one of the Sidhe, seeing so much wilderness with so few humans around to destroy it.

He hadn't had any trouble adjusting; so far as the natives and pit-crew were concerned, Alinor was just another mechanic. No weirder than most, since mechs were a breed unto themselves.

If for some reason I had to hide, this would be the place to come. There's no sign of Unseleighe Sidhe, and I haven't encountered anything hostile. I could set up a woodshop . . .

maybe become a raving Baptist out here in God's country; that would really *throw any pursuers off.* He shook his head, pushing the dismal mental picture away. *Eck. What a truly frightening thought.*

Some of the Folk, the Low Court elves, *couldn't* go too far outside the influence of their chosen power-nexus, and most of the rest were content with the many challenges on their home ground. But Alinor prided himself on the fact that he was not ordinary in any sense, even by SERRA standards; the only other elven mechanic that could match his skill was Deirdre Brighthair, and she couldn't challenge his mastery of metal-magics. Even Sam Kelly had been impressed by what he could do.

Of course, I am a few centuries her senior, give or take a few decades. And I've been a mage-smith for a long, long time.

He wished, though, that he could work some other kinds of magery; a little magic that would loosen Bob's tongue, for instance. Excessive conversation had never been one of the man's character defects, not for as long as Al had known him. He *knew* Bob was no idiot, that quite a bit must be going on in the young human's mind. The problem was that what actually came out appeared to be carefully edited or just doled out unwillingly and uttered with extreme caution. If Bob had said five words since dawn, Al would be surprised.

Their car banked around a corner and screamed past them, kicking up a brief bow-wave of hot, dry, exhaust-tinged wind, motor howling like a Bane-Sidhe. Then the beast of metal and gasoline dopplered away, swinging around for another lap.

"Hot," said Alinor, strolling the few paces away from the edge of the track to where Bob sat on an oil-drum, his red coverall immaculate, despite the hundreds of adjustments made on "their" engine since it first went out this morning. He leaned up against a tire-barrier and pulled his cap a little lower over his eyes, so that the brim met the top of his Ray-Bans.

"Eyah. It's that," Bob Ferrel replied, without taking his gray eyes off the track or the frown off his lean, weathered face.

Al sighed. Bob was in full laconic Maine-mode. *Like talking to a rock. Actually, I might get better conversation out of a rock.* "Nice track, though."

"Eyah."

Considering that this out-of-the-way track was a lush little gem, that was hardly an adequate reply. *When I know people who would kill to work here. . . .* "Guys back at Fayetteville would be green," he offered.

"Eyah."

All right, new tactic. See if he's at least listening to me. Alinor tried the path of absurdity to get something like conversation out of his human partner. "I heard they're going to bring in topless camel races next Saturday."

Now Bob finally turned his head, just barely enough to give Al a hairy eyeball, despite the glasses. "There's a ping in number three cylinder I don't like," he said sourly. "I want you to look at it when they bring it back in."

Blessed Danaa, you might have said something.

Alinor stiffened and instantly became all business. When Bob said he heard something, a SERRA mech listened to him. Bob, like young Maclyn's mother Deirdre, could tune an engine by ear. "I can look at it now," he offered.

"Do that," Bob said, tersely. "We've got a reputation riding on this."

Bob took that reputation a little more seriously than Al did; after all, a High Court elven-mage like Alinor could conjure anything he wished to out of the molecules of the air and earth around him, just by studying it long enough to "ken" it. Bob, when he wasn't partaking of elven hospitality, had a living to make. *The old-fashioned way,* he once joked, in a rare instance of humor. And Bob Ferrel had every intention of dying a wealthy man.

Not that I blame him, Al thought absently. *He's the kind that hates charity.*

The elven mechanic lounged back again, but this time every bit of his concentration was bent on the car careening its way back towards them. Or rather, his attention was bent on what was under the hood; a cast-aluminum engine block of elven make from the "shops" at Fayetteville, another one of the Fairgrove facilities. Al knew this particular block so well he could have duplicated it in an hour. He should; he had kenned it himself.

Not that he wanted anyone outside of a select company of SERRA members to know *that.*

He set his mind ranging inside the inferno of the howling motor, wincing away just a little from the few parts of iron (not so dangerous now, but still uncomfortable), winding his probe into cylinder three. He gave brief mental thanks to Tannim for teaching him those human mageries that made it possible for him to probe through and around Cold Iron at all.

In a moment, he had identified the problem. As the bright red car rounded the far turn, he corrected it with a brief surge of magical energies. He pulled his mind out of the engine and looked up as the car roared by the pits.

Bob was smiling as he pushed his own cap onto the back of his head.

"What was it?" the scrawny mechanic asked, running a hand over his sandy hair before replacing the cap.

"Not the cylinder at all," Al replied. "Piston arm."

"Ah." Bob relaxed still further. It hadn't been a failure of the block, and so he was content. Bob's design had been the one used as a prototype for this block, and he took design flaws personally.

Now I'll get some conversation out of him. . . . Al waited, and Bob remained happily silent, contemplating the track with a smile instead of a frown.

Al burst out laughing, and Bob favored him with a puzzled stare. "You're incredible!" he chuckled. "Anyone else would have been throttling me to find out *what* the problem was and *how* I fixed it, when you know damn good and well the arm's steel and you know we don't handle Cold Iron happily *or* well. But you, you just *stand* there, and say 'ah.'"

"You'd tell me when you got ready to," Bob replied, unbending just enough to give Al a "man, you're crazy" look.

Al shook his head. He was far too used to the volatile temperaments of his hot-blooded Southern compatriots. *Any mech from the Carolinas would have been foaming at the mouth by now and describing my parentage in terms my mother would take extreme exception to.* Not Bob. Not even close. This cold fish from the rocky coast of Maine was just as icy as the elven nordic-derived "cousins" who'd settled there. About the only thing that got Bob's goat around here was the area itself: landscape and the climate. Al thought the rolling hills were marvelous — and the heat was a nice change from the mountainous country of home. Occasionally the residual magic left over from the times when the Indians flourished here came in handy. Though — in fairness, he wouldn't want to *live* here for very long, even if it was a nice change.

Not Bob. He couldn't wait to get back to "where I don't bake and I don't have to look at so much damned sky."

"''E's pinin' for the fjords,'" he muttered.

"Eh?" said Bob.

"Never mind. I was just thinking you're a lot like the *liosalfar* that fostered you."

"Ah," said Bob, his icy gray eyes softening a great deal. "Good people, your cousins."

Al sighed. *Another typical understatement.* At the tender

age of eight, "Bobby" had been rescued by one of the *alfar* from freezing to death in a blizzard. He had been running away from a father who had nearly beaten him black for failing to come *immediately* when called. It wasn't the first time a beating had occurred, but it was the last.

Acting on a tip from a human, Gundar, Bobby's foster father to be, had put the house under snowy owl surveillance for several weeks, waiting, at times in agony, for the right moment to intervene. The beatings had become more severe with time, coinciding with an increased consumption of straight bourbon whiskey, chased with cheap grocery store beer. Even at that age, little Bobby could see the correlation between Daddy's "joy juice" and being beaten; when Father was on a roaring drunk, Bobby made himself scarce, which further angered the old man.

Granted, the father had been under a severe strain; the fish cannery, which was the town's sole employer, had just closed. Daddy must have suspected something going wrong with the company long before that, for the start of the layoffs had been when the drinking started as well.

Ultimately, though, Bobby neither knew the reasons nor cared about them. All he knew was that Dad was drinking, became a frightening, crazy man when he drank, and Mother was just as afraid of him as Bobby was.

In the end she stopped trying to protect him, instead fleeing for the shelter of her mother's house when Bobby's father became "turned on." That meant leaving Bobby alone with him, but perhaps she had trusted in the frail hope her husband wouldn't hurt his own child.

The end came on a bitter December night, when Joe Ferrel was at the end of his unemployment benefits, the cannery closed for good, and at the end of the month they'd be out of a home as well when the bank foreclosed on the mortgage —

But that's no excuse to half-kill your son, Al thought angrily, his blood still running hot at the memory, as would the blood of any of the Fair Folk at the idea of mistreating a child. *Good thing we got him out of there when we did. After the foreclosure, there was no telling what would have happened. . . . "Bobby" probably wouldn't have lived through it. How can they act like that? Treating their own offspring like possessions to be used and discarded at their pleasure —*

He forced himself to calm down; most humans loved their children, treated them as any elven parent would. And for those that didn't — well, there were other possibilities, not all within human society.

Like what had happened to Bob. Bob was grown up now, and safe — *had* been safe the moment Gundar found him. The situation had been perfect for a changeling-swap: take the boy and leave a lifeless, frozen simulacrum in his place. Easily done, and the exchange left no traces in the human world, for why run a tissue analysis on a frozen corpse when it was *obvious* why the "boy" had died?

And Bob found a new home with those who loved and cherished children, even those not of their species. A home where the rules were strict, but never arbitrary, and punishment was never meted out in anger. A place where intelligence was encouraged to flower, and where his childish delight in mechanical things was fostered, nurtured and educated, even if the *liosalfar* were sometimes baffled by the direction it took. Clockwork and fine metal-work they understood — but *cars?*

Still, he was given free rein, though he had been asked to keep his engines of Cold Iron somewhere where they wouldn't cause disruption to fields of magic, and physical pain to his foster relatives.

So things had continued, until as a young man, he eventually got a real job in the human world — for no human could live forever in the elven enclaves. Even Tam Lin had known that. The job had been at a human-owned garage whose proprietor knew about the *liosalfar* and approved of them, an American Indian of full Mohawk blood that considered them just another kind of forest spirit. Soon, thanks to native ability and understanding of physics and mechanics gained from his foster-kin, Bob became the resident automotive wizard.

Things might have rested there, but for Henry Winterhawk. He *could* have kept Bob ignorant of the existence of SERRA and reaped the benefits of having that kind of genius at his disposal. Instead, he asked Bob to bring his foster father in for a conference about his future.

Gundar knew all about SERRA, of course, but he had simply never thought of it as a place where Bob could fully realize his abilities. Winterhawk had been a little surprised that the elves knew about the organization, though — *he'd* thought the magic being practiced down there was entirely human in origin.

I wish I'd seen both their faces, Al thought with amusement. *The Great Stone Face meets Glacier-Cliff, and both of them crack with surprise. Must have been a sight.*

So now Bob was with the Fayetteville shop, and was helping Al baby-sit the first aluminum-block mage-built engine to go into entirely human hands, hands ignorant of its true origin. Keeping the secret under wraps had been a job in itself; more than once Bob had showed ingenuity in the area of creative deception.

Even if you had to pry conversation out of him with a forklift.

"Don't you ever ask questions?" the Sidhe asked, perplexed. "Not about cars, I mean, about us — *my* foster kids have been eaten up with questions every time they've run into a different group of the Folk."

Bob thawed a little more, and some of his true age of twenty showed through. "You don't mind? Gundar said not to be a pain in the ass, but you people are a *lot* different from the *alfar.*"

Al laughed aloud. "Hell, no, I don't mind. Not even close. In Outremer we're Scottish Celts, for the most part, both the human fosterlings and us, and you should know the Scots — if you won't tell us something on your own, we'll find it out. That's why Scots make such good engineers. I'm used to it. Ask away."

"How did you people ever get involved with racing?" Bob asked. "I know about the Flight; Gundar told me about that — but it seems damned weird to me for you people to leave Europe because of Cold Iron everywhere, then turn around and start racing and building cars."

Alinor chuckled. "Two reasons, really. First, we've *always* measured ourselves against you. I — don't suppose you've studied old ballads and stories, have you?"

Bob shook his head.

"Well if you had, you'd find a lot of them with the same theme — the elf-knight challenges a human to a duel, either of wits or of swords, the fight goes on for quite some time, the human wins and carries off some sort of prize. Usually gold, sometimes a lover." *Lost and won a few of those myself, before I got tired of the Game.* "We did that quite a bit, although needless to say, the times when the human *lost* were never recorded in ballads." Al eased the bill of his cap up with his thumb and gave Bob an ironic look over the rim of his sunglasses.

Bob smiled wryly. "What happened when the human lost?"

"Depends on what he — or she, believe it or not — looked like, what skills they had. Usually they had to serve us a year and a day, human-time. Some of the knightly types with big egos and small brains we taught a little humility to, making them act as servants. Generally we had them get us things we needed, news, new fashions — or we had them find the kids that were being mistreated and tell us who they were."

Bob's eyes brightened. "Then what?"

Al shrugged. "Depended on the circumstance. Worst case I ever heard of was a little German town with a real high birthrate. They'd had a witch-scare and killed off all the cats, so the rats had gotten so bad they started biting the kids in the cradles. We stepped in, then, and we got rid of the vermin. But that meant the Black Death missed them entirely."

"So?" Bob said. "Sounds like a good thing to me —"

"It would have been, except that they exported dyed and woven wool, worked silver and other metals, wine — luxury goods. But after the Death, there weren't as many people around to buy their exports. Prices dropped. Food was more expensive, without serfs to till the land. Things got bad. Half the youngsters in the place went around with welts and bruises."

"That sounds familiar —" Bob ventured.

Al snorted. *It should. It's even survived into this day and age.* "Place called Hammerlein. Hamlin, to the English."

Bob shot him a glance that said quite clearly that he thought Al was pulling his leg. Al shrugged. "Ask Gundar. His German cousin was the Piper. We ended up with so many fosterlings we had to spread them out over a dozen Underhill kingdoms."

"Sonuvabitch," Bob said thoughtfully. "Say, when you Folk went up against humans in combat — wasn't that a little one-sided?"

"We did have a bit of an edge where armor and practice was concerned," Al admitted. "But when it came to a duel of swords, humans had an edge too, in that *they* were fighting with Cold Iron." Al smiled reminiscently. *I can still remember the thrill of evading an edge by the width of a hair.* . . . "Put a kind of savor to it, coming that close to the Death Metal. Well, dueling and challenging people at crossroads went out of fashion for the humans, partially because knights were like Porsches — expensive to maintain."

Bob laughed. "Eyah. You don't risk a Porsche on a back-country county-fair drag-race."

Al nodded. "That was when some of us moved. For a while we played at other things, but the Church was making it hard for us to stay hidden, and it just wasn't the same — and besides, there was more Cold Iron around with every passing year. So, in the end, almost all of us moved."

"The Flight." Bob cocked his head to one side and wiped a trickle of sweat from his neck. "Then what?"

"We 'rusticated,' as my father is fond of saying." Al sighed. In many ways, those days had been halcyon, if a little boring now and again. "Then the Europeans followed us across the sea, and rather than compete with them, we went into seclusion, at least on the East Coast. Found places we weren't likely to be bothered. Eventually we set about recreating the Courts in the wilderness." He looked out over the heat-hazed countryside. "For a long time, this was enough of a challenge. It was like starting over, and for the Indians that lived out here already, well, we fit right into their beliefs. No problem. Before the horses came up from Mexico, our elvensteeds would counterfeit deer, bear, or anything else big enough to carry us; it didn't matter that deer and bear *wouldn't* take riders. After all, we were spirits, and our spirit-animal-brothers would do things no ordinary animal would do. For some reason, perhaps that they were closer to natural power than any white man we knew in Europe, picking fights with them just wasn't any fun. It didn't feel right. So we cohabitated, in harmony, for a couple centuries."

Bob gazed at him thoughtfully. Though the human

didn't say anything, Al knew the keen mind was absorbing everything he said. The young man was quite interested — probably because he'd only heard the *alfar* side of the story. The nordic elves never moved from their chosen homes; instead, they had created places where humans passed through without noticing where they were — places that weren't quite in the "real" world, but weren't quite Underhill either.

"Then the Europeans caught up with us. At first we sympathized with them, these settlers who were trying to make homes with next to nothing, and certainly no *magic*, in the wilderness. We had done it ourselves, so we knew it wasn't easy. But with them came Cold Iron, so we had to keep our distance from them. When their settlements came too close to our groves, we played tricks on them, appearing to them as demons in order to frighten them away."

Al saw the hint of what might be the edge of a wry grin of amusement. Like a shadow drowned with sudden light, the hint of a smile faded, replaced with Bob's familiar unreadable expression.

"For a while that kept us entertained. Until they started throwing knives and shooting at us . . . which put an end to *that* silliness. Especially since a lot of their weapons used steel shot as well as lead."

"I can see that," Bob commented. "I'd say Cold Iron in that form would ruin any elf's day — and you people aren't immune to a lead bullet if it's placed right."

Al nodded. "All we could do then was avoid all humans. The Indians were slaughtered, absorbed into the white population, or relocated, so we lost our allies there. As more humans invaded the areas we once inhabited, those Low Court elves unfortunate enough to have located their groves near human cities had serious trouble. The rest of us transported our magic nexuses and Low Court cousins to places even the humans wouldn't want. Isolation, and seclusion, became necessary for us once again. And, once again, we were *bored* silly."

"Bored?" Bob said. "Eyah, I can see that. Live long enough, you do about everything there is to do."

"A hundred times. And get almighty tired of the same faces," Al agreed. "Now the story gets local, though. A few human lifetimes after that, we started seeing those new-fangled horseless carriages around Outremer. And people were *challenging* each other with them." He sighed, remembering his very first look at a moonshiner-turned-race-car, the excitement he'd felt. "Well, what they were doing — races along deserted country roads or on homemade tracks — that was just like the old challenge-at-the-crossroad game, only better, because it was not only involving the skill and wits of the *driver,* it involved the skill and wits of the craftsman. There's only so much you can do to improve armor past a point of refinement, but an *engine* — now, there's another story."

Bob's attention wandered for a moment as their car roared past, then came back to Al. "So you lot began racing? Fairgrove, Outremer, Sunrising, that bunch?"

Al nodded. "I was all for it from the beginning; I was a smith, and I hadn't had anything to do but make pretty toys for, oh, a couple of centuries. Some of the rest wanted to use elvensteeds shape-changed, but the fighters really squashed that idea."

"Wouldn't be fair," Bob said emphatically. "Elven-steed damn near breaks Mach one if it's streamlined enough."

"Exactly. We wanted a challenge, not a diversion. So, we started making copies of cars from materials we *could* handle, learning by trial and error how to strengthen them, and copying *your* technology when it got ahead of ours." Al sent a probe toward the car, but the engine was behaving itself, and he withdrew in satisfaction.

"You wouldn't have dared let people get too close, early on, though," Bob observed. "One look under the hood, and you'd have blown it. So that's why you stuck to club racing?"

Al nodded, with a little regret. "We still don't dare take too much out of the club." He sighed. "Much as I'd love to pit the Fayetteville crews against the Elliot team, or the Unser or Andretti families, or — well, you've got the picture. Best we can do, Bob, is send you fosterlings out there and take our triumphs vicariously."

"You're here," Bob pointed out.

"I'm one of a few that can be out here," he said soberly. "Lots of the Folk can't even be around the amount of iron that's at the Fairgrove complex, much less what's in the real world. I can, though it's actually easier to handle Cold Iron magically when it's heated. That's why I try and do my modifications while the car's running. Cold Iron poisons us, but like any poison, you can build up a tolerance to it, if you work at it. I worked at it. I still have to wear gloves, and it still gives me feedback through my magic to have to 'touch' it, though. And I'd have third-degree burns if I handled it bare-skinned."

Al held up his gloved hands; the Firestone crew thought he had a petroleum allergy. That was a useful concept, since it would explain away blisters if he accidentally came into contact with the Death Metal.

"We could get only so close to the real cars in the beginning," he added. "When the manufacturers began using alternative materials — like fiberglass bodies, carbon fiber, aluminum parts — it became that much easier. Some humans despise the concept of the 'plastic car.' We've been encouraging it for decades!"

"Eyah," Bob said, laconically. "Never could stand disposable cars myself. I always thought a car should last at least twenty-five years. The next time I see a plastic car I'll think differently of it."

Al gloated a little over the "triumph" of getting Bob to speak, with a certain wry irony. *That was actually a stimulating conversation.*

But the respite was brief. The spark of conversation dimmed, and their attentions turned to the track, the team — the unrelenting heat, the hammer of the sun, the fatigue setting over even the best-rested of them. Weariness began to settle in around him again, this time with a vengeance. *How many laps were they going to pull in that car today?* he thought, now with some irritability. *The RV sounds mighty inviting right now.*

He smiled a little at the idea of a Sidhe regarding such a vehicle as a *shelter.* He recalled the time he told Gundar about the RV, the human-made Winnie that was sheathed with the Death Metal. It took some convincing before Gundar finally believed one of the Folk could live in such a thing; Al's friend had yet to build up a tolerance to Cold Iron and shied away.

Al sat down on a stack of chalkmarked tires, a few feet away from Bob. He needed to keep his distance — not from Bob, but from the rest of the team. The Folk had a high degree of sensitivity to energies not usually discernible by humans. Since Al worked closely with humans, his shields had to be much, much better than any of the Folk who never ventured out of Underhill. He had learned when a youngster that he was unusually sensitive to human emotions. His shields had required some specialized engineering to filter out the more intense or negative feelings generated by many humans in order to be able to work around them. Even Bob had caused him a few problems. He didn't have to think about the shields much anymore; the whole process of maintaining them was pretty much second-nature. The only time he remembered the network was there was when an intense emotion somehow managed to breach it.

Like — now.

Now what? Al thought, becoming aware of a nagging feeling of someone in distress, somewhere outside his shields. He reached inside his overalls and withdrew a small package of Keeblers and starting munching absently, his thoughts drifting beyond his immediate world, seeking the source of emotion. The cookie things helped him concentrate, though he wasn't sure why. Maybe it was all the sugar.

He bit the head off an annoyingly cheerful vanilla figure and considered: *Something strong enough to leak through my defenses must be hot stuff. Where is it coming from?* He glanced over at Bob, who was apparently studying an interesting oil stain on the track.

No. It's not him.

Focusing on a broader area, Alinor *reached*, touching the members of the immediate crew. Their emotions paralleled the way he was feeling right now: exhaustion and the heartfelt desire to start stacking a few Z's, coupled with a subtle anxiety over their delicate, powerful creation hurtling its human driver around the track. That wasn't what he wanted. Nothing they were feeling would be strong enough to penetrate the shields.

Too low level. Boy, someone is really hurting *out there. Where is he? Or . . . she?*

Now Al felt a definite female flavor to the emotion, though it was overwhelmed by sheer asexual anxiety. *Ah. A clue. That should narrow the field.* He knew it was barely possible this meant there was some danger at the track, perhaps even a serious problem with one of the cars.

There's always worry, but this is close to hysteria, and we don't need that right now, he thought, regarding the other racing teams around him. There didn't seem to be anything urgent going on, though some of the teams were noticably restless, probably from being out here for so long.

Don't blame them, Al thought, his search distracted for a moment. *I'm ready to go in, too.*

Although the world of racing remained male-dominated even to this day, a fair number of women were on the teams. But none of *them* were particularly upset about anything.

Wives? The few who came to the competition at Hallet were not around today. During test lap days there just weren't that many spectators, either local natives or those cheering the teams.

Odd. He thought. *Maybe I'm looking in the wrong place. Who said the source had to be on the track?* A barbed wire fence surrounded the entire track, forming a feeble barrier between Hallet and the surrounding Oklahoma territory. Immediately behind them, about a quarter of a mile away, was an ancient homestead, little more refined than a log cabin, that appeared to be as old as the proverbial hills. *There, perhaps?* Intrigued, Al reached toward it, diverting his dwindling supply of energy towards the house. Immediately his senses were assaulted by —

A bedroom overflowing with fevered physical activity — brass bedposts pounding like jackhammers against slatted-wood walls pitted and dented by repeated sessions in the warm afternoons and evenings. . . .

Alinor staggered mentally backward as he recoiled from the emotional violence he had inadvertently witnessed, the steamy interplay in the farmer's bedroom. *Whoops! Lots of intense emotion there, but not quite the kind I was looking for*. He felt as if he had been drenched in a scalding shower, and put up every shield he had to protect himself for a moment.

Bob made no comment.

By degrees his mind gradually recovered from the thorough scorching it had received, and in about fifteen minutes Alinor was able to gather energies around him again, retrieving his scattered pieces of empathy from around the track.

He pulled his act together, took a deep breath and

probed again. He sent his thoughts out over a wide area, hoping to pick up the source this way, a method that had proven effective before. The lethargic feelings of the pit crew were again a distraction, especially since they so nearly mirrored his own. *Echo effect*, he thought, shaking his head. *Tends to block what I'm really looking for. Maybe if I got some rest, came after this with a fresh set of eyes . . .*

The moment he considered this, a blast of emotion pierced his reassembled shields once again.

This time he was ready for it; on it as soon as it penetrated. Yes, it was definitely from a female. Now he could sense some other things. The woman was a mother. Images, riding the current of the high emotion, overwhelmed him with a deep sense of loss. But not a permanent loss — the kind caused by a death or irrevocable separation. *She must be looking for something*, Al decided, wishing his powers would provide him a clearer picture. *Or someone.*

Then as if a warm, stiff breeze had blown over his mind, the final image came into focus. Al leaped to his feet, now in a fully alert, combat-ready stance, even though there was nothing here to fight.

She's looking for her child. *And she thinks he's in danger.*

● CHAPTER TWO

A blistering wind dried the tears burning Cindy Chase's face as she stared at the race cars surging across the black, twisting track. She leaned against a tree in a poor parody of comfort. The oak bark pressed uncomfortably through her blue cotton blouse and into her weary muscles. This tree was the only place she had found that was even remotely cool. Her forearms, normally not exposed to the sun, were pink, probably burned worse than they looked. This served only to make her more miserable. It had never seemed this hot in Atlanta.

The heat was only one component of her misery. She'd have gladly traded her long, well-worn jeans for a pair of shorts. *Maybe even a miniskirt*, she thought in an attempt to cheer herself. *Then maybe the men would pay a little more attention than they have been.* She had never felt so totally worthless in all her life.

She'd had less than "no" luck since she'd entered the gates of Hallet raceway. Everything she'd tried had come out wrong. It seemed like the people she'd spoken with thought she was asking them for money, not help. Then again, in her rumpled clothing, washed and never ironed, and not her best, she probably looked like a homeless panhandler, or even a drunk. She had never lived out of a suitcase before and had never realized how difficult that could be. For too long she'd taken for granted things like a fully stocked bathroom, an ironing board, walk-in closets filled with clean clothes . . .

. . . and a family.

Cindy hadn't seen her reflection in a few hours, which was just as well. She knew she probably looked like hell. Her makeup had long ago melted in the heat — if she hadn't washed it away with crying.

Maybe I should go back to the car, she thought dismally, trying not to look at the little color snapshot of her son, Jamie, she clutched in her hand. *Nobody here wants to help me. Nobody cares, and they don't even look surprised! It's like little eight-year-old boys disappear all the time in Oklahoma.* She wasn't normally a vengeful person, but she couldn't help wishing some of these snots would get a taste of what it was like to have a child kidnaped by an ex-spouse and dragged halfway across the country.

Reluctantly, her eyes were drawn to the picture. The lower right-hand corner was wearing away where she had been holding it constantly for the past week. The other corners were folded and fraying. For a week a thousand pairs of eyes had stared at this picture, with varying degrees of interest, or more often, disinterest. A thousand minds had searched memories for a few moments. One by one, they had sadly — or indifferently — shaken their heads: *No, I haven't seen him. Is he your son? Have you tried the police? Are you sure he didn't just wander off?* It was as if they were all thinking: *Daddies don't kidnap their own children. It just doesn't happen. It's just too horrible to imagine.* She wanted to strangle them all.

Yes, I know. Daddies aren't supposed to kidnap their children, take them across the state line, and hide them from their mothers.

But sometimes, they do.

She had carefully mopped up a tear that had splashed on the picture, leaving behind a barely noticeable spot on the photograph's surface. It was a school portrait taken a year before at Morgan Woods Elementary, when Jamie's hair had been much shorter and their lives were much different; normal, almost. *Before his father joined the cult, anyway. The Chosen Ones. Chosen for what?*

Staring from the picture, Jamie's eyes locked on to hers, pleading, and she knew that she wouldn't be leaving the track just then. She had to keep looking now, on this broiling racetrack, just a little bit longer. As long as there were people to ask on this planet, she'd continue the search.

Oh, Jamie, damn it, she thought, crying inside. *Why did your daddy do this to us?*

A car roared past on the track, jolting her from the quicksand of self-pity she was suffocating herself with. The race reminded her why she had come to this place to look for her son. *In Georgia we used to come to places like these, a racetrack, any racetrack, no matter how small. He loved them all, unknown or famous. It didn't matter if it was paved, or a dirt track where they banged into each other until only one was left running.*

James, senior, had been burdened with many addictions, the one most harmless being race cars. Every weekend, no matter what the weather was like, he would trudge to the races with family in tow; Jamie, too, seemed to have inherited his father's obsession. Cindy had resented the incessant trips to the races, the constant shouting over the engines, the near incoherent babble of car techese he shared with his son. "Car racing is a *science*," he had said, over and over, in the face of her too-obvious disinterest. "And a racer is a *scientist*."

"So was Dr. Jekyll," Cindy had retorted, failing then to see the eerie foreshadowing of her words. Though at the time she grew weary of the races, she now dreamed of those days and the unity of their family then. *It was a family Donna Reed would have been jealous of. At least that was what I thought. I never looked under the surface of things, never asked questions; just mopped the floors and made the beds and kept everyone fed and happy*, she thought miserably. *And it was all a lie. I'll be lucky if I ever find my son.*

*   *   *

She'd seen signs of danger, but she was hard-pressed to remember when exactly they had begun. James' drinking, for instance, had increased so gradually that she hadn't even noticed it.

Or, she realized in retrospect, she had chosen *not* to notice.

Then had come the mysterious "bowling tournaments" that took all night, from which James would return with a crazed expression — and a strong odor of Wild Turkey — babbling about bizarre, mystical stuff, a combination of Holy Roller and New Age crystal-crunching. At first she thought the obvious: that he was seeing another woman. Which didn't explain his *increased* sex drive, something he would demonstrate immediately on his return.

That was when she realized something was wrong, but didn't want to admit it. In the beginning she was more afraid of what was going on with him than angry — afraid of the unknown.

The man who James became was not remotely like the man she had married. His behavior just didn't fit into any of her reality scenarios. It was all just too *weird* to understand. The strange books he wouldn't let her see, the things he rattled on about when he came home drunk — it didn't fit any pattern she was familiar with, nothing she'd seen on Sally or Oprah, either.

She gave up on her friends and neighbors when they all carried on about what a good provider James was, and how she should be grateful and turn a blind eye to his "little failings." "Women endure," said her nearest neighbor, who looked like a fifties TV-Mom in apron, pearl earrings and page-boy haircut. "That's what we're put on earth to do."

As things worsened, she lived one day at a time and tried not to think at all. Her son saw that his daddy was not acting normally. She kept thinking it was a phase, like the model-building phase, or the comic-collecting phase. He'd get tired of it and go back to cars, like he always did.

Then came the call from his employer, the owner of an auto parts franchise. James had worked for him as parts counter manager for ten years. That counter had been their version of a wishing well — it was the place where they had met. She had been buying wiper blades, and he'd shown her how to put them on. Fred Hammond, his boss, was calling to see if James had recovered from the surgery, and if so when he would return to work. The place was a shambles; he was sorely missed there.

She had no idea what he was talking about.

Fred explained, in a somewhat mystified tone, that James had taken a leave of absence from his job to go into the hospital for "serious surgery" of an unknown nature. Fred had gone to the hospital the day after the surgery was supposed to take place and, when checking with the information desk, found no record of James' stay, even under every imaginable spelling of "James Chase."

But Cindy knew that James had gotten up at the usual time and, wearing the store's uniform, supposedly went off to work in the pickup. Cindy apologized and said she couldn't imagine what was going on, but she would have him call as soon as possible. She hung up and stared at the telephone for a long, long time.

She remembered that day vividly, and she would always call it "That Day." It was the day her life changed, irrevocably. During a single moment of "That Day" the thin, tenuous walls of denial had crumbled like tissue. It was the day she realized that her husband had gone completely insane. Jamie was in the backyard when his father returned that night, and for a desperate second she considered sending him to a friend's house in anticipation of a major fight. She decided not to. *I don't know that anything is wrong*, she thought, clinging to the last, disappearing threads of hope. *It could be something like in a movie, could just be a mistake, a misunderstanding. Maybe it was even a crank call....*

He had pulled into the garage, as usual, and he came into the kitchen still wearing the uniform shirt with "James" embroidered over the left pocket. He even complained about what a bad day he'd had at the store, something about an inventory of spark plugs that just didn't jive.

She quickly pulled herself together and gently, like a mother, put her hands on his shoulders and kissed him, once. Her expression must have been strained, she would later think, since a cloud of suspicion darkened his face. He also smelled, no, *stank*, of alcohol, though his motions didn't betray intoxication. He fixed her with a raised eyebrow as Cindy blurted out, "I got a call from your boss today."

"Oh?" he said nonchalantly, as he reached for a beer in the fridge. "What did he want?"

Damn you, James, she thought violently. *You're going to make this as difficult as possible, aren't you?* "He wanted to know how the surgery went." She stepped closer, trying to be confrontational, knowing that she was failing. "Actually, I would too. What is he talking about, Jim?"

He said nothing as he started for the dining nook, paused, and retrieved another beer before planting himself firmly in his usual spot at the kitchen table. Timidly, Cindy sat next to him, touching his arm. He pulled away, as if her hand were something distasteful. They sat in silence for several moments, enough time for James to take a few long pulls of beer, as if to bolster his courage.

"I've found the glory of God," he said, and belched at a volume only beer could produce.

"I see," Cindy had replied, though she really didn't. "I thought you were an atheist."

"Not anymore," he said, taking another long drink. "I've seen the light, and the wisdom, of our leader. I haven't been at the store, in, oh, two, three weeks."

"Just like that," she said, starting to get angry. " 'I haven't been to the store.' " She couldn't believe it. "So what am I supposed to do now, throw a party? You haven't been to work and that's okay. Am I hearing this right?"

A serene, smug expression creased the intoxicated features. "I didn't say I haven't been going to work. I have been blessed with new work. I work for God now, and we will be provided for."

As if punctuating the sentence, he crumpled the empty can into a little ball, as if it were paper, and expertly tossed it into the kitchen trash, which was overflowing with the crushed cans. Cindy remembered thinking that he crushed his cans like that so that he wouldn't have to empty the trash so often.

Outside, Jamie had climbed into his treehouse, taking potshots at imaginary soldiers with his plastic rifle.

"Come with me tonight," Jim had said suddenly. She jumped at the suddenness and the fierce intensity of his words. He gripped her arm, hard, until it hurt. "Come and meet Brother Joseph at the Praise Meeting tonight. Please. You'll understand everything, then."

Reluctantly, she had nodded. Then she got up and began preparing dinner for that night.

"Jamie is coming, too," he amended. She had wanted to object then, but saw no way she could get a babysitter on such short notice.

"Okay, Jim," she'd said, pulling a strainer down out of the cabinet. "Whatever you say."

For now, she had thought to herself. *Until I get a handle on this insanity. Then watch out.*

Now she regretted not paying more attention to the particular brand of psychosis preached that night by

Brother Joseph, the leader of the Sacred Heart of the Chosen Ones. Jamie stayed close to her the entire time, apparently sensing something wrong with the situation. They drove for hours, it seemed, far out into the country. James again said little, commenting only on this or that along the road, chewing on his own teeth, biding time. As they came closer to the place of the Praise Meeting, Jim became less talkative. A fog thicker than the alcohol had descended on him, and he stared blankly ahead. Cindy wondered if he wasn't insane but just *brainwashed,* like in a TV movie. That was something that could be reversed, she hoped, and the more she thought about it, the more the brainwashing theory began to make sense. But it made her even more afraid of what was to come; she wished then that she hadn't allowed Jamie along.

The little boy had inched closer to his mother in the front seat of the pickup truck. They had turned onto a dirt road and were immediately confronted by two armed men blocking their way. They were wearing berets and camouflage fatigues; their white t-shirts had a heart pierced by two crucifixes, with some slogan in Latin she couldn't translate. Even with the berets, she could tell they had been shaved bald. They brandished AK-47 machine guns; she knew about the guns from a Clint Eastwood movie she'd seen about the Grenada invasion. The weapon had a distinctive look; banana clips curled from under the stocks. Jim stopped briefly as the men shone blinding flashlights into the truck and quickly inspected the bed, which was empty. With maybe half a dozen words exchanged, the guards had waved them through.

"Those were machine guns, Jim," she'd observed, trying to sound casual and not betray the cold fear that had been clenching her stomach. "Are they legal in this state?"

"You're in God's state now."

Jim said nothing more as they drove on.

Cindy had closed her eyes, wondering what the blazes she was getting into.

Finally the truck slowed, and she had opened her eyes. Ahead of them, at the top of a hill, she'd seen a huge mansion, fully lit, with rows of cars and trucks, mostly pickups, parked in front. More men in berets directed them with metal flashlights the size of baseball bats, and one led them to a parking spot. When they got out, Cindy noticed a .45 automatic holstered at his side.

"Brother Jim! Praise the Lord! You've brought your family into the blessing of the Heart, God bless," the soldier had greeted, slapping Jim hard on his back. Jim mumbled something Cindy couldn't hear, but whatever it was the clownlike grin on the man's face didn't waver.

"Momma, I don't want to go," Jamie'd said plaintively, pulling back, lagging behind. "They got guns, Momma, ever'where. They're *real* guns, aren't they?"

"It's all right, hon," Cindy'd said, knowing it was a lie. It felt like she was pulling the words out with pliers, and all the time she had been thinking, *Please God or whatever you are, let us get through this nonsense intact!*

The main sitting room of the huge mansion had been converted into a churchlike sanctuary. Cigarette smoke hung heavily in the air, amid a low rumble of voices. Jim had led them to some empty metal folding chairs on the end of a row, near a wall. There were hundreds of people there; as she glanced around at those nearest, she found an amazing number of them to be normal country folk, many of them elderly couples. Towards the front of the assembly there was an entire section of middle-class yuppies, some drinking designer-bottled spring water. And over to the side she saw what looked like homeless people, dirty, grubby, lugging ragged backpacks. Drinking out of paper bags. Salt of the Earth.

This guy has all kinds, Cindy remembered thinking, as they awkwardly made their way to the end of the row. *What is it about him that could make him so appealing to these people? These transients over here, they probably have nowhere else to go. But those guys, up in the front. They look like they just walked off Wall Street. What gives?*

More soldiers stood at attention here, thin, lean men in berets, bald like the guards at the gate. Spaced from each other like stone carvings, about twelve feet apart, they watched those around them with their hands behind their backs. Solemn. Unyielding. At the end of their row was a young man, about eighteen, who still had his short, blond hair. He looked like he had been pumping iron since he was eight. Tattooed clumsily on his forearm was a crooked swastika, the kind of artwork kids did to themselves out of boredom, with needles and ball pen ink. He gazed forward icily, solidly, as if cast in steel, looking like he hadn't blinked in a year.

I don't like this. I don't like this at all, Cindy had thought, holding Jamie closer. *And it hasn't even started. This has been one big mistake. I can handle this madness myself, but I should never have brought Jamie into this nest of snakes!*

"James," she'd whispered urgently, tugging at his arm. "I want to leave. Right now! These people are *crazy!*"

"Just relax," Jim had said, yawning. "It will be so much better if you just relax. You haven't even heard what you came to hear. It really does fall into placc. It becomes very clear, once you hear Brother Joseph speak."

At some point during her husband's little rote speech her eyes fell on the stage, and the large emblem on the wall behind it, lit from beneath by candlelight. It was a heart pierced by two crucifixes, the same symbol worn on the shirts of the soldiers around them, and was like no church decoration she had ever seen. It had looked like the kind of "art" that was airbrushed on black velvet and sold at flea markets. Totally tacky.

A hush fell on the crowd and the lights dimmed, ever so subtly. Large, silver collection plates the size of hubcaps were passed around, supervised by the armed men in berets. When one came their way James dropped a crisp, new one hundred dollar bill into the till — one among the dozens there already.

"Jim! What are you *doing*?" she'd gasped, when she saw the money drop. The plate had already passed her, she had realized in frustration, or she would have surreptitiously salvaged it as it went past. Jim said nothing, smiling blandly as the plate continued down the row. People were dropping large bills, multiple bills, watches, jewelry; she watched, stupefied, as the wealth amassed. She sat back in the creaking metal chair and folded her arms, in a mild state of shock. *We don't have that kind of money to give to a bunch of lunatics! Have they drugged him, or is he just suddenly retarded?*

"Only tithing members of the Sacred Heart will be saved. Is this your first meeting?" an elderly woman behind her had asked. Cindy made a point of ignoring her, and the woman sniffed loudly in rebuttal.

"Touchy, isn't she?" the women said behind her.

James laughed in a goofy snort. At what, Cindy had no idea.

Beside her, Jamie whimpered. "Momma, I want to go home," he said. "This place feels icky."

"It feels icky to me, too," she'd whispered in his right ear. "It will be over with soon."

"Hey, what's wrong, buckaroo?" the blond kid said, kneeling down next to Jamie. "This your first time here?"

It's his first and his last, she wanted to scream, but as the boy kneeled down, she noticed the assault rifle strapped to his back. She didn't want to argue with firearms. Jamie's sudden receptiveness to the boy didn't help either. Her son traced a figure eight over the crude swastika on the boy's forearm, apparently fascinated by it.

"It doesn't come off," Jamie said. "What is it?"

"It's a tattoo," the boy said, sounding friendly in spite of the weird trappings. "And it's our salvation." He looked up, meeting Cindy's stare with his soft, blue eyes, a disarming expression that somehow took the edge off the evil she was beginning to feel from him. He smiled at Cindy boyishly, and from his back pocket he pulled out a Tootsie Pop and gave it to Jamie, who attacked and devoured it hungrily. *He's almost normal — at least on the surface. But he has Nazi crosses tattooed on his arm and calls them "salvation." A boy Jamie could look like someday,* she thought, in agony. *Why did I have to bring him to this godawful place!*

The lights dimmed further, and from somewhere appeared the minister of the church. *Brother Joseph, didn't Jim say?* No less than four armed soldiers escorted him to the podium, knelt, and when Brother Joseph dismissed them, took their places at the four corners of the stage, glaring at the audience. The quiet was absolute. Brother Joseph had peered into the audience, his burning eyes sweeping the crowd like the twin mouths of a double-barreled shotgun. In the utter stillness, his eyes tracked through the different faces and settled on Cindy. He smiled briefly then, and continued his inspection, lord of all he surveyed. Cindy had thought she was going to collapse when their eyes locked.

Jesus! Cindy thought in dismay. *Those eyes.*

He really thinks he's God's own Gift. And my crazy husband believes him.

"Momma," Jamie whispered. "Can I have a tattoo like his when we get home?"

"Shhhhhh!" the woman behind them admonished. "Quiet. Brother Joseph is about to *speak.*"

What happened for the next three hours was a vague blur of hate images, from which she retained little. It wasn't a blackout, or even a full lapse of memory. She retained pieces, fragments, of the "sermon," and she wasn't certain if there was any coherent flow to begin with. Brother Joseph vomited a vile concoction of religion and white male supremacy that would have made a Klansman blush. That was what she remembered, anyway. The topic wavered from fundamentalist Southern Baptist preachings, to New Age channeling, to an extended foray into Neo-Nazism, sprinkled liberally with passages Cindy remembered from high school history class — *Mein Kampf*. The audience sat, enthralled; it wasn't the sermon that scared her so much as the unthinking acceptance of the congregation. Brother Joseph could have said absolutely anything, she suspected, and they would have bought it all without question.

After the sermon Cindy had made it clear to her husband she wasn't *about* to stay around and socialize, she wanted out *now*, and when she reminded Jim that she had her own set of truck keys he finally relented and, not particularly angry at having to leave, drove them home. In silence.

The next day, a Saturday, Cindy tried to broach the subject of his employment and, specifically, his income. James brushed her aside, saying that she would never understand, and asked her if she had any Jewish ancestors. She did, but didn't think it wise to tell him. He went out and spent the rest of the day playing with his son, and acted as if she didn't exist. On Sunday, he left for somewhere he didn't specify and returned late that night, almost too drunk to walk, and fell into bed.

On Monday James continued to live the lie, getting up at six and dutifully donning his uniform. He mentioned the problem with the spark plugs and other things she knew he would never deal with that day, and after he was gone Cindy didn't answer the phone, for fear it was his boss. She sent Jamie off to school, the only normal thing to happen in her life, the only thing that made *sense*.

The next day was the same, and the day after. She paid the bills out of the dwindling bank account, made sure Jamie did his homework, and watched her husband deteriorate. Cindy also began contemplating divorce, but taking the first tentative step towards breaking up, like calling a lawyer, was too terrifying for words. It was easier to live the lie along with her husband and hope they would live happily ever after.

Weeks passed, and James Chase began coming home later and later in the evening. For a while she kept track of the odometer, and going by the miles stacking up on the pickup, determined he was probably going out to that mansion where the "Praise Meeting" was held. If not that, then God only knew where he'd been. Up and on the job for Brother Joseph, every day, driving all over on errands for the church, the Sacred Part of the Frozen Ones or some such nonsense. She began to withdraw herself, never going out except to buy food, and that the absolutely cheapest she could find. She prayed the checks wouldn't bounce after every trip.

Then finally Jim stayed out overnight, then two, then three nights in a row. Cindy wasn't terribly surprised; what surprised her was that he returned sober once or twice. Sober, yet untalkative. Whatever he was so fervently pursuing during the day, whatever his life had become as a new member of the Sacred Heart of the Chosen Ones, it wasn't his wife's place to know.

She had taken to sleeping in a bit more each day as her frustration built. She got up long enough to send Jamie off to school, then returned to bed. Sleep afforded her one way to escape the craziness the church had conjured.

She went back to answering the phone and talking to

the neighbors, trying to hide the pain with makeup and forced smiles. Then one particular morning she answered the phone, after James had left for whatever it was he did during the day. It was Jamie's school; with a start she realized she hadn't seen him off that morning. The principal's secretary wanted to know if everything was all right and reminded Cindy that calling the parents was procedure when a child didn't show up for class. Uncertain why she was covering for him, she explained that he was home ill and that she had simply forgotten to notify the school. She hung up and began running through the house, calling Jamie's name, looking for some clue as to his whereabouts.

Just when she thought she was going to lose her mind she found the note taped on the refrigerator door. It was in James' handwriting and it did ease her mind — for a moment. It simply told her not to worry, that he had taken Jamie with him for the day, though it didn't specify exactly why.

Even though she didn't suspect kidnaping then, the note opened up a Pandora's box of ominous possibilities. But before she could think coherently enough to worry about what might be happening to her son, the phone rang again. The bank was calling to tell her that five checks had bounced, and that both the share and draft accounts had been closed weeks before by James Chase.

She hung up, numb with shock.

She ran for the bedroom. A brief, hysterical inspection showed that no clothes had been taken, at least that she could tell. His shaver, shotgun, a World War II Luger, a Craftsman socket set, were all still in the house, and wouldn't be if James had really left. Not wanting to even think about the notion, she decided that it was too crazy even for James. She spent an anxious day cleaning, releasing nervous energy, venting her frustration. Around noon, she had an anxiety attack, and for ten minutes she couldn't take a breath.

Jamie is with those lunatics, she thought, repeatedly. She finally calmed herself enough to breathe, but she knew she could not go on like this, day after day, wondering what twist her husband's insanity would take *this* time.

Late that afternoon the pickup pulled into the garage, its bumper tapping the back wall hard enough to make an audible *crack*. Cindy heard her son crying. She ran to find Jamie in tears, her husband drunk, and a thousand unanswered questions staring her in the face.

"Oh, Jamie, *Jamie*, what's wrong?" She'd held him, getting no sense out of him. "What *happened*? Did your daddy do something to you? Did Daddy hurt you?"

She looked around furtively to see if Daddy was around and within earshot; inside the kitchen, she heard the hiss of a beer tab.

"No. Wasn't Daddy," Jamie blurted, through the tears. "It was Br . . . Brother Joseph." He sniffled, glancing over her shoulder, apparently looking for James. "*Please*, Mommy, don't let him take me back there ever again!"

She held him closer, forcing back some fear and trembling of her own.

James stayed long enough to finish off the last of the beer and left alone with vague promises to return soon. As soon as he was gone she called a women's shelter and briefly explained her situation. Soon a motherly, older woman arrived to pick them up. At the shelter, a young graduate lawyer eager to log some court experience was waiting for them. He took down the essential information and assured her that she had a good case, and would *probably* get full custody. Cindy had a problem with that word, *probably*, but got on with the business of settling in at the shelter and quizzed Jamie on what exactly had happened at the Chosen Ones' church.

On a bed in a common room they shared with

several other women and their children, Jamie sat and
tried to tell his mother what had taken place in the
church, describing an odd ritual on the stage in the
meeting hall, in which he was the central figure. Twice
her son tried to tell her what happened, getting to a
certain point in the explanation, whereupon he would
burst into hysterical sobs.

What happened back there? she wondered, half sick
with fear that they had done something truly evil and
harmful, emotionally, to her son. Divorce seemed to be
the only answer, if she was going to protect her child.

Her uncertainties hardened into resolve. *Never
again. That psycho is never coming near my son again!*

She steeled herself for a fight, for some attempt by
James to counter her actions — but nothing happened.
The court proceedings went smoothly and without
incident. There were twenty or thirty other child abuse
cases pending against the cult in question, some of
which the police were already investigating. The judge
expressed the belief that Cindy had tolerated far more
than she should have, and if James Chase had
bothered to show up for the hearings he would have
no doubt received a severe tongue-lashing. During the
week preceding the hearing Cindy returned to the
house with two large men from the shelter and
retrieved a few missed items, and while there she discovered that her husband had apparently left with his
clothes, the shotgun, the Luger and the tools. Though
the lawyer had papers served to James at the house, it
now appeared he had left for good. Taking no chances,
and at the strong urging of her companions, veterans
of situations like these, she remained at the shelter
until after the hearing. With the help of the shelter, she
got a part-time job at Burger King. The judge granted
Cindy Chase full custody of her son, ownership of the
house, and declared their marriage null and void.
Finally.

She had thought it was over, that they were safe. That *Jamie* was safe.

Then, on Friday of the fourth week following the divorce, Cindy waited on the porch for Jamie's school-bus. Just like always.

The bus squeaked to a halt, disgorged its screaming passengers, and shuddered away. There was no Jamie.

Cindy rushed inside and called the school. The teachers told her that Jim had taken him out of class an hour before the end of the day.

Hysterical, she notified the police, but the response was underwhelming. After an hour an officer showed up at the school to take a report. If the school's principal and Jamie's teacher hadn't stayed to comfort her, she would have gone over the edge right there. There wasn't a whole lot they could do, the officer said . . . there were so many missing children, so few personnel, so little budget. She explained that this was *different*, that she *knew* her husband had taken him, there were *witnesses* for cris-sakes, and the cult was *crazy*, they had to do *something*, right *now* before they . . .

The officer had sadly shaken his head and told her they would do what they could. From his tone, how-ever, it sounded like it wouldn't be much.

From memory Cindy drove to the cult's mansion, where she had been to her first Praise Meeting. She took several wrong turns, but after hours of relentless driving found the huge house. Realty signs in the front lawn declared the property for sale. The house, itself, was empty. Cleaned out.

The police, as she feared, weren't much help. She found herself in the position of thousands of other parents whose ex-spouses had kidnaped their children. Since she couldn't tell them where the cult could have gone, their options were limited. Through the parents of other child abuse victims, she learned that other members of the Chosen Ones had also vanished. Bank accounts and personal property, mostly cars and trucks, went with them. It was clear to Cindy that the cult had staged a mass exodus from Georgia. To where, she had no idea.

The only thing of value that James had left behind was the house. That, Cindy surmised, was only because it was too heavy to take with him. She needed money, lots of it, to search for her son. She double-mortgaged the house and sold everything out of it she could, all of the appliances and Jim's stereo, which miraculously had been left behind. With a certain wry satisfaction she sold her engagement and wedding rings to a pawnshop and used the money in part to pay for the divorce. Robert Weil, "Private Investigator" suggested they first begin by putting Jamie's picture on milk cartons. The Missing Children's advocacy group was very helpful.

The rest of her time and energy she spent keeping herself together. There were any number of times that she could have slipped over the edge and gone totally bonkers, and often she wondered if she had. Occasionally she slept, but most nights she did not. Her employers were sympathetic at first, but as the weeks passed, so did the sympathy. She began receiving warning "talks," suggestions by her male boss that she "pull herself together" and "let the professionals handle it." She sensed an unspoken feeling that her boss felt she was to blame for the entire mess. . . .

Robert Weil, "Private Investigator," turned out to be next to worthless to her search. He just wasn't _doing_ anything, so she fired him. Then the leads began to trickle in from the Center for Missing and Exploited Children, information that was the direct result of the milk carton photographs. From Atlanta they began to track him west, from three different sightings a day apart. She stocked up the Celica with what she could from the house, quit her job (just before they were about to fire her, she suspected), and left, taking up the trail herself.

The money disappeared quickly. She checked in periodically with the Missing Children's group, and finally learned that the two had actually been spotted by several witnesses in northeastern Oklahoma. Driving all night, she arrived in Tulsa around daybreak, and after she caught a few hours of sleep she asked the desk clerk if he knew of any race tracks in the area. Not even involvement in the cult had stopped Jim's addiction to racing and cars before the divorce. The only track the clerk was aware of was Hallet; he knew there were others, he just didn't know where. She made plans to search out each one, provided her money held out.

Right now it looked like she needed a miracle. *I guess nobody's handing out miracles today.*

She stifled a sob, put the picture away in her purse, and started looking for a restroom. *If I'm going to get anywhere with this I've got to make myself presentable. A place to freshen up, maybe. I'm not going all the way back to the motel. I don't have money to stay there much longer, anyway.* She trudged towards what looked like facilities and fought back a wave of dizziness. The heat —

Her vision blurred, seeing blue sky, with the kind face of an aging man in the center, like a Victorian picture of a saint. She blinked again.

"Are you all right, miss?" the man said in a rusty voice. "You keeled plumb over."

She was lying on her back in the grass, and there was a sore place on the back of her head. The man helped her to sit up a little; from his blue coveralls she assumed he was connected to the track somehow. He held a cup of lemonade to her lips, which she gulped gratefully.

"Whoa, now, hold on! Not so fast. You'll make yourself sick again," the man said. Around them, an unwanted audience of gawkers slowly formed in the thick sludge of the heat.

"What happened?" she asked stupidly, feeling

vulnerable in her supine position, the words just coming out automatically. She *knew* what had happened. Her brain just wasn't working properly yet.

"Well, you fainted, little missy! Would you like me to call an ambulance?"

"No!" she exclaimed, not out of fear for doctors, but out of concern for how much it would cost.

"Well, okay then, if you think you're all right," he said, still sounding concerned. "You know, we have a first aid tent near the concession stand," the man said. "If you're suffering from heatstroke the thing to do would be to get over there."

"No, I'm fine, really," she said, and she meant it. With the cooling lemonade her energy returned quickly. "I think I'll sit here a while and drink this, if that's okay with you. I guess the heat just got to me."

"Of course it's okay. If you want a refill, just holler," the man said, winking in a friendly way. There wasn't anything sexual about it, something for which she was glad. *He reminds me of my father, when he was alive,* Cindy thought, looking at the deep wrinkles in the man's face, which seemed to be made of stone. When he winked, the wrinkles fanned out over his face like cracks in a windshield. He leaned closer, looking like he thought he might have recognized her. "I've never seen you at this track before, have I?"

"Well, I've been here all day," she said, trying and failing to keep the frustration out of her voice. "Maybe you can help me," she added, feeling a slight surge of hope. Cindy pulled the photograph of her child out of her purse and handed it to the man. "I'm here looking for my son. His name is Jamie. . . ."

She hadn't intended to tell him her life's story, but he seemed content to sit and listen to her, shaking his head and *tsk*ing at the right moments. *Finally,* she thought, as she prattled on about her husband, the cult, and her missing son, *somebody who'll listen to me!*

Finally the old man nodded. "Miss, you ain't had nothin' but bad luck, that's for sure. Sounds to me like this fella is a pretty hard-core racing fan. And *hard-core* fans tend to hang out with the pros in the pits. I haven't seen your son, but maybe someone else has. Would ya like to come have a look see?"

Without hesitation she accepted, and soon found herself waiting for a break in the race, so that they could cross over to the pits. When the break came, another wave of heat came over her, and she thought with a touch of panic that she was going to pass out.

Not again, she thought, and willed her strength back.

The moment passed, without her new friend noticing. He escorted her — with an odd touch of gallantry — past a short cinderblock wall where a man waited, watching who came in. One nod from her heaven-sent escort allowed them through.

When she entered the pits her senses were assaulted with the sights and smells of racing. Everywhere she walked, she stepped over oil-marked concrete, bits and pieces of race cars lay strewn everywhere, usually in the form of washers, bolts and brackets — she thought irresistibly of a dinosaur graveyard, strewn with bones.

A blast of something aromatic and potent, which she identified a moment later as high-octane racing fuel, threatened another fainting spell.

Too overwhelmed by sight and sound, smell and vibration, she stood, trapped like an animal caught in the headlights.

Then the sound, at least, stopped. In the temporary absence of engine roar, she found her ears ringing, and when she turned to see where her friend had gone she saw him rushing off to a race car that had just pulled in. *I guess I'm on my own now*.

The people she saw were either frantically going somewhere in a huge hurry, or doing nothing at all, some even looking bored. It was this latter group that she tried to talk to, praying under her breath that she wouldn't get in the way. She hoped she knew enough from her racing experiences with her husband to tell when a crew was seconds away from swarming over a car, or when they were just trying to kill time.

She approached one team, who seemed more intent on barbecuing ribs than changing tires on a race car. Men stood around a portable grill, holding beer cans in beefy fists, and stepping back when the grease flared. Some of them were apparently drunk, and while this reminded her uncomfortably of her ex-husband, she went up to one anyway.

"Hi, I'm looking for my son, this is a picture," she said, holding the photograph out. "Have you seen him?"

The man's features softened briefly, but when he saw the picture, they hardened. He said curtly, "No, I haven't," and looked at her as if she didn't belong there.

Another, younger man, who might have even been the driver, smiled broadly and shook his head, and then promptly ignored her presence, as if she had faded into invisibility. She asked the next man, and the next, feeling like a scratched record.

No, we haven't seen your son. Are you sure you're in the right place?

Then, one large man staggered over to join the group, a hulk with a barrel-chested torso that could have stored a beer keg, and probably had.

"I might have," the big man said, belching loudly. *He's so much like Jim,* she thought, wondering if this man might even know him. "But then again, I might *not*. What's the story, lady?"

"He's my *son*," she repeated. *Does he know something?* she thought madly, hoping that maybe he did. *Has he seen Jamie or is he just playing with me?* "My husband, his name is James Chase, do you know him? He sort of took Jamie away, we're divorced and I got full custody. James took him out of school, in Atlanta, and they were last seen in Tulsa."

"Maybe you should go look in Tulsa," he said rudely. But then he continued, his eyes narrowing with arrogant belligerence. "And what's this crap you're saying about kidnaping, anyway? And how the hell did you get full custody? Must have cost you a lot to take a man's son away from him."

Cindy became very quiet, shocked into silence. The man moved in closer to her, exhaling beer fumes in her face.

"What kind of a mother *are* you, anyway? Jesus Christ, lady, if you were a decent mother maybe your son wouldn't have gone away with your old man. *Would* he?"

His unfairness and hostility conspired with the heat to glue her to the spot, unable to move, like a frightened kitten cowering away from a pit bull. The man continued the tirade, with angry enthusiasm — really getting into shouting at a woman half his size — but she didn't hear any of it. The heat was catching up with her again, and a race car started up and was revving loudly nearby, drowning out all the senseless noises the man was attempting to make.

But in the nightmare the day had become, she could read his lips. *Let it go. Just let it go, lady, the boy's probably happier with his father anyway. Go find another hubby and raise some more brats.*

The cars roared away.

"And no real woman would —"

That was the last straw. Unable to take it anymore, without even the noise of the nearby car to completely take away the man's unpleasantness, she turned violently and stumbled away. She didn't want him to have the pleasure of watching her cry.

She walked slowly, so that her blurring eyes wouldn't

betray her into a fall, vaguely aware of the man shouting behind her, unaware of where exactly she was. The tears surged forth now, breaking through a wall she didn't even know was there. She leaned on an oil barrel, faint again from the heat, and let the tears come freely. There weren't many witnesses here, and what few there were didn't care, didn't matter. . . .

"Al, what is it?" Bob asked, moderately concerned. "Anything important?"

Alinor shrugged, feeling the source of the emotional overload coming closer. *She must be in the pit area by now. Perhaps I shouldn't involve Bob yet . . . until I know a little more about what's going on here.*

"Oh, I don't think so," Alinor said, forcing a yawn, but Bob didn't look like he believed him. *He knows me too well,* Al thought. *He doesn't look it from the outside, but for a young human he's darned sharp.*

"I'm sure you won't mind if I tag along. The car's going in anyway," Bob said slyly, as more of a statement instead of a question.

"Yeah, sure," Al said, too casually. To say "no" would certainly tip him off. *Perhaps the gods intend for him to be involved in this one after all.*

"I've got a — feeling. Not sure if it's anything," Al said conversationally, as they walked toward the core of the paddock, the pit area where most of the cars came in to refuel. "Might be nothing, but then it might be —"

Al stopped in mid-sentence as he watched Bob's eyes tracking like an alert scout's, first to the racetrack, then to a group of men clustered around a grill.

Then came the emotion again, piercing his mage-shields like nothing he'd felt in a long time, and he put one hand up to his temple, reflexively.

"Is this what got your attention?" Bob asked calmly, pointing at a large man who was yelling at a small woman holding a photograph. From the emotion and thought-energies he was picking up now, Al knew that the picture was of the child she had lost. He had seen the man before, and knew he was a first-class misogynist, a male chauvinist pig, an egotist, a jerk. A general pain in the rear.

In short, Al didn't like him. And he would be perfectly pleased to have a chance to show the bastard up.

Saying nothing to Bob, he approached the pair. He privately hoped Bob would stay back and remain out of the situation long enough for him to find out precisely what was going on.

The woman paled and turned away from the bully, obviously fighting back tears. When the man took one step after her, Al intervened, wishing he dared land the punch he longed to take, but knowing he had to be far more surreptitious than that.

You don't need to follow her, Al sent, winding the impulse past the man's beer-fogged conscious. *Go back to the party. Leave her alone.*

The man paused, shook his head, and crushed the beer can in his right hand.

He hadn't noticed Al's little thought-probe as coming from outside himself. Now Al was confident enough about keeping his powers a secret that he sent one final nudge: *She doesn't matter. Besides, there's more beer at the barbecue.*

This last item seemed to get his attention away from his victim. He turned and walked uncertainly back to the barbecue, directly for the ice chest, ignoring the ribs being served. No doubt of where *his* priorities lay.

Alinor waited a moment before approaching the woman, who had obviously taken more than she could bear this afternoon. For a moment he thought she was going to pass right out and fall into the barrel she was leaning against.

She is in such pain over her child, Al anguished with her, waiting for the right moment before going to her. *I must help her. There is more about this than is apparent on the surface.*

"Excuse me," Al said softly, coming up behind her. "Are you . . . all right?"

She sniffled, as if trying to get herself under control, then turned slowly around. Their eyes met briefly before she looked away, and he sensed she was embarrassed about her appearance. Her eyes were puffy and red; obviously, she'd cried more than once today. "Yeah, I'm fine," she said, between sniffles.

Al calmly watched her, waiting for her to respond to the fact that he was not buying her story for even a minute.

Her jaw clenched, and she choked on a sob. "No. I'm *not* all right," she said, contradicting herself, but finally admitting the obvious. "Please. I don't know who you are, but I need help. This guy helped me get in here, but I don't know how to get out. The rules. Whatever."

And then she burst into sobs again, turning away from him.

Saying nothing, knowing that there was nothing he could say for the human that could possibly help her at that moment, he took her hand to lead her to a little grassy area near the track that was reasonably quiet and shaded. He sent Bob for cold drinks and told him where they'd be. Bob rolled his eyes, but cooperated nonetheless. Al ignored him.

He'll remember soon enough what it means to help a human in distress, Al thought. *It will all come back clearly to him when he sees what's wrong. He was on the receiving end once. I don't know what it is involved in this yet, but I can tell this isn't going to be light.*

He saw to it that she was seated in a way that would keep her back to most of the track-denizens, and handed her a fistful of napkins to dry her tears.

Then he waited. The revelation was not long in coming. When she had composed herself sufficiently she showed him her son's picture and began her plea, her words tumbling over each other as if she feared he would not give her a chance to speak them. "That's Jamie, my son. My husband . . . I mean, my *ex*-husband kidnaped him from his school in Atlanta, and —"

"Now wait, slow down," Al said softly. "Start from the beginning. Please."

Cindy nodded, took a deep breath, then explained to him what had *really* happened, telling him about the cult and the eerie change that had come over her husband. The parts about her ex-husband's alcoholism reminded him of Bob's past history, and Al was grateful the young mechanic returned with the drinks in time to hear it. He saw Bob's eyes narrow and his lips compress into a thin, hard line, and knew that the human had been won over within three sentences.

The story aroused many deep reactions in him, from the near-instinctive protective urges shared by all elves, to the feeling that this was only the surface of a larger problem. There was more here than just one little boy being kidnaped.

There is death here, he thought, with a shudder he concealed. None of the Folk cared to think about death, that grim enemy who stole the lives of their human friends and occasionally touched even the elven ranks. But he knew it, with the certainty that told him his flash of intuition was truth. *There is death involved, and pain. And not just this woman's pain, or her son's.* He was not one of the Folk gifted with Fore-Seeing, with the ability to sense or see the future — but he had a premonition now. This wasn't just about one small boy.

As she finished the story, Al studied the photograph, engraving the image permanently in his mind. *Now I must help,* he thought with determination. *I could never turn away from something like this.* And, with ironic self-knowledge, *It was time for another adventure, anyway.*

"And that's it," Cindy concluded, as if she felt a little

more heartened by his willingness to listen. "I'm just about at the end of the line. And I think I'm going crazy sometimes. Can you, I don't know, ask around? I don't know what else to do."

"I'll do anything I can to help you," Al said firmly, looking to Bob for support. The human shrugged — both at Al and at his own willingness to get involved — sighed and rolled his eyes again ever so slightly.

"I'll take that as a yes," Al told him, then turned to Cindy. "When you feel a little better, we can start asking around the track. I know the people here who would be sharp enough to notice something odd about your ex-husband and your son." He laughed a little, hoping to cheer her a bit. "Most folks here, if it doesn't have four wheels, it doesn't exist."

She looked from him to Bob and back again, grateful — and bewildered. "Th-th-thank you, Al. And Bob," she said at last, looking as if she didn't quite believe in her luck. "What can I do to, you know, pay you back?"

She sounded apprehensive, and Al did not have to pry to know what she *thought* might be demanded in return for this "friendly" help. "Not a thing," Al quickly supplied. "But I do need a little more information about your son and your ex. We know he likes races. What about some other things he enjoys? What might attract him here in particular, and where else might he go around here?"

No, he had not been mistaken; the relief she felt at his reply was so evident it might as well have been written on her forehead. *Thank God, I won't have to — he isn't going to —*

Al sighed. Why was it that sex could never come simply, joyfully, for these people? Along with the curse of their mortality came the curse of their own inhibitions.

Ah, what fools these mortals be, he thought, not for the first time — and turned his attention back to the far more important matter of a child in danger.

• CHAPTER THREE

Jamie winced. Jim Chase ignored him and banged on the pickup truck's balky air-conditioner, which was threatening to break down for the third time that week. The once-cold air was turning into a warm, fetid blast, and anybody with sense would just roll down the windows. Jamie perched on the sticky plastic seat beside his father, staring glumly at the Oklahoma countryside. He counted cows as they passed a pasture, something Jim had taught him to better pass the time. Meanwhile, the hot air coming from the truck's dash made sweat run down his neck, and he was trying his best to ignore it.

Jim's large fist pounded the air-conditioning controls, which had no effect on the temperature; the interior of the truck was quickly turning into a sauna. Jamie calmly reached over and turned off the blower, then cranked down his own window. The air outside was just as hot, but was drier, and at least it didn't smell of mildew.

His father muttered something about a compressor, a word Jamie barely recognized. It sounded expensive, which meant it would stay unfixed. Jim was still a genius when it came to technical stuff. But when he was angry, or when he drank joy juice, the genius went away. Like now.

Jamie decided to see if at least he could get his father to stop doing something stupid. "Daddy, isn't the compressor in the motor? Under the hood?"

Jim's calm words seemed to come with great effort. "Yes, son. The compressor is in the motor."

"Then why are you bangin' on the *dash* like that?"

Jim laughed, a little, at that. "Good question," he said, leaving the dash alone and unbuttoning his shirt in the heat. Jamie wished he had brought more of *his* clothes on this trip; he'd managed to scrounge around for a used tank top at the vacation place, and it was the only clothing he had that was cool enough to wear on these excursions. Even though it came down to his knees, and felt more like an apron, it was more comfortable than the one shirt he still had.

Overall, this had been the longest and *weirdest* vacation he'd ever been on, especially since Mom wasn't with them. At the vacation place, however, he had been to a kind of school, which didn't make any sense at all. *You don't go to school on vacation,* he tried to tell his dad, but his father had insisted. Jamie attended class in a single room with one strange old lady named Miss Agatha who hated blacks and Jews and had a big gap between her front teeth. She taught them her hate along with readin' and 'rithmatic, or at least tried. Hate was wrong, he knew, but since he was surrounded by adults who seemed to think differently, he didn't question them.

Much.

The classroom was filled with other children who were just as confused as he was. Most of them were there because they weren't old enough to be in the Junior Guard. The kids in the Junior Guard didn't have to go to school, so it was something Jamie wanted to join, if for no other reason than to get away from Miss Agatha. He even lied and told them his age was ten and not eight; you had to be at least ten to join the Guard and use an AK-47. But they hadn't believed him.

Jamie had thought of this vacation as one big adventure, in the beginning. But in the past couple of days, he had begun to sense something wrong. He started asking his father questions — about the whereabouts of his mother, and why he was gone from *his* school for so long. And why he didn't have any spare clothes.

He'd kept up an incessant barrage of questions, couching the questions in innocence so that he would stay out of trouble. He might only be eight, but one thing he knew was his dad. James had bought it at face value, looking pained, not annoyed, whenever his son brought up the subject of his mother.

Finally today his dad had told him that they would be seeing Mom on this trip to Tulsa. Why, Jamie had asked, didn't Mom come to the vacation place? It was a surprise, James had replied, and that seemed to be the end of that.

They had made several trips to Tulsa since they arrived here, each time loading up the truck with big bundles of food and supplies. Sometimes they had to stop at a bank and cash a CD, but Jamie had never heard of money coming out of music before. Besides, they didn't have a CD player; more mystery. James purchased canned goods, mostly; things they wouldn't use right away, food that was put away where no one could see it. This category of grocery was called "in the event of an emergency," according to Miss Agatha. The rest of the food, the "perishables," was for the other people, he knew that much, since he got very little of it himself.

Now they were going to the store again, and like the last time, the air-conditioner quit. No big deal for Jamie, he didn't mind the heat as much as his father did. It didn't matter, as long as he was outside the vacation place. It was a stifling place, especially when Brother Joseph was around. All day Jamie had looked forward to the trip, knowing that Mom would be waiting for him in town. He didn't mention her to Daddy during the trip, since he already felt like a nuisance bringing it up before.

"Miss Agatha tells me you're a bright student,"

James said conversationally, over the wind pouring in through the window.

Jamie shrugged. "It's not like school at home. It's too *easy.*" He wanted to add that it was also pretty weird, some of the things Miss Agatha taught them. And that he was the only one in his class who wasn't afraid of Miss Agatha. He had asked her why it was okay now to hate when it wasn't before. After all, Mommy had always said that it was wrong to hate black people because of the color of their skin, or Jews because they went to a temple instead of a church.

Miss Agatha had not been amused and told him that the Commandments said he had to obey his elders and she was his elder.

Then she went on with the same stupid stuff. Only today she had also mentioned another group, the homos, but he had no idea what made them different. Miss Agatha had simply said to stay away from them, that even saying "homo" was wrong, that it was a *bad word*.

"When am I going back to the *real* school, Daddy?"

Jamie knew he had said something wrong then, by the way his father's face turned dark and his lips pressed together. But it was a valid question, after all. Wasn't it?

"Maybe it's time for you to learn what the big boys know. The truths they don't teach you at that other school, the one in Atlanta."

The boy felt a shiver of excitement. *What the big boys know. Like Joe. The things they haven't been telling me, that big secret the grownups are all excited about but don't tell us. It is time for me to know that big secret now?*

"Listen up. This is a Bible story, but not like any Bible story you've ever heard before. Those other ministers, they don't have it right, never have, never will. We're one of the few groups of people in the world who know it straight, son, and by the grace of God we'll spread the word further."

James paused a moment, apparently gathering his strength, as if summoning vast intellectual reserves. Daddy was having trouble thinking, Jamie knew, because he had run out of beer the day before and hadn't had any since.

"Do you remember Miss Agatha telling you about the beginning of the world? About how God created the world and all the people on it?"

Jamie nodded, uncertainly. *The big secret has to do with that icky stuff?* he thought, suddenly disappointed.

"And the story of Genesis, in the Bible. Most Bibles don't tell you that before Adam, God had created several other species of mankind, the black man, the red man, the yellow. Some had civilizations and some had nothing. Some could live in peace because they were too lazy to do anything else, but most of the inferior races could only make war. God made all these people before Adam, long before he had it down right, you see." James sounded earnest, but he was frowning. "But most ministers, preachers, they don't know all this 'cause their churches didn't want them to know the truth."

Jamie nodded, as if he understood, but he didn't. This wasn't like any Bible story *he* had ever heard, or even read.

"Now remember, and this is important. This is before the white man. God saw that his work could be better, that all these monkey races were turning back into animals. He needed a perfect creature, and that's when he made Adam out of the river mud. Right away he knew he had something there. This one was different. This one was *white*. The color of purity, the same color as God."

Already Jamie was getting uncomfortable. This was *not* what he expected to hear. *All that hate stuff again,* Jamie groaned inwardly. *With big words to make it sound important. Brother.*

"God could see that what he made was perfect, with an intelligence higher than any creature's he had yet created. And that included the black man. The Lord God also saw that his new creation would bring peace to a world filled with war, since it was an inherently peaceful creature he had made. He was a higher being, in every way. He had to be, since the Lord God was creating a race of people to inherit the earth, to be God's direct descendants, to be his children."

"Yeah, Dad," Jamie said, forcing politeness. He didn't like what he was hearing, and he wished his dad would finish. *You made more sense when you were drinking joy juice,* he thought rebelliously.

"Then the Lord God saw that Adam was lonely, and he created Eve. She was of the same race as Adam, and it was God's intention that she bear Adam's babies, to make a perfect race. But Satan, who was an angel rebelling against God, he got involved somehow and mated with Eve instead, and gave her his serpent seed."

"Is this the same Satan the Church Lady talks about on Saturday Night Live?" Jamie asked, figuring this to be on safe ground. Mommy had let him stay up one Saturday, when his father was away, and watch the show with her. Since then, he had always associated Satan and women like Agatha with humor. But now, Daddy didn't look like he was trying to be funny.

"Don't know what you're talking about there, son," James said, puzzled for a moment. "If that's some kind of late-night religious show, it's probably only half right. I'm telling you what's really right, all true. Pay attention now — this made God really angry, since this wasn't what he had in mind at all. Eve wasn't as perfect as Adam, because she had let Satan do this to her — which proved to God that women were going to be naturally inferior to men. Now God's purest race was polluted. Now Satan, since he was part of one of the first races, is black."

Jamie stifled a snicker. *Boy, is that stupid! First he says Satan's an angel, then he says he's a snake, and now he says he's black.*

"Eve gave birth to two sons, but that was how God knew they must have had different fathers, because one was black, Cain, and the other was white, Abel. Cain was lazy and wanted to live off the sweat of other people, through stealth and cunning, which is typical of the way the Jew serpent race thinks. Cain took off to Babylonia and started his own kingdom, and this is where the Jews came from."

Now Jamie *knew* that was wrong; he knew where the Jews came from. The little bitty squiggly place, the one littler than Oklahoma. Israel. And he'd never heard of Babby-whatever. Unless it was that icky lunch-meat they gave the kids here. But James was really enjoying his captive audience, so Jamie sighed and pretended to listen.

"Before long everyone was mating with everyone else, mixing the races, committing sodomy — I'll explain that one when you're a little older — and God didn't like that. So he flooded the Earth with water, and God started a new kingdom, but as it happened some of the Jew serpent seed got onboard the boat anyway. Before long the Jews gained control again. The Jews and blacks are doing that to this day."

Then how come so many poor people are black? Jamie asked silently. *And how come there are people putting bombs in Israel?* He'd learned *that* in his real school. Esther had brought in some scary pictures. . . .

"When Jesus came, it was too late. The Jews were already in control, and they crucified Jesus. The battle between good and evil rages to this day, and now the Communists are pawns of the Jews, and they're just as bad. Any day now hordes of Jew Communists are going to invade the United States, and only a select few are going to be ready for it. That's why we are called the Chosen Ones, and we abide by no laws except *divine* law."

Daddy had completely lost Jamie at this point. Was that why James drove over 70 in the 55 mph zone, because there was no "divine" speed limit? And was that why he wouldn't wear a seat belt?

James was still babbling, like a tape player that wouldn't stop. "The white race will reclaim its lost status, but it will take time, and work, lots of work. The ministers and churches today, they don't want to tell the truth, they don't want to work, understand, but it's all there for anyone to see. The other churches have been diverting energy away from the real work, and that's why we're here. This is what Brother Joseph is teaching us. This is why you're in Brother Joseph's school, instead of that unholy place in Atlanta."

"You mean, we're not on vacation?" Now Jamie was really confused.

James glanced at him sharply. "Of course we're on vacation, but it's the Lord's vacation."

"Are we really going to see Mommy when we get to Tulsa?"

Jim became silent then. It was the first time Jamie had mentioned Mommy that day, and having finally asked the question, he was suddenly nervous.

"Who told you we were going to see Mommy in Tulsa?"

The boy shrank, sensing that familiar anger which often led to his father's backhanding him. "You did," he said, meekly.

James considered this a moment, then said, "That all depends on Mommy. If she wants to see us, she'll be there. If she doesn't want to see us, she'll stay home."

But we didn't tell Mommy where we were going, and we didn't call her or anything to tell her we'd be in Tulsa today.

"What if she's *not* in Tulsa?" Jamie said, holding back the tears at this betrayal of a promise. "What if she's still at home? What if she doesn't know we're going to be in Tulsa today?"

"Then that'll be her fault," James said. "She's a Jew woman or something."

When they pulled into the parking lot of Tom's Wholesale Discount Market, Jamie searched for his mother among the several faces he found there. Boys in jeans, shirts and vests pushed giant trains of shopping carts back to the front of the huge building, where even longer lines of carts, stuck together by some magical glue, awaited shoppers. While they were waiting to enter the store, Jamie continued the search, afraid to ask his father about his mom. James had looked ready to hit him back there, Jamie knew, and figured it was time to be quiet. Through trial and error, he had learned to gauge his father's temper.

James showed the girl their membership card and entered the store, selecting a flatbed cart. Still, no Mom. He followed his father silently, knowing that to lag behind would mean to be lost, and to be lost would eventually mean a backhand to the side of his head. And with Mommy nowhere around, there was nothing to stop James, nothing to restrain him. Jamie doubted these strangers would do anything to stop his father from hurting him; they never had before.

Tom's Discount was the only place Jamie had been to that sold stuff by the case. The store was a big warehouse. To reach some of the stuff, a forklift was necessary.

Cases of canned food began to stack up on the cart, and after a man helped them forklift some stuff down from a high shelf, they proceeded to the freezer section. Daddy had mentioned buying milk and cheese last, because it was a perishable. He hoped, also, the sample lady would be there so he could get some free cheese or barbecue sauce or wieners, he was so hungry. But she wasn't there, and he was starting to get unhappy about that when something else attracted his attention.

The freezer section was a catacomb of glass doors and frozen goods. Blasts of cold, biting air nibbled at his skin whenever someone opened a door. Over here, though, was a row of refrigerators, with milk and milk products stacked up inside the door.

His own face stared back at him.

He opened the door while his father, loading boxes of cheese, wasn't looking. The milk cartons were connected by plastic tape, so he couldn't take that one out. But he read it anyway, recognizing his school picture from the year before. It was his name, all right, and his date of birth. According to the carton, he was last seen with James Chase in Atlanta, Georgia. Jamie stared at the picture for a long time, trying to figure out how he could be on there, and why. According to the carton, he was a "Missing Child." *But I'm not a missing child. I'm right here, with Daddy. Daddy knows I'm here, so there must be a mistake. Is this what he meant about seeing Mom in Tulsa? Or does Mommy have something to do with this picture being on here?*

As he was puzzling over this, he became aware of a large presence behind him, and with a start he looked up at his father. He pointed at the carton, tried to say something, but only a squeak came out.

"What are you looking at there, son?"

James knelt down and studied the carton, taking it out of the refrigerator. He looked at the picture, then at Jamie. Then he looked up and down the aisle; nobody was around just then. The boy noticed that he had the look of someone doing something he shouldn't. He began to feel all funny in his stomach.

"That isn't you," he said, simply. "That's another boy. He's got the same name as you, but it's another boy. Got that?"

Fearful of what would happen to him if he did otherwise, Jamie nodded.

"That's good," he said, quickly going through the

remaining cartons, checking the photographs on each one. Apparently, he was holding the only one with his son's picture; he found no others. "Start putting more milk on the cart. This size, here," he said, indicating a stack of milk cartons larger than the first. "I'll be right back."

Jamie tried not to look, but out of the corner of his eye he watched his father look around quickly before dumping the milk in a large, plastic-lined waste can.

When he returned, his expression was somber. "It was bad," he informed his son. "The milk was bad, so I threw it out for them."

Jamie nodded, meekly, and continued loading the milk.

"Here. Let me give you a hand with that," James said, as he helped his son load the flatbed cart.

For Jamie, the situation was becoming more frightening than he wanted to admit. His first impulse was to trust his father, without questioning him about why Mommy wasn't around, why they were far from home, why his picture was on a milk carton. It was easier to just listen to Daddy and do what he said; this gave some order to his world. It was also the best way to avoid being hit. He loved his mother, but he had to admit that during the divorce he felt very much afraid without his father. When James returned to his school to pick him up for the vacation, Jamie was thrilled, though he didn't understand why Mommy wasn't with him. The divorce was weird; Daddy explained it as temporary, and it didn't really mean they weren't married, even though that's what Mommy said it meant. She was confused, he explained. He would explain it all when she got to Tulsa, whenever that would be.

They drove away from the discount store with the loaded truck, and Jamie stared out the window at the other cars. Ahead was an Arby's, and the boy remembered his hunger.

"Daddy, I'm really hungry. Can we stop at Arby's?"

James frowned, as if the request was too much to be handled. But Jamie saw him stuff the wad of bills and change in his pocket when they'd finished buying things. Money, he knew, wasn't a problem.

"I don't know, Jamie. Brother Joseph wouldn't like it."

"Why?" he wanted to know, flinching. He expected a blow, not only for questioning Daddy, but questioning Brother Joseph, which was an even more heinous crime.

"Brother Joseph knows what he's doing," James explained carefully. "He has tapped the Divine Fire before, and through you he will do it again."

Hunger was gone, immediately, as his stomach cramped with fear. *No, not that again —*

"But Daddy," he protested feebly, "I don't want to."

James shook his head dismissively. "That's because you're just a child. When you get older, you'll understand. It's all in Brother Joseph's hands. Fasting is crucial in achieving the purity to talk to God. Something else the clergy in general doesn't know about. Consider yourself fortunate."

The Arby's came and went. Jamie could smell the odors of roast beef and french fries, and his stomach growled loudly. "Perhaps he'll let you eat something tonight. After the ritual. It will be special tonight," James said, as if savoring the prospect. "Just you wait."

They drove on in silence for several moments, while Jamie tried to concentrate on something other than his complaining stomach. *I'm so hungry*, he thought, and when he saw them pull onto the highway to get back to the vacation place, he realized he wasn't going to be seeing Mommy in Tulsa after all.

So I guess she isn't there, he thought, starting to feel a little cranky instead of being unhappy, and beginning to think he ought to push the issue. After all, Daddy had promised. He was reaching a point where he didn't care if he was hit or not. In a way, he felt like he deserved it. *I must have done something bad, or Mommy would be here by now.*

"There's something I got to tell you," James began, and Jamie sighed.

He's lying again, he thought, somehow knowing that what would follow wouldn't be the truth. He didn't know how he had acquired the talent for spotting lies, but he did know that Daddy had been lying a lot lately.

It seemed like James was waiting to get on the highway before telling him what, exactly, was going on. James gunned the motor, bringing their speed up to seventy before turning to his son.

"I haven't been telling you everything, because I wanted to protect you. You probably think it was a little weird the way we left Atlanta. Took you from your school and everything. There is really a good reason for all of that. Before I explain, I want to be certain that you understand that I do love you, and I wouldn't do anything that would harm you."

Jamie was feeling uncomfortable again, but he nodded anyway. Whatever lie was coming, it was going to be a big one.

"Good. I trust Brother Joseph without question, and *he* wouldn't hurt you either."

Jamie wasn't sure about *that*, but he was too afraid to question it. *Brother Joseph is* really *weird, and he's why you're* so *weird, isn't it, Daddy?* He remembered the last odd ritual, the fourth of a series, in which Brother Joseph made him see and feel things he still didn't understand. Scary things. It was like a big monster on the other side of a wall, like the creepy thing he felt under his bed while sleeping or lurking in his closet. The thing that came to life in his room when Daddy turned the light out. *That* thing; a dark something that made wet sounds when it moved, the thing that watched him when Brother Joseph shoved him through the wall during the rituals. He forced Jamie to see it, sometimes even to touch it. The wall wasn't solid, he knew, but it was still a barrier. *Walls were made for reasons*, he thought, and the reason for this one was *good*. He pushed the memory away, at the same time dreading the coming ritual, where he knew it would just happen all over again.

"I don't mean for you to worry about your mother, but something has happened in Atlanta that's put us all in danger. We were going to see your mom in Tulsa, but I guess she just hasn't made it yet."

Jamie stared glumly forward. "What's happened?" he asked, resigned that whatever James would tell him would be a lie, but hoping for some truth anyway. "What's happened to Mommy?"

"Nothing," James supplied. "Not that I know of, anyway. Back in Atlanta, the police, they came and said that I did something that I didn't. They think that I'm involved in drugs; they accused me of dealing drugs in your school in Atlanta. You know what I'm talking about when I say drugs, don't you?"

Jamie nodded, remembering the cop who had spoken to their class about the bad boys who were smoking cigarettes and other things behind the school during lunch, kids who were only a few years older than him. The cop showed them the green stuff that looked like something Mommy had in bottles to cook with, and another baggie of little white rocks called "crack." That was bad stuff, the cop told them, and they had caught the man who had sold it outside their school. When the cop told them about what drugs did, Jamie was scared and decided that if he was ever offered any, he would refuse. But his dad had nothing to do with it; he knew that much for certain.

"Well, son, it's all a terrible misunderstanding. If it weren't for blessed Brother Joseph and the Chosen

Ones, I'd be in jail right now. See, we've got to hide out with the Chosen Ones for a little while, until things kind of level out. I have a lawyer out there working on the case. Your mother didn't know much about this at first, but when I called her and told her what was going on, she got all nervous about me and said I'd better take you with me; she wasn't sure if she could handle you all by herself. The police were wondering about her, too. With the drugs, and all. But don't you worry none. Momma will be here soon."

The stink of *lie* was thick. Jamie wondered why his father couldn't tell how obvious it was. The boy frowned a little, looked up at his dad, and wondered when he was going to stop lying to him.

"You know I don't sell dope, son."

"I know that, Daddy. They caught who was doin' it. I'm never gonna touch drugs. The police said they make your head puff up and your skin turn green and purple. They make you crazy and do awful things to people."

"Good, son. That's just what I wanted to hear," James replied, absently, as if he hadn't heard a word Jamie had said, once he got the initial answer. "Brother Joseph, he's going to help us through this. He's done a lot for us, and these little errands we run, getting the food for them and all, are a way of helping him back. It'll all work out, you just wait and see."

It can't ever work out, Jamie thought, getting angry at his daddy for making up stories. *Momma doesn't know a thing about this, I just know it. This is all real wrong, I shouldn't even be here, I should be in Atlanta going to my school and not this icky place with these icky people Daddy likes. Sarah would know what's right. She always knows what's right. I'll ask her when I get back. She might even know where I could get some* food, *without Brother Joseph knowing about it.*

Jamie knew they were getting close to the "vacation

place" when Tulsa dissolved behind them, and the terrain became barren of civilization. There were a few cattle in this part of Oklahoma, sprinkled among the scrawny groves of native oak. The sun continued to beat mercilessly against the earth, but now that it was late afternoon, the temperatures inside the truck were more bearable. They turned off to a lesser, two-laned highway, then to a gravel road. After some time across the bumpy route they came to the front gate, a large steel barrier set in a bed of concrete. James unlocked it, and they proceeded into what the soldiers called "the Holy Land of the Chosen Ones."

Soon they reached a second gate, this one connected to a tall chain-link fence topped by barbed wire. At the gate was a sentry box, where two young men in t-shirts, camo pants and combat boots intercepted the truck. There was a brief inspection before continuing into the main compound. Above them two dozen electricity-generating windmills *thwapped*. Joe had told Jamie they were connected to powerlines leading to the vacation place.

The truck rumbled past a series of drab quonset-style shacks. They seemed deserted; once his father had remarked that this was where food and supplies were kept, ready for the "invasion" the grownups were always talking about. Other soldiers, more numerous now than when they first arrived, were patrolling the grounds. At the northwest corner of the compound was an old log cabin that was now a sort of museum. *This was what the freedom fighters first lived in*, he remembered Miss Agatha saying on a field trip. *It stands as a monument to their holy independent spirit and is an inspiration to us all*.

Next was a cluster of plain, cinderblock buildings, and more quonset huts that reminded Jamie of *Gomer Pyle* episodes. Beyond was the entrance to the underground shelters, the vacation place, where Jamie now lived, along with the rest of the Chosen Ones. Miss Agatha said there were almost one thousand of the "enlightened" living in the vacation place; since he was the new kid, he felt like he was treated with a little more suspicion than the rest.

After all Daddy does for them, they still don't like me.

He figured this was from jealousy, because he was allowed outside, a privilege usually reserved for the trusted few. His father's unique function in fetching supplies had its advantages. Nobody else had a membership in Tom's, and Brother Joseph didn't want anyone else to get one. He said it was a "security risk." But since Jim had gotten the membership a long time ago, there was no reason not to use it.

Jim drove the supply-laden pickup to yet another checkpoint. This was at the mouth of the underground, a gaping, dark hole at the base of a concrete ramp. Jamie knew there would be dim lighting down there that would never compete with the searing summer sun outside; his eyes would have to adjust, first. Going in always frightened him. It was like going down the gullet of some prehistoric creature.

There was some consolation, though; Joe was one of the guards working the gate today. He was just coming on duty when they had left for Tulsa, and Jamie figured by now it might be time for his shift to end. The boy had met Joe at his very first Praise Meeting, and Joe had been nice to him — he'd given him a Tootsie Pop and showed off his *tattoo*. There was something so — affable, genial about Joe; they had become instant friends. His father approved warmly, and since Joe was the only one besides Brother Joseph who would have anything to do with him, they spent a lot of time together hiding out in the nooks and crannys of the uncompleted sections of the underground.

At first Jamie thought it was a little weird that Joe could sometimes guess what he was thinking, and sometimes answered his questions before he could actually ask them. And only yesterday, Joe had predicted that they would be going out; in fact, said he would be seeing him because he was working guard duty. When Jamie quizzed him about his ability to read minds and see into the future, Joe got real scared, and said for him to never mention that again. He wasn't reading minds and he wasn't seeing into the future, said it was something called "deduction," like Sherlock Holmes did. He also said that if anyone thought he did read minds they'd both be in big trouble. It was the work of the devil, such things, and no Chosen One could *ever* have powers like that. Jamie let the matter rest.

Sure enough, Joe was standing there, at attention, looking the same as he did when they left. The boy looked up to Joe, admiring him in his uniform. He was every bit a man in Jamie's eyes even though he was barely old enough to be in the Chosen Ones' regular Guard. He was eighteen, one of the few guards who still had hair. Jamie hadn't asked why, because it seemed to be a delicate subject. The rest of the Guard were shaven bald, and it seemed to be some kind of special thing, but he didn't know what it meant.

There were a zillion other questions he wanted to ask Joe today as well, and the top of the list was: why would his picture be on a milk carton?

And besides that, why hadn't his mother shown up yet? He knew he was treading dangerously just to ask Joe, since his father had already provided an answer. If Joe squealed on him, he would be in hot water, and he'd get beaten. Jamie decided to ask anyway, as Joe's overall trustworthiness had never been in doubt, and they shared mutual secrets anyway. And if Joe's answer didn't sound right, there was always Sarah. She knew things most people didn't, and her word was golden. Sarah had never, ever lied to him, or acted as if he was bad or stupid.

James turned off the motor. This was the last and most thorough check in the land of the Chosen Ones, and was used to detect the smuggling of undesirables, spy devices or Communists into the underground bunkers. Jamie had the impression the guards trusted his father but had to do this thing anyway. They went through the truck thoroughly, examining the supplies, looking under the vehicle. His father stood by quietly; this was a sacred ritual, as was any procedure that protected the Chosen Ones from the Jew Communist enemy, who was due to invade any day now. Everything these weird people did seemed to be in preparation for a war, and Jamie didn't understand why anyone outside the compound didn't share this sense of urgency. It must be one of those "truths" that Daddy mentioned, which only the Chosen Ones knew about.

After the inspection Joe spoke briefly with Jamie's father. "You go with Joe," Jim said, getting into the truck. "I have to go unload these supplies. I'll see you at supper, after I speak with Brother Joseph."

Go with Joe! That was exactly what he'd wanted to do. He looked over at the young man, who was grinning as he slung his AK-47 over his shoulder. Jamie had never seen him without it, not even at the big communal dinner hall, and while at first it was a little scary, now he didn't think anything of it. At the vacation place, guns were everywhere. This was not like normal life. *Things are different here.*

Before Jamie could react to the good news, his father was in the truck and starting it up, the conversation apparently finished. Joe's relief had arrived, a scowling man who looked like Daddy did a day after drinking too much joy juice.

"Hey, buckaroo," the big boy said jovially, squatting down to talk to him, "I've got something to show you."

Usually Jamie didn't like it when he knelt down like

that; it made him feel like a little boy, even though he was. But this time was different, he didn't care much; there was a surprise involved this time.

Instead of a surprise, Joe pulled out another Tootsie Pop. Jamie appreciated it, as any eight-year-old would — especially with his stomach growling — but he tried to not let the disappointment show.

"That's not what I wanted to show you," Joe said, trying to conceal a snicker. "Come with me."

Joe led him through a series of tunnels and passageways, some nominally lit, which had been carved into the earth by the Chosen Ones. Some of the digging equipment was still here, Jamie noticed; he had never been down this way before, had in fact been told to stay away from this area of the tunnels, this being forbidden to those under ten. But now the restrictions seemed to have been lifted by his hero.

"You've never been down here before," Joe said, "and it would probably be a good idea if you didn't tell anyone we were here. It'll be our secret. Okay?"

"Awright!" Jamie said, with awe in his voice. "What're we doing down here, anyway?"

"Nothing we shouldn't," he replied. It was hard to keep up with him, he was walking so fast. His legs, too, were that much longer. "I talked to your daddy about this, first, so it's all right with him."

"What is this place?"

They came across a sign, with a drawing of a young soldier holding an AK-47 over his head in triumph, with the caption:

SACRED HEART OF THE CHOSEN ONES
JUNIOR GUARD
FIRST BATTALION

It took a moment for it to register; then surprise spread through Jamie. "Am I joining the Junior Guard already?" It was like a rite of passage here. It had only been a few weeks since Jamie had arrived, but he had come to recognize the importance of some of the ritual elements of the vacation place. The Junior Guard was one of them. "First Battalion? How many battalions *are* there?" He wasn't sure what a battalion was, but from the sign he gathered they were important, and that there must be more of them.

"There's only one right now," Joe admitted, as they entered another large, damp room, filled to overflowing with every type of firearm he could imagine. Jim had taken him to a sporting goods store once, with what had to be a million guns on the wall, but it was nothing compared to *this*. The rifles and assault shotguns were lined up in several racks. Beyond that were thousands of wooden boxes, some of them open, filled with bullets. Along another wall, behind a huge sheet of glass, were small handguns, each with a name affixed to a tag. The room smelled like gun oil and rubberized canvas; the odor gave him goosebumps on the back of his neck. *This is for real.*

"I'm going to show you how to fire a weapon," Joe announced proudly. "Do you want to learn a handgun or a rifle?"

Jamie was struck speechless. *Learn how to use — a* gun? Even the Junior Guard didn't start right away with guns, he knew that much. Joe was providing something special here, and he knew it.

"I want to learn *that* one," Jamie said, pointing at the assault rifle slung over Joe's shoulder, so common it seemed to be a part of him. *"Your* gun."

Joe laughed, but not in a way that humiliated him, the way the other grownups did. Joe was his friend, and his laugh didn't betray that. "Sorry, bucko, you're gonna have to work up to this one. Come over here." He led him to a rack of rifles, smaller and lighter than most of the others. "These are all the right size to start with. Hey, Jamie, I had to start with an *air* rifle when I was your age. You get to use real bullets. *You're* lucky."

Jamie studied the weapons. One stuck out, grabbed his attention. It wasn't quite a machine gun, but it looked a little more grownup than the others. It had a block-letter J carved in its stock. "That one."

"Hmmmmm," Joe said. "Good choice. It used to be my gun, when I was little. Imagine that."

Joe unlocked the gun rack and handed him the weapon. "Never point it at anyone you don't want to kill. Don't point it up, either, when you're down in the bunkers. Always point it down. Roof's usually metal here, and if it goes off accidentally the dirt or wooden floors will absorb the bullet, but it would bounce off metal and hurt someone."

He reached for it eagerly. "All right, Joe. Is it loaded?"

"Always assume it is, even when you know it isn't. *NO — don't point it at me!* There you go, down at the ground. Good boy." Joe's voice took on a singsong quality. "What you have here is a Charter Explorer Rifle, model 9220. Takes eight .22 long cartridges. It's not *fully* automatic like mine, but it'll do for starters." Joe picked up a box of bullets, and his voice returned to normal. "Let's go to the firing range."

They walked in silence to the next room. The long, narrow area was floored thickly with sand, and the roof tapered down at the opposite end. This was, Joe told him, to deflect weapons fire into the ground. Standing in the firing area were several crude dummies, which he thought were real people, at first. They were wearing military uniforms, and some were holding staffs with flags on them. One he recognized as Russia's flag, and another held a flag with a six-pointed star. There were other items to shoot at in the sandy area, but the primary targets seemed to be the make-believe people. Jamie didn't like that very much. He hadn't associated the weapons with killing people until then, though he knew deep down that's what they were for.

Guns were something he was used to; sometimes they were used to hunt animals, but not people. His daddy had never mentioned killing when he was cleaning his Luger. And on the rare instances he had taken Jamie along for shooting practice out in the woods, he always shot at bottles and cans. Never people. And he couldn't imagine Joe shooting and killing someone else. The sight of the dummies standing there, waiting to be shot at, made him feel a little sick inside.

But he didn't say anything to Joe, for fear of being a sissy. *I'm going to do this, no matter what, so nobody will treat me like a sissy no more.*

Joe showed him three different sniper positions before he even let him handle the loaded weapon; as he lay there, belly down in the dirt, Jamie wondered what this had to do with learning how to shoot. Finally the older boy loaded the weapon with eight little bullets and carefully handed it to him.

"This is the safety," Joe informed him, lying prone beside him in the sand. "This keeps it from firing accidentally. Until you're ready to shoot, leave it on."

The lessons progressed from there, and after learning to *squeeze*, not pull, the trigger, Jamie fired his first round. It wasn't nearly as loud as he expected, but then his gun wasn't as large as Joe's. At Joe's urging he selected a target and fired a few more rounds, remembering to *squeeze* the trigger, and promptly picked off one of the objects in the sand. His first kill was a Hill's Brother's coffee can, which went *piiiing* as it flew backwards into the sand.

"Good *shot*, buckaroo!" Joe applauded. Jamie was triumphant. "That's better than I did my first time!"

Jamie was getting ready to draw on another target when he became aware of someone standing behind them. Another weapon went *snik, snik*. Jamie's arms turned to putty, and the barrel of his rifle dropped.

"If I were a Jew-Communist-pig you'd both be dead

now, Private!" an ominous, and familiar, voice boomed. Following Joe's example, he scrambled to his feet, leaving the weapon on the ground.

It was Brother Joseph, standing there with Joe's AK-47 pointed directly at them. As if to make a point, he turned and fired a few rounds into a dummy.

"I'm sorry, sir," Joe stammered in the echo of the gunfire. Jamie could see he was really scared; his face had become whiter than usual, which probably wasn't so bad, since these people seemed to value that color. "I was just showing—"

"*Silence!*" Brother Joseph demanded, and received. The man was wearing a strange military uniform similar to the Guard, but it had a preacher's white collar incorporated into it. Jamie had never seen this particular article of finery and assumed it was new. "On your stomach. Fifty — no, *one hundred* push-ups. Now!" the man barked, and the boy responded instantly.

Joe dropped to the ground, making his lean, muscular body rigid as he began the push-ups, using his knuckles for support. It was how the Guard always did push-ups, Jamie observed, and it looked quite painful.

While Joe was doing this, Jamie could see a thin wisp of smoke trailing out of the AK-47 and remembered his own gun, lying on the sand. He thought it best to go ahead and leave it there, to give himself time to figure out what was wrong, and what Joe had done that was so terrible. Brother Joseph was angry about something, and although the anger seemed to be directed at Joe, he did not feel at all comfortable standing in the man's shadow. Even when he *wasn't* angry.

Joe counted out the push-ups, pumping them off with ease; a slight sweat broke out down the small of his back and beaded across his forehead. The beret had been left on, as Brother Joseph had given him no permission to remove it. Slowly but surely, Jamie was beginning to understand the nuances of discipline within the Guard, though he had never envisioned Brother Joseph as the direct leader of them. The Guard leadership seemed to be comprised of middlemen subservient to Brother Joseph; now the boy knew the weird preacher was probably in command of them as well. His new item of clothing supported this.

It was in moments like these, when the cruelty shone through like a spotlight, that Jamie had second thoughts about joining the Junior Guard. Then he would look at Joe and see him endure the abuse and begin to wonder if this really was the natural order of things everywhere. It certainly was the natural order of things *here*.

Joe completed the punishment and leaped to his feet, standing sharply at attention. His breathing was hardly labored, and only the slightest gleam of sweat had appeared on his forehead. What would have been brutal punishment for most didn't seem to bother him in the least; Jamie was in awe. *Someday, I'm gonna be able to do that.*

"Very well," Brother Joseph said, sounding a little calmer. "Perhaps that will teach you never to leave your weapon where the common enemy can take it and use it against you. I know, son, it probably seems like there's no chance for a Jew-pig to infiltrate, but you never know. They're a cunning bunch, the spawn of Satan."

"Yes, Father," Joe said, looking down at the ground.

Son? Father? Is he Joe's daddy? Or do they just talk like that because of who he is?

"So tell me, young guardsman, what were you doing down here with this *child*?"

The question carried strange, accusatory undertones that Jamie couldn't fathom. Leaving the firearm in the sand didn't seem a good idea, and he wondered if now was a good time to bring that up.

"I was showing this youngster how to use a weapon, Father," Joe said, pride slowly returning to his voice. "He has a fine talent for marksmanship, if I do say so," he added.

"Glad to hear it," Brother Joseph said, and handed Joe his weapon. "Strip and clean your weapon, son," he said. "Your mother will be expecting you at our dinner table tonight. You haven't forgotten her birthday, have you?"

"Of course not, sir," Joe said. "I will attend."

Brother Joseph regarded Jamie with a bemused, patronizing expression, as if he'd just seen him for the first time. "Young James," he said. "So you have a gift. That much was obvious, that first time we touched the Holy Fire together." His eyes narrowed. "Yes. Special. And *very* gifted indeed," he said in parting, and as he walked away his laughter echoed down the metal walls.

The sound made him feel empty, and somehow unclean. As Jamie watched Brother Joseph's back recede he felt a new dread, a growing horror that had no name. The Chosen Ones didn't see it, saw only the bright side of him. They followed Brother Joseph wherever he went. Sarah was the only one who knew about it besides Jamie, that's how hidden it was. And when the preacher made him "channel" the Holy Fire, they both saw this darkness, so scary that Jamie made himself forget what he saw and touched, most of the time.

But every time he saw Brother Joseph he remembered. *And we're going to do it again tonight. Oh, no,* he thought, and shuddered.

In silence Joe finished cleaning his firearm and put it all back together. He seemed humiliated, and justifiably so. But Jamie still had questions to ask. About the milk carton, about his mother. And he was going to ask them; they were alone now, and there would be no better opportunity.

"Is he your daddy?" Jamie blurted, knowing no other way to start.

"Yes. He is. And it's nothing we need to talk about. As far as anyone is concerned, I'm just another soldier, fighting for the cause. I get no special treatment," he said, his eyes narrowing at Jamie. "And don't you treat me no different. If you do that I'll have to rough you up." He added that last, lightly, like a joke.

But in that second, with that brief, angry expression, he looked just like Brother Joseph. *Joe, Joseph. Of course. How come I didn't guess before?* Jamie knew he could get real depressed over this if he let it happen, but he tried not to. *Joe's still Joe. Even my daddy's bad sometimes.*

"Why didn't you know your daddy was coming?" Jamie asked, but immediately knew it was the wrong thing to say. Joe was looking at the ground, apparently not paying too much attention.

"Sometimes I just have to turn it off. . . ." Joe said absently, then looked at Jamie in mild alarm. "No one can read minds. Remember that. And don't call him my daddy. He's my leader, and that's all that matters."

"Oh," was all he said, and Joe looked relieved. Apparently, other people down here made a big deal over it. But then, those other people *liked* Brother Joseph. "Something weird happened today when we were out getting supplies."

"What's that?" Joe asked, brightening up. He sounded glad to change the subject.

"I saw my picture on a milk carton. It said I was a 'missing child.' What does that mean?" he said, waiting for *some* kind of reaction from Joe.

He found none, absolutely nothing. A stone mask went over his face, and Jamie knew something was amiss. It was the same mask he had worn when his father sneaked up behind them.

"Are you sure it was you?" he finally replied.

"Yep," Jamie said. "Sure was."

Joe frowned. "Did you tell your daddy about it?"

Jamie felt a little cold. "Y-yeah, and he said it was someone else."

Joe stopped and knelt again, but it was with an expression of such severity that Jamie wasn't annoyed by it; he was frightened. "Then listen to your father. Do not disobey him. It is the way of the Chosen Ones. It was wrong for you to ask another grownup when your father already told you it wasn't you." Joe held his chin in his right hand, forcing the boy to look directly in his eyes. "If your father said it was someone else, then it was someone else. *Don't ask anyone about it again.*"

Jamie wanted to cry. This was the first time his friend had spoken to him like that, and it hurt terribly. *This is still not right*, he thought. *But he isn't gonna tell me anything else, either. Maybe I'd better not ask about Mom, then. Daddy already told me why she isn't here. It's because she doesn't want to be.*

But as Joe walked him back to his room, he couldn't believe this was the real reason.

Joe walked him back to the tiny cubicle that served as his home. It was in a section of the underground that was lined with sheet metal, forming tubular habitats for most of the "civilian" Chosen Ones. That meant all the women, little kids, and the few men that weren't in the Guard, like Jamie's dad. The Guard and Junior Guard lived elsewhere, in barracks-type quarters, austere living for even a seasoned soldier. At first, Jamie had thought it was a kind of jail, without the bars. Joe had showed the Junior Guard barracks to him once, but it did not inspire the awe the older boy had apparently hoped it would.

Jamie's quarters were cozy in comparison. The cult had found scrap carpeting and had used it to create a patchwork quilt on all the floors. The three pieces of furniture were all used, and none of it matched: a chair, a formica coffee table, a burlap-covered couch with the stuffing coming out in white, fluffy lumps. For the first week they didn't have a bed and had to sleep on blankets and blocks of soft foam that had been in a flood, according to Jamie's dad. The two twin mattresses they had now were an improvement over the floor, but Jamie overheard one of the men who carried them in say they had been stolen from a motel. Their lighting came from one dangling lightbulb that had no switch and had to be unscrewed each night with an "as-best-ohs" rag kept specifically for that purpose. The bathroom and single shower were down the hall and serviced the entire row of ten tiny rooms. Moist, musty air occasionally blew through a small vent, enough to keep the room from getting too stuffy. But since they were underground, the cool earth kept the temperature down.

At first the rugged environment was more exciting than uncomfortable, this secret place where he hid with his dad from the rest of the world. But as a week passed, and he began to miss his mother and wonder about where she was, the experience became disturbing. He missed his things, his toys, and especially his clothes. He missed having three meals, or even *one* meal, a day. He couldn't remember the last time he'd eaten, other than Joe's gift of candy. *It wasn't yesterday. I think it was the day before.* When he went to the dining hall, all they would give him was juice. Orange juice at breakfast, vegetable juice at lunch and dinner, and apple juice at night. Everyone *else* got to eat, but not him.

Joe's answer wasn't good enough, Jamie thought, morosely. *It wasn't even close. Didn't tell me nothin'.*

Jamie sat on his bed and leaned against the curved, metal wall. His father was not here yet, but it would only be a matter of moments before he came and fetched him for supper, which was served in a large, communal hall. *But I've got time to talk to Sarah, before he gets here.*

The wall was cool and pulled some of the heat out of his body. *Good. That'll help me to think real hard.*

He closed his eyes. "Sarah?" he said. "Are you there?"

:I'm here, Jamie,: he suddenly heard in his head. *:I was getting worried.:*

• CHAPTER FOUR

Cindy looked a little better now that she was in the cool, dry air of Andur's air-conditioned interior. Her conversation was certainly more animated.

"Well, like I said, he's a car nut. That's why I was here, looking for him at the track." Cindy repeated herself often, apparently without realizing it, as Al's elvensteed, Andur, pulled slowly through the paddock.

Andur was disguised as a white Mazda Miata, although usually Andur was a much flashier Porsche 911. Andur's choice of form — and Alinor's transportation of choice — had changed through the ages. To flee the Civil War, Andur had been a roan stallion. Some years later he had manifested as a Harley Davidson, but this had attracted the *wrong* kind of attention, and Al had asked him to change to something less conspicuous. On a racetrack the little sports-car fit in quite well; though it was an inexpensive one, anything more ostentatious might have attracted questions.

Besides, Al rather liked Miatas. Their design was rounded, purposeful and sensual, like a lover's body or a sabre's sweep.

Andur in this form had only two seats, but Bob claimed there were last-minute things to do at the pits before calling it a day and sauntered off to check on his precious engine.

Al didn't spare a second thought for the man, who seemed just as happy to deal with metal and machine-parts, rather than an unhappy lady on the edge. In some ways, Al didn't blame him; Cindy seemed very close to the end of her resources — mental, emotional and physical. Bob was young and might not be much help with an emotional crisis. And he certainly couldn't be counted on for sparkling, cheery conversation if Cindy got too morose.

The summer sun was setting, casting an orange glow on the Hallet raceway, silhouetting Bob against the red-and-gold sky. He appeared solid. Someone to be depended upon. Al was very thankful Bob was here, as he pulled away from the pit area, heading for the nearby campground.

Cindy clenched her hands in her lap, as tense as an over-wound clock-spring. Al's senses told him that her anxiety attack had yet to run its course. She was not paying much attention to things outside of herself, which was all to the good for him, but that wasn't a healthy state of mind for a human.

She was surely running on pure adrenalin by now. Her hands shook slightly, and she still had trouble catching her breath, and that also concerned him. He wasn't a Healer, except maybe of metals. If she were to become ill, he wouldn't know what to do with her.

How am I to calm her down? She can't have been eating well, lately — and the heat hasn't done her any good, either. I have to get her settled and balanced, or she won't be of any use at all.

Alinor frowned as he considered her distress. From the moment they began talking he had been forced to put up an array of shields usually reserved for the most intense of emotional moments. There was no doubt that she was in dire need of some kind of release, and out of consideration for her state of mind, he allowed a small amount of her anxiety to seep through. She wouldn't know what he was doing — not consciously — but even though she was only marginally psychic, her subconscious would know that someone was "listening" to her, and cared enough to pay attention and not block her out. It was simply common manners among elves not to shut someone out completely, unless absolutely necessary; what he had done so far was enough to keep Cindy from pulling him in with her. Later, when he could concentrate on the task, he would see what he could do to apply some emotional balm to her misery.

On the other hand — so far as keeping his "cover" intact was concerned — in her present state she probably wouldn't notice that the Miata had no ignition, or that it was driving itself. Al rested his hands on the steering wheel, to make it look as if he was in control, but the elvensteed knew where they were going.

"I think I left the air-conditioning on in the RV," Al said conversationally, reaching forward with a tiny touch of magic and activating the air-conditioning switch. With any luck, it would be cool by the time they got there. *Let's see . . . Gatorade in the fridge? Yeah, plenty of that. And ice. We should be in good shape when we arrive.* "It has a shower," he added, hesitating. Al realized what this might sound like, and he glanced over at Cindy for a reaction. She offered none, gazing blankly forward, apparently unaware she was tying the edge of her blouse in a knot.

At least she didn't take exception to that suggestion. That is, if she even heard it. It wasn't as if he was trying to *seduce* her in any way —

Even though she was attracted to me, I could feel that. . . .

But he wasn't *demanding* sex — he wasn't even expecting it. It was just —

Damn. I am trying to seduce her. Am I trying to prove to her that I'm attractive, or to myself? This is something that a good session of sweat cannot fix. I should know better.

But she was very vulnerable at this point, and in obvious need of comfort. Comfort which could be physical or otherwise — and if physical, could take any number of forms. And he was skilled at offering that kind of comfort. He'd had lots of time to practice, after all —

Stop it! he scolded himself. He was tempted to reflect on the last time he'd had any kind of relationship, but he knew it would only heighten his desire. In his childhood, so many years ago, the maxim had been drilled into him by his father: *never get involved emotionally with a human, except on the most casual of terms.* There was a good reason for this guideline, as evidenced by centuries of elvenkind's experience. First of all, going by most definitions of a "relationship," the human involved would eventually become aware of the existence of the Folk and want to know what was going on. With the exception of humans like Bob, the foster children who were brought up Underhill, this was seldom a good idea. Word could get out, and if enough humans became convinced that elves were "real," the elves in question would have to go into strictest hiding. This was usually done with concealment spells, but in the more dangerous cases of hostile humans, an all-out retreat to Underhill often became necessary.

But that wasn't the real danger. One way or another, those situations could be handled. The Folk were experts at hiding from the humans, and throughout their long history had even enhanced their disguises with "fairy tales" they had written themselves.

The main reason the Sidhe avoided relationships with humans was simply that humans grew old and died.

However, when Alinor was younger, he had decided to ignore this advice. Being young, he had convinced himself that he was immune to such pain —

And I told myself that killjoy adults didn't understand love. They couldn't see how it meant more than life or death.

Or so he thought.

It had been around a century and a half ago. After falling head over heels in love with a young pioneer girl, Janet Travis, they settled in what was now North Dakota. They were one of the few settlers able to maintain a homestead in that area, as they were the only *wasichu* who could get along with the Lakota Sioux living there.

It helped that they honored the beliefs of the Sioux themselves, hunting rather than farming, never taking from the land more than they could use, never wasting anything, and giving thanks for what the land gave them. Alinor's magic, carefully disguised as earth-medicine, brought the deepest respect from the tribes.

The years passed, the seasons turned, and Alinor and his human bride enjoyed what seemed in retrospect to have been an idyllic existence in the Plains. It was the longest stretch of time he had ever spent away from his own kind, and if it hadn't been for this periodic sojourn Underhill, he might not have survived with his sanity intact. Janet only knew that he was going out hunting — to trap furs to trade for the things they needed. He never told her that he went off Underhill to reproduce the flour, salt, bolts of linen . . . and that the few things he *did* trade for, he went to the Lakota for. Men did that, and she understood. He would go off and return with three elvensteeds laden with enough to see them through another six months or so.

The problem was, it was hard work reproducing enough goods to last six months. He could be gone as long as a month. And time did not pass Underhill the same way it passed in the real world. He never knew exactly when he would emerge. . . .

One bright winter afternoon, Alinor came back from his semi-annual trip and discovered his beloved Janet was dead.

He had never learned the cause then; and the reason was still a mystery. The Lakota might have been able to tell him, but they were in their winter hunting grounds, and no one had been near the cabin. She could have been hurt — she could have caught an illness — he had no way of telling.

She was forty years old, advanced age for humans of that era, but she had been healthy and young-seeming, without the burden of producing a child each year as women of her time usually did. She had been fine when he left her, and from the condition of their cabin, whatever had killed her had sickened her so quickly that she hadn't had time to do more than close the door, put out the latchstring, and get into her bed.

He'd thought in the first month that he would join her, dying of grief. He'd thought in the second month that no one of the Folk had ever suffered so. In the third month, he burned the cabin to the ground with his power, gave his furs and treasures to the Lakota, and returned to North Carolina and Underhill.

A little older, a little wiser, Alinor sought out the High Court of Elfhame Outremer. He returned to his brethren with his grief. There he learned that others had made the same bonds to mortals as he had, and understood.

Janet was many years ago, he told himself. *I promised myself I would never do that again.*

Still, it had been a very long time since he had taken a human lover; despite her distress he found Cindy appealing, and sensed that she was attracted to him as well.

But not now. There is a time for everything, he thought, *and the time hasn't arrived yet.*

The RV was parked on a section of the Hallet grounds reserved for campers. The camaraderie was as evident here as at the races; the temporary city of tents, campers and rec vehicles provided some sanctuary from the frantic pace of the track. The portable communities followed the races much like the ranks of carnies did at the state fairs, and the faces were always familiar. Al could have walked the distance, but Cindy had seemed ready to melt — and Andur had been right there. And, truth be told — human women found sports-cars exciting. He'd been strutting like a prize cock, hoping that she would admire his "Miata," and that some of that admiration would spill over onto him.

They pulled up next to the RV, near a copse of trees that offered some shade. "My parents had an RV like this. A Winnie, isn't it?" Cindy said as she got out of the Miata.

"Class C Winnebago. With a bunk over the cab," Al said. "Did you say you have parents?"

"Had. They died last year. I had to sell the RV to help settle their estate or I'd still have it," she said. Her words trailed off, and she seemed to withdraw a little.

I guess I'd better not pursue that one, Al thought, realizing that he'd touched on a sensitive subject. *Sounds like this poor girl is all alone in this mess. Without even parents to fall back on.* Hearing that surprised him somewhat. For the most part, his small sphere of friends, though far away, were Sidhe. Al thought in terms of the Kin's longevity, not humans'.

The interior of the RV was pleasantly cool, to Al's relief. But as they entered the door, he found himself embarrassed by the state of the interior. He wished that he had cleaned the place up a little; he couldn't even see the second bed under all the animal, vegetable and mineral flotsam that somehow migrated into the cabin, seemingly of its own volition.

I think junk breeds in RVs.

He scooped up an armload of dirty clothes — and other things less identifiable — then dumped the entire load in the tiny bathroom to be sorted. Later. Then he popped the table up, making the bed into a place they could both sit.

"Cozy," Cindy commented, but it sounded like she was trying to be polite. He noticed her nose wrinkling at an odor.

Yes, I know. The place smells, Al thought apologetically. But at the moment she looked like she didn't care too much. *Why clean the place every day when I can effortlessly make it into my normal nest?* Being one of the Sidhe had its advantages; Al could conjure whatever he wanted for the interior. On most days, his digs would make a Pharaoh envious. Silk sheets covered the beds, and intricate, woven tapestries draped the walls and ceiling of the compact RV, giving it more depth, an illusion of space it just didn't have. Bob certainly never had any complaints about it. But all that luxury would have to stay in magical "storage"; at least until Cindy was safely stowed away somewhere else.

His harem of illusory dancing girls, complete with fans, grapes and feathered garments, would also have to remain in hiding, stashed away in the netherlands of his magical universe. Only his statue, an ornamental metal reproduction of an art-nouveau Phaeton mascot, could remain the same. When "activated," it became a graceful, liquid-chrome servant. In its inanimate state, however, it looked like something that had been stolen from someone's lawn. He'd have to do without her as well.

He sighed. For the time being his home would have to remain a plain, unaugmented recreational vehicle, complete with a monumental mortal mess.

"I don't think I have to ask if you're thirsty," Al said, pulling a large square jug of orange Gatorade from the fridge. "Despite appearances, the cups are clean. I promise. And so is the ice."

Cindy settled down at the smallish table, letting the cool breeze of the air-conditioner brush across her face. "That feels so good," she said. "I don't know how to thank you for all this. Are you sure your friend won't mind if I stay here tonight?"

"Positive. We'll work something out," Al said, though he didn't know what it would be. He sat at a second place at the table with the other plastic cup of Gatorade. "Feel better?" he asked, as she gulped the orange potion.

That much we have in common. We both need this magical stuff after all that heat. It always tastes good when you really need it.

"Much," Cindy said, sounding like she really meant it. "Tell me, what exactly do you do at the racetrack? You're not all dirty and grubby like most mechanics I know."

Like her ex, Al thought with hostility, but set the feeling aside. *You don't know he was a mechanic. Parts store, remember?*

"Originally I'm from the East Coast." *I've come from many places. I'd better tell her one she'll believe.* "North Carolina, mostly. That's where the South Eastern Road Racing Association is based. SERRA, for short. And the firm I work for, Fairgrove Industries. We're running a test-project for the Firestone team." He didn't mention he had conjured an engine block from thin air, and was here with Bob to watch how it performed.

"So what, exactly, are you doing here?" she quizzed. "This must be small time compared to what you're used to."

"Well no, not really," Al lied. "Hallet is unique. It takes skill to keep our cars on this one at the speeds we're traveling. This is a good venue to heat-stress test the cars and their engines. I'm on loan to the Firestone team as I said — what I'm actually doing is monitoring one of our cast-aluminum engine blocks. Different drivers, different conditions, out in this neck of the woods. A good way to make sure that what works at Roebling Road or Road Atlanta will work everywhere."

"I see," Cindy said, but it looked like he was losing her again. A faraway, distant look fell over her. Thinking other things.

"Do you think I'll ever find him?" Cindy finally said, looking at him as if he was the original Sibylline Oracle, or an Archdruid.

He spoke from his heart. "Yes, I think we will. But first things first. Are you tired?"

"Exhausted," she said, yawning. "This cold air. Feel's good, but . . ."

"Putting you to sleep, isn't it?" Al observed, wryly.

"Some," she admitted. "What time is it, anyway?"

"Eight something, probably. Why don't you go ahead and crash? I have to go check some things before I turn in."

"You're sure I'm no trouble?"

"I'm certain. Go ahead, scoot. Take the bunk over the cab. That plastic curtain pulls across for privacy and snaps at the corners. I can make this table back into a bed for myself."

Which should reassure her as to the purity of my intentions.

Cindy finished off two more cups of Gatorade before she climbed the ladder into the overhead and finally gave in to sleep. It didn't take long. *She* must *be dehydrated,* Al decided, leaving a fourth cup of iced Gatorade in the well at the head of her bed, in case she woke up thirsty.

Before leaving the RV, Al stood in the doorway, looking back at Cindy, lying there asleep. *So trusting of strangers,* he thought. *She doesn't know anything about me, yet she falls asleep so easily, leaving herself vulnerable. Either I look completely harmless, or the poor girl is very, very naive. Or else she's so desperate she'd take an offer of help from anyone.*

Alinor left the RV, locking the door and making certain it was secure. He seldom locked it, having his own devices for safeguarding the Winnie, but this time he made an exception.

Night had fallen on the track, and locusts and crickets were out in full force, replacing the race-car roars that had dominated the daylight hours. Around him were small impromptu parties, barbecues, none of which would last very long. Racers tended to respect the next man's sleep time, and brought the noise inside after about nine or ten at night, adjourning to quiet poker games or TV. Some of them traded videotapes, and a couple had Nintendos casting *their* spell. A tranquil atmosphere fell over the little makeshift city of tents and campers at night, reminding Al of why he liked racing in general, and these humans in particular. It was as an RV marketer had advertised once, "a community on wheels," where the people next to you were your neighbors, even if for only one night at a time.

Al walked beyond the campers to an emptying parking lot. Not a lot of spectators on trial days. Only hard-core racing fans showed up for days like these, and those that were not friends of someone here were long gone. *This was a good day to look for her child*, Al thought. *If he had been here, he would have been easy to spot. Too bad they weren't here. Maybe tomorrow . . .*

Maybe — but he didn't have a lot of hope that they really would show up.

Cindy looked a lot like Janet; flyaway brown-blond hair, freckles over the bridge of her nose, direct, blue eyes. Really, allowing for the differences in clothing, she looked amazingly like Janet. He guessed that her sense of humor would be very similar too — and that if she ever really smiled, it would light up her face and make her dazzlingly lovely.

And he was afraid of the effect that would have on him.

He told himself that he had other things to think about, and plenty of them. *I will deal with that later.*

So, what should they do about this missing child? Sit around and wait for him to appear on their doorstep? It didn't seem a very logical way to handle things. *We could keep an eye out for her child tomorrow, but it sure* feels *like a longshot. I didn't want to tell her that, since this is her only hope. What if they* don't *come tomorrow? What then?*

Feeling tired, and just a little depressed, Al sat on a tire-wall, watching the sparse traffic on the nearby Cimarron Turnpike. His vision blurred as he gazed at the occasional retreating red taillights, and he began to see how tired he really was. His thoughts turned to his partner, Bob. *He's not going to like this one bit. And I didn't even ask him if she could stay. It's my RV, but it's his home, too. I just took it for granted that he wouldn't mind.*

But then, what else could he have done? She was alone and broke, and a child was involved. . . .

How could he turn his back on a child — or on someone as childlike in her distress as Cindy?

But then again, he didn't know exactly what he was getting into and was beginning to feel a little put out with himself for getting so deeply involved so quickly. *I know what Bob will say: leave it to the Sidhe to stick their noses in where no one else would.* But that thought simply catalyzed his resolve again. *Well, so be it! That's why we get things done.*

Al paced the edge of the parking lot; the asphalt radiated heat and the scent of baking petroleum, still warm from the day's sun. Portions were cracked and dry, the result of years of weathering. A lone Hallet employee wandered the empty parking lot with a bag, picking up litter. *If I had lost a child in this part of the country, how would I go about finding him?*

It didn't take long for him to see that he knew very little about how the mainstream of human society worked. He might as well have been from another planet. For years, especially recently, in modern times, he had relied on humans like Bob to provide a smokescreen for him, concealing him from suspicious eyes and coping with the intricacies of the modern world for him. In fact, of all the Folk Al knew, only Keighvin Silverhair in Savannah knew enough of the modern world to move about in it unaided.

Even at Hallet, Bob played interference for his partner. This was a world within a world, essentially transparent to the rest of the population. His niche as a SERRA and Fairgrove mechanic made him part of the landscape; nobody asked questions around the track if you were an insider, and SERRA automatically qualified him as that. Only outsiders were subject to suspicion. Outsiders — like Cindy, which was probably the reason she'd had so much trouble this afternoon.

When anything went wrong, if an accident happened, there was always a human there to pick up the pieces, to drive the ambulance, to call the hospital. Al had never had to do any of those things. On the rare occasions that police were involved, Al had observed from a distance, preferring to keep his presence as discreet as possible, even throwing in a concealment spell for good measure. But out here, there were no police to call — those were attached to cities, and Hallet hardly qualified as that. There was someone else in authority in these parts, but he couldn't remember who, or what, they were.

Blessed Danaa, Al thought, throwing his arms up in helplessness. *Where does one go for help around here?*

He had no idea. Back at the RV he had felt rather — superior. What was it Bob said? *Macho,* that was it. Macho to be able to help Cindy out like he did. Then he was in control of the situation. And he was also on his own territory, the racetrack, the Winnie. But now, faced with the prospect of going Out There, into the humans' everyday world, he was at a complete loss.

Then he remembered an ad he'd seen once. *Can't find it? Try the Yellow Pages.*

"The phone book. Of course," he whispered, barely realizing he'd spoken aloud.

Near the observation tower was a row of public telephones. Al had generally avoided such devices, even when they were in their infancy. There was something inherently wrong about one of the Folk using such a contrivance, when he could send his thoughts and messages to faraway places without them. It was like using crutches to walk when nothing was wrong with your legs. But he went in search of one, and spotted it by the lighted symbol built into it, with the phone book attached by a chain. Some of the pages even *looked* yellow.

"Let's see, her ex-husband's name was Jim Chase. That's the same as James Chase, I think," he muttered to himself. He fished out the last of his cookies and ate them while he thumbed through the book. The phone book was a bit thinner than the ones he had seen, which might have been a clue to its usefulness had he been operating on the proper wavelength.

Nothing. Not even a "Chase" was listed.

Ok, then. Be that way. Can't find it? How about "missing children" in the yellow pages?

No luck. Hallet wasn't exactly a large town. In fact, the directory listed several other towns in the same directory. Frustrated, and tired, he gave up on the phone book. *Time to find Bob,* Al finally admitted. *Maybe he'll have an idea. After all, it's his society.*

Bob wasn't very talkative, as usual, and suggested they tackle the missing child situation in the morning. They had both had a long day, he pointed out, and besides, tomorrow their crew had a day off. Good time to play private investigator. Al agreed, finding it difficult to stay awake. He'd been short on sleep last night, and his body knew it. A few hours from now, he'd be alert, his mind running at top form. Now was not the time to try to solve problems.

But there was the need to figure out where to put Bob—

He solved the sleeping logistics by having Andur turn himself into a white van, complete with bed — truth be told, a much nicer environment than the Winnie was at the moment. Bob volunteered for it without Al having to ask; Al retired in the table-turned-bed, with Cindy chastely asleep in the loft, and instantly fell asleep, the woman's proximity notwithstanding.

* * *

Dawn brought something besides the crowing of roosters in the nearby farmyards. There were sounds of someone stirring in the RV. Not unusual; Bob often got up before he did, and sometimes even started breakfast, if he felt motivated enough. But the sounds he heard were different, not of someone making a new mess, but of someone . . . cleaning an old one up.

This was terribly out of place. Alarmed, Al sat up abruptly.

"Good morning," Cindy greeted him cheerfully, from an arm's-length away. "When was the last time you guys cleaned this dump?"

Egads. A morning person, Al thought muzzily, as the evening's events came flooding back at him. *I took this Cindy under my wing last night, didn't I? If she's going to be awake and active this early in the morning, maybe I'd better think about putting her somewhere else.* Al fell back on an elbow, watching her sweep the narrow aisle of the RV. The place smelled strongly of ammonia and Lysol, in spite of the fact that the windows were open, the air-conditioner off.

"We have a broom?" Al inquired, yawning.

"Yes, you do," she replied. "It was in the back of the closet. Still wrapped up with the cardboard thingie on the back. Never used."

Horrified, Al watched her sweep up the dust into a shoebox and begin wiping down the plastic runner with a sponge.

"We don't have a . . ." *What was it called? Oh, yeah,* "A mop. Didn't know you could do it that way."

She paused, then looked up with a faint smile. "I can tell. Don't worry, I'm almost done. And I guarantee you won't be able to find a thing."

"That's nice to know," Al said, uncertain of what exactly she meant. He realized that he was still fully clothed, either because he had been too exhausted to remove his garments the night before, or in his foggy state he was too modest around Cindy to get comfortable. He'd even left the track cap on, with his hair pulled back into a thick ponytail, so as to better hide his ears. *Good. Saves me the trouble of getting dressed.* He glanced out the little side window at the white van that was his elvensteed, and reached with his mind to the sleeping human within. Bob wasn't sleeping; in fact, he wasn't even there. *Must be off doing something.*

He sat up and regarded his small — but now spotless — home. The sink and stove had been cleaned, as had the microwave and refrigerator. These items were now new colors, ones he didn't recognize. Even the cabinets had been wiped clean. He was suddenly ashamed that this human had had to stay here without the usual concealing spells that made its squalor into splendor.

She deserved better. He began moving the foam-block cushions to make the bed back into a breakfast table, pondering the changes in the RV, and the more unnerving ones deep in himself.

Something was missing, but in this unnatural state of cleanliness, he didn't know what. It was all so . . . different.

My clothes! he realized, in panic, remembering the crumpled, smelly pile of fabric that was developing a life of its own, a fixture that was moved from one location to another without ever really being dealt with. *What did she do with them?*

"Bob is at the laundromat," she said, as if reading his mind. "I had to show him where it was."

Which answered two questions. "It is sort of hard to find," Al said, wondering where it was himself.

She eyed him strangely, then said, "Would you like me to make coffee?"

Caffeine! Blessed Danaa, no. . . .

"Uh, no thanks, Cindy. I don't drink coffee." Or anything else with caffeine. "Hard on my stomach. I'm — uh — allergic to it. To caffeine. Badly." Al checked his wristwatch. Ten-thirty. "It's early. And it looks like you've got a lot done. Why don't you take a break?"

"I think I will. Oh, I wanted to ask you. Where did that white van come from?"

Al feigned nonchalance. "Oh, that's ours. The crew's. It kind of gets traded around," he said, hoping she believed him. *I meant to have that changed back to the Miata before anyone got up,* he thought, and hoped that Bob told her the same, if not a similar, story.

Cindy dropped into the tiny booth the bed had become. Al opened a Gatorade, his standard breakfast fare. "How do you feel?"

"Much better. Since it was cool this morning, I went ahead and opened the windows. The cleaners, and all." Al nodded; it was still an uncomfortably strong scent. *Guess that's what clean smells like.* "Thank you for letting me stay here. Hope you don't mind the cleanup."

"Oh, not at all. I'm glad you did. Forgot what the place really looked like."

Bob came into the narrow door, first shoving in a huge laundry bag that Al was distantly aware of owning. It was stuffed to its maximum capacity with, he assumed, clean clothes. A rare treat. It caught in the doorway, and with a visible effort Bob wedged it through.

"Just set it up there," Al said, indicating the now vacated loft. "We have things to do today."

Bob looked around at the RV and the sparkling results of Cindy's work. "Jesus," he said, and sat. "You've been busy. I've been asking around about your boy, Cindy. Nobody here knows anything. Might be they've never been here."

Cindy looked down, to hide the sudden surge of despair. Al felt it anyway. "Oh well. It was worth a try," she replied, sounding defeated. "I don't know what else to do now."

"Have you called the sheriff's office?" Bob asked.

"I've talked to the Tulsa police. There wasn't much they could do about it. Then I called the Tulsa County sheriff's office, and they were sympathetic, but not much help either."

"Eyah," Bob said. "But we happen to be in *Pawnee* county here. What you say we give 'em a call? If those nutsos that your ex is involved with set up shop around here, you can bet the Sheriff will know it. And in a place this small, everybody knows everybody else. A new man in town with a small boy is likely to get noticed."

Al finished his Gatorade and all three trooped to the pay telephones to call the Pawnee County Sheriff's office. Bob gave Al a nod and a significant look; Al shrugged and stood aside to let Bob make the call.

"Well, I think we might be in luck," Bob said, hanging up the phone. He had spoken for several minutes in a hushed monotone that was hard to listen to. The one-sided conversation shed little light on what the person on the other side was saying. "Deputy named Frank knows about some kind of whacked-out religious cult in this area. Actually, it's closer to Pawnee than Hallet, from what Frank says. He wants to talk to us."

"Well, then," Alinor said. "Let's go."

"In what? The Miata's only a two-seater," Bob said.

Al gave him the hairy eyeball, cleared his throat loudly, and continued. "The crew gave us the van. Re*member*?"

"Oh, yes. The *van*," he responded, while Al wondered what he had told Cindy about the elvensteed and the mysteriously appearing and disappearing van.

But at the moment, Cindy didn't seem to notice the awkward exchange, or care. She had a gleam in her eye, excitement that could only be a glimmer of hope.

Pawnee was a tiny little burg nestled among the rolling hills of Northeast Oklahoma, similar to a dozen

other towns that Bob and Al had passed through on
their trip to Hallet. Pawnee itself was built on a series of
hills, giving it an uneven, tilted look. It looked old, and
for Oklahoma, which had been granted statehood in
1907, that meant sometime early this century. The
dates on the masonry of some of the buildings confirmed this: 1911, 1922, 1923. City Hall was behind an
elaborate storefront, on a red brick street unevened
with time. Across a street-wide gulf of time and technology was a Chevy-Geo dealership, displaying the latest
Storms and Metros in the same showroom window that
once must have hawked carriages, Model T's, and
Woodies.

Al had a definite feeling of *déjà vu*, thinking maybe
he had been here before, in his youth, when horses
and sprung carriages were just starting to replace
horses and buckboards. Even in modern times the
town maintained a tranquil, relaxed atmosphere.

They passed a Texaco, a mom and pop steakhouse, a
tag office, a Masonic temple and assorted city blocks of
ancient brick structures that had no obvious function,
their windows boarded or bricked over. Pickup trucks
and enormous cars from the sixties and seventies
seemed to be the preferred mode of transportation
here. Townfolk strolled the sidewalks, casting annoyed
or disdainful looks at the few hopped-up teenmobiles
haunting the streets. *Lunchtime*, Al noted, thinking
there was probably a high school nearby.

In the center of Pawnee was a grassy knoll, surrounded on three sides by brick streets; Al had
forgotten such anachronisms still existed. The seat of
Pawnee County government sat atop the knoll,
guarded by a large piece of artillery, a museum piece
forever enshrined on the front lawn. Behind this stood
a WWI memorial, a statue of a soldier with flowers
spelling "PAWNEE" at its feet. The courthouse was a
three-story brick building, surrounded by a few cedar

and oak trees. Carved in stone, across the top of the structure, were the words: PAWNEE COUNTY COURT-HOUSE.

As they approached, Al could see a single car in the parking lot, with the traditional silver star of authority painted proudly on its side.

"This is *it* for the whole county?" Bob exclaimed as they climbed out of the van. "Doesn't seem like much."

"Pawnee County is *not* highly populated," Al reminded him, then jibed, "I thought you didn't like metro areas."

"I don't. I just expected more, is all."

Cindy held her purse closer, as if it were a teddy bear. Then she checked to be sure the photo of Jamie was still inside. "I don't care if it's a shack, as long as they can help me find my son. Is the Sheriff's office in there?"

"Should be. That's where the car is. Let's have a look."

The courthouse smelled old; smelled of dust, layer upon layer of ancient floorwax, more layers of wood-polish, of old papers stuffed away in boxes and forgotten, and of heat-baked stone. There was no air-conditioning in the central part of the building. The floor was hand-laid terrazzo, cheap and popular in the thirties, and worth a small fortune today. In the hallway, handpainted signs hung over battered, wooden doors, thick with brown paint applied over the years. There was not a person in sight in the over-powering silence. Al began to wonder if they were in the right place.

"Is there anyone here?" Cindy said, as they walked uncertainly down the hallway. "No people."

"This is it. Look," Bob said, going towards a sign that said "SHERIFF'S OFFICE," with an arrow pointing down. They took a short flight of stairs to the court-house basement, and found the Pawnee County Sheriff's office behind a glass door.

Again, the place seemed to be staffed by ghosts. They looked over a receptionist's counter into a well-furnished office. The walls were half-faded government-blue and half-wood paneling. Then, from an adjacent office, a chair squeaked, and a deputy appeared.

"Yes? Can I help you?" the young man said. "Are you . . ."

"We called a half an hour ago," Bob said.

"You must be Cindy Chase, then," he said to Cindy. "Please come in. I'm Frank Casey, I hope I can help you."

Frank was exactly what a deputy in Oklahoma should look like, Al decided. He was sizable, with short, coal-black hair, dark skin, high cheekbones. He was without a doubt part Native American, a *large* man who barely cleared the doorway to his office. He wore a dark brown uniform with tan pants, and had a deep, booming voice that commanded immediate attention. He moved slowly, as if through water, and had a gaze that suggested he was drowsy. But Al saw he was anything but dim; his eyes shone with subdued intelligence, an intensity that seemed appropriate for anyone in a position of authority. He was capable, and concerned about Cindy. Al decided that he was an ally.

Frank pushed open a creaking brass-trimmed door and led them to his office. Three ancient varnished-oak folding chairs had been set up, apparently in preparation for their visit, in front of a pressboard computer desk with a gleaming-white IBM PC sitting incongruously atop it.

"Have you filled out one of these?" Frank asked right away, shoving a piece of paper across the desk to Cindy, a form for a "runaway or missing person report."

She nodded without taking it. "In Atlanta, and again in Tulsa. Last time they said it was already in the computer."

"Good," Frank said, sitting at the computer. "That

will save time. Lets see what the NCIC has to say about it."

"NCIC?" Al asked.

"National Crime Information Center." Frank tapped away, and soon a menu filled the screen. "If you filled out a report in Atlanta, then it was entered there. This will tell us if anything else has developed lately that you don't know about yet."

After a few moments he frowned and said, "James Chase, Jr. Kidnaped from school by one James Byron Chase, your husband—"

"Ex-husband," Cindy quickly interrupted.

"And last seen in Tulsa, a week ago. Hmm. And now you think he's in Pawnee County?"

"I thought he might have been at Hallet. You know, the races. They're big car fans, the both of them. . . ."

"Tell me about it," Frank said calmly. "Tell me the whole story. From the first time you thought something was wrong. There might be something there I can use to help you, and we've got time."

Al paid no attention to the words; this time he narrowed his eyes as he tried to sort out the feelings involved. As Cindy told the deputy about the changes in her husband, Al had the feeling she was somehow trying to justify the search for her son, emphasizing that James Chase was no longer the man she married, that he had become a monster and was nothing like the caring, giving father of her son that she knew. Almost . . . apologetic. *For as many years as those two had been married, there must have been some kind of ongoing emotional abuse for her to feel so responsible about the situation. Emotional abuse results in emotional damage. Great Danaa, look at Bob when we rescued him. Gundar thought he was autistic until he peeked out from under that thick, defensive shell.*

When she got to the part about the Chosen Ones, Frank became visibly more alert. "After that first meeting I knew I had to get Jamie to a shelter, but I was too afraid to do anything. Then, after James dragged him off the second time, he came home in hysterics. Something happened — I still don't know what. But it was the last straw."

Frank's eyes burned with an intensity that made Al think of the Lakota warriors he had known so many years ago. "I see. And the leader of this cult, what was his name?"

Cindy bit her lip. "Brother something. Brother *Joseph*, I think it was. Totally nuts."

Frank calmly got up and went to a file cabinet. When he returned he held a thick file, and opened it out on his desk. He handed Cindy a glossy photograph from a stack of others. "Is this the man?"

Cindy stifled a gasp as she looked at the picture, holding it by the edges as if it were tinged with poison. "That's him, all right," she said, half in fear and half in anger. "Those eyes. I could never forget them."

"Then it is true. More evidence. Another angle to this mess."

"What mess?" Al asked.

"This cult," Frank said, speaking the word as if it tasted vile. "They've set up shop right here in our county. There's hundreds of them, perhaps thousands. For the past three years they've been building this damned thing right under our noses and we never knew about it until recently. Here. Look at these."

Frank handed her what looked like an aerial photograph. Bob and Al, sitting on either side, leaned in closer for a look.

"What am I looking at?" Bob asked.

"We asked the State Highway police to fly in and take some pictures a few months back." Frank's eyes continued to smolder, and Al sensed a deep and abiding anger behind the calm facade. "The construction you see there is pretty much done by now. But there you can see the equipment in use. From what I can see from these, and it's not much, it looks like they're digging bunkers for World War III."

"That would make sense," she said thoughtfully. "I remember something from that sermon, or whatever it was, about an invasion that was going to happen any time now."

Frank raised one eyebrow. "From any particular direction? Any special enemies?"

Cindy shook her head tiredly. "The Soviets, the Jews, the blacks, the gays, the Satanists, pick a group — any or all together. They didn't seem to differentiate one from the other. But from the sounds of that bunch, I don't think it would matter. He could say hairdressers or Eskimos and they'd still believe him."

Frank sat back in his chair and fingered one corner of the file folder. "We've tried to get a search warrant to kind of check things out. No luck. They have a tight-assed lawyer — pardon my language, ma'am — who has filed injunction after injunction, blocking the warrants. The judge has no choice but to grant them. We don't have enough evidence. The lawyer, as crazy as he is, knows his business. Especially the loopholes in our legal system. You'd think he wrote 'em, he knows them so well."

"What about building codes?" Bob asked. "Those bunkers look a little questionable."

"That's the sad part about it," Frank said. "That part of the county is unincorporated, so there aren't a lot of permits you have to get. We already cleared them, including the Environmental Impact Assessment, years ago, without really checking it out. The inspector in charge back then has since retired, when we found out he had serious problems of a nature I'm not at liberty to discuss. We even have the blueprints to the place they filed when they applied for the permits. It *looks* like they built more than originally declared, but it's all underground, and we can't tell from outside. And we can't get a warrant to go in."

"Can we see the — blueprints?" Al asked, though he wasn't sure what a blueprint was.

"Nothing much to see," Frank said. The blueprints were in a desk drawer, and he spread them out over the open file.

"All this here, and here, looks like living quarters. The area isn't zoned so we couldn't get them on zoning violations. The rest, I don't know. But it's legit. All of it. At least everything they actually filed for." He folded the blueprint up and returned them to his drawer. "After they scared the EPA guy off with a squad of six armed bald goons following him around, nobody wants to go in and inspect. And there's nothing leaking into the aquifer or spilling into the creek, so we can't go in there on *that* excuse."

"They had guns. Lots of guns. What do your laws say about that?" Cindy asked.

"They're legal, on private property. To own and to discharge. They're not within any city limits. They're their own city. Unincorporated, of course, but a city nonetheless. And if they ever incorporate — they can make their own laws."

"Even machine guns are legal?"

Frank gazed at Cindy a long moment. "Are you referring to assault weapons?"

"I guess," she said doubtfully. Frank got to his feet, amazingly agile for such a big man.

"I'll be back in a minute," he said.

While Frank was gone Al leaned forward and glanced through the file. On top was a map, crudely drawn, which seemed to be of the cult's hideout in relation to the land and roads around it. He leaned back in his seat before Frank returned.

"Did they look anything like this?" Frank said, brandishing a fierce-looking rifle. "It's a Colt AR-15. If they have too many of these I'll be most displeased."

"Well, they had some of those." She frowned. "But

there were other kinds, too. Can I have something to write with?"

"Here's a pad," Frank said, shoving a notepad and pencil across the desk to her. "Can you draw what you saw?"

She was already sketching. Frank stowed the assault rifle and returned; she gave him the rudimentary drawing of a weapon.

He frowned. "This looks like an AK-47. The clip curled out, like this?"

She nodded vigorously. "Uh-huh. They had other guns — .45s, shotguns, 30-30s. My husband owns a World War II Luger. He has it with him. But I saw an awful lot of the ones with the curled clip."

"Christ on a crutch," Frank muttered. "Just what we need. A nest of crazies with assault guns in our hills, waiting for Commies."

"It's the same group," Bob interjected. "The same ones we *know* James Chase was with. And we know he took the boy and vanished when they did. Isn't that enough for a search warrant?"

Frank gave him an opaque look. "To search for what, exactly?"

"To search for Jamie. That's why we're here today," Al pointed out.

Frank frowned, and said slowly, "I'll talk to the DA, but I don't know. I *would* have said 'yes,' but that was a while back. I've already locked horns with these crazies and come off losing too many times. There were some things about this cult that I thought were cut and dried, but I was dead wrong. Can't shut someone down for their religion, no matter how weird, and their lawyer knows every angle of religious-discrimination law. And they've tied themselves in to being a Christian group, and Christians have the swing around here. That's the story."

"How much evidence do you need?" Cindy said, sounding mystified. Al was just as frustrated, a hard ball of tension forming in the pit of his stomach. He could not believe this group was getting away with so much, as Frank phrased it, right under their noses. *Brother Joseph is a shrewd one, to have picked this community. He did his homework.*

"I understand your frustration, Miz Chase," Frank said, rubbing his temple with his knuckles, as if his head hurt. "And I have my own set of frustrations. I'm the only one around here who wants to get excited about it. I think part of the problem is folks around here, they don't quite grasp the magnitude of what's taking place. Those people don't come into town, not even to shop. They do that in Tulsa, by the truckload. Most of them stay cooped up in that complex. Those that do leave, they leave their guns behind, except for maybe rifles in the gunracks in the cab window and big crucifix stickers, and you see that everywhere." Frank shifted in his chair, looking thoughtful. "What I've seen up close I don't like either. They have guards at the gates leading into the complex, and they politely ask me to leave whenever I show up. There are probably more children in that place than we realize, but I've only seen a half-dozen of the kids go to the schools here."

"They what?" Cindy said, sitting up. "Is Jamie one of them?"

Frank shook his head, and motioned for her to calm down. "Don't think so, ma'am. I mean, I can't be sure without checking, but I truly don't believe they'd let him off their grounds if they have him. I've talked to some of the teachers. Kids seem to be from all over the country, complete with school records. They're legit, all right. But, the teachers say the kids are basically quiet; sort of keep to themselves, don't say much about religion or anything else. They don't trust the other kids. They move around in a tight little huddle, staying together. You can talk to them, but they won't talk to you. They just stare at you till you go away. And that pretty much describes everyone at the compound."

"Could *I* talk to one of them?" Cindy asked hopefully.

Frank shook his head. "Even if you could get one to talk, might not be a good idea. Could tip them off. If they sent your husband and Jamie out of this county, there's nothing we could do about it. My guess is these kids are brainwashed to the point of being 'safe' to let outside the group. Doubt you'd get much more out of 'em than I have."

Soon, after more dead-end discussions, both parties came to the conclusion that there wasn't a great deal that could be done right then. Cindy's frustration was obvious even to the deputy; Bob had his jaw clenched tight, and Al felt the muscles of his back and shoulders bunching with the need to do *something*. But there was nothing to be done.

Legally.

And that's the real trick, isn't it?

Frank wished them well and gave them each his card, with his home number on it, along with instructions to call him "if anything came up." Al noted later that the deputy seemed embarrassed that he couldn't do much. Something else was holding him back, but Frank wasn't saying what it was. He also had the feeling that if *they* did something a little on the wrong side of the fence to get information, Frank would look the other way, even cover for them. He didn't come out and say that, but he kept giving both him and Bob significant looks whenever he mentioned how much *his* hands were tied.

That doesn't matter; we don't really need him now. We know their location, some of their habits, and we have a lead, he thought, plans of his own beginning to form, as they left the county courthouse. *I think I should go check out these people myself.*

• CHAPTER FIVE

The day after Jamie and his father had gone to Tulsa for supplies, Jamie gave up the search for allies, especially regarding the question of his missing mother. Nobody, including Joe, wanted to discuss it.

That negative reaction from Joe had been a disappointing surprise. He'd always thought he could tell Joe anything — and he *knew* how much Joe loved *his* mother, even though he never said much about it. He was always taking her bunches of wildflowers. He'd thought Joe would understand how much he missed her. . . .

Anyone he'd even mentioned his mother to specifically forbade him to bring the subject up with anyone else; so by the time he talked with Sarah, he had already decided to keep quiet about it, even with her.

But today he was having second thoughts about that, as the situation at the vacation place began to weigh more heavily on him. They still weren't letting him eat anything, and the juice they gave him never came close to filling him up. Hunger pangs came and went, with increasing frequency and intensity. Sometimes lately he had trouble standing up, and he always got dizzy if he walked too far. If he was getting sick, he knew it would be his own fault because he didn't have faith in Brother Joseph; at least, that was what everyone else would tell him. Then they'd tell him he had to confess his lack of faith and be healed.

Not a chance! He'd rather just suffer. Brother Joseph was too frightening to trust, but try to get the rest of *them* to see that! If you had faith, everyone told him, you wouldn't get sick. If you didn't, you did.

So he didn't tell anyone about the fainting spells, but he knew the time would soon come when he wouldn't be able to keep them secret.

In the meantime, he drank all the juice they'd let him have, and lots of water. He was still allowed to do that, and if you drank enough, the hunger went away. For a little while.

He had trouble sleeping again that night, and not just from the hunger, since Daddy had brought several bottles of joy juice to their room, the strong, amber kind, in funny-shaped bottles. The only word he could read on the label was Kentucky, and why it was on there he didn't know, 'cause that was a state. When Daddy drank that kind of joy juice something happened to his throat that made him snore real loud, and he rolled around on the bare mattress in his sleep. To keep from getting squished Jamie slid off the mattress and curled up in the corner with a blanket that was covered with tiny bugs.

But that didn't really matter to him. He just wanted to sleep. The bugs didn't bother him as much as usual.

He got up before Daddy did and went down to the showers, where other kids were getting ready for school, too. He had forgotten to wash his clothes out the night before, so he would have to wear them again, with that funny smell they got when he slept in them. A week earlier one of the other boys had stolen his clothes and hidden them down the hallway while he was in the shower, but his daddy caught him and whipped the living tar out of him. Jamie overheard some of the things they said, things he didn't like. The daddy told the boy that Jamie and his dad were poor and homeless before joining the Sacred Heart, and that it was wrong to pick on needy people like that. Jamie never thought of himself as poor, and he knew they had a home; Mommy was there, or at least that was what he thought, since she wasn't in Tulsa.

Now the boy would have nothing to do with him, and had turned the others against him as well, because he'd been punished. The other kids said nothing as they got cleaned up, and Jamie started to feel a little bit to blame for the whipping the first boy got. It hurt when they ignored him, although it made him even more grateful that he had Sarah for a friend.

School that day was a little different. They didn't talk about Jews and blacks much, or Israel or the divine plan Brother Joseph had in store for them. Part of the day was spent studying a machine for making drinking water. The process was called "reverse osmosis" and Miss Agatha made them memorize it and spell it fifty times on the chalkboard. "There will come a time when we will need this," the teacher admonished; Jamie didn't understand the need for the machine when you could just turn a faucet on, but he didn't ask any questions. Miss Agatha would just have made him write something else fifty times on the chalkboard, and it would probably be nasty and full of hate.

During lunch break, Jamie was sent to a room all by himself with his juice while the other kids went on to the cafeteria. He was still under orders to not eat until they summoned the "Holy Fire," Miss Agatha reminded him.

He tried to make the juice last, but it was gone all too quickly. Funny, he'd never liked V8 before, but now he would have drunk as much of it as he could have gotten. He wished that Brother Joseph would go and get it over with. His stomach was not hurting as much anymore, but he did feel weaker today. Daddy had slipped him some crackers and cheese the night before, and that helped a little, and there had been Joe's Tootsie Pop. But sitting here alone in the empty, thick-walled room, with nothing but a chair and a lightbulb, made him want to cry. He heard Miss Agatha say something about "sensory deprivation" and this room, but didn't understand any of it. He just knew it was boring in here.

Nobody was around, not even Miss Agatha. After a while, he realized that would make it easy to talk to Sarah.

"Sarah," he offered cautiously. "You there?"

:Right here,: she said, her voice filling the space between his ears. Jamie had put a pair of stereo headphones on once, and this was the same kind of effect. *:They're all gone?:*

"To eat," Jamie said dejectedly. "There was something I wanted to talk with you about yesterday. But I was afraid to."

Jamie sensed anger, which quickly dissipated. *:You don't have to be afraid to talk to me. You know that.:*

"Sorry," he said. "It was just, I was confused, you know? First Daddy gets weird, then Joe yells at me. . . ."

:It was about the milk carton, wasn't it?:

"How did you know?"

Silence.

"Okay, okay," Jamie said, a little sullenly. After all, she was only a girl — she didn't have to rub it in how much more she knew. Everybody here said girls weren't as important as boys. "You know a lot more than I do. You already told me."

:I see more, is all,: Sarah said, impatiently. *:And you know everything else they tell you is a lie. Why shouldn't I see more than you do? Because I'm a girl?:*

He blushed with embarrassment at getting caught thinking nasty thoughts. "Sorry," he mumbled. "Just, they keep *telling* me —"

:And it's hard to keep remembering how much they lie. I know, Jamie. What's bugging you?:

Jamie had the feeling she already knew, but he told her anyway. "I haven't seen my mother in a long time.

Daddy said she'd be in Tulsa, but she wasn't there. Nobody around here wants to talk about it. What's going on?"

:I'm not sure, right now,: Sarah said, hesitantly. Jamie didn't know if he could believe her or not. It wasn't like her to not know everything. *:Look, it's not 'cause I can't tell or won't find out. I need more — stuff. Think about your mother. Think about what she looks like.:*

Jamie did, fully aware that Sarah could see exactly what was going on in his mind. This once made him uncomfortable, when he remembered all the bad things he used to think about girls, and even some of the mean tricks he used to play on them at school in Atlanta. But if Sarah saw these things, she didn't let on. She accepted him unconditionally, the only one besides his mother to ever do that. He reminded himself just how much he trusted her. Hey, she'd even been nice when he was thinking girls weren't as good as boys. . . .

:She's not here, not at their Sanctuary anyway,: Sarah said suddenly. *:But I think . . . she's close. Nearby. She's not as far away as Atlanta, anyway.:*

Hope flared. "In Tulsa?"

:I don't know. Don't give up, all right? I'll keep looking. Until I find her, though, you can trust Joe. I think I could even talk to him directly, if he didn't close his mind off the way he does. He has . . . things he can do, but he doesn't want anyone to know, because of what they would all think about him. They'd figure it was the work of the devil, and there's no telling what they would do about it.:

There was a warning in her voice that made him shiver. Miss Agatha had hinted some horrible things about what was done with people who were "possessed of the devil."

"I dunno," he said doubtfully. "I mean, his daddy is Brother Joseph. I don't think he'd snitch on me, but —"

:His father might be Brother Joseph, but that doesn't mean

Joe's like him. There's a lot of good in Joe, and he doesn't agree with much of what his daddy does. He'll help you, the same way he tried to help me.: She sounded very positive, and very tired.

But he hadn't known Joe had been helping Sarah. "What happened, you know, with you and Joe?"

Again, silence. Jamie had learned that this usually meant she didn't want to talk about something, and he let it rest. He sat on the crude chair for some time, wondering if she had left, when she spoke again.

:Joe will see you after school. Go with him.:

And she was gone. Her presence vanished, like a candle blown out by the wind. In the past he had tried to get her back, but once she was gone, he knew that it would be a while before she would return. He wished he could have had time to say good-bye. As usual, he didn't. That was just Sarah's way. Maybe she didn't like saying good-bye. . . .

Joe will be there, after school. We'll get to go do something, maybe go outside, Jamie thought, as the lingering traces of Sarah disappeared. The prospect of being with his "big brother" was enough to dissipate the misery, even enough to make him forget his hollow stomach. *Oh boy!*

And even though his gnawing hunger made him forgetful, so that he made mistakes when Miss Agatha asked him questions that afternoon, talking with Sarah must have brought him luck. Miss Agatha just nodded indulgently, said something to the others about "the special Gift Jamie has is coming through," and prompted him until he got the answer right. That didn't earn him any friends among the other kids, though, because Miss Agatha was even harder on them as if to make up for being easy on him —

But in the end, he didn't care. He had Sarah, he had Joe. If the other kids were going to be dumb-butts because of something *he* couldn't help, let them. They were jerk-faces anyway. If he'd been home in Atlanta, he wouldn't have hung around with any of them. All they did was parrot Miss Agatha's hateful stuff and play games like "coon hunt" and "burn the nigger." That was what they called blacks; niggers. Jamie *knew* that wasn't right — his teachers in Atlanta, the ones he trusted, said that calling a black kid a "nigger" was like calling a kid in a wheelchair "cripple" or "freak."

After school was over, Joe was waiting outside for him, just like Sarah said. It wasn't the first time Joe had met him afterwards, but since his guard duty usually ran past the time school was out, it was rare to see Joe right after class. As always, he was wearing his uniform, with his AK-47 slung over his shoulder alongside a backpack.

The other children coursed around him like a flooding river around a solid rock. Some shot him angry glances, including Miss Agatha, who sniffed as she walked past. Jamie had sensed the contempt earlier, some sort of jealousy over his relationship with Joe, and as usual he disregarded it.

"Wanna go fishing?" Joe asked right away, and instantly, Jamie's world lit up.

"Sure!" he replied enthusiastically. Then he frowned, not knowing where exactly you could fish around here. Unless Joe wanted to go to a park somewhere else; but that would mean leaving the vacation place, and he had never been allowed to do that, unless he was with his father. After drinking as much joy juice as he had the night before, James wouldn't be very good company today. "Where?" he asked doubtfully.

Joe chuckled. "There's a pond over near the north side of the complex. Only a few of us know about it. We'll have to stop and get a bow to fish with, though."

Jamie had thought the only way to fish was with a pole, or maybe even a net. But as they walked, Joe explained how it could be done with a bow and arrow, if you were good. There were plenty of hunting bows in the armory. Joe had a special bow in mind, one his dad had purchased for him when he was Jamie's age.

After the revelation that Joe was Brother Joseph's son, Jamie had begun to see that his friend had a few more privileges in the Guard than others his own age. They were, he realized, exercising some of them now; nobody else had unlimited access to the armory. At least, not among the kids.

"Let's walk," Joe said. He had talked about borrowing a motorcycle, but had apparently decided against it. "It's not as hot today. Rained this morning."

Living underground, you didn't notice things like rain or sunshine. Jamie squinted at the bright glare of the sun. It reminded him again how dim it was below. They passed by guards periodically. Joe waved and they waved back, letting them out of the complex without question. The boy knew that the story would be different when they came back through, when they would be searched. But he wasn't going to worry about that yet. When they came to the final gate, Joe told the guard they would be fishing a while and would be back before too long. The guard wished them luck and locked the tall chain-link gate behind them.

It occurred to Jamie that if they caught fish, he might be able to get a bite to eat. But eating meant cooking, and cooking meant a fire and things to cook with, things they didn't have. Jamie remembered something called sooshee that was raw fish, and before today the idea never appealed to him. Today was a different story. If Daddy could cheat and sneak him some cheese and crackers, maybe Jamie could do the same with the fish they could catch.

So he asked him, "Hey, Jamie, when we catch the fish, can we make sooshee out of it?"

"Naw," he said. "We have to cut them up for the other fish and throw them back." Then he eyed the boy warily, as if suddenly understanding the purpose of the remark. "You know you're on a strict Holy Fire fast. I'd get in big trouble if I let you eat anything."

Somehow Jamie wasn't surprised. Even though Joe was his best friend, next to Sarah, he was still under orders from Brother Joseph. Now that he knew Brother Joseph was Joe's father, that added a new dimension to the threat. Jamie knew you couldn't get into nearly as much trouble with other daddies as you could with your own.

He dropped the subject about food, remembering the vehemence with which Joe had responded to the milk carton question. He didn't want a replay of *that* miserable scene.

The barbed wire fences receded behind them as they took a trail through the oak forest skirting the northern edge of the complex. Jamie felt a little happier, knowing the other kids, who would kill for a chance to go into the woods and play, were sitting somewhere underground dreaming about what he was doing now. Birds called and flew overhead, and something skittered through the grass and leaves along the path.

Presently they came upon a clearing.

Jamie suddenly felt cold. There was a foreboding sense of dread attached to the place, a feeling of evil, or suffering. He was sort of seeing things inside his head. The vague images flowing through his mind were shifting and confusing; having been told by Brother Joseph not to share these impressions with anyone else, he didn't tell Joe about his feelings or what he was seeing.

"You've never been to this place before," Joe said firmly. "And don't you never tell anyone you were here."

Jamie nodded, feeling a little sick to his stomach. The images grew stronger, and he began to wonder if Sarah was feeding them to him. She had done that before, when they first met, but that was a long time ago and they were good friends now. Sarah could talk to him in person now. That is, if she wasn't afraid of coming to this place.

"We had to bury somebody here," Joe said suddenly, and the words shocked Jamie. "She died real young, but the Chosen Ones, we bury our own here."

"This is like a graveyard?" Jamie asked, hesitating.

Joe nodded absently. "Yep, but no one knows about it."

Jamie looked about in alarm. "What 'bout the headstones?"

"Like I said, nobody knows about it. If there were headstones, everybody would know, wouldn't they? Daddy was afraid of putting tombstones up because he was afraid they'd be visible from the air—" Joe suddenly cut his sentence off, sounding like he'd said something he shouldn't have. Jamie acted like nothing was wrong, even though the bad, dark feeling was getting stronger. It was different here than it was with the Holy Fire, and not as bad. The feeling was more a terror of something that had already happened, as opposed to something that was *about* to happen to *him*, as during the rituals with Brother Joseph. But he also suspected the two feelings were related, in a distant sort of way.

They went over to a mound of dirt about as long and wide as a beach towel. The earth had been turned sometime recently, maybe this spring, but Jamie could see that it had been more than a few weeks. Wild weeds had sprung up, while the more permanent grass, which took longer to grow, came in around the edges. It was plainly somebody's grave, and the revelation left him feeling hollow and icky inside.

Joe knelt and took off the backpack. From within the front pouch he pulled out a battered bouquet of wildflowers. *Must have picked those while I was in class,* Jamie thought, surprised. *Must have been someone important, whoever this was.*

"I hate to think nobody remembers Sarah," he said as he lay the flowers on the mound.

Sarah? My Sarah?

Joe sighed. "You wouldn't remember her. She died long before you came here."

"But . . . " Jamie blurted. He didn't know what to say, other than: *Sarah can't be dead, I just talked to her! In my head!* But that sounded too strange and unbelievable, so he didn't. Besides, Sarah was his secret, and lately Joe was showing basic problems where certain topics were concerned. Not untrustworthiness yet; but, well, there were things he just wouldn't discuss with some- one who had blown up the way Joe had over the milk carton.

Joe just knelt there, staring at the grave.

Suddenly, despite the fact that he didn't want to believe it, Jamie knew this was the *same* Sarah. *Had* to be. As he looked at the mound of dirt, images formed mistily in his mind, a gust of something, a spirit, a smell, like baby powder, only a little sweeter. Sarah's scent. Jamie watched Joe in concealed horror, finally accept- ing that all along he hadn't been talking with a person, exactly.

He had been talking with a ghost. And ghosts were supposed to be scary.

But Sarah's not scary, he thought, in confusion. *Sarah's my friend!* He stared at the grave, while Joe bowed his head like he was praying.

The images that had been lurking at the periphery of his mind now sprang into full, vivid life, coalescing, condensing, forming a story, a kind of movie in his head. A scary story — the kind his mommy wouldn't let him watch on TV. He knew that without knowing how he knew it. And he knew he would have to watch *this* story, because it wasn't just a story, it was real.

Jamie saw her clearly now, standing just beyond the clearing on a short, grassy knoll. Sarah was a girl his age with black hair and delicate brown eyes, in a calico dress that fluttered slowly in the windless afternoon. Joe didn't see her, and Jamie knew that was only because she didn't want to be seen.

Her mommy and daddy had joined the cult, too, only they had disappeared suddenly, and nobody knew where they were. Brother Joseph told Sarah that they would be back, that they had just gone to Tulsa for a little while. Sarah didn't believe it then, but played along because she feared Brother Joseph, just like Jamie did now.

And for the same reason. Brother Joseph had been starving her just like he was being starved, and had used her as an instrument for communicating with the Holy Fire. At first her parents had objected. Then they went along with it, or at least they told her to do what Brother Joseph said, until they worked things out. Then, they disappeared. Sarah was afraid Brother Joseph had something to do with that. The weeks went by slowly, and still no parents. This was starting to sound familiar to Jamie.

Meanwhile Brother Joseph held the Praise Meetings, and the Black Thing came closer to Sarah no matter how hard she tried to keep it away. Sometimes, during the same rituals that Jamie dreaded, she actually touched that dark, horrible thing, but most of the time she pretended to see it, telling Brother Joseph what he wanted to hear.

The preacher said it was a good thing, this Holy Fire, but Sarah knew better, and kept it at bay as best she could.

Then one night it came too close, and she couldn't repel it. The hunger had been intense, and the lack of food had weakened her will as well as her body. Brother Joseph yelled at her to touch it — and, unable to fight him, she did.

The suffocating thing tried to pull her in. She cried hysterically and broke with it. Brother Joseph ordered the congregation to leave, informing them the Praise

Meeting was over. When they had gone, and his personal bodyguards had locked all the doors, he turned to Sarah and grabbed her throat with his perfectly white manicured hands.

"You will do what I say, you little slut, always!" Brother Joseph screamed, and the images became shaky as Sarah lost consciousness. Then the series of images ended, and Jamie was vaguely aware of . . . a different kind of darkness. . . .

"Jamie! Jamie, what is it?"

When he opened his eyes Joe was looking down at him, his face contorted with concern. "Are you okay? What's the matter?"

Jamie's vision blurred again; he closed his eyes to keep from being sick, and he felt Joe pick him up and carry him away from Sarah's grave. He felt something wet and cold at his lips, and he drank deeply. The water had a funny metal taste to it, but he didn't care as he guzzled all that was offered.

He opened his eyes again. Joe was kneeling in front of him, his expression a mixture of concern and fear. The clearing where Sarah was buried was in sight but further away, making it tolerable now. Above, an enormous oak shaded them from the summer sun, and nearby he heard water running.

"You passed out back there." Joe frowned. "Weak?"

"I guess," he said, and admitted to Joe what he hadn't told anyone else. "I feel funny."

Joe felt his forehead. "You're warm, but that ain't nothin' in this heat. Are you going to be all right? You wanna go back?"

Jamie sat up, finding his strength returning — as much of it as there was, anyway. He didn't want to go back, so he forced a smile and said, "I'm fine now. Let's go fishing." He looked behind him, toward the sound of running water. "That a creek back there?"

Joe seemed to be having second thoughts. "No, I'd better get you back. I don't like the way you just dropped like that." He paused, as if considering something. "You said you knew Sarah, back there. After you passed out. What didja mean 'xactly when you said that?"

"Dunno," Jamie said. "I'm okay now," he added, trying not to let the disappointment show in his voice. "We'd better hurry, if we're going to get to supper on time."

About halfway back to the vacation place, Jamie remembered he wasn't going to be getting any supper.

Frank Casey felt his tired eyes drying. He'd stared at the computer screen for a solid minute before blinking. There it was, right in front of him, all the information he needed to find a kidnaped little boy. And not a damned thing he could do about it.

The three people who had just left his office, the boy's mother and the two oddball road-warriors, were the only people in the county who seemed to care about this peculiar cult setting up shop in their backyard. When he first learned of the Chosen Ones, Frank had been willing to live and let live, until he saw the clues that people were being controlled in some obscure, sinister way. And after listening to Cindy talk about the assault weapons, and the other implements of destruction the cult seemed to take a keen interest in, not to mention the power that one man had over the whole lot . . .

It was all just too damned dangerous. Frank Casey could almost smell the grape Kool-Aid and hear the zipping of body bags.

The cutbacks in the department couldn't have come at a worse time. Given that the county's economy was mostly tied to the price of a barrel of oil, the decrease in revenues from real estate and other taxes was inevitable. With fewer men, he couldn't collect evidence and be discreet at the same time. But if he spent enough time — some of it his own — he would probably see something that would justify a warrant, something that their high-powered attorney couldn't block.

Frank Casey remembered the glint he had seen in Al's eye when he mentioned the stakeout, and smiled. The man was smart; so was his partner. They'd seen the hints, he was sure, just as he was certain they'd act on them. *Yeah, you're hungry for it, too,* the tall Cherokee thought. *I can't authorize civilians to do stakeouts, but if you find something I'm sure gonna back you up on it. Every inch of the way.*

Al waited, his arms crossed over his chest, projecting every iota of authority he had — not as Al Norris, Fairgrove mechanic, but as Sieur Alinor Peredon, Knight-Artificer in the service of Elfhame Outremer, who had once commanded (small) armies.

Now all he had to do was convince one human of that authority. . . .

Bob sighed, finally, and shook his head. "All right," he said, though with a show of more reluctance than Al sensed he really felt. "All right, I'll cover for you here, and I'll keep Cindy from asking too many questions, if that's what you really want."

"It's what I want," Al said firmly. "Absolutely. I don't want to raise her hopes that I'm one of your foolish movie-star corambos —"

"That's *commandos,* or *Rambos,*" Bob interrupted.

"Whatever. I don't want her thinking I'm going to charge into unknown territory and carry her boy off. I want to get the lay of the land and check defenses." Al frowned, though it was not intended for Bob. "The fact is, there is a very odd feeling about that place, even at a distance. The Native man, the deputy sheriff, he feels it too, although he considers himself too rational and civilized to admit it. I am not going to stumble about blindly in there—"

"Fine, fine," Bob interrupted again. "But while you're off with Andur, where am I supposed to be sleeping?"

"Ah," Al said, grinning with delight. "I have solved that small problem. Behold—"

He took Bob around to the side of the RV; parked there, beside the Miata, was a white van. He enjoyed the look on Bob's face; enjoyed even more the expression when he opened the door to reveal the luxurious interior. *Not* as sybaritic as the RV would have been had Cindy not been with them, but a grade above the RV in its current state.

Bob turned back to him, his incredulity visible even in the dome light of the van. "How in hell did you do that?" he demanded. "I *know* you didn't ken the van, you'd need more time than a couple of hours to make the copy—"

"This is Nineve," Al informed him smugly. "Andur's twin sister. I called her from Outremer last night, when I realized that we would need two vehicles. You rightly said that the elvensteeds can crack Mach one in forms other than four-legged; she arrived here as soon as darkness fell." He permitted himself a smile. "Now you have lodging *and* transport."

Bob regarded Nineve with a raised eyebrow. "Hope she was in 'stealth' mode, or there's gonna be UFO reports from here to Arkansas." Then he unbent and patted the shiny side of the van. "Thanks, Nineve. You're here in right good time. And you sure are pretty."

The van's headlights glowed with pleasure.

"Now listen," Bob continued, "I got an idea. How 'bout we put Cindy in Nineve, and you an' me go back to bachelor quarters, eh?"

Al thought about that; thought about it hard. Not that he had any doubt that a strong reason for Bob's request was his inherent puritanical feelings —

But with Cindy in the van, he would be able to transform the RV into something far more comfortable — so long as he remembered to change it back before she entered.

And I won't have to wear a hat to sleep, either.

He sent a brief, inquiring thought to Nineve, who assented. Andur's twin spent a great deal of time with the human fosterlings of Fairgrove and liked them. Just as she had liked Janet. . . .

"Good idea," he said, thinking happily of a long soak in a hot shower when he returned, and a massage at the skilled hands of his lovely chrome servant — small as she was, her hands never tired.

Doubtless Bob was thinking of the same things.

Better to get Cindy out of the way of becoming a temptation. Bob is right about that much.

"Well, fine," Bob said, a slow grin spreading across his face. "I'll move her things now. Soon's she gets back from the laundry with her clothes, I'll intro — I mean, show her the new quarters. That oughta keep her busy enough that she won't be asking too many questions."

"And I had best be on my way," Al observed, "if I am to learn anything of these people tonight."

Andur revved his engine a little, as if the air-conditioner compressor had come on, to underscore his eagerness to get on the road. It had been a long time since he and Andur undertook a rescue mission. It would be good to get back into harness again.

Andur popped his door open as Al approached the driver's side of the car and shut it as soon as he was tucked into the seat. Al let the four-point seat-harness snake across his shoulders and his lap, and meet and fuse in the center of his chest. Not that he often needed it — but no one allied with racing ever sacrificed safety.

Or an edge.

Andur flipped on his lights, turning everything outside the twin cones of light to stark blackness by contrast. Despite the impatient grumble of the pseudo-engine beneath the hood, Andur had more sense than to spin his wheels and take off in a shower of gravel. Such behavior at a track was the mark of an amateur, a poseur, and would earn him and his rider as much respect as Vanilla Ice at a Public Enemy concert.

Instead, Andur prowled out with slow grace, making his way to the single unlocked gate for the after-hours use of mechanics and drivers. They proceeded with courtesy for the few folk still about and on their feet after the long day. Alinor thought briefly that it was much like being back at Court; it was considered good form to be socially graceful as a means of preparing one's mind before an imminent battle, and the coolness displayed gained one more status than strutting or worrying.

Al did not have to touch the steering wheel; Andur was perfectly capable of reading his mind to know where they were going. Down the gravel access-road to the roughly paved county road that led to Hallet, and from there to the on-ramp for the turnpike —

And there he paused, while Al read the map of the area and matched it with the one in his mind; the one that showed the rough details of the cult enclave. The turnpike was one possible route —

But there was a better one; so in the end they passed the turnpike and took another county road, then another. Andur knew precisely the route to take, so Al leaned back into the embrace of the "leather" seat, and let his mind roam free.

This was a land like a strong, broadwinged bird — with a deadly, oozing cancer. In this area's heart hid a festering wound in the power-flows of the earth, a place where energy was perverted, twisted, turned into something it made him sick to contemplate.

He might not have noticed if he hadn't been looking for it; it was well-hidden. He might have dismissed it as a stress headache. There was no doubt in his mind that this was the work of "Brother Joseph"; it had that uniquely human feel to it, of indifference to consequences. There was also a hate, an anger, and a twisted pleasure in the pain of others.

He opened his eyes and oriented himself, calling back the suppressed elven night-vision that made the darkened landscape as bright as midday sun. Andur had long since darkened his headlights; *he* certainly didn't need them to see his way. And now as Al watched, the shiny white enamel of the hood darkened, softened, going to a flat matte black. The engine sounds quit, too — they rolled onto a gravel-covered secondary road with no more sound than the crunching of gravel, which also quieted as Andur softened the compound of his tires. The sound of the cicadas in the trees beside the roadway drowned what was left.

Then Andur turned off the road entirely —

And Al was sitting astride a matte-black stallion, who picked his way across the overgrown fields like a cat crossing ice. The hot, humid air hit him with a shock after the cool of the wind and Andur's air-conditioner.

Al realized that his white track-suit was not the best choice of outfits for a scouting mission. With a moment's thought, he changed the Nomex to a light garment of matte black silk; then blackened his face and hands as well with a silken mask and gloves. His feet he shod in boots of lightweight black leather, easy to climb in. In this guise they approached the first of the three fences surrounding the complex.

This far from the road, there was only the patrolling guard to worry about — and the trip-wires and fences.

He felt Andur gather himself and hung on while the elvensteed launched into an uncannily silent gallop, the only sounds muffled thuds when his hooves hit the ground. Then he felt Andur's muscles bunch —

He tightened his legs and leaned forward, as Andur leapt.

No human would ever have believed his eyes, for the elvensteed began his jump a good fifteen feet from the fence, cleared the top of it with seven feet to spare, and landed fifteen feet from the fence on the other side.

Without a stirring of power-flows. The magic of good design, sweet Andur.

They passed the second fence the same way, but halted at the third, innermost fence; the one that surrounded the compound itself. This was as far as Al wanted to go right now. There was no way he was going to go nosing about an enemy camp without scouting it first.

Andur concealed himself in a patch of shadow, and Al climbed a tall enough tree that he was able to see the compound quite clearly. Whatever the sheriff might have imagined at his most pessimistic, the situation was worse.

The guards prowled within the fence like professional soldiers. There were a lot of them, and the number of life-essences Al detected below ground indicated that this "Brother Joseph" must be fielding an army.

There was Cold Iron everywhere, low quality iron which disrupted his senses; it was difficult to concentrate when using his Sight, and even more difficult to find ways around the barriers. And deep inside the complex was that evil cancer he had sensed before. It was not a spell or item, but it *was* magical. It wasn't elven in origin, nor was it human . . . no, something old and experienced had created the magical "taste" he'd sensed. There was something alive and not-alive shifting its enchanted form inside the compound.

It was quiescent when he first approached it, but as

he studied it, the thing began to rouse. He drew back, thinking that *he* had caused it to awaken and stir — but then his questing thoughts brushed the thoughts of humans — many humans — in the same area, and he realized that *they* were the ones waking it.

He withdrew a little further, heart racing despite his wished-for cool, and "watched" from what he hoped was a safe distance.

The humans were gathered in one of the underground areas for a spectacle of some kind.

Could this be one of the "Praise Meetings" that Cindy described?

Something — someone — moved into his sensing area. Another human — but where the life-fires of the others burned with a smoky, sullen flame, more heat than light, *this* person's burned with the black flame of the devourer, who feeds on lives. Even more than lives, this human thrived on the *hate* of those around him. Al knew him without ever seeing his face. This *must* be Brother Joseph.

With him was a tiny, fitful life-spark, so close to extinction that Al nearly manifested in the full armor of an elven warrior-noble and carved his way to the child's side. For it *was* a child, who had been so starved, so abused, that his hold on life and his body was very tenuous indeed.

Jamie. It had to be Jamie.

And as Al held himself back, with anger burning in his heart, the evil thing at the heart of the gathering woke.

And reached for the child.

● CHAPTER SIX

By the time the Praise Meeting started, Jamie was having a hard time keeping himself from throwing up even though there was nothing in his stomach but water. And he couldn't stand up for very long; he shivered and his skin was clammy, and he had to lie down on the floor because sitting in the chair made him dizzy.

He knew the Praise Meeting had started, because he heard the organ; it vibrated the walls all the way back here, in the very rear of the building. The vibrations disoriented him; he had his eyes closed when the door to the little room finally opened, and the two big guards came in to get him.

Brother Joseph always sent two huge men with AK-47s to get him. It was just one of the hundreds of things Brother Joseph said and did that didn't make any sense. But maybe it was a good thing they'd been sent this time; when one of them ordered Jamie to stand, he got as far as his knees before that soft darkness came down on him again, and he found himself looking up at their faces from the ground.

He was afraid for a minute that they'd hit him — but they just looked at one another, then at him, then without a single word, picked him up by the elbows, and hauled him to his feet. His toes didn't even touch the floor; that didn't matter. The guards carried him that way down the long, chilly corridor to the door that led to the back of the Meeting Hall.

They came out on the stage, at the rear. The four

spotlights were focused on Brother Joseph, who was making a speech into a microphone, spitting and yelling. Jamie couldn't make any sense of what he was saying; the words kept getting mixed up with the echo from the other end of the room, and it all jumbled together into gibberish.

The two men didn't pay any attention, either; they just took him to an oversized rough-wood chair in front of the black and red flag that Brother Joseph had everyone pledge to and dropped him into it, strapping down his arms and legs with clamps built into the chair itself.

Jamie let them. He'd learned the first time that it did no good to resist them. No one out there would help him, and later his father would backhand him for struggling against Brother Joseph's orders.

Brother Joseph continued, so bright in the spotlights that Jamie had to close his eyes. It seemed as if the only light in the room was on the leader; as if he sucked it all up and wouldn't share it with anyone else.

Brother Joseph's voice, unintelligible as it was, hammered at Jamie's ears, numbing him further. He was so hungry — and so dizzy — he just couldn't bring himself to think or care about anything else.

Finally the voice stopped, although it was a few moments before the silence penetrated the fog of indifference that had come over Jamie's mind. He opened his eyes as a spotlight fell on him — light that stabbed through his eyes into his brain, making hot needles of pain in his head. But it was only for a moment; then a shadow eclipsed the spotlight, a tall shadow, with the light streaming around the edges of it.

It was Brother Joseph, and Jamie stifled a protest as Brother Joseph's hand stretched out into the light, a thin chain with a sparkling crystal on the end of it dangling from his fingers. Jamie knew what was coming next, and for a moment he struggled against his bonds.

But dizziness grayed his sight, and he couldn't look away from the twirling, glittering, sparkling crystal. Brother Joseph's voice, a few moments ago as loud as a trumpet, now droned at Jamie, barely audible, words he tried to make out but couldn't quite catch.

The world receded, leaving only the crystal, and Brother Joseph's voice.

Then, suddenly, something different happened —

This was the part where the Black Thing tried to touch him, only it didn't this time. This time he was somehow standing *next* to himself; he was standing on the stage, and there was someone between him and the boy strapped to the chair.

Sarah. And she stood as if she was ready to fight something off, in a pose that reminded him of the way his mother had stood between him and his daddy the first time he'd come home after Brother Joseph had —

:After Brother Joseph used you, like he used me,: said a familiar voice in his head. *:For that — :*

The girl pointed, and he saw the Black Thing slipping through a smoky door in the air, sliding towards the boy in the chair.

Only now he could see it clearly, and it wasn't really a shapeless blot. It was — like black fire, swirling and bubbling, licking against the edge of the door. Like a negative of flames.

It was bad, he felt that instinctively, and he recoiled from it. But he found he couldn't go far, not even to the edge of the stage. When he tried, he felt a kind of tugging, like he was tied to the boy in the chair with a tight rope around his gut.

:Don't worry, Jamie,: said Sarah. *:I'll keep it away from you. It won't mess with me now.:*

The Black Thing moved warily past her — then melted into the Jamie-in-the-chair.

Jamie jerked, as pain enveloped him.

Sarah stepped forward and grabbed something

invisible — and then it wasn't invisible, it was a silver rope running between him and Jamie-in-the-chair. And the minute she touched the rope, the pain stopped.

"Speak, O Sacred Fire," Brother Joseph cried out, as the boy in the chair jerked and quivered. Brother Joseph's voice sounded far away, and tinny, like it was coming from a bad speaker. "Speak, O Holy Flame! Tell us your words, fill us with the Spirit!"

Jamie-in-the-chair's mouth opened — but the voice that came out wasn't Jamie's. It was a strange, hollow voice, booming, like a grownup's — like James Earl Jones'. Gasps of fear peppered the audience when he began speaking, outbursts which the people quickly stifled. The audience reaction turned to awe as the echoing voice carried into the crowd. It said all kinds of things; more of the same kind of stuff that Brother Joseph and Miss Agatha were always saying. All about how Armageddon was coming, and the Chosen Ones were the only people who would be saved from the purifying flames. About the Jews and the blacks and the Sodomites — how they ran everything, but after the flames came, the Chosen Ones would run everything.

But then the voice said something Jamie had never heard Brother Joseph say —

"— and you, Brother Joseph," boomed the voice. "You are the Instrument of the Prophecy. You will be the Bringer of Flame. You will be the Ignitor of the Holocaust. In your hand will be the torch that begins the Great Conflagration —"

Brother Joseph began to frown, and his frown deepened as the voice went on with more of the same. *This must be new* — Jamie thought.

:*It is new*,: said Sarah, relaxing her vigilance a little, and turning to look over her shoulder at him. Even though he knew she was a ghost now, he was somehow no longer afraid of her. In fact, in his present state, he felt closer to her, like they were the same kind of people now. And it helped to be able to see her. He moved a little closer to her, and she took his hand and smiled.

:This stuff is all new,: she said without moving her lips, cocking her head to one side. *:And Brother Joseph doesn't like it. Look at him.:*

Indeed, Brother Joseph's face was not that of a happy man, and Jamie could see why — for out in the assembled audience there were stirrings and murmurs of uneasiness.

But when the voice stopped, Brother Joseph whirled and raised his hands in the air, his face all smiles. "Halleluia!" he cried. "Praise God, he has chosen me to lead you, though I am not worthy! He has called me to witness for you and lead you, as John the Baptist witnessed before the coming of the Lord Jesus and led the Hebrews to the new Savior! You've heard it from the mouth of this child, through the instrument of His Holy Fire — I am the forerunner, and it is my coming that has been the signal and paved the way for the end — and *our beginning!*"

Cries of "Praise the Lord!" and "Halleluia!" answered him, and there were no more murmurs of dissent. Brother Joseph had them all back again.

:Now comes the part they've really been waiting for,: Sarah said, an expression of cynicism on her face that was at odds with her years. *:The miracles.:*

"Half Hi to win, Saturn Boy to place, and Beauregard to show in the second," boomed the voice. "Righteous to win, Starbase to place, and Kingsman to show in the third. Grassland to win, Lena's Lover to place, and Whatchacall to show in the fifth—"

:Miracles?: Jamie said, puzzled.

:Those are all the horses that are going to win at Fair Meadows tomorrow,: she replied. *:They're going to make a lot of money by betting on them.:*

"Fifth table, fourth seat, Tom Justin," said the voice. "Tom should get in line behind the fat woman in a red print dress and take two blue cards, two red, two yellow and two gray. Sixth table, twelfth seat, Karen Amberdahl. Karen should get in line behind an old man with a cigar, a turquoise belt buckle and a string tie with a bearclaw slide, and take one of each color."

:And those are the people that should go to bingo tomorrow night, where they should sit, and what cards they should take. If they do that, they'll have winning cards.: Sarah's lip curled. *:But it won't be a lot of money. They're just making the seed money for the real stuff. The horse races, and what comes later.:*

Finally the voice stopped; Jamie felt dizzy, and when he looked down at himself, he was kind of — transparent. He could see the floor through his arm. Had he been able to do that when he first found himself here? He didn't think so.

:You're fading,: Sarah said, looking worried. *:I don't know why. I think the Black Thing is using you up, somehow —:*

She didn't get a chance to elaborate on that; the guards were escorting everyone except for a chosen few out — those few filed up to the front and waited in a line just below the stage. Jamie noticed, as they arranged themselves and waited for the guards to get everyone else out, that he was getting solid again. So — the Black Thing used him up when it spoke. And if it wasn't talking, he got a chance to recover.

"All right," Brother Joseph said, in a brisk, matter-of-fact voice that was nothing like what he used when preaching, "We got the El Paso crack shipment tonight on the airstrip. Bill, you're new; hold your questions until the Holy Fire is done speaking."

What came out of Jamie-in-the-chair's mouth then, was not anything like what he had expected.

"Apartment 1014B over in the Oaktree Apartment Complex is a new dealer, he'll pay top prices to you because he's been having visions. His line dried up. Sell him a quarter of the shipment. You've got enough regulars for another quarter. For the rest, take a quarter to Tulsa, peddle it Friday on Denver, on Saturday over by the PAC, Sunday on the downtown mall. The narks will be elsewhere. *Don't* talk to anyone in a blue Ford Mustang, license plate ZZ611; they're cops. Get off the street on Friday by two in the morning, there's going to be a bust. Take the other quarter to Oklahoma City and —"

:Is he talking about drugs?: Jamie asked Sarah, bewildered. *:Like dope? Like they said to say no to in school?:*

She nodded grimly. *:That's where the real money is coming from,:* she replied. *:Brother Joseph is a dealer, and the Black Thing knows where all the cops are, and where the best place to sell is.:*

The man Bill, who had been designated as "new," looked unhappy, and as if he was trying not to squirm. As the voice finished — and another wave of dizziness and transparency passed over Jamie — he saw that Brother Joseph was watching this man very closely. And before the man could say anything, Brother Joseph spoke, in still another kind of voice. Friendly, kind, like Daddy used to be before all the joy juice, back in Atlanta.

"Now, Bill," Brother Joseph said, "I know what you must be thinking. You're wondering how we, the Chosen of the Lord, could *stoop* to selling crack and ice, this poison in the veins of America. How we could break God's law as well as man's."

Bill nodded, slowly.

"Bill, Bill," Brother Joseph said, shaking his head. "This is part of our *mission.* The Holy Fire *instructed* us to do this! We aren't selling this to innocent children — it's going to Satanists and Sodomites, uppity Jews and niggers, Commies and hippies and whores — all people who'd poison themselves with the stuff anyway, whether we sold it to them or not. They're killing *themselves;* we're no more to blame than the man that sells a suicide a gun. And what's more, we're drying up the trade of the regular dealers, godless nigger gang members. The ones who *do* sell this poison in schoolyards."

Sarah snorted. *:No they aren't,:* she said angrily. *:That's a lie! They're* supplying *the guys who sell dope to kids. White and black.:*

Jamie nodded, remembering the stuff about "the dealer whose supply line dried up."

Bill looked unconvinced and replied, hesitantly, "But — what about the bingo games, the horse races —"

"Peanuts," one of the guards scoffed, in an insulting tone. "Grocery money."

"Now Tom, that's not fair," Brother Joseph told him, in the tones of a parent mildly chiding a child. Then he turned back to Bill. "He is right that it's really just the cash for our day-to-day expenses," the preacher said. "Bill, *you* know what an AK-47 costs these days, I know you do."

Bill nodded, reluctantly.

"And we have hundreds — thousands. And that's just one of the guns we have stockpiled. Then there's the anti-tank weapons, the grenade launchers, the SAMs — that's just weapons. We *bought* those tractors and bulldozers, outright —"

"I was a farmer," Bill said slowly. "The gear you — we — have is about a quarter mil per tractor, and I dunno how much them earth-movers run. But — we never win big at the track or the bingo games, and I know there's big pots —"

"And there's IRS agents waiting right there at the track and the parlor, waiting for the big winner," Brother Joseph interrupted. "We *can't* let the gov'ment know what's going on here, and if a lot of our people start winning big, not even our fancy lawyer is gonna be able to keep them off our backs. Hell, Bill, that's how the gov'ment got Al Capone, didn't you know? Tax evasion!"

"Dope money's big, it's underground, and can't be traced," said one of the other men, complacently. "And nobody in this state would put dope and a church together."

Bill thought for a moment, then nodded again, but this time with a lot less reluctance. "I guess you're right —"

"It was *I* who ordered them," boomed the voice of the Black Thing, unexpectedly, startling them all. "Holiest Brother Joseph was reluctant, but I showed him the way, the way —"

"The way to acquire the money we needed without hurting innocent children," Brother Joseph took up smoothly, when the voice faltered.

"Well, I guess it's all right, then," Bill said, looking relieved, and glancing out of the corner of his eye at Jamie-in-the-chair, nervously. "If the Holy Fire ordered it."

"That will be all, then, soldiers of faith," Brother Joseph said in his old, commanding tone of voice. "You have your marching orders. Tomorrow you will be assigned and go forth to implement them, in the name of the Holy Fire."

The guards herded the last of the Chosen Ones out, leaving Brother Joseph alone with Jamie. And the Black Thing. And Sarah — but he didn't know she was there.

Brother Joseph turned to Jamie-in-the-chair, with a terrible, burning hunger in his eyes, a hunger that looked as though it could have devoured the world and not been satisfied.

"Tell me," he ordered, in a harsh voice. "Tell me about the End. Tell me about my part in it."

The voice began again; more of the same kind of stuff it had told the crowd at the beginning, but more personal this time. About how Brother Joseph was the One True Prophet of the age, how he would lead the

Chosen Ones in a purge of all that was evil on earth, until there was no one left but his own followers. How he would be made World President for Life in the ruins of the UN Building; how he would oversee the building of the Promised Heavenly Kingdom On Earth.

There was a lot of that stuff, and Brother Joseph just ate it up. And Jamie faded and faded —

Finally even the hunger in Brother Joseph's eyes seemed sated. The voice stopped when Jamie was like one of the transparent fish he'd seen in the aquarium at school, or like a boy made out of glass.

And so dizzy he couldn't even think.

"Blessed be the Holy Fire," Brother Joseph said, standing up straight and making a bow that was half adoration and half dismissal. "Blessed be the Sacred Flame. I thank you in the Name of God, and in the Name of Jesus —"

The Black Thing started to dissolve from Jamie-in-the-chair, pulling out of him, and Sarah let go of the silver cord. She stayed protectively between it and him, though; until it went into that door in the air —

The door in the air shut — and another kind of door opened behind it. And the Black Thing somehow dissolved into the *flag*.

Or the flagpole —

That was the first time Jamie had ever seen *that* —at least, that he remembered. But then, a lot had been different tonight. He'd never been shoved out of his body, either. He turned to Sarah, suddenly desperate to ask her questions —

But Brother Joseph clapped his hands three times — and suddenly he was *back* in the chair, in his body, and as nauseated and dizzy as he had ever been in his life.

His gorge rose, and he couldn't help himself or control it anymore. As Brother Joseph released his arms from the straps, he aimed as best he could and made Brother Joseph's white shoes not so white.

*   *   *

After Brother Joseph had Jamie taken away, the preacher retired to his private quarters. Exhausted, he stood in the clothes closet that was as long as a hallway, the aroma of cut pine overpowering in the bright fluorescents. The evening's events swirled in his mind like a lazy tornado, and he knew he was on an emotional roller coaster, swaying between doubt and conviction; as soon as he thought that the Sacred Fire had turned against him, he saw that it was, indeed, still in his court, shucking and jiving to mark his way to the top, spewing the useful information like a self-digging gold mine.

Hanging from brass rods were a hundred or so suits, worth anywhere from two hundred to a thousand dollars each, wearing a thin plastic wrap from the dry cleaners, each embodying its own, distinctive memory. Brother Joseph often surveyed his collection of expensive clothing in times of turmoil and change, to remind himself of the tribulations and triumphs that had already taken place. The suits reassured him and quelled his doubts, reminding him that he still held power, that his gifts were infinite.

Much of his preaching, especially after the founding of the Sacred Heart of the Chosen Ones, incited his crowds to violence. These suits had seen riots and marches and demonstrations against the unholy, and had born witness to his struggle. They felt like faithful supporters, always there when the important things happened; like the protest of the godless Unitarians, who questioned the Bible, slandering its very truth. The demonstration his people staged at the YMCA (so weak was their minister that they couldn't even raise the money to build a decent building!) was a wondrous thing, especially when the riot broke out. Joseph spotted the suit he'd worn that day, a conservative gray Oxford, and gloried in its cleanliness. The bloodstains which once darkened its immaculate surface were now only a memory. His suit, like his ministry, emerged from the wreckage of that incident unblemished. A good lawyer could prove — and disprove — anything.

At the end of the closet, hidden where only he could find them, were his white Klan robes, where it all began.

Ah yes, he thought nostalgically, savoring the sudden memory the robes brought. *The beginning of my struggle. The end, alas, of my youth.* The smell of gasoline and burning wood, the secret meetings, the handshakes, the passwords. The hillsides filled with the faithful, their pointed hoods aimed heavenward, toward God. The sweet hatred that flowed in the gatherings, lubricated with cheap beer and even cheaper whiskey.

Those were the glorious days.

He'd joined the KKK as a teenager, and insisted early on that he be permitted to participate in a real nigger lynching, that nothing else would hold his interest. He just wanted to kill niggers. The old-timers, they seemed to find him amusing if overly rambunctious. He had been all of seventeen when he joined. He looked older, and was able to pass as a twenty-year-old, not that it would have mattered if they'd known his true age. The Klan loved new, young blood. His raw hate sustained him for some time, but as he matured, he began to need specific reasons for the hate — he began to doubt, when he saw others his age burning with the same fervor for causes the very opposite of his.

Justification came bound in faded black leather; the Grand Dragon began quoting scripture. In the light of a burning cross, somewhere on a hillside in Mississippi, he saw the glimmer of his true destiny. The feelings of hate he had for the godless actually had a *meaning* behind them, reinforcing his beliefs. He could attach names to the things he hated, and they were impressive names, all of them: Satan's spawn, heathens, the non-believers. His soul had swelled with pride. His feelings, after all, were *justified*. And others enabled him to act them out.

It was the first time the Bible had any meaning for him, the first time its truth made any sense to him. *There is only one right way, and I know what it is.* So he had believed, and the Bible provided proof. The Bible was all the justification he needed.

After all, look at how many people lived by it.

He thought he had found his place, his kindred. But as the months progressed, he had participated in only two lynchings. *Any more, and the FBI will come after us*, one of the senior members of their Klan said.

But Brother Joseph knew it wasn't prudence that had spoken; it had been cowardice. They didn't have the guts, he knew then, and his faith in the Ku Klux Klan faltered.

By the time he had turned twenty, the Klan began admitting Catholics for the first time in its history, and he realized it was time to leave. They just didn't have it straight, was all. Time to forge a new organization, a new group.

A . . . *church*.

He never attended a formal seminary; he earned his sheepskin through a four-week correspondence course. All he needed was a piece of paper to hang in his "office," to point at when anyone questioned his credentials. He knew it was a facade, but a necessary one needed to carry out his work. He knew the *real* truth, and in his hands he held the secret to the One True Church. He stumbled across a passage in the Bible, and from this he produced a name for his movement: The Sacred Heart of the Chosen Ones.

He studied the Bible night and day, highlighting the passages which lent particular weight to his beliefs. These were the passages he emphasized in his sermons, adding some flourishes of his own.

He preached hatred. Hate was cleansing; the Sword

of the Lord — didn't the Bible speak over and over about the Wrath of God? Hate purified. Hate separated the weak from the strong, the *doers* from the idle, the pure in spirit from the dissenters, the doubters. Hate separated the men from the boys — and from the women. He knew about women. They were too weak to truly hate. They were inferior to men.

There were many men who came to him just on that basis alone. And women, too, the *real* women who liked being told their place and liked a strong man who'd keep them there. Like his own wife, who went where he told her and never lifted her voice or her eyes. . . .

He claimed credit for the killing of Martin Luther King during an especially rousing sermon before a congregation of a dozen men and twenty elderly women. The next day the FBI came by, asking him to expand on that sermon. Nervously, he explained to them that he meant it in a *spiritual* sense, that he hadn't pulled the trigger after all. Not *really*.

This was back in the sixties, and the ball had barely begun to roll.

His congregation slowly built to around a hundred, and peaked there for several years. He had masqueraded as a Baptist minister because he'd heard those people could sure fork out the money if you pleaded hard enough. With a minimum of hassle he found the necessary contacts to forge the proper documents to become a "bona fide" Baptist minister. After skimming the till for five years, stashing a good chunk of it in gold and CDs, his credentials came into question when he refused to attend an annual Baptist minister's conference in nearby Atlanta.

Before the darkness could gather completely he absconded with what he could and assumed a new identity in California, where he took to the airwaves as a radio preacher. As "Father Fact" he had enjoyed a sizable following for close to a year.

Then, as the spirit moved in him, his sermons took a more radical slant. More and more often, his true feelings began to overcome him in the midst of a sermon, raising the ire of the Federal Communications Commission. Soon "Father Fact" became "Father History," and after several unsuccessful attempts to find similar employment with other stations, he holed up in a cheap hotel in Los Angeles with one hundred thousand dollars in the bank and a fire in his gut.

At the San Jose Hotel he had a revelation, sent to him directly from God. At first he interpreted the message to mean that he was to become the second Christ. Then, as he mulled it over a bit, he decided instead that it was time to write a book, a *manifesto,* for his new church. It was time to come out into the open, to preach his new school of thought unfettered by anyone else's rules. The time of hiding behind the "established" order of religion had come to a screeching halt. He started using the name "Brother Joseph," which at first was going be a pseudonym only, since he suspected the authorities in Georgia might still be looking for him. But he liked the sound of it, and it stuck. "Brother Joseph, leader of the Sacred Heart of the Chosen Ones," was a fitting title. But the movement would need a users' manual, and over the next fourteen months, with an old Underwood, he hacked out the *Manifesto of the Sacred Heart of the Chosen Ones.* Editing or retyping, he had decided, would not be necessary. After all, this was the divine word of the Lord; who was he to decide what the Lord wanted left in and what He didn't? Had the Apostles edited the books of the New Testament? Had Moses edited the Ten Commandments? Those were not choices for a mere mortal, he reasoned then and now, so he let the work stand as written.

Unwilling to trust the task of *publishing* his holy book to anyone else, the Brother Joseph purchased an old offset press and developing equipment. Stray lumber and cardboard became a darkroom. For weeks, after typing God's Word on nine by eleven rag, he shot the individual pages directly from the single-spaced typewritten sheets.

The manifesto wasn't simple; Brother Joseph required 1532 pages to explain his leap of intellect, excluding the table of contents and index. On the "reference and bibliography" page the word God appeared seven hundred and seventy-seven times. In all-caps.

With some basic binding equipment, which was used to make cloth-bound books the old-fashioned way, he went to the next phase of his project. Between inexpensive meals of Discount Dan's macaroni'n'cheese and cold Van de Camps Pork and Beans, selected from his immense survival cache, he lovingly handcrafted each volume. They were easily the size and weight of an unabridged dictionary. On a good day, he could produce three to five books, which were soon given away. The preacher sent the very first volume to the newly elected Ronald Reagan, with a simple note reading: "Have your men read this immediately."

Six months later he signed and numbered the five hundredth volume. The four hundred ninety-nine volumes preceding it had been given away to Klansmen, defrocked ministers, congressmen, mayors, governors, shriners, a hundred right-wing organizations, and anyone else he thought would be interested. But that day, holding volume number five hundred, Brother Joseph frowned and scratched his head. Despite the address he had clearly printed on the title page, no tithes were pouring in to finance the new movement. Not even a letter or a postcard. Nothing. Although he had close to seventy thousand left in the bank, he didn't want to dip into that yet. He simply couldn't understand the lack of interest. He had thought that by now *someone* would have seen the wisdom in God's words.

Fifteen years and a thousand miles away, Brother Joseph stood in the closet of expensive suits, regarding with a sense of melancholic nostalgia the box of books marked, in purple crayon, "original manifesto." There was only one of the hefty tomes left, and it was stored here. The time would soon come when he would have to publish the full-length manifesto again. With new plates, of course — hell, in fancy, scrolled type, scanned from the original book and set by computer and fed directly into the bowels of his own printers. Now he owned his own little publishing empire. Never again would he have to type a word.

During the early years of the Chosen Ones, someone convinced him to condense the book a little, to where it was only about eighty pages long. It wasn't even an *outline* of the original masterwork — it was a mere *pamphlet*. The decision angered him, but he permitted the sacrilege in order to attract more followers.

In 1983 Brother Joseph purchased a stolen mailing list from *The Right Way,* an ultraconservative monthly which featured articles on assault weapons, Israel Identity theory, the Jewish Question, survival tactics, quilting tips and home cooking recipes. With the pilfered list he mailed, at great expense, one hundred thousand copies of the condensed *Manifesto.* The new edition contained simple instructions on how to start your own Sacred Heart chapter.

The ruse worked. Almost overnight congregations began to pop up all over the country, mostly in the South and Midwest. Ten in all, in the beginning, and he kept himself busy ministering to each. Money poured in. A few of his larger CDs, left over from his Baptist preaching days, began to mature. In the conservative atmosphere of the Reagan Administration, his church flourished. Congregations swelled. Finally, his message was receiving the attention it deserved. Humanity might survive after all.

Reluctant to end his brief jaunt down memory lane, Brother Joseph disrobed and hung his latest acquisition, a tailor-made Sacred Heart uniform with all the relevant religious markings, in a separate valet in the closet. The coat alone was a work of art, with Sacred Heart insignia, military decorations of his own creation, gold cord and epaulets. The severe black shirt and white collar gave it a religious look, and despite its Catholic undertones he let the creation stand. It looked more impressive, after all. The entire outfit cost nearly two thousand dollars to have made and it fit perfectly; it was his most treasured possession.

Nothing too good for the founder of the Sacred Heart, he thought.

As he selected one of fifteen bathrobes, each a different shade of blue, gray or black, he noticed a plaid suit. He hadn't worn this one very long because of a certain place in the trousers where it was too tight, but nevertheless, he remembered the circumstance of this particular outfit, and scowled.

That reporter will never stand on Sacred Ground again, he seethed, tying the robe. He meant to have the suit burned, to erase the bad memories it represented, but had never got around to it. He had worn it once during the early growth of the church, about six years before, when he was attempting one of the first channelings during what he would later call "Praise Meetings."

There had been a new lamb in the fold, a young man who had been to the meetings for the past three months or so. Brother Joseph had picked him to be the vehicle for the channeling session, and he had agreed. The young man was an admitted Democrat, and that alone should have tipped him off, but in those early days followers were coming out of the woodwork from every conceivable direction, and he hadn't really cared. The "channeling" went well, and the subject had shown every indication of the holy trance. The original plan was to channel John the Baptist, but somewhere it all got sidetracked and the subject recited passages from the Bible, claiming to be one of the twelve disciples. He never said which one, an omission which should have been another clue. The response from the gathering was questionable, but Brother Joseph declared the session a success and adjourned the meeting. The subject vanished soon afterward, and after a cursory asking around, nobody seemed to know who he was.

The next day, on the front page of the *Wichita Eagle*, Brother Joseph saw an article prominently displayed in the upper half of the paper. "Eagle Reporter Infiltrates 'Channeling Cult,' " read the headlines, and accompanying the article was a photograph of the reporter. He was, indeed, the same subject who had "channeled" the night before.

Aghast, Brother Joseph read on. The "sting" had taken three months, and while it had been unplanned, the leader of the cult had picked him to be channeled. In detail the reporter described the "high visibility" of firearms and the "gullibility of the audience, who seemed to come from rural, uneducated backgrounds." As the final insulting touch, it seemed that the "scripture" he'd quoted while in the "trance" was all fabricated, but had been accepted as "fact" by Brother Joseph and his followers.

Brother Joseph, staying at the house of one of the flock, packed his bags and left Wichita, Kansas, in a hurry. He left the situation in the capable hands of one of his followers, hoping the brouhaha would remain local. During the next month it appeared that it would, but the preacher had learned his lesson. To the best of his ability and the ability of the chapter members, each new member had a thorough background check.

The incident had happened many years before, but

still it grated. He had been *so certain* he had a true medium sitting before him. In time it would become clear to him that a true channeling would be much more compelling and believable than an agent of Satan spouting made-up scripture.

Putting the distasteful experience behind him, Brother Joseph entered the bathroom adjacent to the long hallway, finding one of his servants sitting at the makeup table, reading a Bible. Brother Joseph recognized him as one of the Junior Guard, with beret, t-shirt and camo pants. Within the walls of his private living quarters full assault rifles were waived; this youth wore what appeared to be a WWII Luger sidearm. The young man looked up expectantly, closing the Bible.

"Your bath is prepared, Brother Joseph," the boy said, standing and bowing slightly.

The leader nodded, noting the perfect way in which he had been addressed. *I must remember to compliment his CO when I see him,* he thought complacently.

"Have a seat. Make yourself comfortable, young man," Brother Joseph said fondly. It felt good to have servants, especially the faithful young followers who were so bright, so energetic, so enthusiastic for the Church and what he wanted to accomplish with it.

To call this room a "bathroom" would be a disservice, Brother Joseph mused, as he eased into the immense marble bathtub. The bath, which was installed on a raised platform surrounded by roman columns, could have held at least five people at once. But such a thing would be wanton and sinful. This was his solitary pleasure, his just reward for serving the Lord, to be shared with no one.

"More patchouli," Brother Joseph said, and the boy poured more pink powder into the swirling baths. "More air in the jets," he added, as an afterthought, and the boy adjusted the knob to make the water more bubbly. The flowery fragrance rose from the steamy bath. To call this heaven would have been a sacrilege. But then, the preacher speculated, maybe God provided a tiny piece of heaven for his top workers.

Once Brother Joseph's needs were seen to, the Junior Guard lad bowed and returned faithfully to his Bible. *Fine young man,* the preacher observed, trying to ignore his own shriveled skin, the liver spots, the flab, and other nagging signs of aging. He thought of his age in terms of what he had told his congregation, not the date on which he was born. Instead of being fifty-nine, he was actually forty something. Nobody questioned him. Being leader of the Church had its advantages.

So much accomplished, so much more to do, he thought, glorying in the evening's events. These Praise Meetings energized him in ways nobody even suspected; he felt years younger after a successful night like tonight, and if there had been time he would hold one every night. But it was late when the meetings concluded, including the little private meeting afterwards, and his people needed rest to be able to put in a full day for the Church. The information he had gleaned from the Holy Fire would take days to process. Any more meetings, and the data would be wasted. Such a waste, the preacher calculated, could well displease the Holy Fire, and that was the last thing he'd wanted to do.

Overall it was a pretty good Praise Meeting. At least until the little brat threw up on those shoes, Brother Joseph thought, melting further into the hot, steaming bath. *I didn't like throwing that pair out, but I didn't exactly have a choice. Oh, well. Plenty more where they came from.* Adjoining the long closet was another closet, which held around two hundred pairs of fine dress shoes, each pair assigned to its own cubby-hole in the extensive shelving he'd had built.

Despite that disgusting display of nausea there at the end, the boy is a remarkable tool. The fasting had been so effective that the preacher was contemplating extending the fast until the next Praise Meeting, three days hence. No resistance to the Holy Fire this time — and that seemed to please it a great deal.

And what it *said* . . . Brother Joseph was still wallowing in that praise, an honor bestowed to *him*. Now he knew what Christ felt like: powerful, right, still the obedient servant of God, yet also the Sword in His hand.

This was, he reflected, all he ever really wanted to do, since the days of the burning crosses and the dangling niggers, and throughout his long days in the San Jose Hotel. Yes, *this* was all he wanted to do, this service to the Lord.

Especially now that he was much *more* than a mere servant. The Sacred Fire surpassed his wildest expectations tonight. It not only affirmed his position in the Church, but in the God/Man hierarchy. Tonight, his status went up more than a few notches. The memory warmed him like a fine glass of burgundy. He raised his arms out of the steamy, fragrant water, half expecting electricity to arc between his hands.

Life is grand. It's good to be the one on top.

Until now, everything the Holy Fire had allowed him to do had been mere parlor tricks. He reminded himself that the parlor tricks had convinced many a borderline believer in his power, and in his ability to call forth the glory of Jesus and God.

But the boy — the boy — that his key to glory should be one small boy, who might not ever have come into his hands. . . .

He suppressed that thought. It *would* have happened. The Lord willed it. Just as the Lord had willed that he find that flagstaff.

He had been looking for a suitably impressive staff for the church flag, the symbol of all they stood for, the banner under which his armies would eventually march to victory. But the stores that sold such things had only the same wooden poles, topped either with brass spearheads, eagles, or round knobs. He had wanted something more.

And something not so . . . expensive.

Surely God had directed his steps to the little junk shop in Lafayette, Indiana, a place run by two senile old people, so identical he could not tell which was the husband and which the wife. One of them had directed him to the back of the room when he answered their vague mumbles with "I'm looking for a pole."

Wedged in a space between two enormous oak dish-cupboards, pieces that would fit only in a room with a fourteen-foot ceiling, had been a selection of poles. Curtain poles, fishing poles, poles for punting —

And yes, flagpoles.

Standing tall among the others was a grime-encrusted flagpole of indeterminate age and origin. It stood taller than the two dish-cupboards that flanked it, its top ornament hidden in gloom. When he reached out to heft it doubtfully, he received a double shock.

First — it was *heavy*. Too heavy to have been made of wood.

Second — a real, physical shock, like a electrical spark that arced from it to his arm. It only lasted a moment, but in that moment, he knew he *had* to have it.

He carried the thing forward to the old couple — who, when they learned it was to be used for a church banner, refused to accept any money for it.

He remembered thinking as he carried it out that even if it wasn't *quite* suitable, the price was certainly right.

Back at the revival tent, he began cleaning his find — and discovered that under the years of dirt and grime, the pole was of hollow brass, three sections fitted together like a portable billiard cue. He had expected that the threads would have corroded together, but they unscrewed smoothly, as if the pole had just been machined and put together for the first time.

But it was the top ornament that took his breath away and made him realize that the piece had been waiting for him — for decades, perhaps even for centuries. A flat piece of brass, it proved to be engraved — with the Church's own emblem, the Sacred Heart pierced by twin crucifixes, the sole difference being that this heart was engulfed in flames. There was writing around the edge of the plaque, but it was in Latin and what he thought might be French, so he had ignored it.

And it was from that moment of discovery that the Holy Fire began whispering in the back of his mind, bringing the Word of God directly — if imperfectly — to him. It was then that he had decided to try channeling again, after that disastrous incident in Wichita. And that was the first time he had actually *gotten* something, through the medium of little Sarah.

And now, even more effectively, the Fire *acted* through the medium of young Jamie.

The boy had proven to be an effective bridge. On the very first channeling he allowed the preacher to invoke a ball of flame, which he held in his unprotected hands. The Fire spoke then, but he later learned that only *he* had heard it. The next Praise Meeting he had arranged to have a bed of hot coals ready, and at the appropriate moment, to the horror of those attending, he walked barefoot over it. Only once, though. He didn't want to try the patience of the Sacred Flame by showing preference to another, lesser flame. That one time though had been enough. The congregation flocked to the stage to examine his unblemished feet. And then, surprisingly, to kiss them.

As he thought back on his career in the light of the Sacred Fire's words tonight, Brother Joseph began to see a pattern emerge, one which placed him at the very center of things. Gradually, since the lynching days of the KKK, through his rise in the Baptist Church to the present, God had slowly but surely been revealing truth to him, and only him. Those other would-be leaders, as he was so fond of preaching, didn't have it right, never did, never would. This latest revelation, for it was truly a *revelation*, put him in a position only slightly lower than Jesus himself.

Though he hadn't felt that way when the boy threw up on him. Had Jesus had people throw up on his holy robes and sandals? At least nobody had been around to see it. If anyone noticed the condition of his shoes after leaving the altar, they had politely, and intelligently, withheld comment. Still, he didn't like how that memory played in his mind. It seemed like Satan might have had a hand in this —

No, that wasn't possible, since Satan was too afraid to mess with personal friends and agents of God Almighty. Satan's tools didn't projectile-vomit no matter what was in the movies.

It couldn't have been interference. The boy simply lost his control, and whatever it was he drank last, from the sheer excitement of channeling the Holy Fire.

At least, he hoped that's what it was. But as he considered this, an alarming thought came to mind. What if this was some kind of *signal*, sent by God, to warn him that the boy was going to be trouble? A similar signal had been sent in the case of the little brat Sarah, in the form of a sickness during one of the Praise Meetings. That had been embarrassing, and it had required maximum use of his silver tongue to quell the audience. It had looked like some sort of epileptic seizure at the time. Eventually the congregation returned to their seats, including her parents, and watched as the girl flopped around on the stage; *possession*, that's what he'd said, he remembered. This incident had happened weeks before he had to actually kill her, and now it seemed to have been a sure sign that trouble was to follow.

Time will tell, he thought, with a sigh. The water's heat was making him dizzy, but he stayed in nevertheless. He didn't feel clean, not yet. The preacher had made sure that the boy had been taken back to the isolation room, away from his father. It had come to his attention that Jim Chase had been drinking a bit heavily in his private room with his son. That just didn't seem right. Also, he wasn't sure if he could trust the man to maintain the integrity of the fast and had suspicions that he'd slipped the boy some food. Tonight, at least, Jamie would have to be separated from his father. Perhaps the separation should be permanent. The boy seemed more exhausted and muddled than the last time, but the preacher didn't worry; God would see to it that the boy survived. His body, anyway. It really didn't matter if the boy had a mind or not. He was only a mouthpiece, to serve the Holy Fire as an object, not a thinking being. And his soul would surely be purified from contact with the Holy Fire. Why, if the soul could talk to him directly, it would probably be thanking him right now.

"After all," he'd told the boy's father, while escorting the boy to the isolation room. "Children are the property of the parent who gave them life. And now, Jim, you owe me your life. You should rejoice that I have a use for your son."

Jim had agreed, nodding numbly, shuffling off to his room after locking the door on Jamie's new home.

The Holy Fire would protect the boy, as it always had, despite the apparent exhaustion he was displaying.

The Holy Fire always survives. He knew that, as surely as he knew his own name. Brother Joseph.

If the boy became unsuitable, there would always be others. The boy could even be buried beside Sarah and her parents.

As could his father, if he objected in any way. This, however, was unlikely; the man was a faithful, unthinking servant. The best kind. Meanwhile, so was the boy, though he had little choice in the matter.

Neither did Sarah, he reminded himself.

The pitiful creature never once understood the importance of her sacrifice, and that in itself was a tragedy. It was ironic that he hadn't even been trying for the Holy Fire, didn't even know that it existed. He remembered Sarah's parents telling him how *receptive* she was, how *special*. And he remembered how the voices whispering in the back of his mind had urged him to try channeling again, that this time it would be different. So he had tried using Sarah to shoot for a garden variety prophet, like Elijah.

But instead, he got *it*. The Holy Fire. The same fire that had spoken to Moses from the burning bush.

Never, ever, had he thought he would reach something like *that*. It had all come about so casually — almost by accident.

Channeling was very big, he had realized, after reading an article about Shirley MacLaine. Californians were making lots of money with this idea, and while he didn't believe for a second that MacLaine was telling the truth, it had a certain macabre appeal. And surely in the hands of the God-fearing, if anything happened, it would be with God's will.

So he gave it another try. Sarah seemed pliant, her parents appeared cooperative, and he staged a "channeling" one night where there were few in the audience, before he had moved all of the Sacred Heart chapters to this central location. After several unproductive tries at contacting "Elijah," it happened. The Holy Fire spoke through the girl, in a voice that made her sound like Satan. As the girl spoke, it dawned on the preacher that it was not Satan but God, the *real* God, that was talking to him directly.

Cunning, the Holy Fire was; in its first message it told the preacher what he would have to do for it so that it could aid him in his mission. It could assist the Chosen Ones in attracting new members, give them information on gambling, tip them off when the police were nearing their operations. All sorts of helpful things, meant to bring wealth to the faithful and to confound the unbelievers. And money meant power, in anyone's language.

But the girl proved a disappointment. She resisted any further attempts to channel the Holy Fire again, much to his humiliation and, later, rage. Oh, the Fire came through, but it was a struggle, and the information it was able to convey was meager compared to what he *knew* it wanted to give.

Yet Brother Joseph had not given up. He knew enough about the Holy Fire to begin seeking another suitable subject.

It didn't take long. In fact, the father had practically dumped Jamie in his lap. Jim had been attending the Atlanta Praise Meetings intermittently at first, but then he began appearing on a regular basis. He had mentioned to the preacher that he had a son, a trusting, receptive child. Something about those words triggered an excitement in him. "Would you like to bring the boy to the next meeting?" Brother Joseph had asked, and Jim did.

Along with his mother. *She* should have been left behind, the preacher realized instantly when he first saw her. She sat stiffly in the audience, full of resistance, looking scared and angry at the same time. Over the years the preacher had learned to spot that type, the unbeliever who would always be an unbeliever, a wife or a husband who had been dragged along. The infidel who would compete with God for the ear and soul of the newcomer, and sometimes even win.

But the boy — the *boy* was special, more than Jim realized. And from the first moment he'd set eyes on Jamie, he knew that the Fire wanted him.

Jim had brought Jamie by himself one day, and Brother Joseph seized upon the opportunity. The faithful were anxious for a good channeling, and he had prayed earnestly for success before it began. He wasn't disappointed. The boy proved to be a superb conductor of the Holy Fire.

Then the mother had intervened, before he could get Jim to turn the boy over to his hands.

The divorce came as a surprise, to both himself and Jim, he had to admit. The preacher hadn't thought she'd had it in her. *The whore,* he thought, seething. The woman and her son went into hiding before he and Jim knew what was happening, but when the divorce papers were filed by that smart-assed lawyer, Brother Joseph knew what to do next: wait. Eventually, she would have to let her guard down. Just let her think Jim was gone, and then go in for the boy. Once she thought she was safe, she'd go back to the old house, the familiar surroundings. The preacher assigned a private in the Guard to discreetly watch the school for Cindy, and a few days later, after she showed up, Jim went in to pick up his son.

The father had been wired with a remote microphone, which they used to monitor the situation. Fifteen Chosen Ones waited beyond the school's perimeter in three separate vehicles, ready to go in and take the boy by force, if necessary. It wasn't; the school had no idea what was up. In fact, they had been downright *helpful,* to the delight of those listening in. Within moments Jim emerged with his son and quietly drove off in their pickup, followed close behind by a Bronco, a Cadillac and Brother Joseph's God-given stretch Lincoln. The convoy of Chosen Ones were well on their way to Oklahoma before the mother had any idea of what had happened.

A brilliant mission. Brilliantly planned and brilliantly executed, just . . . brilliant, gloated Brother Joseph. He looked up from the swirling waters, just in time to see the young guard bring a snack in on a silver tray. Cheese, crackers, caviar. A kind of salad he didn't immediately recognize. *And the police in this county* still *don't suspect a thing.*

He knew this was primarily because of their lawyer, Claudius Williams III. The old man came down with the Detroit flock three years ago, a true believer in God, Country and AK-47s. In his collection of assault weapons he had fifteen of the Russian-made rifles, all of which he cheerfully donated to the Sacred Heart armory. As a citizen of Detroit, Williams had practiced law during the week, favoring the male side of divorce proceedings. On Saturday, he had participated in a white supremacists' organization. On Sunday, he had been a church preacher, teaching the Israel Identity to hungover auto workers. *All in all,* Brother Joseph thought, *a well-rounded individual. Even though he wanted to continue preaching. He saw, with God's help, the light of wisdom. After all, we needed his expertise in the legal field. And his performance in that capacity has been exemplary.*

Once the underground lair of the Sacred Heart was discovered by the county's law enforcement, Claudius Williams III went into action. For months prior to moving to Oklahoma, he had studied the local laws in books acquired by Guard agents, finding loopholes, exploiting weaknesses. Pawnee County turned out to be ideal for their purposes. Since the building permits had already been granted, it was a simple matter to keep the sheriff off their property. What the law didn't cover, court injunctions did. In Pawnee County, it was difficult to obtain a search warrant.

And it didn't hurt that the district judge was an old college buddy of Claudius. The judge had been battling with the DA and sheriff for years now, over run-ins with his *own* friends and relatives, so naturally the granting of injunctions was a simple matter, reduced to a rubber-stamped formality. The judge and lawyer smiled and shook hands, the DA and sheriff fumed and scratched their heads, and the Sacred Heart of the Chosen Ones existed, more or less, as a sovereign state.

Brother Joseph chuckled at the sheer perversity of it all; his young servant looked up quizzically from the Bible. Their eyes locked for a brief instant before the boy looked away, apparently embarrassed.

"I must awe you," Brother Joseph said. "I know that service in my private quarters is a rotational thing, but you must feel a *chill* of excitement to be here. Am I correct?"

"Of c-course, sir," the boy stammered. "Is there anything I can get you?"

"My bathrobe, my boy," the preacher said. The boy scrambled for the robe, lying on a chair on the other side of the immense bathroom. "And a towel. I'm through here for the night. Secure the area and report to your CO. You will be commended."

The boy blushed when he handed the preacher the robe. *Such a young face. And such dedication to one he worships. What, Oh Lord, have I done to deserve such favor?*

Jamie was only vaguely aware of the two beefy fists gripping his arms as he was led away from the Praise Meeting. Behind him he could hear Brother Joseph talking some icky stuff to his father, none of which really made much sense. It was just more gobbledygook. More of the same.

When the man grabbed his arm he realized that his arm had gotten smaller, and that he felt lighter. These facts didn't register immediately, but somewhere along the way he saw what it meant, and wondered if he would go away if they didn't feed him. His body, he reasoned, must be feeding on itself, and pretty soon he would be all gone. Would his real body fade away like the ghost-one had during the Praise Meeting, going all see-through, until there was nothing at all? Or would he turn into a stick-figure, like the pictures of Ethiopian kids?

Then Jamie was dimly aware that he was going someplace different, that he wasn't going back to the old room. In a way that made him glad. He wouldn't have to worry about being rolled over on, and he wouldn't be using a blanket full of little white bugs. He didn't really care where he was going, though he was fully aware that it could be far worse than his room, if Brother Joseph was taking him there. His consciousness was fading, and he wondered if you could walk and sleep at the same time.

Somewhere in his schooling he had heard about the place they took bad boys who ran away from home, played hooky or used drugs, the place called "juvie detention." If that was where he was being taken, he now knew that you didn't have to do something bad to get there. But he wasn't scared about it, and he wondered why.

Finally they put him into a little room that had a little bed in it, but no carpet or other furniture. The blankets on the bed smelled clean, something he had barely noticed when they put him down on the bed; all he could do then was lie there and pant, and look at the stars that sparkled in his vision.

The darkness became absolute when they slammed the door on him. Jamie let out a little whimper before falling asleep, into a world of nightmares he was too tired to wake up from.

● CHAPTER SEVEN

Al climbed a little higher in the tree, further away from the chain-link fence. The added distance he'd put between himself and the steel decreased the interference that disrupted his senses, and made it easier to get around the metal barriers, but it didn't make him feel any better about what was taking place down there at the "Praise Meeting."

In fact, the impromptu fine-tuning made what was happening down there all the clearer, and it took every ounce of his willpower to keep from dashing to the boy's rescue.

No heroics, he lectured himself. *I can't do Jamie any good if I'm shot full of holes. Lots of holes, by the look of those automatic weapons they're lugging around.* But anxiety knotted his stomach, and the urge to get over there and *do* something kept him in a state of nervous tension.

When he remembered what he looked like, in black clothing, boots and mask, he couldn't help but grimace; he looked either like a Ninja or a black-power commando. With this group, who hated black and Oriental people as much any other scapegoat, he wouldn't last very long. In the bright lights he would make an easy target. He didn't think he could dodge that many bullets, even with Andur's help. The elvensteed could run fast, but not *that* fast.

When the gathering began, and his brief glimpses into the humans' minds gave him more and more information, Alinor quickly identified this as the same kind of "Praise Meeting" that Cindy had told him about. Everything matched what she'd described, including the peculiar flag in the stage's background. What he hadn't expected was the evil thing that Brother Joseph summoned as soon as Jamie arrived. Al had not expected ritual magic, not here. He had assumed that the dark power he'd touched had been something the cultists didn't know about, or something that was using them without their knowledge. It seemed he was wrong — terribly wrong.

Given the magical power of the entity, he was still afraid that it might have detected him, there at the beginning of the ritual. He couldn't shake a sense of familiarity, a haunting foreboding that he had, indeed, seen this thing, or something like it, in the past. Alinor had to admit that it wasn't often these days that he ran across such things. One was more likely to encounter such things in the halfworld, beyond the borders of Underhill, not in the technological environment of the "real world." But here it was.

And it threatened Jamie's very survival. It would have to be dealt with, destroyed. At the moment, Alinor was most likely to be the one to face the beast.

Provided it didn't find and devour *him* first.

After he'd withdrawn his probes from the immediate vicinity of the entity, he studied its reactions. Soon he was satisfied that it hadn't sensed him, and that the humans who had gathered were responsible for its waking. And then the creature saw the tiny life-spark that had to be Jamie, and reached. . . .

But instead of devouring the boy, the child's soul *switched* with the dark thing. Alinor did a double take; suddenly, outside the boy's body, stood the boy — or rather, the boy's spirit. And speaking through the body was the evil force, in full control of mouth, tongue and vocal cords.

The elf's first reaction was awe at the expertise this human, Brother Joseph, had with the magics of the halfworld. But as Alinor surreptitiously explored this "expertise" he found the preacher wasn't responsible for the shift at all. In fact, the switch took place in *spite* of the preacher and all he did. He saw the interference the emotional energies were creating: strong, gusty waves of hate and fear, intermingled with the human excitement of the Praise Meeting. Brother Joseph didn't engineer the switch, the evil force did, deftly sidestepping the waves of psionic energy the meeting generated, shunting them off.

Alinor narrowed his eyes and frowned, gathering his thoughts. His perch in the tree was getting uncomfortable, but he dared not move. If that *thing* didn't notice him, the guards down there might. The entity might even see him then, a complication he quite easily could live without.

I'm assuming too much, he decided. *I don't know that it perceives magics and energies the same way I do. In fact, it probably doesn't see it the same way. It seems quite alien — and it's not like an Unseleighe creature, either. The emotion-driven psychic force that Brother Joseph is raising may be acting as food to it, not a loud distraction. I wish I had someone with more experience here with me. . . .*

As the darkness enveloped the boy, Alinor became aware of yet another creature, creeping quietly out of the halfworld.

Who is she? Alinor wondered, suddenly aware of the being's gender. This was not something cut from the same fabric as the present occupant of Jamie's body.

She was quiet, yet strong. And the fact that she retained a sex, and a vaguely human semblance, finally gave him the clue he needed to identify *what* she was, if not who.

A human ghost.

Al sighed. A ghost tied to this place could only mean that it was bound somehow to Brother Joseph or the cult. Such bindings were rarely anything other than tragic. *So much unhappiness in this place, invoked by a crazed human preacher who doesn't even know what he's done!*

And now there was another complication to what had seemed straightforward last night. That this was a ghost with Jamie told him a great deal. The woman, no, *girl*, had evidently died a violent death. Spirits with that kind of ending frequently lingered near the earth-plane, still not convinced that they had died; wandering about aimlessly, knocking things over and making a general nuisance of themselves. The very tragedy of their death acted as a burden, an anchor weighing them down until the conflict surrounding their demise was resolved.

Yet even as he thought that, he knew that wasn't the case here; he could sense it. This spirit had a purpose, and the purpose involved Jamie.

Was this her way of dealing with her own death? Al wondered as he watched the flicker of light take form. The girl sent Jamie's spirit a thin tendril of energy, which began blocking the boy's pain.

Well done! Alinor complimented silently. *I hope that before this is all over and done with I'll get to meet this little one, and perhaps help her leave this plane....*

But this was getting more complicated by the moment; not the simple "snatch and grab" of the usual elven rescue. His premonition had been correct. There had been death, sadism and violence here, and there was more to come.

He resisted a particularly strong urge to contact the ghost-child. Allies in this situation could only help to tip the odds in his, and Jamie's, favor. But to reach out to her could alert the beast to his presence and, conceivably, to hers. How she had managed to aid Jamie was something he would have to ask later.

Alinor listened, and watched.

The thing began to speak through Jamie, and the reaction from the audience was dramatic and varied.

The thing fed on the roiling emotions of the preacher's flock. *A true parasitic spirit,* Al thought. Parasites in any world were disgusting things to him, *especially* when they attacked children. This one seemed particularly insidious, in view of the total possession the thing had of the boy's body. He wondered what would happen if it weakened Jamie to the point where it could make that possession permanent.

The entity spoke, ranting in the same vein as Brother Joseph, and an outpouring of racial hate and convoluted biblical theory that was enough to make him ill. It made even less sense than Brother Joseph, something Alinor had to hear to believe.

And he could not shake the nagging sense of familiarity.

Where else have I seen this thing? Al asked himself, now certain he'd encountered *it,* or perhaps a relative of *it,* before.

It began saying things, things the preacher seemed unprepared for. The man stood back, apparently trying to form some kind of rebuttal to what was coming out of the boy's mouth. *You, Brother Joseph, you are the instrument of the Prophecy. You will be the Bringer of the Flame.* . . . The boy's distorted voice ranted on, while the preacher just stood there, open-mouthed, slack-jawed, for once at a loss for words.

Alinor took note of how the preacher reacted to this unexpected tirade. Brother Joseph did not like what he heard — but more importantly, the words disturbed the audience as well. The congregation shifted nervously, and the deep wrinkle between Brother Joseph's eyebrows deepened.

But like the professional orator he was, he bounced back from the uncomfortable moment as soon as the entity gave him the chance to speak, replying with a rambling continuation of his previous sermon.

Within moments he had reconciled everything the

creature had said with his own words, exerting a powerful charisma to charm the flock and lull them back into their feeling of comfortable *belonging*. Apparently relieved that what the Sacred Fire had to say was no real surprise, they responded with mindless shouts of "Praise the Lord," resolutely erasing any lingering doubts from their own minds.

A guard passed by the tree Al was sitting in, startling him and catching him unawares. He pulled his attention back to his immediate surroundings. *Need to watch that,* he thought, as his stomach lurched in alarm. *I am, after all, sitting in a tree in hostile territory.*

But the guard continued his patrol around one of the buildings. Apparently he had not noticed Alinor perched above him. This time he'd been lucky, but luck could only stretch so far.

Al checked cautiously for other guards, found none, and eventually sent his mental sight back to the Praise Meeting. But now the hall had been cleared of all spectators, except for a handful of men gathered at the foot of the stage. The boy continued speaking, but *what* he was saying . . .

Alinor smiled sardonically. *Now we get to the practical part of this evening's programming,* he thought, making mental notes on the kinds of information the entity produced for Brother Joseph. *Bingo. Horse racing. Gambling. What else?* he wondered. And then he heard what else—

Drugs. Information on the police. *Great Danaa, this thing has a lead on just about everything. It knows more about the humans and their world than they do. Not only that, but it's engineering the sale of drugs . . . to* children!

Now he was not only sickened, he was outraged. *The man is a monster. He has the ability to manipulate whoever listens to him — and he uses it for this. And beneath it all, he's still a puppet, a tool. The thing that controls him, that's the culprit, the blackness behind this entire charade masquerading as faith . . . some Christian, he hasn't got a clue. . . .*

Then, with a cold shock of recognition, Alinor finally remembered where he'd seen this *thing* before. *The church and all its esoteric trappings*, he chided himself angrily. *Brother Joseph, and all his blithering religious lunacy, should have been a dead giveaway. Of course — of course. I know where this thing came from — what it is. It's been nearly a thousand years, but I shouldn't have forgotten, no matter how long ago it happened. This dark creature, this blackness, this thing, this blot of evil, this . . .*

Salamander.

It shouldn't be happening again. But it *was*.

Only this time, the Christian soldiers weren't toting shields, swords and arrows. They were armed with the latest in automatic weaponry, killing tools designed to exterminate humans by the hundreds.

Yet how could it be happening here, now? When he had witnessed the creation of the United States, Alinor had thought that the Constitution would prevent religious crusades from destroying lives and souls ever again. The Constitution was, after all, designed to protect *all* religions, not just the Christian one. At its inception the new nation was easily the freest place in the world. It still was, though the Folk still needed to remain concealed.

The Salamander is behind it. Blessed Danaa — he thought angrily; wishing, as he had so many times before, that he had found a way to do away with the creature, or to at least send it back from where it came.

And nothing has really changed since the last time.

The last time, ten centuries ago.

I was only a child. . . .

It was his first excursion outside Scotland, to the home of his mother's people. He'd looked, at the time, like a teenaged human boy, and although he was considerably older than he appeared, he acted and thought like the sheltered youngster he was.

His father, Liam Silverbranch, had taken him to meet his mother Melisande's kin in Elfhame Joyeaux Garde in France.

His mother's mother had been Elaine du Lac, who had fostered the famous Lancelot du Lac, and both parents had deemed it high time that he meet his celebrated relatives and learn the Gallic side of his heritage. But there had been no one near his age there, not even human fosterlings, and the older elves had gotten involved in hunts and Court gossip and politics. Eventually they had left him to his own devices. He had run off on an exploration of his own as soon as the idea occurred to him.

It was his first chance to see mortals in any numbers, humans other than the fosterlings. The humans were so — bewildering. He had wanted to see them up close, to see the way they really lived; their capacity for violence astonished and intrigued him with morbid fascination. They seemed to throw their short lives away on a whim, to court injury and death for the strangest of reasons or no reason at all. He *had* to learn more.

He had slipped off in human guise when his father and King Huon were off on a three-day hunt. He had planned to stay human for several months, knowing that the time-slip between the human world and Underhill would make it seem only a day or two — five at the most — for the elves. He had even picked out a human to imitate.

His intent, originally, was to pass as a tanner's apprentice. The boy was being sent from a cousin in another village — the tanner had no idea what the boy looked like, only that he was coming. What he did not know — because his cousins didn't tell him — was that the boy was much younger than he'd been led to think; instead of being an adolescent, the proper age for an apprentice, he was only six. The cousins had hoped to fob the boy off on their richer relative; since he was already foregoing the usual apprenticeship fee, they figured once the boy was in his custody, he wouldn't turn him away. He'd lost his way and been found by one of the fosterlings, who'd taken him Underhill with her.

Alinor turned up right on schedule. For a few months all was well; the tanner was relatively prosperous, and since he catered to the wealthy with his finely tooled leather horse-goods, Alinor got to see all the violence he wanted, quite close. But in the third month of his apprenticeship, his master had died of a madness that, he later learned, had been caused by a poisonous mold in rye bread. Knowing that it would be unwise to be associated with a human who had gone mad, he attempted to return to Elfhame Joyeaux Garde.

By that time, he was weary and sick of the mortals and their unfathomable ways, and he had seen enough of the humans' world by then to extinguish any lingering desire for adventure. The bloody battling of the humans, their insatiable desire for conflict, was all very fine in a ballad or tale — but when you stood close enough to the scene of the battle to be spattered with blood from the combatants, it was another case entirely. He was tired of the poor food, the unsanitary conditions, the coarse garments. He was tired of being either too hot or too cold, and very, very tired of rising before dawn and working until the last light had left the sky.

But the ruling council of Joyeaux Garde forbade his return. And that had come as an unpleasant shock.

After all, he had left on his own, without asking leave of the ruling elven royalty, without even telling his parents. Such carelessness had led to exposure in the past — led to the deaths of elves at the hands of mortals, led to witch- and demon-hunts. Or so the ruling council said.

So he was to learn a lesson about the consequences of selfish and unthinking behavior. Alinor suspected that his own father Liam Silverbranch had something to do with the "exile." Liam had admitted to being worried sick over his disappearance, and Liam did not care for being inconvenienced or discommoded in any way. He especially was not amused at his son's audacity in addressing the council without even a touch of humility. And since Alinor was too old for a switch to his rear, he would receive a punishment equivalent to the crime.

It was, King Huon explained (looking much like one of the pictures the humans painted in their churches of a stern and unforgiving God), time for him to get a good dose of the humans. Especially since he had left his rightful home and Underhill without regard for rule of elven law or the feelings of his elven kin.

Alinor knew that he had not been mature in any sense, back then. *I was such a little — what do they call it these days — "rug rat?" Trying to be an adult, without the mental equipment to do so. It's a wonder I didn't get into more trouble than I did.* The Court gave him a year, human time, before he could return to the elves' world, and in that year he was told to survive as a human, not as one of the Folk, and face death if he was exposed as Sidhe. Which meant, in so many words, use your wits, not your magic. Fortunately the humans were wearing their hair long in those days, and most peasants wore hats or hoods night and day, making it easier to hide his conspicuous, pointed ears.

Rebuffed, Alinor did as he was told. To a point. He wandered aimlessly, in the guise of a peasant, which wasn't too difficult since he didn't have a pot to pee in anyway. For a few days he managed to convince himself of the romantic nature of his travels, living on the edge, evading the Death Metal of humans' weapons by a hair's breadth. Great adventure for a youth, and it would have gone on for some time, except for one thing.

Alinor was cold, tired and *hungry*.

In any of the elven enclaves, food was available in abundance. But in the humans' world, starvation prevailed — at least for the lowest classes. Drought and floods regularly wiped out much of the agriculture, and what the weather left, insects and plant diseases ravaged. Small game was difficult to catch without a bow — which, as a peasant, he was not permitted to own — and it was nearly impossible to find a forest that some human noble hadn't already staked a claim to, a claim which was enforced by sword- and arrow-wielding sheriffs. His early attempts at kenning eatables resulted in a tasteless, unpalatable mush that mules would turn up their noses at. Before a week was out, the youngster knew he was in trouble, and began searching for a human he could influence and to learn the mundane ways of making a living as a freedman of some kind. Not even he was romantic enough to think of the life of a serf as something to be pursued.

Alinor had been contemplating pilfering and slaughtering a chicken, and wondering if it was worth the risk of being caught. The farmer in question had several fierce dogs guarding his property; Alinor had thought he would be able to lull them into sleep, but what if he missed one? He finally decided that it wasn't worth the risk and was going in search of a field he could loot for turnips after dark. That was when he came across an elderly man wearing a peculiar robe and a towel around his head, muttering something to himself as he trudged along a dirt highway. He was leading a sickly mule and cart, and nearly walked into the youngster.

The old man had stopped dead in his tracks and gazed at him strangely for a moment. Where he had come from, and what he was doing here, Alinor had no idea. And at the time Alinor couldn't have cared less; he was *starving*.

And whoever the old man was, he didn't speak French, Norse, Saxon English, or Gaelic, the four tongues Alinor knew. After several aborted attempts at communication, the elf finally conveyed his need for food, and to his surprise, the old man gave it to him. Though it was only a bit of bread and a stick of dried meat, gamy and heavily seasoned, Alinor had devoured it hungrily. Only after finishing the meal did he realize that, by accepting the gift, he had become an indentured servant to the man.

Not that it really mattered. Here was the help he'd been looking for. Alinor had even felt very clever, knowing he could leave at any time, since the old man was weak and helpless. Besides, he had reasoned, this had the potential to be interesting.

Over time Alinor learned that the man was known in the region as Al-Hazim, also called the "Mad Arab," though he was neither Arabic nor mad — he was, in fact, a Moor from Alhambra. After some time, he wondered how Al-Hazim escaped being set upon by the other humans — he was, after all, an infidel and fair game. He finally decided that most humans thought the old man was a Jew, not an Arab — Jews had a tenuous immunity from persecution, since when a noble needed money, he had to go to the Jews for it, his own fellows being forbidden to lend money by the Church. This led to a kind of dubious safety; no one wanted to kill the man who would lend him money, but when the debt came due, sometimes it was easier to end the debt with the life of the creditor. . . .

And those that knew the old man was Arabic had another reason to fear him and leave him alone.

He was a magician. He might traffic in demons. He might be protected by horrible creatures. No one human wanted to chance that, and by the time the local Church authorities were alerted to his presence, or the local nobleman was told the Arab was on his property — or a mob was gathered from the braver folk of the village — the Mad Arab was long gone. He never stayed anywhere that he was known overnight. Alinor had the feeling he'd probably learned that lesson early in his career as a wanderer.

Al-Hazim was an alchemist by trade and possessed a handwritten copy of the *Emerald Tablet* a rare and eagerly sought-after book. Though the book was a famous treatise on Arabian alchemy, it had never been translated because it was knowledge that had been uncovered by the infidels, and for a fee the Mad Arab would read it aloud in broken but understandable Latin. To Alinor it was only so much gibberish, but "scientists" in the towns they passed through would provide food and shelter for the privilege of transcribing while Al-Hazim spoke.

The elf couldn't understand the reverence other alchemists paid the *Emerald Tablet*. It was all just half-mystical nonsense compounded with human ignorance, and Alinor privately thought the work and its owner equally ridiculous.

They fell into a pattern of traveling from town to town, usually in search of "scientists" and the very few churchmen who were interested in the *Emerald Tablet* and its secrets. Alinor listened to them debate the secrets of alchemy, and absorbed this "great wisdom" to the best of his abilities, at least until he couldn't stand the cryptic nonsense anymore.

Alchemy, he learned (albeit reluctantly), was considered to be more than just a science, it was a philosophy that supposedly represented mystic, occult knowledge. Al-Hazim's goal was to produce the "elixir," which could be used to convert cheap metal into gold. Alinor knew something of metals; every Sidhe did. What the alchemists were talking about was possible, but not in the way that was outlined in the *Tablet*. When Alinor was able to examine a nugget of pure gold, payment from an isolated monk from the Saint Basil Monastery, he kenned it thoroughly. The gold was the purest Al had ever actually touched, for the Folk preferred ornaments made of silver over those of gold, and the contact enabled him to ken it well enough to produce a perfect replica.

Now he could assure the prosperity of his "master" — and not inconsequentially, himself. And all without risking the exposure of his magic-use by the Folk.

Of course, he couldn't claim responsibility for doing so. It had to appear to be the work of Al-Hazim the Alchemist, not Alinor of the Sidhe.

So he produced a nugget of gold in the crucible at the appropriate moment, the next time Al-Hazim made the attempt for some of his fellow scientists.

Needless to say, it caused a sensation.

This would not have been the first time the Sidhe had produced gold for humans — though usually, it was as a gift to a mother with hungry children, or a father with girls to dower and no money. But Alinor had been specifically forbidden to work this kind of magic by his elders. . . .

He decided, rebelliously, that he didn't care. If he had to substitute gold for a few worthless lumps of lead in order to fill his belly, then that was what he would do. After all, *he* wasn't getting the credit—and notoriety. Al-Hazim was.

Word of the Mad Arab's success filtered down through the countryside, and as they neared towns the populace cleared out of the streets, avoiding them at all costs. Only the few who sought knowledge, power or greater wealth — often at risk to their souls, according to the Church — ever sought them out. Perversely, this increased their safety. The lowborn were terrified of the demons Al-Hazim *must* have had to protect him; the highborn were well aware of the tale of the goose that laid golden eggs and were not inclined to risk either the demons or the loss of the secret of making gold to the hands of a torturer. Al-Hazim was careful with his "talent," changing only the "choicest leads" to gold, and small nuggets at that.

Meanwhile, Alinor worked the magic that created the actual miracles, while Al-Hazim conjured the "elixir" over the tiny brazier they carried with them. Chanting passages from the *Emerald Tablet*, the Mad Arab carefully heated the vessel, a small copper pot with tubes running back into it, like a still, while his tiny audiences watched.

In a trance, the Mad Arab held the vessel over the coals, sometimes for hours, often in conjunction with astrological conditions, while onlookers stared at the flames, mesmerized. Alinor became a little uncomfortable in the intense emotional energy generated at such gatherings, but he held his youthful impatience in check, reminding himself what this was all for.

He had to work stealthily, so that his "mentor," Al-Hazim, got the credit, and sometimes he was a little jealous at the attention the decrepit old Moor received. But the astonished looks and hysterical applause when a little chunk of lead "turned into gold" was well worth a little discomfort and unrequited envy. This was the most fun he'd ever had, and behind the curtains of the wagon the youngster would break out in unrestrained laughter, holding his sides, chortling until he wept.

All this, for a little lump of yellow metal. Alinor would shake his head and chuckle, as the gold was scrupulously divided between the Moor and whoever had provided the costly ingredients of the elixir. Soon they were able to buy a healthy pair of horses and a full-sized wagon, so they could ride instead of walking. They began to wear decent clothing, and Alinor took on the look of a young nobleman. They stayed in a well-appointed tent instead of sleeping in the fields. Life was a little better, when alchemy worked the way it was supposed to.

"Everything comes from the One and returns to the One," the Mad Arab chanted from memory, as they traveled. They were on their way from Toulouse to

Clermont in the southern part of the Kingdom of France, in early November of what — these days — was denoted as the year 1095. Back then, calendars were few, and dates a matter of guess. "It is truth and not lies. What is below is what is above, as all things have been from One by the mediation of One," he continued. From that he went into a recitation in what Al had determined was his native language. Al-Hazim had been particularly pleased with himself lately. They had received word from none other than the "king" of the Catholic nation, Pope Urban II, that their presence was requested in the city of Clermont-Ferrand. The messenger had been sent with a considerable sum of gold coin, with promises of more when they arrived.

The youngster had gotten the distinct feeling that the old man's excitement had more to do with who they were seeing than what they were receiving for coming. Alinor had only a vague understanding of the humans' religions at the time; to him, it all seemed completely nonsensical, whether it was Al-Hazim's brand of Mohammedism or the local variant of Catholicism.

Still, it could not be denied that the Church had considerable significance; indeed, most of the towns and villages they'd passed through seemed to be governed by the Church, with a king or lord installed as an afterthought. The Pope seemed to be a particularly important figure. Al gathered that it wasn't the man's religious significance, though, that Al-Hazim was ecstatic over. He was, after all, a follower of a different faith. It was the man's *political* power that interested the Mad Arab.

Alinor studied his strange mentor as they traveled the mountainous terrain south of their destination. *Not quite as mad as he would have us think,* he observed, wondering if this was something he had overlooked, or if the man had actually changed. The recent sessions with the "elixir" — a mixture of blood, ground pearl, mercury, sulfur, and several herbs Alinor couldn't identify — had generated vast amounts of psychic energy, powers which Al-Hazim could not see, and which Alinor had thought at first that he was probably not aware of.

Alinor had known just enough to be a bit worried about that. Such situations, or so he had been told, were dangerous in the extreme. Most humans could not see these powers, or what they could do, but that didn't stop pockets of power from forming, usually in places where they could do the most harm.

This seemed different somehow, as if Al-Hazim, in spite of his apparent lunacy, knew what he was dealing with. Alinor could not be sure, and it worried him now and again. But he was easily distracted by the novelty of their journey, and he kept forgetting to be concerned.

The last town they stopped at before Clermont was not much more than a church and an inn that served cheap ale and sour wine. Here, as at the other towns, Al-Hazim's fame preceded them, but this time the locals were less afraid and more in the mood to be entertained, as if the Moor were some kind of showman. Alinor was tired and a little irritated, and his usual envy for Al-Hazim's fame had become amplified in proportion to the size of the new audience. When the Moor agreed to perform his usual transformation ritual, the youngster decided for him to have a lapse in abilities.

The villagers gathered around, determined to see the miracle occur, as Alinor stood in the shadows. For hours Al-Hazim gazed at the little brazier, occasionally adding coal to keep it going. As night fell, more villagers, now finished with their work in the fields, wandered into the inn to witness Al-Hazim's Great Work. Some became impatient and began ignoring him in favor of the strong, sour wine, but the Mad Arab continued with his tedious task unperturbed.

Alinor gleefully listened to the villagers murmur dissatisfaction with his mentor's work.

See. He's not the great wizard you thought he was, is he? It was me all along, and I still have the power to make him look the fool!

The copper vessel simmered and boiled, and when Al-Hazim tested the elixir on a sample piece of lead, nothing happened. The Mad Arab frowned but continued his chanting, while the villagers around him became more and more vocal in their dissatisfaction.

Alinor found this increasingly amusing. He considered giving the poor Moor a break and producing an unusually large nugget of gold. *When the time is right,* he promised himself. *Let the old fool sweat first.*

Finally the villagers got downright disgusted with the whole thing and began jeering at the old man, threatening to pelt him with refuse, although none of them quite dared to do so. The grumbling went on for some time, growing in intensity, and Alinor became a little nervous himself. Before he could give the audience satisfaction and produce the gold, the Arab's mood suddenly changed.

The old man looked up sharply from the brazier, fixing the peasants with a dagger-like glare for a moment, and the noise dropped somewhat, but did not entirely cease. Then he snarled, silently, and his chanting changed to an evil-sounding, gutteral verse that Alinor hadn't heard before.

Suddenly a sense of impending danger fell over the gathering; a feeling of a vast shadow creeping over the audience, a shadow that held the chill of death in its depths. In panic Alinor tried, in vain, to exchange a large lead weight at the Arab's feet for gold, but something, something strong, was blocking him. Nothing ever raised by a mere human had ever been potent enough to do this before, and at this point Alinor was well and truly scared witless.

What is *that thing?* Alinor had thought, in a state of panic. Normally sensitive to what humans were thinking around him, his mental gifts also seemed to be impeded. But the humans' expressions of cruel mirth, now turned suddenly to fright, said it all. The evil essence seeped into every corner of the inn, sending them into silence, while the elf tried desperately to determine where it came from and, most importantly, what it *was*.

For the first time since being cast from Joyeaux Garde, Alinor considered calling for help. King Huon, certainly, would know how to deal with this thing; it was probably beyond Alinor's abilities. As the youngster considered this option, however, it seemed less and less feasible.

First of all, they might not come in time, or come at all.

Secondly, though it might solve the immediate problem, it would make Alinor seem incompetent, and very much the child the other elves apparently thought he was. *No. That wouldn't do at all. It would only show them that they were right all along, that I couldn't handle the humans' world.*

The Mad Arab turned his attention to the fire blazing in the little brazier, which itself was beginning to glow red. In the fire Alinor saw a dark shape take form, a creature that writhed and exulted in the flames. Al-Hazim apparently saw it, but no one else seemed to take notice of it besides Alinor. As the thing grew, the youngster saw what it was; it looked like a large, black salamander, moving in the fire but unscathed by the heat. Indeed, the thing seemed to thrive in the flame, and Alinor flinched when the black shape turned and *winked* at him.

He sees me, and he's letting me know it, he had thought in alarm. He remembered the elements of alchemy, in particular the animal symbols, which represented the four elements of Earth, Air, Water, and Fire. Fire was represented by the *Salamander.* Until this moment, he had thought the Salamander was a creature of complete myth; he'd never seen one Underhill, and he'd certainly never seen one *here*.

That only he and Al-Hazim could see the thing told him that it was not of the humans' world, that it was from the halfworld of spirits. So far, everything he'd seen had made him more and more alarmed. And it didn't help that it could also see *him*.

The essence of the Salamander wafted into the inn as the Mad Arab continued with his dark chants, as if he was adding power to the creature he had conjured. Fights began to break out — apparently spontaneously — over minor things, and he and Al-Hazim might just as well have been invisible. No one seemed to remember they were there at all.

Alinor knew the Salamander was behind it. And in a few more moments he watched it actually take possession of a few of the younger men, whose minds were more malleable than their elders, whose emotions flared with a little less urging. It seemed to avoid the older men altogether, perhaps because they weren't resilient enough.

The fights quickly escalated. Mugs, then bodies began to fly through the air. The innkeeper locked up the liquor, corked the keg, and disappeared.

Alinor began to look for an exit, not liking the dangerous state of things one bit. He could feel the creature probing *his* shields briefly, looking for a way into his soul —

Before he could move for the door, a newcomer blocked his way. It was a monk wearing a long dirty robe, bald and disheveled, like a hundred other mendicant friars on the road. He wouldn't have warranted a second glance ordinarily.

But there was something unique about the man and the handful of peasants that had followed him in. The monk was definitely the leader, as the others deferred to him. The monk and his entourage had an air of presence about them —

Or at least, they acted as if they were vastly more important than they seemed.

The Salamander seemed startled, as if it had seen them too — and didn't like their presence at all. Now Alinor was puzzled and abruptly changed his mind; he had to see what would happen.

The monk cleared his throat and made some kind of an announcement —

And the fighting stopped. Gradually, but it *did* stop.

The monk spoke again; it was in some tongue Alinor didn't understand. What he heard instead was the muted whispers as the inn's clientele slowly noticed the monk. "Peter the Hermit," they muttered, turning and pointing. They seemed in awe, as if he really was as important as he was pretending to be.

Now the elf noticed what he carried with him; a small copper box just large enough to contain an apple, with intricate metalwork decorating it. Alinor admired the work, but assumed it was a reliquary for a religious object and dismissed it as unimportant. There was a much more interesting conflict shaping up — between his master and this newcomer.

He still might have to run for it — so far they hadn't had any trouble with religious types, but Al-Hazim *was* an infidel, and as such, was likely to come under the censure of the Church and its agents. This Peter might just give them some trouble.

Now Al-Hazim looked up, his eyes narrowing as they met the Hermit's. They silently exchanged something between them, something not particularly polite; it was as if they had seen each other before and had some unpleasant dealings. The monk held the copper box out and opened the lid. The container was empty.

With a resigned air about him, Al-Hazim began chanting again, only this time it was something different, more intense. The foreign words did not resonate with the same dark evil as the ones before, the passage which had summoned the Salamander in the first place. But the Salamander responded, albeit reluctantly; the box the monk held seemed to act like a magnet, pulling the creature towards it.

The peasants of the inn became quiet and looked confused, as if they weren't certain if they should be angry with each other or turn on these newcomers. Dark powers fluctuated violently in the room, giving Alinor a screaming headache.

Gradually, the Salamander was sucked into the copper box. As soon as it was inside Peter the Hermit sealed it tightly with the lid, tying it with a strip of leather and a crucifix on a silver chain.

With that, the atmosphere changed again. The people even seemed to have forgotten their disappointment in the Moor's performance; seemed, in fact, to have forgotten the Moor altogether. The fights that erupted ceased, the opponents now slapping each other on the back and wandering out together.

Whatever this thing is, Alinor thought, *it brings out the ugliest feelings from humans, makes them hate. The hate was not directed anywhere, so the nearest person became the object of it.* He shook his head at the pure insidiousness of the thing. *And Al-Hazim must have had it tucked away somewhere. The peasants angered him, and he set this thing loose to cause mischief.*

He's a crazy old man, but he's dangerous. Now, I think, is the time to leave him. He doesn't know I could see what he did. After all, nobody else saw his pet. If I let on that I did, no telling what he might turn on me!

While the monk was holding the copper box, as if savoring its contents, Alinor stole away through the kitchen, leaving behind what few possessions he'd acquired while in the Mad Arab's employ.

Then he encountered another obstacle. Outside the door a large number of peasants had gathered, some with packmules.

He slipped out of their way as silently as he could,

thanking Danaa that their attention was all on the inn door and not on anything else. Within moments, he had attained the road and was heading for the forest, congratulating himself on a successful escape.

Then he stopped — feeling suddenly guilty.

He pondered the unexpected reaction as the raucous sounds of the inn faded behind him, giving way to the more familiar and comforting sounds of the forest.

Where to go now? Returning to Joyeaux Garde still wasn't possible; his year of exile was barely half over. And now he had a better understanding of how the humans' world worked. It wasn't so hard to make your way about, if you were clever. Perhaps he could even set himself up as an alchemist and turn lead to gold, just as he had been doing with Al-Hazim.

I can get by just fine without him, Alinor had told himself. *I don't look like an infidel, I can speak the language better than he does, and as long as I can wear my hair long I can keep my ears concealed. Or I can even chance the spell being detected and disguise myself.* On the surface, it sounded like a good plan: ken the appropriate objects for "alchemy," perform the proper "rituals" while heating and cooling the "elixir," and he would soon be able to support himself quite well.

But — he would have to be very careful that the Folk didn't find out about his exploits.

Would that be possible? The result was tempting; to return home dressed in human finery, showing them all that he knew how to take care of himself and that he was a real adult, not just a naughty child.

But what about the Salamander?

That was a real problem and, he had realized, the source of his guilty feelings. Leaving the situation at the inn felt like he was leaving behind a responsibility. He had heard Liam and the other older elves talk about the evil things they came across in the humans' world, and what they did to eliminate the problems before they threatened Underhill.

It wasn't just a tradition; it was something that was ingrained in each of them, Alinor realized. He had to admit that he felt a distinct tugging as he walked away from the Salamander, a tugging that became stronger, not weaker, the further he moved away.

It would be so easy to just walk away from that evil thing back there, he thought. *Nobody would know the difference. Nobody in the elven kingdoms would know that I ran from the thing. A Salamander . . . this entity, a foe far beyond anything I can handle anyway!*

Nobody would know . . . except me. *I'm telling myself I'm grown up — a full adult. But can I really believe that if I don't at least try to do something about this — creature — before it becomes a danger to me and my kin?*

Alinor stopped walking. Slowly, he turned back towards the inn, still visible at the side of the winding dirt trail leading from it. *Oh great Danaa,* he thought, at length. *Does this mean I'm getting a "conscience"? That thing the Court sages claim raises us above the beasts, makes us greater? Whatever it is, it makes me feel larger, stronger — and frightened. Think of the trouble it could lead me into. . . .* Alinor smiled. *Trouble indeed.*

He watched the monk leaving the inn, followed by the handful of followers who had escorted him. Outside, a hundred or so peasants gathered around him and cheered.

Who is this Peter the Hermit, with all these followers? he wondered. *Now that he has the Salamander, what is he going to do with it?* The thought of this man in control of so many people made him nervous, to say the least. Add in the Salamander, and there was no telling what would happen. *The humans' world is my world, for the time being,* he accepted, grudgingly. *I've partly caused the Salamander's summoning, and now the thing is in the possession of this monk, whoever he is. A man who had no*

trouble capturing the Salamander. There's no point in return-
ing to Al-Hazim, he no longer possesses the thing. He might
have other powers, but that can be dealt with later. Peter the
Hermit, on the other hand . . . Alinor frowned, knowing
then what he would have to do.

Peter the Hermit had a following far larger than the
group accompanying him to the inn. They were,
Alinor later found out (after blending in with the rest of
peasants), some of the first to throw in with him and
were escorting him for protection. Alinor had no
trouble joining ranks with the motley crew that
wandered back to the encampment along another dirt
road; they accepted anyone and everyone who was
willing to follow their leader. For the time being, Alinor
kept his questions to a minimum, choosing instead to
look and listen carefully to what was going on around
him. The bulk of the monk's people were at a camp
some miles away, and cheered loudly as the ragged
procession reached the edge of the assemblage of carts
and crude tents.

It was just as well he had left behind what valuables
he owned; from the villainous look of some of these fellows, he guessed that a fair number of "followers" were
thieves as well.

He learned he was right, after fending off the pluck-
ing hands that tried to take his clothes when he "slept."
And not just thieves; the gatherings that sprung up
every night in the encampments were the loudest he
had heard yet in this land, and the religious meetings
often turned into drunken orgies once the Hermit had
retired for the night. Apparently all the rules of Good
Christians had been suspended for *this* lot. And the
monk was a different sort from the priests Alinor was
familiar with. The more he saw, the more confused he
became.

After some searching — and a few misunderstandings

as to his intentions — the youngster found a lad who appeared to be around his own age and fell in with him. The boy was talkative and spent most of his waking hours with a skin of ruby wine constantly at hand. He seemed to be better dressed than the majority of the Hermit's company, and Alinor soon discovered he was the son of a knight. He was quite at ease with Alinor, probably because the Sidhe was dressed in similar wealth and style, and spoke with the accent of the nobility rather than in a crude peasants' dialect. Alinor had left the Mad Arab with literally the clothes on his back — but they were fine clothes, and clothing in the humans' world marked one's status in life.

The boy had done nearly the same as Alinor, running off from home with little preparation. The boy's name was Albert, Alinor learned, and when he told the young man that he had just joined the group that day, Albert launched into a lengthy paean to the holiness and mission of Peter the Hermit.

Occasionally his words slurred, but for the most part he was coherent. Coherent in spite of the wine he gulped at every pause for breath from the skin tied at his side.

"Peter the Hermit is God's true prophet, incarnate," Albert said, though in a hushed toned that suggested that not everyone in the camp shared quite that same belief. "The Turks tortured him when he went to Jerusalem on a pilgrimage. He brought back monstrous tales of barbarians seizing the Holy Land. He'll take anyone in, as long as they follow him on his journey and pledge to fight beside him."

Where then, Alinor asked delicately, was this journey leading?

"Why to the Holy Land, of course!" Albert announced proudly. "To free Jerusalem and return it to Christian rule. He doesn't have full support of the Church yet, but he will, when he goes to Clermont. He's to see the Holy Father, the Pope himself."

Alinor remembered that Al-Hazim had been summoned to Clermont by the Pope, and wondered if this had anything to do with the Salamander. Cautiously, he inquired about the dark entity and the copper box — and the visit to Al-Hazim that had ended with the Hermit's capture of the creature.

"Salamander?" the boy said, obviously puzzled. "Don't know anything about a salamander. Today Peter went to reclaim something that had been stolen from him by that Arab, Al-Hazim, but I don't know what it was. Some kind of power to fight the infidels, they say. Why an infidel like Al-Hazim would be in possession of it — well, who knows what an infidel will do, or why. Unless he took it to keep Peter from using it." He took another gulp of wine and grew bolder. "He should be burned. They should all be burned, the heretics, the Jews, the Turks, the Arab dogs — they're all in league with devils."

Which explains the odd exchange between the two men, Alinor thought. *The Salamander was stolen.*

When Alinor turned his attention back to the boy, Albert was happy to continue the conversation, especially when the Sidhe asked him about himself. "Where we come from, it's been dry for three years. Witches, again, I think. Drought wiped out the crops. Our fief isn't doing well, father says. He's gone back to tournaments for prize money to pay his knight's fees and everything. My older brother went with him as his squire. They left me at home, and I was sick of it, sick of hearing Mother and the rest whine about money. This pilgrimage, this *crusade,* is a godsend. I mean, besides being holy and all. Anything would have been better than staying *there.*"

The next morning, as it turned out, only a portion of Peter the Hermit's followers went on to Clermont. The majority remained as before, preparing for the long journey to Jerusalem. What they were going to do

about the "invaders" once they got there was a point
Alinor must have missed, since most seemed unsuited
for warfare. Beggars, children, old women made up a
large part of the mob, and those young men, including
Albert, who were fit for combat did not seem to be
armed. However, those who were picked to go with
their leader were the few knights and noblemen who
were armed. Alinor volunteered to go, and was offered
a ride by a very young knight, newly dubbed, who had
little in the way of armor. A leather tunic, a helm and a
short sword was his entire outfit, so riding double on
his mare would not add too much weight.

The ride took two days, with an overnight stop near
a brook where all (for a wonder) bathed. Afterwards
Peter the Hermit told them great stories about the holy
city and the barbarians they were to battle. Alinor made
himself inconspicuous, but spied on the monk whenever possible, seeing the little copper box either in his
possession or somewhere nearby. He never let the
creature escape while talking to his men; Alinor
suspected that he was saving the Salamander for future
use. He had an idea what that use might be — but he
couldn't be sure. He tried not to think about the fact
that once he did know, there *still* wouldn't be much he
could do. . . .

The group following Peter the Hermit didn't attract
much attention, as there were similar groups of armed
men converging on the city of Clermont. The town was
larger than Alinor expected. There were whole streets
of houses and taverns, and *pavement* beneath their
horses' hooves. On the other end of the town where
the houses thinned, they came to a field where a large
number of people had gathered. Nearby was fountain
and a huge, partially built church; someone whispered
that it was the Notre-Dame-du-Port, but Alinor wasn't
sure if it was the building or the fountain they were
talking about. In the center of the gathering a throne

had been erected on a platform, where a king sat, surrounded by bishops, fully armored knights and more religious clerks and monks than Alinor had ever seen in his life. After listening to the hushed whispers, he discovered the king was not a king but Pope Urban II, the very Pope that had summoned Al-Hazim. Nervously, the Sidhe cast surreptitious glances around him, looking to see if the Mad Arab had appeared after all. Gratefully, he saw no sign of the Moor or his cart.

The Pope was giving a speech, but it was difficult to hear in the open field. Alinor caught parts of it, enough to gather that the Pope was raising an army to fight the Moslems, who had apparently invaded his Holy Land. This was a holy crusade to save Jerusalem from the hands of the infidel.

"Now that the barbarians have taken the holy city of Jerusalem, of what use is our religion?" Pope Urban II shouted over the not-quite-hushed masses. "The Church of the Blessed Mary, the Temple of Solomon, the very streets where trod Christ Almighty! Taken from us, by the godless!"

The people did not seem particularly upset by the revelation. Alinor didn't understand why, unless they did not value their religion as much as the Pope thought they should. *More human folly,* Alinor thought. *To construct a religion, and then fail to abide by it. I wonder if their god knows about such stuff? Perhaps he's busy. This Holy Land is too far away for most of them; they're far more worried about their neighbors than the Arabs across the sea. They look ready to walk off at any moment.*

But the Pope didn't give up so easily. His voice rose as he chastised all those present for being sinners, for fighting and robbing their neighbors, for taking the Lord's name in vain. He invoked the name of a warrior of the past, Charlemagne, who had also defended the Holy Land from invading pagans. Alinor flinched at that last statement, remembering that no few of the

Sidhe of Joyeaux Garde had gotten involved in that
little altercation. And that Charlemagne had inadvertently mistaken a few elves for demons and had them
burned at the stake when he could capture them. Only
King Huon had managed to settle the mess with a min-
imal loss of life. The whole thing was beginning to
make Alinor just a little nervous, especially after
Albert's ranting about "witches and Jews and demons."
Nearly everyone he'd seen in his travels had been
unhappy, hungry, ill-clothed and ill-housed. It didn't
take much to start a witch-hunt among people as dis-
contented as these were.

The reactions of the people around him were mix-
tures of boredom and suppressed hostility; either the
men didn't like being lectured like little children, or felt
that the Pope could have condemned others — such as
the nobles who guarded him — with greater cause.
Alinor realized what the Pope was trying, without success, to do: whip the crowd into a frenzy, so that they
could storm off to the Holy Land and pound others
into the dust. This was exactly the kind of enthusiasm
Peter the Hermit had managed to invoke in his own
people, and in large numbers. But this Pope didn't
seize the imagination of these people the way Peter did.

Peter the Hermit smiled smugly; there was no doubt
in Alinor's mind that he was well aware that the Pope
was failing where he succeeded. In that moment the
monk's old face resembled one of his mules, and
despite the gravity of the situation, Alinor fought to
keep from laughing. *Meek and defenseless as that old monk
may appear*, the elf thought, *he's managed to do what the
Pope has not.*

But then his blood chilled; for without a word, Peter
the Hermit pulled the little copper box from beneath
his cloak.

Of course! he could have shouted. *That's why he needed
the Salamander. Now he's going to release it in this mob!*

Fighting an urge to dismount and run for the wilderness outside the town, Alinor watched with dread as the monk opened the copper box.

Magic had been at work to imprison the Salamander; now the bond was released, and the creature escaped from its cage.

Alinor felt the rush of magical wind wash over him as the Salamander dissolved into the air, and its essence dispersed into the crowd. As before, it was invisible to all but himself — and the monk.

I can't let them know I see it, he reminded himself.

The effect of the Salamander's presence was immediate. It was as if the crowd had been doused with a bucket of ice-cold water from the Allier. Utter silence made the Pope's words clear and thunderous; suddenly he was the center of all attention, as if he spoke with Divine inspiration.

"Are you men, or cowards?" the Pope continued, angrily, not yet realizing that the crowd had changed its mood. Even to Alinor, the Pope seemed larger, and the throne itself began to glow, ever so subtly, drawing more attention to its occupant. "Prepare yourselves for battle. It is better to die fighting for the Holy Land than it is to tolerate this invasion of your sacred places. Arm yourselves, if you are Christians!"

The cheers were as sudden as they were deafening. Alinor could feel, beneath their horses' hooves, the ground shake with the cries for battle. Peter the Hermit stepped back at the heartfelt outcry, but quickly regained his composure. Alinor expected him to take command of the situation while the Pope was still surprised by the sudden turn of mood, but the monk remained quiet, with a subtle smile creasing his bland features. The Salamander, with its insidious power, was doing all the speaking for him — and it seemed that he did not care *who* roused the crowd, so long as it was done.

Knights rallied around the Pope, dismounted, and

began taking vows on their knees, their hands shaking with fervor. Ordinary townsfolk began dismantling a cart, converting it to staves and clubs, apparently not knowing their Holy Land was thousands of leagues away. All around were cries for war and conquest. At the Pope's feet, a wooden bowl began filling with coins and jewelry, contributions for the glorious crusade.

A crusade of anger and hatred, fueled by the Salamander.

Peter the Hermit made no attempt to retrieve his little demon, and that was ominous.

Alinor learned, to his dismay, that the monk had several of the dark creatures in hiding. Back at the camp, Alinor spotted him rummaging about a wooden trunk, which contained an array of oddly shaped copper boxes. Orders among his followers were that none of these containers were to be touched by anyone but the leader. And those orders were enforced with fists and cudgels.

Before he had left Clermont, however, the monk had rallied all those townsfolk the Pope would not accept as fit for battle. Pope Urban wanted only young knights for his sacred army and would not take ordinary folk. Very well, then; Peter would take those who had been rejected by the Pope in disdain for their lowly status, and *they*, not the over-proud knights, would be God's Army, the *true* instrument of freedom for the Holy Land.

Peter sowed hate for the nobility right along with hate for the infidel, and the common folk devoured it all with glee.

The Salamander had done its work well; Jews had fled their path, for fear of being "converted" in the knights' wake. By the time they left Clermont, the Hermit had assembled a small army from those rejected by the Pope. He had led the mob back to the camp, looting and pillaging the houses identified as belonging to

"Jews and heretics" along the way. "We will begin the crusade *here!*" he had shouted. "We will first purge *our* land of the unholy, then take the purifying fire to Jerusalem!"

Alinor was profoundly grateful that he had not been with Al-Hazim; they would have arrived at the scene just in time to stand in the path of that unruly mob. And he had no doubt how *that* would have ended.

The high number of noncombatants continued to amaze Alinor. *They're going to fight some of the greatest armies in the world, and who do they take with them? Women, children, old men, boys barely old enough to think about growing beards. The Salamander has poisoned everyone with hatred and anger.*

It was insane. Utterly insane. Not even religious fervor could account for it. *This entire venture is hopeless. They gladly march into battle with this Salamander riding their backs, as long as they're promised a direct trip to heaven when they die.*

Then there was the question: Why was *he* still tagging along?

It wasn't a sense of responsibility, since now he knew he wasn't to blame for the Salamanders. Peter the Hermit had obviously been keeping several for years. In fact, the Salamander Peter released was probably not the same one Al-Hazim had conjured, judging by the collection of copper boxes.

If anything, Alinor was following the army of crazed idiots out of curiosity, or at least that was the most comforting thought for a young Sidhe not yet used to his nagging conscience. After all, what could he do? *One* Salamander was too much, never mind the nightmare stashed away in the wooden trunk. Following this ragtag bunch out of conscience — well, that was as foolhardy as their quest, wasn't it? Must be curiosity.

The army was a little better behaved when they marched to Cologne in April. Armed guards appeared when they passed through certain territories, but the townspeople welcomed them graciously, and even added more volunteers to their ranks. More armies were meeting in Cologne, most better organized and better equipped than the Hermit's. The French army started off immediately after Easter while the peasants' army organized and stocked themselves as best they could. Alinor noticed that the monk was carrying an empty copper box immediately after the French left, apparently having "seeded" their ranks.

Peter the Hermit and his army set out across Europe, gathering strength and attracting volunteers along the way. Their pace was slow; it was no trouble to keep up. Alinor stayed at the head of the group, shadowing the guards that watched over Peter, and as a result, shared in their relative prosperity.

It was amazing. Chests filled with gold and silver wherever they went. Food was not a problem. The townspeople, having heard of the looting — or holy provisioning — elsewhere, put all of their goods outside the city walls in full view, for the crusaders to help themselves as needed. Then they closed themselves behind their stout gates and city walls.

Alinor helped himself along with the rest, accumulating bedding, clothing, even weapons — but he wondered about those in the rear of the army; mostly very old or very young, female, weak or crippled. Here at the front there was no suffering, plenty for all. But there were thousands of people in this so-called army. How were the ones behind faring? This march across Europe was tiring even for him; he slept long and hard these days, and the journey was turning him from the soft, spoiled elven-child he had been into a hardened and seasoned traveler, wary and cunning. What about those for whom this was not as "easy"?

They proceeded to the Kingdom of Hungary without serious incident, their army now amounting to twenty thousand. Alinor had seen the monk release Salamanders to encourage volunteers in Vienna, and then again in Budapest and Belgrade. They ran into resistance at Nish, when a Salamander seized control of some of the knights, who in their anger set fire to houses and farms. The local militia, city guard and army responded, rounding up a fair number of the crusaders. Meanwhile, Peter hurriedly captured the renegade Salamander and returned it to its copper prison. It was the first time Alinor saw the monk lose control of one of the creatures.

It was not to be the last.

The majority of his troops intact, the "army" marched to Constantinople, where they set up camp beyond the city walls.

And that was where the Hermit's troubles truly began.

By this time, Peter appeared to have lost control; his people looted and pillaged within the walls of Constantinople on any pretext — only now it was all the time, instead of just at the Hermit's behest. Alinor guessed there were still three or four Salamanders loose in the camp. The monk gave all the signs of being unable to catch his little monsters, and now they were inciting his troops to ever-increasing excesses and violence. Angered, the Byzantine Emperor Alexius told Peter the Hermit to take his people out of his domain. Faced with the prospect of seeing the emperor's troops — real troops, armed and trained — descend on his own "army," the monk readily complied, although it took all of his eloquence and promises of further riches to coax the mob outside the city, towards Jerusalem.

And there they stayed, camped far enough outside the walls that it was not possible for the Hermit's followers to wander into the city to loot at will. The sun beat down on them by day, and scorpions and snakes crept into their shelters by night. Food was becoming scarce even for the Hermit's followers, and when food could be found, it was full of sand, half-rotten or withered. The Hermit couldn't seem to get his troops to move on, nor could he turn back to Constantinople. Alinor became more restless as the days went on. He yearned to return to the Kingdom of France and Joyeaux Garde. By now he knew only too well that there was nothing he could do, either about the hundreds of thousands of innocents in the ranks of Peter's army, or the Salamanders that drove them here. He was no longer even curious about the humans and their ways; he was sickened to the heart by the useless violence, the pettiness and the waste of lives. As long as they were letting themselves be led about, the humans never had a clue of their potential. It was sad, so unlike the ways of Underhill. All he wanted was to go home.

Unfortunately, he had no way to get there. The army was in the middle of nowhere, camped on the shores of the Sea of Marmarra. There were no horses to be had at any price, and no ships to carry him back across the sea. Peter the Hermit had gone back to Constantinople to parley with the emperor.

Alinor privately thought he had done this not to gain shelter for his followers but to escape the effects of the Salamanders running rampant through the camp. Isolated groups from his army began sacking and burning the Byzantine Christian churches along the shores, killing Christians and infidels with a blithe disregard for anything other than blood and loot. Alinor was deeply afraid and withdrew into himself, becoming sullen, speaking to no one. On a day when he realized he had not heard singing or laughter for a month, he decided to leave for Constantinople, trying to avoid the madmen of the crusade until he got free of them. He planned to blend in with the locals once he reached the city. The prohibition against magic — and his year-long exile — were long since expired. He could cast whatever illusions he chose, replicate some of the local

coins until he had enough money to travel properly —
perhaps even buy comfortable passage on one of the
Italian ships. *There's nothing I can do about the
Salamanders,* he told himself. *It's not my doing, and it's not
my responsibility. I'd better get out of here while I can.*

He had the strange premonition that something terrible was going to happen. And he didn't want to be
around when it occurred.

That night he slept fitfully under a cart in which a
human couple did what passed for lovemaking. He
was afraid the rickety thing would collapse, after all the
stresses of the journey, but at the time it was the safest
place to be. Orgiastic drunkenness ruled the camp
these days, and he was soul-sick with it. *These humans are*
terrifying *when intoxicated,* he observed, as the cart
above him rocked and squeaked with the humans' rut-
ting, *and there is no passion in their lovemaking in that state.
They're like dogs making puppies in the fields.* Staying under
the cart ensured some privacy, however dubious.

When the horizon had begun to lighten, Alinor was
up and around. *Enough light to see by, at least. All I have to
do is follow the shoreline back to the Bosporus. Provided the
Turks don't kill me first. After what we've done to their land
and their people, I wouldn't blame them.*

We?

The Sidhe slipped silently across the field of sleeping
bodies. There were a few others who were slowly waking,
some with more energy than others. Somewhere he heard
a priest saying the morning mass to a flock of early risers.

Peaceful. And totally unlike the way the camp would
be in a few short hours.

He thought he had cleared the camp when he was
confronted by something in the half darkness that rose
up to block his path and spoke to him, mind-to-mind.

:What are *you?:* the voice hissed. *:You can see me, where
the others cannot. Who sent you here, and why have you been
watching the Hermit?:*

Alinor stifled the scream that tried to claw its way out of his throat as a Salamander materialized before him, an outline against the sand that gradually became solid. There was only one, but it was enough; it grew as he shivered before it, until it was easily the size and mass of a warhorse. Half shadow, half dark fire, it seemed slightly transparent — but Alinor was not going to be fooled into thinking it couldn't hurt him.

But it's not solid, he told himself, debating whether or not he could flee the thing. After all, he had never felt its effects. Maybe he could evade any magic attacks it made so long as he ran from it rather than confronting it.

:You were with Al-Hazim,: the Salamander continued, and Alinor realized this was the same creature that the Mad Arab had conjured, and the Hermit had seized, at the inn. *:You owed him servitude, but instead you abandoned him for this,:* it hissed, and the stubby, black head jerked towards the camp. Then the creature gave him a wry, intelligent look. *:But you are not a fool. You have been following me, observing me. That you can see me means . . . you're not human? Is that why the detachment, boy?:*

Alinor fought the urge to run, barely winning.

:I cannot feed on your anger like the others. And you smell like a spirit.: It drew closer, so close that the Sidhe could smell its foul, stinking breath.

:I ask you again. What are you?:

It was the breath that did it. Alinor turned to run towards the beach — he heard waves pounding the shore, and that gave him direction. But then, behind him, from the camp, came screams which increased in volume and number.

What — the elf thought, and the Salamander was gone, bounding towards the screams, which were now coming from everywhere.

Without thinking, Alinor sprinted for the beach, then looked back to see what was going on.

The camp was being rushed by an army of Turks.

The remnants of what must have been a raiding party were running back to the camp in terror, pursued by Turks on foot and on horse. The camp, undefended, vulnerable, not even all awake, was a prime target for a well-organized force.

And this was a real army, not a handful of Moslem traders or Byzantine monks.

Peter's followers were doomed. Alinor watched in horror as entire regiments of mounted, armored and sword-wielding Turks rush the camp, killing everything in sight. Turkish soldiers put everyone in their path to the sword, without regard to sex or age. A sea of horses poured into the camp like locusts as blades and arrows bit deeply into anything that moved.

His first instinct was to fling himself into the midst — to save the little ones from the swords, the arrows —

But he was only one. And *they* were wielding Death Metal.

A stronger instinct — that of survival — overcame his initial impulse. He could grieve later that he had been unable to act. *Great Danaa, I have to run! They'll just as quickly kill me!*

And he did run, with a desperation and speed he didn't think was possible. *Even the Salamander couldn't have inspired that run*, he would later think. But that was many years and miles later. . . . *Perhaps it was my own conscience I was trying to outdistance?*

Alinor struggled to sit up. He hadn't realized he'd almost nodded off on the tree bough until he'd teetered, and the sudden shift in gravity urged him awake. The Sidhe looked down at the ground, seeing gravel and fallen oak leaves instead of sand, wondering briefly why he didn't hear waves washing over a beach.

Time check. This is the twentieth century now, he thought, wondering why he suddenly felt so exhausted. *I must have gone into a light Dream*, he decided, still shaking the confusion. Down on the ground, in the compound of Brother Joseph's domain, soldiers stood guard, but instead of Turks waving bloodied swords, radical Christian crazies waved AK-47s and AR-15s.

Even after nearly a thousand years, it's amazing how some things simply don't change for these humans. The elf's thoughts turned grim, however, when he remembered what else was inside the Chosen Ones' complex.

Something that wasn't human at all.

What he saw the Salamander doing with Jamie was much more subtle than its crude manipulations back in 1096, when it simply reached out for young, flexible minds and started brawls in a tavern. Or, on a larger scale, when it possessed the thousands of peasants during Peter the Hermit's crusade, inciting them to go forth and reclaim the Holy Land for Pope Urban II. No, not now; the times had changed dramatically since then. A fine degree of stealth was required to operate in this modern world, where communications were instantaneous, and strong, central governments had formed, accompanied by equally strong and effective law enforcement.

To be a Salamander, one still had to find niches, gaps in the fabric of society to operate in relative freedom. Gaps like Pawnee County.

And niches like Jamie.

Alinor seethed as he began to piece together the creature's true nature; not only did it need a place where laws were not easily enforced, it chose a vehicle, a resilient vehicle, far younger than the brash, sword-toting hotbloods led by the Pope. He remembered the effect the child had had on the Praise Meeting crowd, saw it for more than the stage show he had thought it was. Using Jamie, the creature had seized control of those people just as surely as it had seized control of the crusaders, using religious hate and intolerance as the catalyst.

The girl, with as much skill as she's showing in the spirit world, must have had a medium's abilities before she passed over. Didn't Cindy say something about Jamie being sensitive? This would explain why he was chosen, and kidnaped, instead of Brother Joseph using one of the other kids who were already in the cult. The Salamander is now speaking *through its vehicle, baiting its followers directly with wealth and power, something I don't remember it doing before.*

I think we are all in deep, deep trouble.

• CHAPTER EIGHT

Al closed his eyes, and reminded himself that not even an elven warrior and magician could take on an entire army of humans single-handedly. He was not a movie hero, or a superman, who could charge through waves of men with machine guns. If his captors had *planned* to keep the boy protected against elven meddling, they could not have chosen better. He was walled away from the outside by Cold Iron; to get at him, Al would have to go inside one of the steel-sided bunkers and past several iron-reinforced walls. His magic couldn't hold up under that; iron pulled Sidhe spells awry.

And he had no real-world proof that the boy was there, nothing he could bring to Deputy Casey to invoke the human authorities. They needed evidence in order to act; a change in human legal process that now turned out to be a hindrance. *Used to be, we could stir up a population to do just about anything, just by convincing them that what we said was the truth. Damn nuisance, this need of hard evidence for due process, sometimes. Still, it means there is no room for doubt — guilty is guilty this way.*

In point of fact, there was very little he could do, either with his own powers, or with the humans'. First of all, there was the Salamander; his powers were not equal to taking it on. He had never been one of the greater warriors of the Folk; he'd never been one of the more powerful mages. *His* success these days lay in his adaptability to the humans' world.

There was nothing he had learned in all of the

centuries since he had first encountered such a creature that could be used to counter it. Nothing. In fact, all he had learned was that he didn't want to meet it on its own ground. And this, without a doubt, was the creature's own ground. The last time he'd seen a Salamander, he'd turned tail and had run away. The second time, he'd headed for the nearest walled fortress. But this time he couldn't run.

He ground his teeth together in frustration. Up until now, whenever he'd had to pull a rescue, it had been a fairly simple operation. He would find the child in question, spirit it away from its parents, take it Underhill, and one of the others would cover his tracks.

Quick. Easy. Painless.

So all right, what can I do? he asked himself, angry at his impotence. *How can I at least give the poor little lad a respite? Give them something else to think about?*

First, he had to calm himself; find the quiet place deep inside himself where his power lay.

He took two long, slow breaths. By the time he exhaled the second, he had achieved the calm he needed. He called up his mage-sight, and opened his inner eyes on the world.

Everywhere he looked, Cold Iron thwarted him, standing like dull, barbed barriers against his Sight. This was the Death Metal at its worst; if his power touched it, the metal would drain energy from him, spinning his spell-traces away into shreds too fine for him to collect back. It would be very difficult to insinuate his powers into this stronghold in anything other than a passive manner. Cold Iron protected their machineries, their storage places, themselves — even their weapons were of Death Metal. And *here* was an unpleasant surprise. Even some of the bullets were sheathed in it. Now he not only had to fear a direct hit, but a *grazing* hit might poison him.

But wait — he extended his senses a little further,

frowning with concentration. A headache began just at each temple, but he would not let it distract him, reaching a little further into the maze of threatening metal and humanity.

Everywhere there was Cold Iron, there was also something else that might provide an insidious pathway for Al's power to penetrate Brother Joseph's citadel; a network of copper tendrils weaving through the complex in an elaborate network of support. The electrical wiring system, of course; it hummed with the power coursing through it, and was as obedient to Al's touch as the Cold Iron was hostile.

A frail enough pathway, and one that had severe limitations, but it was better than nothing.

Perhaps Al didn't know a great deal about ordinary, day-to-day living for humans — but he knew electrical systems and knew them very well. He'd amused himself long ago with his "playing with lightning," but tonight there was nothing funny about it. He sent a little tendril of power questing curiously along the network, testing it, seeing where it went, how it was constructed. This system was mostly new, and all of it was less than five years old. Humans tended to distrust the very new, or the very old; this network of wiring was neither. They wouldn't be expecting any troubles out of it. And they depended on the electricity it carried so completely that he found himself smiling grimly.

He explored further. There weren't any voltage regulators except on the main circuit breaker; even the computers had only the simplest of surge protectors on them. Those would protect against sudden surges; they wouldn't protect against something a little more — subtle.

Al opened his mind and his magic to encompass the entire system, holding it in his metaphorical "hands" like a cat's cradle. Then, slowly, he began decreasing the resistance of the wiring across the entire network.

This was the sort of thing that happened naturally with age and generally never caused any harm. But then, few people ever had the voltage regulators that maintained the level of power in their systems fail on them.

Soon the system was running "hot"; capable of carrying voltage of around 140 instead of 110. Which didn't matter, since 110 was all it was getting. Of course, *that* was about to change.

Al carefully skirted the iron clips and bolts around the aluminum main breaker box, and adjusted voltages at it. Slowly, so no surge protectors would trip. Eventually he brought the voltage all the way up to what the system would carry — and there were few pieces of equipment here meant to operate on 140 volts.

Now motors would run faster, burning themselves out. Electrical circuits would overload and blow. Computer equipment would be fried. But none of this would happen all at once; a lot would depend on how delicate the equipment was. Whatever; they would have to replace everything that burned out — then the replacements would fail — again and again, until they thought to check voltages. They would have to replace every bit of wiring before he was through, from the breaker boxes outward. They wouldn't discover this until they had lost several more machines and had replaced everything else. This meddling was going to cost the cult a lot of money. And time, and trouble; unfortunately, it would not be as difficult to pull the wiring as it was in a normal building, but it would be troublesome enough, and they would have to do without power in the entire circuit while they replaced the wires.

If something happened that forced them to use their emergency generator, it would all happen that much faster. Al took out the voltage regulator entirely on *it*.

Power levels would fluctuate wildly as pumps and air-conditioners came on- and off-line.

He contemplated his work with satisfaction. Already, all of the electric motors in the complex were running a little faster. Pressure was building in some equipment, several water-pumps, for instance.

Hmm. They are using common white plastic pipe. There is no more resistance to my magic than wood or leather would give. A little weakening of the pipes at the joints . . .

There. In a few moments, the joints would burst, at least in those portions of pipe that were under pressure. There was some kind of elaborate arrangement in one corner, for instance, that was going to go up like a water festival before too long.

Using his magic — finally *doing* something — had cooled his temper enough that he could think again. With luck, the fanatics would be so hard-pressed for money by his sabotage that they would act hastily, perhaps get caught by the police. It occurred to him that the more havoc he could wreak that Brother Joseph *himself* would have to attend to, the more likely it would be that the bastard would believe some outside supernatural force was opposing him.

Of course, it is. And for once in his life, he will be right.

When that happened, Brother Joseph would be kept so busy trying to find the source of the interference that he would have little time for anything else.

He might leave the boy unguarded, or relatively unguarded. At the least he would leave the child alone, give him a chance to recover. If Al could not get in, perhaps the boy could escape on his own.

So, it was up to Al to make Brother Joseph's life as miserable as possible. This, of course, would make Al's life infinitely more pleasurable. A man has to have a hobby he enjoys.

He only wished he could tell the boy's mother about this — that he could tell her he knew for certain that

Jamie was here. But if he did, not only would he betray that there was something supernatural about himself, he might inadvertently tempt her into going into danger to save her child.

No. No, for all that it would comfort her, he could not tell her Jamie was here. Not until he had something more concrete to offer her than that information alone.

So, back to work. *How about a bit of blockage in some of the pipes that are not under pressure? That should be amusing.* He knew those pipes that were attached to pumps, but the rest — only that they carried water. The Cold Iron interfered with his perceptions too much to be more specific than that. Right now Al could not tell whether the pipes took fresh water into the complex, or wastewater away, but in either case, there would be problems if he blocked the pipes — say, by reaching out, just *so,* and touching the pipes to make them malleable, then — pinching them, and letting them harden.

There. That should do it. Not all at once — but like the electrical failures, these should cascade.

He withdrew his senses — carefully. He couldn't detect the Salamander, but that didn't mean it didn't have ways of watching the world from wherever it was hiding. More than Cold Iron, he feared *it.*

I couldn't defeat it back then; I don't think I can do so now. The best way to deal with it for the moment is to avoid it. It can do nothing without human help and a human to work through.

He considered what he had accomplished, as he molded himself to the trunk of the tree he had chosen and scanned the area for more guards.

Another pair of them passed about twenty feet away from his tree, peering from time to time through something attached to the top of their rifles. It wasn't until after they had passed that he realized what those instruments must have been.

Nightscopes.

He belatedly recognized them from the action-adventure movies he'd watched over the years, in city after city, racetrack after racetrack, late at night when the humans slept and there was little for him to do.

Nightscopes: instruments that gave humans the ability to see like an owl or one of the Sidhe at night. He wasn't exactly certain how they worked — but he shivered, realizing that the only reason the men had missed sighting him was that they simply hadn't been looking through the nightscopes when they passed him.

And what would they have done if they'd seen him?

The answer to that question didn't take a lot of reasoning. They'd empty those clips into him without a second thought.

No illusion he knew of would fool nightscopes —

But he could reproduce — on purpose — what had occurred by accident.

He closed his eyes again and took a deep, deep breath, and as he exhaled, he *pushed* the outermost layer of his shields, expanding it outwards, slowly, until it reached about thirty feet from where he sat. Then, within that shell, he set a compulsion: *don't look at me.*

It was just that simple. Once guards reached the perimeter of his defenses, they simply would not be able to look in his direction. Any further away, and the trees would hide him, even from the sophisticated scope. He wasn't worried about Andur; if the guards saw the elvensteed, they'd simply assume he was a stray horse. They could try to catch him, of course, but the operative word was *try.* Andur would happily lead them a merry chase over half of the county before vanishing to return to Alinor.

Feeling a little more secure, he turned his attention back to the Chosen Ones' compound. There was still plenty of night left; surely he could do more than he had.

The problem is, everything I've done to them can be fixed. It'll cost time and money, but it can be fixed. I need something that can't be undone.

Well, the one thing that mankind still hadn't completely conquered was — nature. What was there about this area that Al could meddle with?

There was a spring running under the property; it was the source of the cult's water, and came to the surface to form a pond and a stream leading from it at the far end. But that wasn't the only place where it could surface, if the conditions were right.

There was a crack in the bedrock just under one of the cult's buried buildings; the building itself rested a few inches above the surface of the bedrock, on a cushion of sandy soil. If Al widened it just a bit and extended it down to the channel of the spring, the water would gradually, over the course of the next few days, work its way to the surface and emerge at the rear of the building.

This was a storage building of some kind; not one for guns or ammunition, but full of heavy wooden crates piled atop each other. The crew that had built this place hadn't known what it was going to hold, evidently, for the concrete floor wasn't strong enough to support what was resting on it. The concrete had already cracked under the weight in several places. When the spring water worked its way up through the crack in the bedrock, it would soon seep into the building through the cracks in the floor, soaking, and hopefully ruining, everything on the bottom layer. By the time they found the damage, the entire floor of the building would be under a six-inch-deep sheet of water that no pump would ever cure.

That was something they could neither replace nor repair. They would have to abandon the building. He contemplated other possibilities, but there weren't many at the moment. He could induce mice to invade, of course; plagues of bugs —

But that would mean a certain amount of hazard for the rest of the children. Mice could get into their things; *would* bite if cornered or caught. Insects could bring disease . . . some of the insects native to here were scorpions, whose sting was poisonous and painful, and could be fatal to a small child.

And there were snakes aplenty around here; he'd been warned about them when he first arrived. Three kinds of *them* were poisonous: rattlesnakes, copperheads, and water moccasins. No, he couldn't turn those creatures loose where there might be children.

Well, maybe just that one area where there seems to be a lot of plumbing, of electrical circuits. Where there doesn't seem to be a lot of people. That might be Brother Joseph's quarters, or those of his high-ranking flunkies. If it is, it's about to become unlivable over the next couple of days.

He widened cracks in foundations, opened seams, created hundreds of entrances for insects and other vermin. Then he created another kind of glamorie — one that would attract anything small, anything hungry. From there the insects, mice and reptiles would work their way into the rooms, and there were no children in this bunker. Adults, he reckoned, would get what they deserved.

That should settle the account a little more.

It was scarcely more than an hour or two past midnight. If he and Andur got out now, he'd even have a few hours to sleep before he had to get to the track.

If only he could tell Cindy what he knew. . . .

Well, he couldn't.

He opened his eyes again, on a world still dark and full of night sounds: cicadas, coyote howls, the bark of foxes, the cry of owls —

And, far off, too far for human ears to hear — footsteps, trampling methodically through the grass.

Brother Joseph's perimeter guards were still on duty.

He called Andur with a thought; the elvensteed slipped out of the shadows of the trees like one more cloud shadow, ghosting across the fields of grass, chased by the night breeze.

Al didn't bother to climb back down the tree; he wasn't that far up. As Andur positioned himself under the branch, he simply dropped straight down onto the elvensteed's back, a move copied from late-night cowboy shows.

Then, in a heartbeat, they were away, retracing their path over the fences and out to the road.

Once again, Andur became a sleek, matte-black, Miata lookalike. Once again, Al was cradled in air-conditioned comfort. And yet it provided no real comfort to him.

He was restless and unhappy, and only too glad to leave the driving to Andur. For all that he had done, he had accomplished so little.

So damned little. . . .

He brooded all the way back to the track, by which time Andur had bleached to white and acquired headlights again. When he got out of the elvensteed, with a pat of gratitude, he remembered that Cindy had gone to sleep in Nineve, rather than the RV. In a way, that was something of a relief. It meant he didn't have to hide what *he* was, and it meant he could convert the RV into something like its usual glory — and comfort.

Ah, well. He sighed philosophically as he entered the door and locked it behind him. *Perhaps it's better this way. Bob always tells me that it is a human proverb not to mix business with pleasure — and she is business of a kind.*

He held perfectly still for a moment, standing in the narrow aisle between the stove and the propane furnace, and mustered a little more energy. It wasn't going to matter how keyed up he was; when he finished this, he was going to be so exhausted there would be no chance insomnia would hold him wakeful.

He held out his hands in the glow of the tiny overhead lamp and whispered a cantrip.

Power drained from him like water running out of a sink.

And the RV rippled and flexed, like an out-of-focus movie — and changed.

Now there was a full bathroom with a whirlpool tub behind him; he stood beside a counter loaded with the delicacies of Underhill. Beyond him was his silk-draped bed and one of his construct servants, a lovely animated Alphonse Mucha odalisque, to massage his weary shoulders. Beyond that, where a set of curtains waved in a lazy breeze from the silent air-conditioner, was what had been the overhead bunk. Now it was Bob's cubby-bedroom, with a bed as comfortable as Al's own.

Al snatched a handful of grapes and a bottle of wine from the bounty beside him, and shed his uniform and cap by the simple expedient of ordering them elsewhere. With a nod to his servant, he headed for the bathroom and the whirlpool. Between the bath, the wine and the massage, he should sleep very well.

My father, Joe Junior thought, *has finally gone* wacko.

He stormed down the narrow, steel-covered passageway that only he and a select few knew about, fists clenched. Ready to explode. Motion detectors activated lights and deactivated them in his wake. The illuminations winked on and then off, as if seeing his sour mood and sulking back into the darkness to avoid him. His boots echoed hollowly on the damp, concrete surface, as he dodged the worst of the puddles and splashed angrily through the rest. He wanted to punch a hole in the wall, but to do that down here he would need a jackhammer. He contemplated finding one.

His anger continued to simmer, just below the surface, ready to blow at any moment, as he pushed himself further and further away from the others. And, especially, away from his father.

He recalled that when digging this tunnel they had come across a small water source of some kind, a seep or a spring, and had partially rerouted the tunnel to avoid it. But the attempt hadn't entirely worked. Ahead he heard the steady drip, drip of water that had no obvious source, hidden behind one of the walls. Periodically, workers had to bail the passageway out — from the look of things, they would have to do it again soon. He remembered the fit of rage his father had when they were building the tunnel and couldn't get the drip to go completely away. *It's as if he thought he could control nature*, he thought, still furious with what he had seen at the Praise Meeting. *And it was betraying him by not doing* exactly *what he wanted.*

The boy was putting as much distance as he could between himself and the Praise Meeting, which by now was probably adjourning to smaller, special-interest groups. *Like the one dealing drugs*, he thought, biting his tongue against the anger. He was afraid to even think these treasonous thoughts around the others, in part because his body language often gave him away. In spite of the fine physique he'd been cultivating since before he could shave, he hadn't quite learned how to *control* his body, and often it revealed his emotions. A rigid stance, a certain frozen look in his face, had both conspired to betray his thoughts to his father and those close to him. He was hiding his body, at least temporarily, so that it wouldn't reveal what he was feeling *now*.

Then there was that *other* liability, the one he had been stifling since he was a little boy. It was something he tried to forget about but couldn't, because it went with him everywhere.

Everywhere, waking or sleeping. He heard what other people were thinking, whether or not he wanted to, *especially* when he, or they, were emotionally wrought up.

The ability had appeared at puberty, and for a while he was too busy sorting through his newfound raging hormones to properly assess it.

Then his thoughts began to intrude on his mother's;

just a little at first, then with greater strength and clarity as he battled with the roller coaster of emotions any thirteen-year-old experiences.

He discovered to his mingled apprehension and delight that he could read his father's mind as well as his mother's. If father was angry, he knew it and could avoid him in time to save himself becoming the target of his father's frustration. That was useful; it made up in part for some of the other things he read. That his father thought about other women besides his wife was a little distressing, especially since he was a preacher, but Joe began to form the opinion that half of what his father said in church was for show anyway.

That would have been enough, but a few weeks later came the next revelation. Not only could he read people's minds, he could decide more or less what their thoughts would be.

At first it was funny, to send thoughts into his father's head, get him stirred up and watch him make a fool of himself. After the first few trials, however, he began to feel a little sick about it. It didn't seem right, actually; as if he was using his physical strength to bully weaker people, and he stopped playing around with other people's heads — on purpose, anyway. And he began to wonder where this power came from, since his father preached that any "ESP" was the work of the devil.

Was he being influenced by Satan, or was his father just being paranoid?

Whatever the cause, Joe had learned through trial and error that whenever he was angry he ran the risk of intruding his own thoughts on the minds of the people around him. These thoughts, especially when they were as treasonous as they were now, could get him into deep trouble. They would sound as if he had said something out loud, since emotion was behind them, rather than guile and stealth.

If anyone is being influenced by Satan, it's my father, he thought angrily as he came to the end of the tunnel. Here stood a tall metal door which looked something like a walk-in safe. Joe inserted a card with embedded chip data, identifying him as Brother Joseph's son. The huge metal door swung open, allowing Joe entrance to the private health club. Here only the elite branch of the Sacred Heart of the Chosen Ones could enter.

It was empty, as usual. His father certainly never came here, and rarely did the officers of the Guard and Junior Guards. The others who came here, the first lieutenants and one of his father's personal body-guards, used the place occasionally, but that was generally before dawn, before his father had risen; while Brother Joseph was awake, they were always on duty. And during a Praise Meeting, and shortly after-wards, he was almost guaranteed solitude here.

Much of the new Universal and Nautilus equipment had been moved from their mansion in Atlanta. Other items had appeared recently, including one puzzling piece of equipment he'd never understood or seen used, which looked like something used to balance tires. The room was decorated with chrome-rimmed mirrors, red and black velvet wallpaper, and black vel-vet trim, reminding Joe of a funeral home.

Joe stripped out of his uniform. He peeled it off, quickly, handling it like a dirty surgical glove, now a lit-tle disgusted with what it represented. His glance fell briefly on the sloppy swastika he'd tattooed on his forearm while inspired by a fifth of Wild Turkey. *Wish I'd never done that,* he thought regretfully, now noting how the swastika had crept down his arm, almost to his wrist, as he'd grown to maturity.

Wasn't even sure what a swastika was, when I did it. Knew it had something to do with the war. Knew it had something to do with kill-ing Jews. Daddy hated Jews, so I guess I thought it would be cool. Didn't even remember doing it until I saw it the next day. How old was I? Thirteen? No, I think I was twelve. Not a teenager yet.

He threw on some tattered shorts, not bothering with a tank top. He needed dead weight, and lots of it, to vent his anger tonight.

The fifty-pound barbells were shiny chrome, reflecting halogen light in bright arcs as he lifted them high overhead in short, intense repetitions. The wall was one huge mirror, and he stared at his own snarling face, at the veins that bulged from his temples. Muscles swelled. Perspiration broke, beaded, dripped. He repeated the exercise, this time lying back on a bench, shifting weight, working different muscles.

They warned me not to get attached to the little boy, he seethed. *Even Father, after he'd managed to kidnap Jamie. He didn't seem to mind before! He wanted me to be friendly while the poor kid had a chance to get away — but now that he's ours — he's just another tool, another toy, another magic-trick for the crowd. I played right into it!*

Weights clanked angrily as he brought them together over his head, making a satisfyingly aggressive sound. Though this was normally not good form when doing reps, he clanked them again. The sound felt good, appropriate.

Luke never liked it, the way I favored the boy, Joe thought, remembering the reaction of one of the lieutenants, one of the first followers in the early days of their church. *He told me it was going to be a problem. He pretended to be my friend, but I know he went to my father. The first time I objected to the channeling, when Jamie was still new.* He winced when he remembered the crack of his father's riding crop, the liquid fire that poured across his naked back. He remembered his own screams exploding from his mouth, and the hoarse voice he spoke with for days afterwards. *Some of those welts never seemed completely healed,* he thought to himself, painfully aware of the ridges flexing and hurting even as he exercised. *Father said they should be a reminder.*

What he was thinking now would qualify him for

such punishment again, but he guessed that next time, if it came to that, it would be more severe. If such a thing were possible.

They can't do that to Jamie again, he thought, his attention turning from himself to the boy. *I'd gladly take another whipping if that would get Jamie away.*

Normally at a Praise Meeting he would have been on the stage, guarding the proceedings with the others. But not tonight. Apparently his father, at Luke's urging, had seen what a liability he had become when dealing with Jamie. Tonight he had been given "leave," to observe the channeling if he so desired, but not to participate in any way.

Guess he figured I'd just get in the way. Weights clanked. Joe counted. *Seventeen, eighteen. Guess he figured right.*

He exhaled explosively, as weights flopped out of his hands onto the padded floor with a muffled *thud*.

He didn't starve Sarah like this. At least not for this long. The boy had become visibly thinner over the past few days, and weaker, and his eyes had developed a vacant look. *Like someone on drugs*, he thought. *Only, I know he's not on drugs.* Jamie didn't smile now, except for a few moments when Joe greeted him. Then the smile faded quickly, like a candle's flame blown out by the wind.

Joe closed his eyes. *It's the guilt, isn't it?* he thought. *I'm not angry at my father. I'm angry at me. Jamie has looked up to me like a little brother, and I haven't done a thing but manipulate him. I'm the one who's lured him into this, told him it was all okay when I knew what was going to happen. And now he's starving to death. And worse, he's being used by that thing that Father thinks is God. I think he's wrong. It's not God, it's not even close.*

He crawled into the bicep curl machine, sitting on the short bench and reaching under the bar where the weights connected. No one had used it since he'd been there; no one else could pull eighty pounds. Luke certainly couldn't. But Joe used Luke's image to fuel his strength, using the anger to pull the bar up under his chin.

Luke sure has risen in status in the past few weeks, he observed cynically. Joe had always resented the man, even back when he was very little and Luke was still a newcomer. He had been around their family for as long as Joe could remember, being one of the few followers who remained faithful to his father, even when his ideology shifted from one political spectrum to the other. Not surprisingly, his loyalty had been repaid in high rank within the Chosen Ones hierarchy. Joe was beginning to see how much he really resented that. And how much power Luke's position had.

A year earlier, his father had suggested they form a special security division separate from the Guard, one that would oversee internal threats from within the United States and the Church itself. He had hinted, rather strongly, that Joe would be offered the position of security chief, as he would be eighteen by then and a man. As a member of Brother Joseph's immediate family, he would also presumably be trustworthy, more so than the any rank-and-file Chosen One. But Joe had learned recently that when such a division was formed, Luke would be in charge, not himself. He had yet to confront his father about this, and when he thought about it, he knew that he probably never would.

"He doesn't trust me anymore. If he ever did," he whispered aloud, and looked around in panic, to see if anyone heard. Of course, no one was in the club at the time, but he was still uneasy. Microphones were everywhere, and he wouldn't put it past them to put one here. *None of them trust me,* he said, this time to himself.

But Joe had something on Luke, something that went way back, when he was only a child and still respected the older man. He had never used it — but the time might be coming when he had to, to save himself and Jamie.

Joe's parents had gone away to some tent revival in Oklahoma and Luke was put in charge of baby-sitting. Luke didn't like being left behind, he had wanted to stand at Brother Joseph's right hand and bask in reflected glory. But, being the faithful follower he was, he accepted the task cheerfully and without complaint. Joe liked it even less, as he'd wanted to get away to see a forbidden movie, *The Last Temptation of Christ*, with a friend.

Luke's presence, of course, screwed these plans up royally. But when Luke got into Brother Joseph's liquor cabinet and started to drink, putting a serious dent in the whiskey supply, Joe thought he might be able to get away if he drank himself to sleep. He'd seen Luke do that before, and there was a good chance he'd do it that night, too.

But this time was different; Luke became drunk and started talking, saying strange things. Then he started to make advances — sexual advances. At first Joe had no idea what he was doing until the man grabbed him when he stood up to go to the bathroom, groped him, and stumbled forward.

Joe just froze, then, unable to think.

Luke's thoughts poured through the booze and struck Joe's mind at full strength; the images were so strong, it had felt like a flame had just licked his brain. Joe jumped back, squirmed out of his grasp, and found temporary refuge in a corner. But it was only temporary; he knew he was trapped.

Joe hadn't thought about his other ability, that of making people think what *he* wanted them to, for some time. It had a way of coming and going, and lately it was doing more going than anything else. But Luke's thoughts were so clear they seemed to be super-charged, and the lust that poured over Joe was a slimy thing that made him ill.

When their eyes met, Joe could see exactly what

Luke wanted to do to him. The images were clear and well-defined. Joe had reached further into Luke's mind, more in a reflex than a conscious action, and saw that Luke had done this to other boys before.

It would hurt, he had realized. What Luke wanted to do to him would hurt *real* bad. He could already feel the pain, as if it was already happening; he began to whimper, like a dog, as he froze in fear and shock. Luke had stumbled forward, one hand on Joe's leg, the other on his own belt buckle.

Joe screamed — but not just with his voice.

The old man stumbled back for a moment, as if he'd been slapped, and Joe had screamed again, but only with his mind. Luke had crumpled to the floor.

Joe scrambled away and ran for his bedroom, which had a lock. Luke lay on the floor, yelling at Joe to come back, he wasn't *finished* yet. Joe locked the door and waited, afraid to even breathe. Soon Luke fell asleep, snoring loudly from a few feet outside the door, and Joe felt safe enough to cry himself to sleep, with a pillow muffling his sobs.

Or at least he had tried to. He didn't sleep much, and when he did he would jolt awake at any little noise from where Luke was. The next morning when they woke up Luke said nothing about the incident and went about nursing a hangover. Joe was too mortified to bring it up and wondered if he would tell his parents when they got back.

That afternoon, Brother Joseph and his wife returned. Joe was watching them drive up the hill to the mansion when Luke had turned to him and said, soberly, "If you tell them about what happened last night, I'm gonna kill you. No questions asked."

Joe believed him. So he didn't tell them about Luke's attack. Then, or any time since.

After that horrible experience he began stifling his ability to see into other people's minds. What he saw coming at him from Luke's drunken brain was something he never wanted to see again. The man hadn't physically raped him, but after seeing the images of what Luke wanted to do — and had done before — Luke might as well have, since he lived through it all, every horror Luke had planned for him. He felt hollow and wooden after that night, and made a vow to himself to leave other people's minds be. He told himself that most thoughts are better left alone.

And, he had to admit then, his special power could have been the work of Satan. It sure *felt* like it.

Over the years Luke had provided several more reasons to be hated, reasons that went far beyond what happened that night while his parents were away. The way he treated Jamie was one of them.

In fact, Luke was "guarding" Jamie now, he'd overheard at the meeting. *Guarding against people who might bring him some food. But then, I have privileges. I could take him somewhere. Fishing, or —*

His thoughts stopped there, when he remembered the *last* time they'd gone to the pond, or at least in its general direction. *I could have fed him then,* he told himself. *He hinted that we could eat fish there, and I ignored him.*

He wasn't sure why, but the incident reminded him of Sarah and what his father had done to her. *He didn't know I was watching, from a distance, when he did — that.* His arms grew a little weak and he paused, forcing the image away from his mind. *I wasn't supposed to see that. No one was suppose to see that!* He had been hiding and had been unable — or unwilling? — to betray himself by bursting out and coming to the girl's rescue. He recalled with clarity the morbid fascination that had seized him, how he had watched his father grab the girl's thin, delicate neck. The blue color her face turned. The sudden weakness that came over the girl, the absolute limpness of the body. The brief surprise of his father. The lack of remorse. Then, or now.

And remembered Jamie, withering in the isolation room.

Joe saw what he would have to do. Resolutely, he put the weight-bar back down and went back to the lockers. The scar tissue on his back throbbed in a strange sort of sympathy as he thought about whips.

He's not going to do that to Jamie, he thought as he pulled his hated uniform back on. *I'll never let him do that to Jamie.*

Joe hadn't really considered how he was going to approach this. In his pocket he carried a piece of beef jerky and some dried fruit, which in itself was not very substantial. But it was *something*, and it was easier to conceal than, say, a sandwich. As he came to the sector where the isolation room was, his lack of planning now added a new, frightening dimension to what he had in mind.

He had, however, thoughtfully left his sidearm in the health club. It was a .44 Magnum and its size was enough to raise the hackles of any gun enthusiast — as any Chosen One was likely to be. Once, that model had been considered the most powerful handgun in the world. That was before .577s with Glaser slugs, and the other toys around here. He'd left his Rambo knife with the gun. He had nothing but his hands and his body —

But that body was hard and lean, in itself a formidable weapon.

Especially when fueled by *anger.*

The place where they were keeping Jamie was a hodgepodge of interconnecting rooms that originally were to be used as warehouses, but to date had only partially served that purpose. One of those huge rooms was where they kept the drugs, but he was never privy to which one — or the times they were full. He had gathered that the storage was only temporary, usually only overnight, and changed from one room to another. The blueprint of the sector, and what was actually built, never completely jived either. There were formations of rock that were either too hard to chip away, or served as strategic supports for the upper strata, and had been left alone. Where possible the rooms were paneled with sheetmetal and were further divided with chain-link fencing. The entire sector had a cold, metallic atmosphere about it. But then, Joe reflected, so did the rest of the underground complex.

Joe peered around a corner at Luke and another guard, someone whose name he didn't immediately remember, standing in front of a double door with a padlock. This was probably where Jamie was, and he ran through his mental map of what adjoined this particular room.

Back wall is solid rock; room would have been a little larger if they'd had the right equipment. Room itself is large, divided into storage bins with fencing. Jamie must be in one of the bins. Get in through the top? Joe racked his brains for what was in the level above them, and came up with: *That's Father's private quarters up there. Well, scratch that.* Other rooms beside it had sheetmetal walls, and although cutting through would be possible with a saw, the *noise* would be prohibitive. Overall, a good, secure place to imprison someone.

Time to deal with Luke and his partner, he thought, and shivered with mingled apprehension and tension.

Luke was reading a Bible; his partner, a man Joe now recalled was known only as Billybob, was reading a weapons manual on the Colt AR-15. The gun itself was lying across his lap as he sat reading. Joe hadn't intended to sneak up on them, but his footsteps simply didn't make any noise. When they finally did see him, they jumped into action and had their weapons drawn on him, cocked and ready. Bible and weapon book fell to the ground, forgotten.

"Oh Lord," Luke said, relaxing some. "It's *you*. Why you sneaking up on us like that?" He didn't seem at all pleased and continued to aim his gun at Joe.

Joe shrugged, feigning innocence. "Wasn't sneaking up on you." *You just weren't paying attention, you lazy puds,* he wanted to add, but chose diplomacy by default. "Just walk kinda quiet in these tennies."

Now that the immediate crisis was over, Luke relaxed into his accustomed superior attitude. He was about forty years old with an immense potbelly that made him look like a giant lightbulb. Even after the brief excitement of being surprised, he was breathing with difficulty, and his face was flushed from the exercise of getting suddenly to his feet. *Not surprised, after seeing what he eats for breakfast. A slab of greasy bacon the size of a brick, fried potatoes, scrambled eggs. Every single day. Gonna have a heart attack before too long. Too bad it's not right now.* He didn't seem to notice the bad effects of poor health, or the fact that he was woefully out of shape. Instead, Luke put on his normal, superior sneer, an expression more-or-less permanently carved into his fatty features. Buck teeth protruded prominently from his face, and he looked like a pig doing an Elvis imitation.

"Do you have any idea what time it is?" Luke asked, slowing his breathing with a visible effort.

"I dunno," Joe replied, intentionally sounding stupid. "Late, I guess."

"It's two A.M." Luke said, arrogantly. "Any idea why your father put me on duty here?"

Joe gazed blankly and shrugged.

"To keep people away from our little treasure in there," Luke said, jerking the barrel towards the room they were guarding. "Who, by the way, is sleeping. What do you want, anyway?"

"I wanted to see Jamie," he replied. "I kind of promised him a bedtime story. I was gonna tell him about Daniel in the lion's den."

"You know what your father said," Luke said, shifting the assault rifle in his arms. "He wants no one near the boy. That includes everybody. That includes *you.*"

"He's real lonely." Joe said, but he knew how helpless that sounded. "You could —"

"No. I *couldn't*."

Luke advanced menacingly, quickly, as if he was considering shoving Joe away with his own massive weight. Joe stepped back automatically as his body began to go into defense-mode, automatically tensing some muscles while relaxing others, a well-honed response due to years of self-defense training. Training, in part, received from Luke, before he'd put on the weight.

And Luke saw it. "Go ahead. Try it. I have a witness. You don't. Your father will believe me, whatever you do."

Billybob made several snuffling noises that approximated laughter. Joe absently toed a rock with his right combat boot.

"That is, if you lived," Luke continued. "Why are you here, Joe? You don't mean to tell me you actually *feel* something for the little lump of shit we've got stashed away back there?"

"Well, no," he lied. Now he regretted not having a plan. *But this will only help me if it makes me look like a fool. Luke is less defensive if he thinks he's dealing with someone more stupid than he is.*

"I just wanted, you know, to study him. See what kind of effect food deprivation has on a person. Look, if we're going to be doing this we need to see how far we can push."

"Depri-what?" Luke asked, seriously confused. He always did have trouble understanding words with more than two syllables.

"Means *starving*," Billybob informed him.

"Oh," he said, with a knowing look. But he frowned anyway while a rough, blistered thumb toyed with the safety. "Still don't like it. Listen, you go get permission from Brother Joseph and I'll let you see him. I mean, how am I supposed to know this isn't a test and all?"

"You don't. But I guess you're right," Joe said,

knowing that to push now would only arouse more suspicion. "I'll go talk to my dad now."

Luke nodded. Billybob made more snuffling noises, this time sounding like a hog rooting for food, sounds that had no clear meaning.

"Where is he, then?" Joe asked, with a touch of anger.

Luke shrugged. "Back in his quarters, I guess."

Joe saw an opening. "You mean you don't *know*?"

The superior sneer faltered; Luke knew the rule as well as anyone else; *the first lieutenant must always know where the leader is, for security reasons.* Not knowing was a punishable offense. Luke stammered. "I — I — he must be in his quarters now. He is. Yes, he is. I know it."

"That's better," Joe replied, privately delighted at the tiny victory. He turned to leave, effectively terminating the conversation.

He's a fool, if you know what buttons to push. No wonder he followed Father for so long. He glanced back, catching Luke as he stood there, mouth hanging open, apparently still trying to piece together what just transpired. *You'd need a brain like a sponge to stay on with Brother Joseph all these years.*

Joe smiled — but only to himself.

Luke qualifies.

Out of range of the two idiots guarding Jamie, Joe's thoughts turned dark. He was, after all, no closer to getting food to the boy. The giant piece of beef jerky jabbed him in his pocket, reminding him of his failure.

I failed because I didn't have a plan, he reminded himself. *I can try again, but this time I'd better be smart.*

In the Guard, one was taught to use one's assets to their fullest advantage. Being the son of the founder of the movement, he had barely scratched the surface of those assets. For example, he could go places where very few, even within the Guard, were permitted. He went to one of those places now.

Using the card again, he entered one of several remote security stations, small rooms paneled with heavy-gauge metal and stuffed to the rafters with high tech surveillance gear. Against one wall was a pickax, a firehose, and a set of bolt cutters behind a glass pane. Along the opposite wall, ten tiny black and white screens blinked back at him. This particular station, he knew, was redundant. These same feeds were going to the main security station, which had a wall of screens that dwarfed this rig. This station served only this sector of the underground, whereas the main station had camera feeds to everything. The Guard monitored the main station, and at least one member would be there now. Eventually, when they had more manpower — women didn't count — all stations would be manned, giving redundant security everywhere. The small screens here had various views of the hallways and tunnels. Some angles, he saw to his surprise, were new. *Looks like they've put new cameras up. Gotta watch that. Must assume I'm being watched at all times.*

Which prompted him to look up. *Good. No cameras here.* Every time he used his card, a record of where and when it was used was stored in the cult's computer, also located in the main station. *They'll know I was here. And they might want to know why.* He knew, however, that it would be at least a week before they ran the reports that showed security card usage. For the time being, anyway, he was off the hook. In a week, surely, he'd be able to come up with a plausible excuse.

He studied one screen, which gave the view right outside Jamie's isolation room. Luke and Billybob sat reading their respective books. The other nine screens didn't show anything particularly interesting: empty hallways and views of the storage rooms, and other things that weren't important. One screen was turned off. When Joe turned it on, a camera view from within the isolation room came to life.

Jamie was lying on a mattress, sleeping fitfully, having what appeared to be nightmares. Joe was stunned at first; he hadn't expected to find a camera inside the child's room, but when he thought about it, it made sense. Jamie was important. Jamie had to be watched. On the little black and white screen the boy seemed thinner than he'd been at the Praise Meeting. Joe remembered when, as a little boy, he'd found a kitten swimming frantically down a stream. He had plucked the animal from the water, and for several fascinated moments watched it stretch out and go to sleep in his palm. Wet, it had looked like a dying rat, its tiny lungs heaving against a frail rib cage. That was what Jamie looked like, lying on the mattress.

As pitiful as the boy looked, the sight only cemented Joe's resolve. *The question is, when am I going to be able to get in there without Luke knowing?* He debated over whether or not to wait until their shift changed over. They might even put Junior Guards down there, though this was unlikely. At any rate he might have more leverage with their replacements, being the son of the leader. Some members of the Chosen Ones held him in awe, prompting some enthusiastic followers to speculate out loud that Joe was the grandson of God.

He had never taken full advantage of these attentions, this being one of the assets he couldn't fully exploit while keeping a clear conscience. *Not that my conscience has been too clear lately anyway,* he thought, remorsefully. *Taking advantage of those people who think I'm divine might be tempting. But that wouldn't make me no better than my father. God, what a prick he is! He manipulates them so well, especially when he uses Jamie to invoke that thing. If I start doing the same crap, what's to stop me from becoming just like him? Do I really believe in what he's doing?*

Which prompted another distinct stab of doubt. *Do I really have faith?*

As if on cue, the power failed briefly, then returned.

Lights in the security room blinked. As one the ten screens went to static, as if switched to a dead channel. In the distance, Joe heard an alarm that he couldn't immediately identify. Water gurgled nearby, as if a pipe had ruptured behind one of the walls.

Down the hallway, someone shouted. Running footsteps followed the shout, came near, then retreated into the distance.

Wide-eyed, Joe stood perfectly still, keenly aware of every sound around him. His faith in God, now, was completely restored.

Four of the screens flickered to life. One of them displayed the view of the hallway outside Jamie's isolation room. Luke and Billybob had abandoned their positions, it seemed; their books lay idle on the empty chairs. The two guards were nowhere in sight. Frantically, Joe banged on the screen that had the interior view, getting no results. The screen continued to display snow, with an occasional horizontal line.

He must still be in that room, he thought. *They just ran off to see what the commotion was.* Then, *There was a reason for this to happen now.* Joe eyed the bolt cutters on the wall, saw what a perfect tool it was for dealing with padlocks. Joe found a rag, wrapped it around his hand, and punched out the pane of glass. After removing the major shards from the frame, he took down the pair of bolt cutters and made for the door.

The alarm was a little louder now and seemed to originate at the end of a long corridor. The shouts became more numerous and confused, and it sounded like whatever happened would keep the two guards, along with many others, busy for some time. It never really occurred to him that whatever the emergency was could be a danger to himself or Jamie. His only impulse was to move, and move now.

Abruptly, the power went off altogether. For several moments he stood in total darkness, unable then to see his hand in front of his face. In the security room behind him, muffled by the thick steel door, several electronic gadgets whirred to a halt. The alarm cut off completely.

Good Lord, Joe thought, taking a tentative step forward. *What a time for this to happen.* During the early days of living in the underground, when all of the bugs in the electrical system hadn't yet been worked out, he had carried around a flashlight on his belt just for such emergencies. But it had been months since the last blackout, and since then everyone had become complacent about the power system, taking it for granted.

Then, further down the passageway, a light winked on. From the ceiling a thin finger of light touched the concrete floor below. *Emergency backup,* he remembered. *This is going to work even better.*

Somewhere in the underground, he heard someone shout "Fire!" followed by a scream and the blast of a fire extinguisher. Again, he felt strangely calm, although it occurred to him that maybe he should feel a little more alarmed. Since there wasn't much that was burnable in the underground caverns, not much attention had been paid to drills should a fire occur—

It didn't matter. What was important was to get a piece of beef jerky and dried fruit to a starving boy.

He knew the passageways from memory and was able to navigate back to where Jamie was being held. Emergency lights periodically illuminated the way. Still, there were sections of darkness that most people, unfamiliar with the floorplan, would have balked at. Presently he found himself in front of the unguarded double doors. Inside, Jamie whimpered.

"Jamie?" Joe said, careful to watch his volume. "It's Joe. Sit tight, I'll be inside in a minute."

In seconds he had clipped through the padlock with the bolt cutters and opened the twin doors.

Joe immediately saw by the light creeping in from

behind why the boy was crying; there was no emergency lighting inside, and he had been lying in total darkness. Before doing anything else, he reached up and turned off the security camera. The power wasn't on yet, but when it did come on he figured this would be one of the first rooms security would be most interested in investigating.

"Here, partner," Joe said, holding out the jerky. "Eat this. If you see them coming, hide it. Don't let them know you have it."

But Jamie was too busy hanging onto Joe's knee to eat. "Where have you been?" the boy managed to blurt out.

The effort of sitting up and talking seemed to exhaust him. Jamie flopped back down on the mattress, sitting up on one elbow. Slowly, he took the jerky, regarded it for a moment, then started stuffing his face with it.

"Whoa!" Joe said, nearly grabbing the boy's arm to keep him from wolfing down the gift. "Slow down. You'll make yourself sick eating fast like that."

"I'm already sick," Jamie pointed out. "When did they decide to start feedin' me?"

Joe stared at the boy until finally their eyes met. "They haven't. I'm doing this on my own."

Jamie gazed at him severely. "You're gonna get your ass whipped for this."

"Probably. But I don't care. It ain't right to be starving you like this. And then making you talk to that thing. . . ." Joe froze then, wondering if he should have mentioned it. Instead of the fear he expected to see in the boy's face, he only saw blank incomprehension. *He either doesn't remember, or he's too tired to think straight now,* Joe speculated.

Jamie was paying attention to other things. "Is that fire?" he inquired innocently as he gnawed on the stick of jerky.

"It's . . ." Joe said, momentarily confused. *That was a fire back there, and I wasn't even paying attention. I was concentrating too damned hard on finding Jamie. If the place is on fire, then maybe I should get him out of here,* he thought stupidly.

Joe looked up and saw the thin film of smoke licking across the ceiling. He sniffed and smelled the smoke for the first time. But it wasn't like any smoke he'd smelled before; this stench was laden with plastic and synthetic smells, sort of like when an alternator on a car is about to go out, or when a fuse box overloads.

That's easy. It's an electrical fire, he thought, frowning. This didn't make the situation easier to handle.

This room is no longer safe, he declared. *I'm taking him out now and to hell with the consequences!* After all, this was what he wanted to do all along.

"Come on, buckaroo," Joe said, scooping him up in his arms. He felt the difference in the boy's weight immediately; ten, maybe twenty pounds. "We're getting out of here."

"Okay," the boy replied calmly. "Got any more jerky?"

"Not with me," Joe said. "Too much food will make you sick right now. Hang loose for a while." He remembered reading about concentration camps in Nazi Germany, and the prisoners who, once liberated by the Allies, ate themselves to death. He wondered about this when he saw Jamie, but didn't think he was that far gone. *A little food. No more. At least until I figure out what kind of condition he's in.*

And what I'm doing here, and how I'm going to get him out, and what I do then.

Joe carried him out of the isolation room with a distinct feeling that he was being watched. *Paranoia,* he decided. *The power is off. The cameras are out. There's not enough light in here to see by if they weren't.*

The commotion at the end of the hall was still in progress, but now seemed farther away. From the melee he was able to pick Luke's voice out, an insistent, frantic wail trying in vain to seize control of the situation.

What is going on up there? Joe wondered, becoming a little more interested in the emergency Luke and Billybob ran off to tend to. *Soon I may just find out. Those two, they'll be back soon. I need to make this look innocent if they find me. No, when they find me. There's no way out of this place, even if I did try to make a run for it.* This last thought disturbed — and intrigued — him more than he thought it should. *Have I completely lost my mind?*

He took Jamie to another wing of storage units, where the lighting was still next to nonexistent. He found tall stacks of boxes piled on pallets, their contents unknown. *Probably food,* Joe thought. *But no more for Jamie. It could kill him.* They were well hidden here, and in the darkness he felt like it would be a less likely place for Luke to find them. *Luke is afraid of the dark. I remember that. Could be why he left Jamie and ran for the fire. The fire has light.* Had they gone further they would have walked into a highly traveled area; somewhere around here Joe remembered an access tunnel that would take them to the garage, where he could take a truck and maybe even crash the gate. . . .

There I go again. Thinking crazy thoughts. They'd shoot me and Jamie both, if I tried to get away. We'd be so shot full of holes there wouldn't be anything left.

"Try to stand up," Joe said, setting the child down on his feet. "How do you feel?"

"Sleepy," Jamie said, yawning. "But I don't wanna go to sleep." He looked up at Joe with brown, questioning eyes. "What's going on, Joe?" he asked. "Why won't they let me eat?"

Joe sat down on a bare pallet, which rocked a little as his weight settled down on it. Now they were on eye level, making it more difficult for Joe to talk to the boy. He wanted to shrink into a little ball now, the responsibility for this predicament pressing a little more firmly on his shoulders.

"I'm a little confused right now," Joe admitted.

Jamie's look became puzzled. "I don't know what they're trying to prove back there, making you talk to that thing like that, but it ain't right and it's not good for you. There are some things that just aren't meant to be messed with, and that thing that took control of you tonight is one of them." *Jesus,* Joe thought. *Where are these words coming from?* He listened to his mouth rattle on, uncertain if it was him who was talking, or someone, or something, else.

"But I can tell you this," Joe continued. "It's not right what they're doing. And I'm partway to blame for it. I don't know if I can get you out of here now, but I will someday. I promise you that."

Jamie gazed at him solemnly, his lower lip curling out into a pout. Then the expression changed to anger. Eyebrows arched, his forehead wrinkled.

"Joe, *where is my momma?*"

Joe tried to gaze directly into his eyes, but his look wavered and glanced away. *He doesn't know what's up and what's down anymore. Everyone in authority has been feeding him lies, and now he knows it. He's looking to me for the answers. I've got to tell him the truth, or he'll never trust me again. And if he doesn't trust me, he doesn't have a chance in this place.*

"I don't know where your mother is," Joe said slowly. After saying it, it was a little easier to look up. "I never did. Look. The grownups around here, they haven't been telling you the truth."

Joe had expected tears; he got a dull resignation. "I guess that means she's not coming here. To the vacation place."

He uttered the sentence with such a total lack of emotion that Joe shivered a little. *It's almost like that thing was talking through him again. Like maybe a little bit of it stayed behind or managed to burn out some of his emotions. Or else that he's so used to disappointment that he doesn't care anymore.*

"That's right, Jamie," he said with effort. "She

probably doesn't even know where you are." He looked up. "You stay here a second." Joe got up and peered out of the storage room, down the corridor. The sounds that echoed through the corridor indicated that fire was gone, but that other things were keeping the guards busy. *We're safe for a little while longer*, he decided. *Better make the best use of this time I can. After this it will be impossible to get close to Jamie again.* When he returned, he continued. "Your mother didn't know you were being brought here. Your daddy, you see, he took you away from your school so she wouldn't know, and brought you here so that you could be with him."

Jamie looked confused. *Why shouldn't he be?* Joe thought, resisting an urge to pull his own hair out. *God, I hope I'm going about this right. This had better not be causing more damage than good.*

"But *why*?" was the logical response.

A simple question with a damned difficult answer. It's too late to back out now, I'm already ass deep in this one.

"Your ma and pa stopped getting along together. You're smart, even you could see that." Meekly, Jamie nodded. "And well, he heard about the Chosen Ones and started to come to meetings. And before long he was a believer, and a follower, of Brother Joseph."

"Your daddy."

Joe winced. *You could have gone all night without saying that,* he thought, cringing inwardly. *That's one thing I would really like to forget right now.*

"Yeah. My daddy," Joe said. It felt like he was admitting to a crime against humanity. "He needed someone who could talk to the Holy Fire. Someone young, and smart, like you. Do you remember the Holy Fire?"

"I remember," he said. If the memory was frightening, the boy concealed it well. "But it was okay. I had a friend to help me out."

"Good, that's good," Joe said condescendingly. *I had an imaginary friend, too, a funny fox. Sometimes, he was the only one I had to talk to, when one of Dad's flunkies wasn't around.* "When you're hungry, you can talk to the Holy Fire better. That's why Brother Joseph is doing this. He wants to know things from the Holy Fire, things that will help the Chosen Ones."

He had nearly said, "help us out," but that didn't feel right. He didn't really feel like a Chosen One anymore. *If I'm not a Chosen One, then who am I?* came the thought, but he shelved it for later consideration.

"You don't understand, do you?" he sighed, when Jamie didn't react with anything but acceptance.

But Jamie shook his head. "Oh, I understand," he said matter-of-factly. "Sarah explained everything to me."

Joe felt the room get fifteen degrees colder. *Did he say — Sarah?*

He stared at the little boy, unsure what he should say, or what he could say; it didn't help to ask him again. He heard the name right the first time. *He said Sarah. But it can't be.*

"She's dead," Jamie supplied, with his head cocked to one side as if he was listening to two conversations at once. "She says not to worry, she doesn't blame you for what happened. But she would like to know why you didn't do anything to stop him. She says you were standing right there. When he did it."

"I —" Joe said, but the sound came out a weak gurgle, the kind of sound someone would make when strangling. *Like the sound she made. Oh God, this can't be happening! Is he talking to spirits? Spirits that can read my mind? Is this Satan's work?*

He felt the walls of his father's religion closing around him, warding off the fear of the unknown that this conversation was invoking. *I can't go back to those beliefs,* he wanted to scream. *It's all nonsense, I've already decided that, or why else would I go against him, take Jamie out of his prison and feed him. But this, with Sarah, this is what the demons do. It's what the devil does! What else do I have to protect myself with, besides the Church?*

But — once again, his father had lied.

He told me she went to heaven!

She couldn't have, not if she was talking to Jamie —

Or was she an angel, some kind of sword-wielding, avenging angel, cutting down anyone who had anything to do with her death?

Jamie continued the conversation, like he was on one end of a spiritual telephone. "Sarah says that the forces of darkness are what your daddy attracts, not what she is. She also says you aren't in danger. At first she was mad at me for telling you about her, but now she says it will help all of us, letting you know she's still around. You can help me, she says." For the first time, Jamie showed some spark of interest. "How can you help me?" he demanded.

Joe had fallen off the pallet and was now on his knees, praying. He wasn't even certain what he was saying, but he hoped the emotion of what he was feeling would convey his message.

Jamie peered down at him. "Joe, whatcha doin' down there? You gettin' sick?"

"He's going to be a lot worse off than that," a loud, booming voice shouted from somewhere behind him. Joe jumped up and turned around suddenly, habitually reaching for his sidearm, a .44 that wasn't there.

Luke. Oh good God.

From the darkness came the *snick, snick* of a shell being pumped into a shotgun. Another, softer *snick* betrayed the presence of a pistol.

"I suggest that if you've rearmed yourself to drop it. But I don't think you have. You're not that smart."

The large man's weight shifted the pallet as he stepped on one of the bare wooden platforms. The pallet creaked, protesting loudly. More footsteps; one set no doubt belonging to Billybob. A third person shined a bright spot in Joe's face, panned back and forth between him and Jamie.

"Yep. That's them. They're both here," Billybob

said. It was the first coherent sentence Joe had heard the man utter.

"What the hell did you think you were trying to do?" Luke said, taking a few steps forward. The spotlight continued to shine, silhouetting the huge man. "How far did you think you were going to go with him?"

Joe glanced over at Jamie, who had — thank God — eaten everything he had given him. *If I play my cards right, I can get out of this one untouched. If.*

"Not sure what you mean, Luke," Joe replied. "I was just getting the boy clear of the fire. That is what you abandoned your post to go tend to, isn't it?"

Luke's expression wavered slightly. A flicker of concession passed over his face and then was gone.

"Guess that's what it was," Billybob said. "Wasn't sure."

"Shut up!" Luke screamed. His intensity startled Joe. "What I want to know is what you were planning to do with this kid?"

Joe assumed an expression of surprise. "I wasn't planning anything. What I did was take him to safety. It was pretty clear to me that he was in danger, and that you left him in danger."

"Enough of this crap," Luke said, cutting him off. "Billybob, you and Jimmy take the kid back to his room. I'll deal with Joe."

"But Luke —"

"But nothing. No arguments," he replied, a little softer.

Joe didn't like this one bit. It began to feel like a setup, and when he looked around at his surroundings, he had a creepy feeling he might not walk out of there alive. *This is the kind of place where people die,* he thought, trying hard not to let his fear show through.

Billybob hesitated, something Joe had never seen him do in Luke's presence. Luke's eyebrow raised in response.

"I said now," he said, quietly.

"You're not going to, are you?" Billybob asked, somewhat fearfully.

Joe could tell he was getting impatient. "Just take the kid back to the room now," Luke ordered. "I'll see about you later."

That last statement had an ominous feel to it, and Billybob took the boy by the hand and led him away out of the darkness of the storage room. Joe couldn't see Luke's expression very well, as the light from the hallway emergency light came in behind him. Jimmy followed Billybob out, casting a glance behind him that turned his blood to ice.

He's going to kill me, Joe thought. The realization left him feeling vaguely calm, in a detached sort of way. The fear he would have normally expected just wasn't there. *He's going to kill me, and it's not going to make any difference. He'll make up some story about how I tried to take the gun away from him.*

"You've gotten awfully uppity lately. Who do you think you are, anyway? Seems like you think you're better than me these days." Luke shifted his immense weight, cradling the shotgun carefully. The barrel never wavered.

"I know I'm not better than you," Joe pleaded, trying hard not to grovel. "Its just, things are happening so fast around here. The drugs and all, seems like something's going on there all the time."

"Why don't we just talk about that," Luke said. "Why don't you help with the deliveries? Distribution? You think you're a prince or somethin'?"

"I'm just busy with the Junior Guard," Joe lied. "You know that's what Brother Joseph wants me in. There's no time for nothing else." *If I keep him talking, maybe I can get out of this.*

Luke sneered. "I've been waiting for you to screw up for a long time. I knew you were trouble a long time ago. Knew you would never follow orders from your superiors. You know what I'm talking about, *don't you?*"

He knew all too well. "I think so," he replied, not wanting to get specific. *What is he leading up to?*

"The Chosen Ones will be purified by this," Luke said, raising the shotgun to shoulder level, and taking careful aim at Joe's midsection. "You just sit still, it'll be over with before you . . . "

At that moment the power returned, at least partially, to the sector. Fluorescent lights flickered on overhead as something went *wuuummmmph* in the distance.

"Shit," Luke whispered, looking around him furtively.

Above, located behind Luke, a remote camera whirred back to life. It panned back and forth, its red LED light blinking. Luke spotted it at the same time Joe did and dropped the shotgun to his side.

"There's someone watching us," Joe said. "If you killed me now there'd be witnesses."

"I wasn't going to kill nobody," he said, forcing a smile. "Where'd you get that idea anyway, son?"

"Sure looked that way to me," Joe said.

"What's going to happen now," Luke said, starting for the entrance of the storeroom, "is this. I'm going to report to your father, see, about how you tried to kidnap Jamie and take him out of our little sanctuary here, into Pawnee. The whole story. I'll just let you worry about that."

Joe shrugged. "That's fine with me," he said, not sure where his cockiness was coming from. "But I'll tell you one thing. And I'll let you worry about this: my father is going to find out about what you tried to do to me when I was a kid. Do you remember? Or should I refresh your memory?"

Luke froze in his tracks. "What are you talking about, boy?"

"You know exactly what I'm talking about. He might understand you fooling around with little girls, but little *boys*? And his *son*?"

Luke actually looked white. "He won't believe you."

Joe kept his eyes locked on the older man's. "Are you real sure about that?"

Indecision tortured his face. Joe could almost see the gears turning, however slowly, behind the man's eyes. *Brother Joseph might not believe his own son on something like that, but then he might,* Joe imagined him thinking. *Can I take that chance? As hot as things are around here? Brother Joseph, he likes to kill things when he's under a lot of pressure. Like now.*

"I got a better idea," Luke said, after long moments of consideration. "Why don't we just forget this whole thing ever happened and pitch in and help with the mess we got going back there?"

Joe exhaled a breath he didn't realize he was holding in.

"Yeah, Luke. Sure. Let's go."
Prick.

Al couldn't decide if it was the massage, the bath, or the wine that put him out, but whatever it was he slept like the dead. He barely woke as Bob got up and passed his couch, chuckling over something known only to the human; he thought he said something, but then went right back to sleep. He woke a little after that, with the realization that he had only an hour to track-time.

No matter. The rest had done him a world of good, completely restoring his energies.

After helping himself to bread and fruit from the sideboard, he ducked into the bathroom for a quick shower. Then, with a sigh of regret, he tapped into one of the local energy-foci, and transformed the interior of the RV back to its usual mundane appearance.

Pity. But I can't have someone walking in on this.

He left his favorite servant, the Phaeton mascot, in animated form, however. He had his hands full with breakfast and a brush, and he needed one extra hand to hold the blow-dryer. The mascot provided that, readily enough. She never tired and never got bored; she would hold the hair-dryer for him until the Trump of Doom if he asked it of her.

A quick peek out of the curtains showed the van was quiet and the Miata was gone; that meant that in all probability, Bob had taken Cindy somewhere before track-time. With her out of the way, it was safe enough to let this little evidence of his power remain active long enough to give him a little help.

But just as he thought that, the door opened.

Cindy had gotten up early, but even so, one of the racers had beaten her. The Miata was gone — although there was evidence by the slight motion of the RV that there was someone still inside.

She was glad now that she'd talked Bob into taking back his bed last night. Al was an attractive man; *too* darned attractive. It would be easy to fall right into bed with him. And she didn't want that — or rather, she did, but not right now. If she were to indulge herself — and that was the only phrase that described it — with Al right now, she would be betraying Jamie by taking away time and energy that could be used to search for him. The fantasy also had a slight edge of fear with the desire, which fluttered madly in her stomach; her ex-husband Jim had been her first and only bed partner. Just leaping into bed with someone she had recently met, who she wasn't even in *love* with, grated against her upbringing. She could almost hear her mother lecturing her for even considering it.

But she wasn't a virgin, wasn't at home, and her mother was dead. Al seemed to be a very nice man, and he was definitely a hunk. She wasn't even married anymore — and she'd kept taking the Pill even after the divorce, as a kind of reflex. There was no reason not to —

No. No, that would only make her feel more guilt, and she had plenty of that right now; she didn't need any more.

The van had a kind of friendly feeling about it; a sheltering quality. Cozy, that was what it was, and welcoming. As if she'd spent the night in the arms of some kind of nurturing earth-mother. She hadn't slept so well or so dreamlessly since Jamie had been stolen.

But her stomach woke her, soon after dawn, reminding her that she hadn't had much lunch and only a salad for supper. Maybe Al had come back last night with a little more food. She'd even cook it for him, or rather, for them both.

I wonder what he usually survives on: Gatorade and concession-stand hot dogs? I'd hate to see his cholesterol count.

She pulled on her old jeans and another t-shirt, slid out of the van, opened the RV door, and stepped up.

She poked her head around a corner — and froze.

Al was stark naked, combing his wet hair with one hand, and eating with the other, while blow-drying his hair. Holding the blow-dryer was a little silver statue of a woman; an odd sort of prop, but if it worked —

Dear God, he's a hunk, she thought in one analytical corner of her mind. Al still hadn't noticed her; the noise of the blow-dryer must have covered the sound of her entering. She felt like a peeping Tom —

She'd seen professional body-builders with better bodies — but not many. Did racing build muscles like that?

If that was what Gatorade and concession-stand hot dogs did, maybe she ought to change her diet.

Caught between embarrassment and an undeniable attraction, she started to back out and ran into the corner of the cabinet instead. "Excuse me!" she blurted, as Al suddenly looked up into the mirror and met her eyes.

She froze like a deer pinned in a car's headlights. The little silver statue was alive and moving. It turned to look calmly at her, still holding the blow-dryer. The dryer cord dangled straight down, and though the dryer was running, it wasn't plugged in.

The startled eyes that met hers in the mirror were emerald green and slitted like a cat's. And the ears, standing up through the wet hair, were pointed.

At first, as she took in the sight of Al's reflection, she felt calm. The strangeness of what she was seeing took several moments to sink in, as there was nothing in her experience, beyond cheap horror sci-fi movies, that she could relate this to. Her mind became a total blank and unable to assign this anywhere to the reality she knew.

Then it suddenly dawned on her: Al wasn't human.

She yelped and backpedaled into the Winnebago's interior as Al swung around, grabbing wildly for — not his privates — but his ears, confirming her suspicion that he wasn't human. His elbow hit the blow-dryer and knocked it out of the little statue's hands as he lunged for Cindy; she found herself trapped against the sink, and she acted instinctively. She kneed him, right where it counted, then froze again.

He might not be human, but the salient parts of male anatomy were in the same place. He gasped and folded, giving her a clear view of his ears. They *were* pointed.

In the bathroom, the tiny silver lady had picked up the blow-dryer and was calmly turning it off. Cindy's mouth was dry and her hands were shaking — and she was sure, now, that she had somehow gotten into some place that wasn't on earth. That, and she was finally losing her mind. Or — was this RV some kind of disguised flying saucer?

Al still had her blocked in, and the moment she broke her paralysis to shove past him, he moved like lightning, recovering much faster than any human could have.

He grabbed her arms and held her, this time pinning her legs as well, his strange eyes glaring at her with an anger that made them burn like twin green flames. He was angrier than anyone she had ever seen in her life. Even Brother Joseph hadn't frightened her this way.

She shrank back, so terrified she couldn't speak, her teeth chattering like castanets, wondering when, and how, he was going to kill her —

An expression of disgust passed over his face, and the glare of rage in his eyes dimmed. Suddenly, he pushed away from her, stalked into the bathroom, and pulled the vinyl curtain shut violently.

Before she could move, he jerked the curtain back again; now he was wearing pants, at least, and was pulling on a shirt. "You try my patience and my temper more than you know, human," he snarled, his hair standing out like a lion's mane. "If there were not a child involved —"

"Human?" she blurted. "What are you, a Vulcan?"

He stared at her a moment, shirt half on and half off — and began laughing. First it was a chuckle, then a full laugh, then loud roaring howls of laughter that reverberated in the RV.

Now Cindy was confused. Hell, if he was laughing, he couldn't be a Vulcan. So much for Star Trek. She stared at him as he tried to collect himself. Was she being overly sensitive, or did the laughter have a strange hollow sound that just wasn't human? At some point his eyes went back to being "normal," but the ears remained the same. Al managed to get the shirt buttoned on, and when he looked down, it was one button off. He seemed to find this even funnier and began laughing more.

I guess he isn't going to kill me yet. He rebuttoned his shirt, still chuckling, and she amended that. *Maybe he isn't going to kill me at all.*

As some of the initial shock wore off, Cindy began to

relax. But it seemed as if Al now found the situation — and her terror — quite amusing.

Cindy had been afraid, but that was shifting to anger. *She* didn't think this was anything to laugh at.

"And what is so damned funny?" she finally said, fuming. Then something else occurred to her — and her anger faded as it occurred to her what she had sounded like.

There was a long silence as Cindy sat down at the table, and Al remained standing. The silence thickened, and neither of them could find a way to reach across it. *He sounds different now,* she thought. *He's not coming across as the techie racing mechanic anymore. I can't place his accent, but it's not from North Carolina — he sounds like he was from that Robin Hood movie. What is he?*

"Well," Cindy finally said, after she couldn't bear the lengthy pause anymore. "What are you then?"

"It would take a long time to explain," Al said, then stopped. She had the feeling now that he really didn't want to reveal anything to her, but that he didn't have much choice.

"I've got all the time you need," she said, and crossed her arms over her chest. *This should be* very *interesting,* she thought. "Go right ahead. Nothing you say is going to surprise me more than what I've already seen."

"Perhaps. But an explanation has become necessary. I would have preferred to keep it a secret," Al said, and shrugged. It appeared, at that moment, to be a very *human* shrug. "But, as you say, the cat is out of the bag."

Cindy waited for him to speak, patient as only the mother of a young boy could be in waiting for an explanation.

Al sighed and poured himself a Gatorade. "We go back many thousands of years, our folk. Your people call mine elves now." He waited, as if assuming she'd laugh at the word. She only blinked.

I suppose that makes as much sense as space aliens.

"We have . . . "

"You don't bake cookies, do you?"

Alinor glared. "No. We have known about your people from the beginning, and have always known we were a minority, and were in many ways physically inferior to humans. We have — weaknesses, vulnerabilities, that you do not have. But we have magic. We have always had magic. For a while that was a protection, and even made us superior."

"And it isn't anymore?" she asked, matter-of-factly.

He shook his head. "No, and now we are even more in the minority. As your human civilization grew, we isolated ourselves even more. Some of us were careless, were discovered. The humans quickly put them to death. We were never tolerated. We have learned the fine art of being invisible."

Al gestured to the orange jug of Gatorade, offering. Cindy shook her head. The mechanic — or whatever — took a seat opposite her, his motions careful and precise, as if he was trying not to arouse any more fear. The act was reassuring. The tale he was telling, however, was not.

"We appear in mythology, folklore, fairy tales. Some of these we planted ourselves. Some, though these are few, are true accounts that have been distorted with time. We call ourselves elves because in your language there is no other suitable alternative. 'Sidhe' sounds just like 'she,' after all."

As Cindy listened, she realized her mouth was hanging open.

"Are you sure you don't want anything to drink?" Al asked, starting to sound concerned.

Again, she shook her head. "You mean all this time you and — ? What about Bob? Is he one, too?" The prospect added another uncomfortable dimension to the situation.

"No, Cindy. He is as human as you are," Al replied.

"Which takes me to another aspect of our existence. The children."

Cindy suppressed a shudder and tried to make her expression as bland as possible.

Al seemed to read her mind, which did nothing to put her at ease. "No, no. Nothing sinister. We have a low birth-rate, and we treasure little ones — perhaps more so than you humans do. We often step in to save them from a variety of fates, from drowning, from fires, from falling. We always have." His expression darkened. "Sometimes we save them from their blood-parents. Sometimes we save them from other things, like Brother Joseph."

Cindy relaxed a little. For some reason, she believed him. Well, why not? There was certainly no other reason for him to have come to her aid.

"Children are most precious to us," Al explained, his compassion reaching her through her fog of confusion. "For reasons that extend beyond survival of the human race. Despite some ways we have been received, we need you." He chuckled a little. "Children. You could say that it is the way we are hardwired. No one really knows why. The children we save do grow up, of course — and if it is their parents that we save them from, it is often to other parents, loving ones, that they are given. It is true, we have human helpers, like Bob, who help us fit into society and also help keep us concealed — and some of those were human children who were so badly hurt that *we* were the only folk fit to raise them."

"Hurt, how?" she asked. Fear began again. Would this creature save Jamie only to take him away again?

"Abuse — profound abuse. Physical, emotional —" He gave her a hard look. "Sexual. You might not believe some of the stories. You would not want to. For some children, there is no way that they will find healing in your world. For them, there is ours — a world from their fairy-tale books, a world where no harm from 'the real world' can intrude to touch them. A place where they can learn that there is such a thing as love and caring, and where they can learn to defend themselves so that the real world can never hurt them again."

Cindy thought about one of the women who had shared the shelter with her — a woman with three young girls, and all four of them testing positive for syphilis. Only when the doctor had confirmed the fact — and confirmed that the children had been brutally, repeatedly, molested — did the woman believe what they had been trying to tell her about their father.

Their *father*. She had wanted to throw up. But — wasn't that the same thing that Jim had allowed Brother Joseph to do to Jamie's mind?

She swallowed. "All right," she said, "But what about other kids? The ones who've got at least one good parent?"

"Like Jamie?" He looked at her solemnly. "We would have helped as soon as we realized there was a problem. Your husband: classic case of abusive alcoholism. That alone would have qualified your son for our help, if you are in any doubt. But this Brother Joseph thing, that goes *well* beyond what we would consider acceptable. I can only hope that when we retrieve Jamie, he will be able to forget what has happened to him. If he cannot forget, then we can help him deal with it intelligently. A child must never be underestimated."

They regarded each other in silence for several moments, and the refrigerator started making sounds she hadn't noticed before.

"You must believe me when I say that we only want to help your son, and to return him to you." There was a distinct emphasis on that last that comforted her. "It is only a matter of time before I think we can accomplish this."

Cindy slumped against the backrest. There it was. Things hadn't changed that much. At least Al wasn't something from another planet, or from hell. She still didn't know how to handle the elf thing, though. . . .

Never mind. The important thing was Jamie.

As incredible as the story sounded, she knew, somehow, that it was all true. She'd seen the eyes, the ears —

The little silver lady sashayed across the floor towards Al and tapped his knee. He looked down and handed the creature a plastic cup filled with Gatorade. She took it, then hip-waggled her way to Cindy's knee and offered it.

Trying not to lose her jaw, she accepted the cup, and the silver lady sauntered back into the bathroom, hips swaying gently from side to side.

Well, there's nothing wrong with his hormones, if that's what he keeps around instead of pinups. . . .

"Is that —" She faltered.

He raised an eyebrow. "Magic? Yes. It is."

She swallowed a large gulp of Gatorade.

It could have been worse, she thought. *He could have been a giant bug in a man-suit, or something. . . .*

She saw then that his eyes had gone back to the slit-pupiled green they had been when she barged in and sensed that Al was presenting himself now as exactly what he was, and that he was no longer holding back anything that would distort the true image of himself. She noted, idly, that his ears continued to protrude through his hair even as it dried straight, and remembered that she had interrupted his grooming.

"I should let you get back to what you were doing when I came in." Her eyes fell on his right ear. It was hard to resist. "You don't mind if I — ?"

Al's eyes shifted momentarily, as if he was about to object. Then he smiled warmly.

"Go ahead. But don't *pull* on it. It's very sensitive."

Gently, she touched the tip of the pointed ear,

relieved for some odd reason that it was, indeed, real. It sprang back, as soft and as warm as any human's. This simple act of touching the feature reassured her that she wasn't going mad after all.

"This is going to take some getting used to," she said. "I mean, it's not every day that I meet an elf."

He chuckled. "It's not every day that I get to acquaint a human with our species."

Cindy frowned. "You make it sound like you're from another planet or something. Really, now, you don't look that much different than a human." She blushed, seeing that she was flirting, although indirectly. *What is it about him, even with the pointed ears, that is so compelling? Christ, if we ever had children they would probably all look like little pink Yodas. But then, you know what they say about men with long, pointed ears . . . or was that noses?*

"You're being kind," Al said, and Cindy looked at him askance. *Is he reading my mind, too? No, that was to something I said earlier. But what if he can read minds?* "But there is a great deal of difference between our two races. It wouldn't be wise to introduce you to all of these things now, especially the things we can do. It has already been quite a shock, whether or not you realize it."

"Of course I realize it," she objected, but she knew her words were falling on deaf, if pointed, ears. Cindy couldn't help but notice her sudden calmness and the distinct feeling of somehow being manipulated into losing her fear.

But then her thoughts returned to Jamie, and the darkness came again, swooping over her like a raven that had been waiting in the shadows to rouse her depression. And for all of Al's self-assured words, his *magic,* she couldn't see how she was going to find him, much less get him back.

Are we really any closer to saving him from those crazies? Can little magic statues do anything besides hold blow-dryers? All that talk about saving children, and holding them in such esteem — that's nice, but if Jamie's in there, there's an army between us and him! How can this elf *really help us when the county Sheriff can't get inside that compound?*

"Well. Now that we've got *that* out of the way," Al said, though Cindy was not entirely certain what *that* was, "there are some things you could tell me that would help me locate your son. Unusual things. The things someone else might not believe."

"Like?" she asked.

Al waved a hand in the air. "Psychic experiences. Sleep walking. Talking in his sleep, especially if it seemed as if he was having a lucid conversation with someone. Anything at all?"

"You're talking about the Praise Meeting," she said in an accusatory tone she was trying not to use. "The weird stuff that happened there."

He shrugged. "That and, well, other things. Similar experiences that may have happened at home. But if you like, you can start with the Praise Meeting."

She sighed and straightened up, looking down at her hands while she gathered her thoughts. Though her first impulse was to reject the notion, she knew that, in a way that only Al would know, this was important. *He mentioned other abilities. Could that be why that monster wanted Jamie in the first place?* "Like I'd told you, I didn't want to go to that church thing at all."

Al shook his head. "No, not the first meeting you went to. I mean the time Brother Joseph did the channeling. You told me about it, but I don't know if you were there or not."

"I wasn't. That was the time — *he* — just took off with my son." She had difficulty mentioning her ex-husband by name, so she didn't. "When they got back, Jamie was terrified —"

Something suddenly occurred to her, a connection she might never have made if Al hadn't mentioned psychic phenomena and Jamie in the same breath.

"That's really strange. Now that I think of it, that reminds me of a time a few months earlier, when Jamie had a high fever. He was having hallucinations, or something close to it, when his fever spiked. The doctor only recommended Tylenol and bed rest, so that's what we did. He was sick for a week, but during all that time there were a few — I don't know — incidents. And after that, after he got well, he kept having these experiences. In his sleep."

Al's interest sharpened visibly. "Could you tell me a little more about these?"

Cindy paused, suddenly realizing how much she had tried to forget what had happened, as if by forgetting them she could make them unhappen. If it hadn't been for the channeling and the whole sick mess with the Chosen Ones, she suspected she would have managed to dismiss them from her mind already.

She shrugged, unpleasantly aware that her hands were shaking. "His father wasn't — interested. He kept saying Jamie would grow out of it. But I would hear him at night, sometimes crying, sometimes singing to himself, or even talking to some imaginary person in the room. At least, I thought it was imaginary. Sometimes I could rouse him awake, but on most others, I just couldn't wake him. He would go on, crying or singing or talking. This was after the fever, you see, so I was a little worried that there might have been brain damage or something, but the doctor said it would pass, it was just a part of growing up. And Jim said the doctor knew what he was doing and that I was being overprotective."

"What was he saying?" Al said, leaning closer.

She shook her head, helplessly. "It was in a different language. French, sometimes. I think it was French. I don't speak French, so I don't know. Sometimes he sang things that sounded like hymns in some other language. Most of the time it just didn't make any sense at all. When I asked him about it the next day, about the things he was dreaming, he would tell me the most frightening stories about dragons or lizards, and about castles and these huge mobs of people, women, children, knights, all marching endlessly across a wilderness. Going somewhere, except they never got there. I never understood the details. But then, dreams are like that, aren't they? Just sort of vague and flowing, like someone is pulling what you want just out of reach."

Al's expression had changed, but she couldn't put her finger on what it had changed *to*. It was a little creepy, seeing him staring like that, with those strange eyes — brilliant emerald green eyes.

"Anything else?" he asked, after a bit.

Cindy thought about it. The memory popped out of nowhere with the force of a blow, nearly hitting her between the eyes.

"How could I have forgotten?" she cried out, with an intensity that made Al visibly start. "The day the school called me! Jim was at work, I guess, and so I had to go to the school. Jamie had gotten sick or something, they wouldn't tell me exactly what had happened over the phone." She shook her head and put the cup of Gatorade on the table; her hands were shaking too hard to hold it. "When I got to the nurse's office, he was just sitting in a chair, staring straight ahead, not even noticing me, it looked like. The principal, he was there, and first thing he said was he thought Jamie was on drugs or something. I told him that was ridiculous, that Jamie would never have done something like that. I told him we never had anything in the house stronger than aspirin — the principal just gave me this look, but he gave up, since he didn't have any proof anyway. But the way Jamie acted, I could see why he would think that. He was just staring off into the distance, like one of those little kids I'd seen on TV that was in one of the houses that got hit by SCUDs in Israel, like he'd seen something and was too afraid to talk about it."

As she babbled on, Cindy wondered why in the world she had forgotten *that*. The incident had scared the life out of her, and she'd taken Jamie straight to the doctor. The doctor hadn't been able to find anything, either — he'd said something about "juvenile epilepsy" and that Jamie would probably never have a fit like that again. . . .

It was almost as if something had come in and taken the memory away, and it was only just now returning, bit by bit. Was it was coming back only because Al had asked her for details?

Was I trying to hide it from myself, and trying not to remember it? Or is it that something else didn't want me to? She wasn't being paranoid — not after elves and magic statues, and God only knew what was being done to Jamie. This wasn't the Twilight Zone. Or even if it was, she was *in* it, and she'd better start handling it.

"How long ago was that?" Al asked, piercing the silence that had fallen between them.

"Last year," Cindy said automatically, though on a conscious level she wasn't sure when it was. "I can't remember if it was before or after he got sick. Do you think it's important?"

"Any information is important," the elf replied. "It sounds like he went into a sort of trance." He began to say something, but visibly held back. Realizing he was probably withholding information about her son, she felt a little prickle of anger rise up her spine.

The more Cindy talked, the more concerned Al became about the whole situation. Her recollections of what Jamie had said and done were too similar to his own experiences — hundreds of years ago — to write off to coincidence.

The boy is a medium. Has been, probably all his life. Perhaps Brother Joseph, who has no real ability of his own, didn't

*actually select him. Maybe he was only a middleman. Perhaps
something selected* him*, as a pipeline to a medium.*

*And those dreams about what could have been the
Crusades . . . what must have been the Peasant's Crusade. . . .*

• CHAPTER NINE

In perfect formation, the First Battalion of the Junior Guard stood at attention, their assault weapons held rigidly at their sides, eyes forward, chests out. The tension was like a piano wire pulled taut, threading through the boys' tense muscles, waiting to break. Only moments before, just as they did at this time every day, the battalion of boys had scurried onto the sand-covered drill area in their underground bunker, adjacent to the firing range.

It was the same battalion, the same uniforms, the same weapons as yesterday. Only Joe was different. And he felt the difference, coursing through his veins, pulsing even at the ends of his fingers. He wondered that they didn't see it, but there was no indication that any of the boys noticed anything at all.

This was a routine drill, one they did every day. Joe had been in charge of training the boys for months now, drilling them every moment they weren't in the Junior Guard School, learning the non-physical skills they would need in the world of the New Order. His drilling had paid off, and they had become a well-oiled fighting machine, with a discipline that rivaled the Guard itself. For weeks now Joe's battalion had been the center of his life and the source of his pride —

And even after he began to doubt, at least the Junior Guard had been a diversion from the insanity that surrounded Jamie. Now, with his new vision of the way things were, they were a source of personal embarrassment.

But since it appeared that none of the boys was

going to run out and denounce him, he did not dare change so much as a single lift of an eyebrow. Eyes were on him; Luke's for one. Probably others. Watching for the least sign of difference, of dissension.

Of treachery? That was how they would see things.

"Who are we?" Joe screamed into the silence.

"The Junior Guard!" the battalion screamed back, with voices that cracked with puberty, voices that were deepening, and voices that were still high and tinny with childhood. But the response became a single sound, shaking the walls, reverberating down the concrete tunnels.

"Who do we protect?"

"God and Country!"

"Who else?"

"Brother Joseph!"

"Who from?"

"The Jew Pig Commie Enemy!"

"What do we train for?"

"Armageddon!"

"WHEN'S THAT GONNA HAPPEN?"

"REAL SOON!"

The ritual followed the same script they had all memorized in their first day in the Guard. They learned the routine while half asleep and stumbling into formation during "surprise" drills in the middle of the night. Joe remembered the faint puzzlement on the boys' faces the first few times they repeated the litany, as if they were shouting slogans they didn't really grasp for reasons they didn't fully understand. But now, Joe could see as he surveyed his creation, they understood it all too well. The hate had become real. They believed it. They lived for it. And it was all they lived for; before friends, future, or family.

Brainwash complete, sir.

Today's drill took them outside, to the recently completed obstacle course. The course itself was disguised and camouflaged from the air. The ever-present guards watched for aircraft, in particular a small plane belonging to the Oklahoma Highway Patrol. When the guards spotted anything in the air, even an innocuous ultra-light, someone would blow a signal whistle and the battalion would go into hiding, concealing themselves in oil barrels and fox holes. Normally Joe would be keenly aware of anything that might be flying around in the air, right down to the ever-present turkey vultures, but today he just didn't care. The daily drill was a responsibility, nothing more. Meaningless. *Less* than meaningless. The enemy, he now knew, existed only in someone's fevered imagination.

His father's.

He hadn't slept last night, either. This wasn't terribly unusual, since he had to be up for the late-night surprise drills, and after the drills it would often be late enough that he wouldn't bother going back to bed, instead filling his time with five-kilometer runs and weightlifting. He had found a way to summon a second wind out of habit, but he was glad *he* wasn't required to run the course.

Joe watched the boys crawl under barbed wire, climb up ropes and over walls, run through tires and snake through conduit. And none of it made any sense anymore. *We're doing this for nothing,* he thought in disgust that sat in the back of his throat and made every swallow a bitter one.

Out of the corner of his eyes he saw a familiar shape. *Luke.*

He stood at the corner of the obstacle course, and all evidence showed that he had only recently awakened; he yawned frequently and had the rumpled, disgruntled look he generally had until lunch. *Father must have given him time to sleep,* Joe mused. *He never sleeps when Father is awake.* He found it disturbing, though, that Luke was here watching the Junior Guard. *Is he letting me know that he's watching me?*

The more he considered this, the more it made sense. Joe caught him making furtive glances in his direction, which Luke quickly diverted when their eyes made accidental contact. Then Joe saw him nod towards one of the guards in the tower. The guard returned the nod, then began scrutinizing the area where Joe was.

He's having them keep an eye on me, too, Joe realized.

Dismaying, but not, after all, surprising. Unless —

For a paranoid moment the boy considered the possibility that his *father* could be reading his mind. After all, the "gift" had to come from somewhere! What if his father had known, all this time —

He mentally ran through everything that had happened so far, and his panic subsided. *They were only reading the signs,* he finally decided. *There was nothing supernatural about it. My father is still a fake.*

Still, it was unnerving to be watched so blatantly. He had hoped to be able to sneak away and get more food to Jamie, but as he stood there, watching the watchers, the flaws in that half-formed plan became evident. For one thing, it would not solve the overall problem. Jamie was a tool, one his father was going to use until it broke; and the boy seemed well on his way to breaking. He might be able to get him some more food today, but what about the next day, next week? How long before every opportunity, every chance was cut off? Not long, with Luke in charge.

And that didn't solve the real problem, because meanwhile his father was using him to talk with that godawful thing, *whatever* it was.

That wasn't the last of his problems, either. The drug dealing had also begun tugging at his attention, and he found that he could no longer look the other way and still have anything like a conscience. He taught the Junior Guard that drugs were poison — and meanwhile, his father sold the stuff to kids no older than these.

But with all of these eyes following him now, there wasn't much he could do about the drug ring, or Jamie.

As a child, he had toyed with the idea of running away. That had been when his father first began taking notice of his son, attempting to mold him into a little miniature version of himself. He resisted, at first — after all, so much of what the public schoolteachers taught him ran against everything his father preached — but obeying his father was just too much a part of him to resist. Finally he accepted his father's word completely, and whatever urge he'd had to run away seemed like the most treasonous insanity.

That had been many years ago, when he was a child of fourteen or fifteen. *When I didn't know any better.* But now he was an adult, responsible for his own actions. He couldn't hide behind "my father said" and "my father told me to" any longer. And there was another person involved, a kid, an innocent; someone who was going to die, perhaps even the same way Sarah died. That, he knew after last night, was something he could never live with.

If he could not summon the strength or the means to help Jamie from within the camp, he would have to go outside for the help. He knew enough about the outside world to realize that, once he had gone to the government, there would be no turning back. With the drugs involved, he suspected they would be all too willing to help rescue the boy in trade for busting the drug ring.

Maybe he could strike a deal.

He blinked, and for a moment his sight blurred. *Too little, too late?* he wondered. *Still, if I don't do something now, there won't be a chance to do anything at all. Luke's ready to get rid of me. It won't be long before he succeeds. And then where will Jamie be?*

Then came another horrible thought. *What will happen to him if I can't get him help? I don't have any real evidence to show anyone — just what I can tell them. That little bit of food I brought him was the first thing he'd eaten in a long time, and if I'm gone no one else will be here to help him.*

Meanwhile, the Junior Guard ran through their paces like perfect little robot soldiers. When the exercise was complete, Joe summoned then dismissed the First Battalion. For a brief but oddly sad moment, he wondered if this really was the last time he would ever lead them in exercises. If he did leave, these boys which he had helped convert into fighting and hating machines would have to come to their own conclusions about the Chosen Ones, their beliefs, Brother Joseph. Perhaps, he hoped, it wasn't too late for them to change. Would the defection of their leader make them think — or make them decide that Satan had corrupted him and vow that the Evil One would never touch them — closing their minds off forever?

As the battalion filed back towards the bunkers, shouting a cadence his mother would have taken extreme exception to, Luke gestured for him to *come here*. The gesture seemed calculated to annoy him. It was as if Luke was ordering a dog.

Joe knew he was tired and tried to get beyond his own foul mood when he walked up to Luke. *Don't let him get to you,* he told himself. *You're tired, you're hungry, and it'd be easy for him to make you say something stupid. And he knows it. He's trying to get your goat, you know he is.*

But as he came closer, he sensed something different about the man. The sneer was a little more pronounced, smug. Luke stood in a particularly haughty pose, and there was dark laughter in his eyes.

Something happened, Luke thought. *He's talked with Father about last night, must have. Maybe it's too late for me to do anything about Jamie.* He wanted to blame the weakness he felt in his knees just then on his lack of sleep, but it was fear, and he knew it.

"Brother Joseph wants to speak with you right now,"

Luke said, and it sounded like he was suppressing laughter. With great difficulty. "Boy, kid, you sure have screwed up."

"Where is he?" Joe replied, completely deadpan, as if Luke's words hadn't made any impression on him.

"In his office," Luke said — a trap, since Joe knew "the office" could have meant any of three separate places.

So he asked the right question instead of charging off by himself. "Which one?" he asked. "The one near the meeting hall, the security booth, or the conservatory?"

"Near the security booth," Luke said brightly. "He knows everything."

"No," Joe corrected, meeting Luke's eyes directly. "He doesn't. At least not yet. That can always change. Remember, I was only thirteen at the time. A little *boy.*"

This last statement actually seemed to frighten the man, as if it was a blow that had been completely unexpected. Luke blinked once, then stepped backwards. *As if he forgot all about last night,* Joe thought. *I'll bet this isn't as bad as he's making it out to be.*

It was, however, an effort to keep from shaking. He had been called before Brother Joseph often, as he was a high ranking officer as well as his son, in that order. Each time in the past it had always been an experience with varying degrees of unpleasantness. But today — well, he'd rather have faced a root canal.

What did *Luke say to him?*

Joe realized that Luke was accompanying him. "Did he say to escort me?"

"Why, no," Luke sneered. "We're just one big happy family. Got something to hide?"

"No, I don't. But you *are* a soldier of the Chosen Ones." He gave Luke a level stare and felt a brief flush of success when the man couldn't meet his eyes for more than a second. "Seems to me you have duties. I just thought you might have more important things to do, like see to Jamie. Who do you have guarding him now?"

"That's got nuthin' to do with you no more," Luke said. "You'll see."

Joe shrugged and walked on, pushing the pace, not looking to see if Luke kept up. Short and stocky, the older man had to walk nearly double-time to keep up with him. They entered the dimness of the complex, accompanied by the familiar *whirr, whirr* of cameras panning across them as they passed. *He's watching me,* Joe thought, with certainty. *They all are.*

They came to the main security station, the mother of the smaller one Joe had operated the evening before. *Do they know I was there?* he wondered, but he had no time to fabricate an excuse. Or — did he?

They entered a room full of video screens much larger and more numerous than the little ones he'd used at the backup station. Along one wall was a variety of radio equipment, through which senior members of the Guard monitored police, emergency and aircraft transmissions. One officer was listening to a short-wave broadcast from Russia, another monitoring what sounded like an African station. Since neither of these were in English, Joe wondered why they had it piped through. No one in the Chosen Ones spoke a foreign language, or at least admitted to it, for fear of being labeled a spy or a witch.

His father was standing in the middle of the room, arms crossed, eyes narrowed. He appeared to be displeased with everything around him, but then as far as Joe knew, he always looked that way.

"Good afternoon, sir," Joe said, his voice cracking. The fear he was trying to hide came through anyway. *He likes it when I'm scared,* he reasoned. *That way he knows I'm still under his thumb.*

Brother Joseph did not respond. He seemed to feign an interest in the screens, which displayed nothing particularly unusual; empty hallways, views of the grounds above. One showed the elementary school class, though Joe had no idea why. He cautiously looked for a screen with Jamie and saw none, although some were turned off. The silence continued, and Joe waited patiently for his father to acknowledge his presence.

In his own time, he did. He picked up a computer printout, turned it around, and held it up to Joe.

"This says you were in the auxiliary security station south this morning around two A.M. Care to tell me why, soldier?"

Joe stared at the report that he hadn't expected for days, and at first could think of absolutely nothing to say. *What was I doing in there at two A.M.? You see, Dad, I was just trying to liberate Jamie, see, and take him to the cops and tell them everything. No problem, okay?* His eyes blurred momentarily. *After that, I was helping put a fire out,* he thought, and he seized upon that as an inspiration. His father couldn't possibly know the exact timing of everything that had happened last night. If he just rearranged events a little —

"First, I had checked the storage area nearby because there were lights on down there, which there shouldn't have been at that hour. It was Luke and Billybob; they said they were guarding Jamie, so I started to leave, but there was a disturbance, and I smelled fire," Joe said calmly. "I was near the station. I entered it to examine the security cameras, to see if the detectors had picked up anything or if it was just someone sneaking a smoke. Once I was in there, I saw that there was a fire somewhere in the quadrant — and even more important, I saw that Jamie had been left unguarded, since Luke and Billybob had gone to neutralize the fire. It seemed to me that the fire might move into his room. In order to preserve our assets I took it upon myself to break him free and move him clear of the area, to somewhere secure and safe, where we could be found easily or get out if the fire started to spread."

His father stared at him for a long time. His expression then was totally unreadable.

After what seemed like an eternity he cleared his throat. "That's what Luke here tells me. I just wanted to hear it from you first. Remember next time, that whenever you enter a security station, you must fill out a report describing why you had to enter the station. File it promptly with the watch commander."

"Yes, sir." Joe waited for something else to drop, but soon it became evident that nothing would. Other things seemed to be on Brother Joseph's mind, and Joe glanced over at Luke, who appeared to be disappointed.

"I've been thinking about our new security branch," Brother Joseph finally said. "For some time now we have been lacking in some means to protect our organization from internal threats. I know, our admission standards are quite high, but there's no way to tell when Satan might infiltrate and sway one of our own. It's happened before. It will be an internal affairs matter, investigating and prosecuting those who veer from the one true path."

Joe sighed inwardly. Now that he had escaped the trap Luke had set for him, all he could feel was — tired. *Fine. He brought me all the way into the security booth to tell me that the position he once promised me is going to Luke. Swell. Anything else you'd care to rub into my face while I'm here? It'll save time and trouble to go ahead and get it over with now.*

"And it's been a tough decision, but I've narrowed it down to one." His eyes softened a bit and looked at Joe with what appeared to be admiration. "Son, how would you like to take the post? I've had you in mind all along, but I wanted to be fair to the rest of the officers. Luke here was a close second, but after hearing what you did last night, and the smart snap decisions you made, I've decided to make you the next head of Internal Security."

Joe was speechless. From Luke, who was standing off to his right, he heard gurgling sounds. Then the noises turned to grunts, which further articulated to: "But — But — But —"

Brother Joseph nodded with something approaching sympathy. "I know, Luke, this is a real disappointment. But I know you'll take this graciously. Like a man! You're still important. You're still in charge of that other little project we talked about."

Other little project, Joe thought briefly, but he was still too flabbergasted for it to really register. *He's going to make me the head of Internal Security after all Luke must have been telling him. Does this mean he trusts me after all, or is this just another elaborate test? Look at him. He's handing me the post in front of witnesses, and if this is a trick, Luke doesn't know about it. Sounds like he's about to piss his pants!*

"But —" Luke said again, but Joe's father didn't seem to hear him.

"Another thing," Brother Joseph said. "Any idea what caused all that ruckus last night? That little fire wasn't the only disturbance, as I'm sure you know."

"No, I don't. Perhaps it was the work of Satan," Joe responded automatically, not certain if he believed the words or not. "From what I saw in the security room, it all seemed to happen at once, power failures, cameras going out, pipes breaking, fires — I was concerned with Jamie's well-being and safety. Maybe — I don't know, maybe Satan wants to get at him so we can't channel the Sacred Fire anymore."

His father gave him a funny look at that. "Perhaps. Perhaps you're pushing that part of your responsibility a little too far there." He smiled benignly. "Since you are now a senior officer, let me show you your new quarters."

Joe had little to say as they walked a long corridor to the adjacent quadrant, then went up one floor to a wide, carpeted hallway that announced, with flamboyance and no subtlety at all, *rank*. At the end of the hallway was a set of flags, one American, the other, a little larger and taller, of the Sacred Heart. Not *the* Flag, that one stayed in the Meeting Hall; this was a copy. Brother Joseph unlocked a huge oak door, one of several along the hallway. Slowly, majestically, it swung open, like the gate to a castle.

Joe realized, on entering, that he hadn't really known how well the officers of the Guard lived. Now he did, and he was amazed at the luxury and opulence he saw here. Carpeting, track lighting, a computer terminal, presumably one directly linked to the main computer, and a big screen TV stood against one wall. In the corner was a small kitchen, with every modern convenience including a microwave. The place looked and smelled newly remodeled.

Luke was standing in the doorway. "But you promised me this one!" he wailed, but his words apparently went unheard.

"In here you have an added feature that the others don't," Brother Joseph said, leading him to the bathroom. Or that's what he thought it would be; when he turned the lights on, it looked like something out of ancient Rome. "A jacuzzi, just a bit smaller than my own." And indeed it was, rising out of the middle of the room on a pedestal, surrounded by plants and Roman columns. "But no hanky panky," his father said, winking. "This is for you alone. After a long day of drill, it's good for your muscles. It'll help you keep in shape."

They walked back into the bedroom, where they found a huge antique bed with a canopy. "This was your bed in Atlanta, father," Joe protested, but his objections were a bit feeble. He couldn't deny that he had wanted digs like these all along, but never thought his father would consider him worthy enough. Within a few minutes, all that had changed.

"I will have a few privates in the Guard help you move," Brother Joseph said, watching him with an odd expression on his face. As if even this gave him power over his son.

That was *too* much. "No, please, father. Let me get some help from my Junior Guard battalion. . . ."

"You will not do that," Brother Joseph said fiercely. "They are no longer your responsibility. You are an officer now, with full rank of lieutenant."

"Lieutenant?" Joe said, confused. That was jumping rank, something that just didn't happen. "But why?"

"Because you are my son," his father replied. "And you will be treated as such. Provided, of course, you remember where you stand in the organization." He turned to leave the room, then said, as much to Luke as to Joe, "I have the power to appoint and promote whomever I wish. The Chosen Ones belong to me first, and God second. Do not ever forget that. That applies to both of you." He hesitated at the doorway, then said, "There's something else I must show you. Come."

As Brother Joseph led them to yet another surprise, somewhere deep within the bowels of the underground, Joe tried to cope with his world turning upside down. He didn't think much about where they were being led. All his attention was taken up by these latest changes — not only unexpected, but unprecedented.

What got into him? Shoot. An hour ago I was thinking about running away, but with all this, who could? Head of Internal Security . . .

Now that he thought about it, he wasn't even qualified for something like that. He was just a foot soldier. It was so unlikely that it roused his suspicions. . . .

But his father had said that it would be an easy post, more figurehead than anything, unless a situation came up that would need his special attention. Maybe it wasn't so unlikely. After all, Brother Joseph *was* going to put Luke in charge, and Luke didn't know shit from shampoo.

Nevertheless, figurehead or not, this new job meant rank. It meant being promoted over Luke's head. *And the room! It's amazing!* Joe's present room was little more than a cubicle in a dormitory, with a simple bed on an unfinished wooden floor, a table, a lamp and a dresser. A little more than most of the Chosen Ones had, but still pretty basic. *I think I could get used to this. . . .*

But Jamie—

He tried to keep Jamie, and Jamie's danger, in the front of his mind, but with the sudden change in his status, it was becoming more difficult. He had a taste of the things that only the elite enjoyed. For a moment he was dismayed at how easily he had been manipulated—

But it was a short-lived dismay.

Now I can help Jamie more, if I can sneak around my father's back. That makes more sense than running off. It would be different if he hadn't promoted me, but that changes everything. And the more he thought about it, he knew he couldn't run away. What would he have on the outside? Nothing. He didn't even have a high school diploma, at least not one this state would consider valid. There were no assurances that anyone would even listen to him out there, and given the Chosen Ones' security, he knew he wouldn't be able to change his mind once he defected. They would know, immediately, what he had done. In fact, they would probably assign someone to "eliminate" him. They had done it before, killing a former member who knew too much about the organization. And the man they'd killed wasn't even an officer.

Shoot, they killed Sarah's parents, just 'cause they tried to run off. I wouldn't have a chance.

He would have to contend with Luke as best he could. It would be easier to evade Luke than the entire army. Besides, with this new and unexpected change in status, he doubted Luke would come near him now.

In fact, Luke wasn't even a real threat — no matter what he'd promised before. In order to rationalize killing him, Luke had depended on proving some questionable, if not treasonous, behavior. Now that Joe was head of Internal Security, that would be more difficult, if not impossible, to do. The game had turned completely around, this time in Joe's favor.

Why screw everything up by running away?

As he thought these things over, he had paid little attention to where his father was leading them, or what Luke was doing. Now Joe glanced over at him, walking a few feet behind his father, and saw the characteristic smug grin on the man's face. Whatever was up now, it was going to be nasty enough to revive Luke's spirits entirely.

Now what? Joe thought, but had no time to puzzle over his expression. They had apparently arrived at their destination.

His father turned toward him with a sanctimoniously sober expression. "What you're about to see, Joe, is going to be hard to take. But just remember, it's God's will. To interfere with God's will is to do the will of Satan. And that we *cannot* have."

Then, from behind a set of double doors, he heard the whimpering of a child in terrible fear.

Jamie?

The doors opened, as if by themselves. Then he saw a disheveled, drunken man holding the door open by a crossbar.

"It's been nearly thirty minutes," the man said, visibly swaying as he struggled to stand up. Joe recognized him as Jamie's father. "Should we let him out now?"

Joe could barely see into the darkness of the room, which he now saw was a large storage facility, one of the newer ones. He smelled the damp odor of the fresh plaster and caulking. He hesitated before stepping inside, knowing that he *really* wasn't going to like what he saw. If Brother Joseph had warned him — it was going to be bad, real bad.

Behind him, Luke laughed. Brother Joseph stood in the doorway and beckoned all of them to enter.

The room was dark, except for a few Coleman lanterns sitting on the floor, illuminating two regular Guards who stood at attention. Something that appeared to be a huge box was standing in the middle of the large storeroom. But there was a dark object in the box, and when the *whimpering* came from it, he knew who it was.

"Jamie?" Joe asked, but he was more confused than afraid, since he couldn't quite see the boy or what was happening to him. Then his eyes adjusted, and the darkness retreated.

Jamie lay in the box — or at least, Joe figured he was lying in the box, though all he could see was part of the boy's head. Just the mouth and nose. The rest was covered with an enormous helmet. And the kid's body, from the neck down, was buried in some kind of white substance that looked soft.

Held this way, Jamie could breath, but he couldn't hear, see, or feel anything. If they'd blocked his nostrils with nose-plugs, and they might well have, he wouldn't be able to smell anything, either.

A sensory deprivation box — Joe recognized it from a PBS documentary. It was cruder than the one he'd seen; this one used foam or something, rather than gel or warm water. It didn't look cruel — but it was. Grownups had trouble in the sensory deprivation box. How could a little kid cope with it?

Joe immediately went for the box, but the two Guards stood in his way, holding him back with their assault weapons, denying passage.

Joe shook his head violently. This didn't make sense! Why were they doing this to the kid?

"It was God's wish," Brother Joseph said simply, walking closer, staring down at the suffering child the way anyone else would look at a tree that needed pruning. "I wouldn't worry. God will take care of him, if that is His will."

"His will?" Joe said stupidly.

"God has asked me to do this in order to make the boy even more malleable to His will. He has been resisting of late. I heard the word of the Lord," Brother Joseph said, casting his eyes up in false piety. "So I obeyed. 'The Lord moves in mysterious ways.' I'm certain the reason will become clearer, but until then I must carry out the order he has given me, and only me."

Jamie whimpered again; in that helmet, his ears filled with white noise, he wouldn't even be able to hear himself crying. Joe remembered what Jamie's father said. *Thirty minutes? How long do they plan on keeping him in there?*

Joe turned and faced his father. "May I respectfully ask how this could possibly help us? He was already communicating with the . . . Holy Fire," he said, with an effort. "The latest channeling was the most successful of all. Might this push him over the edge? He is still mortal, Father. Might this overstep the bounds of mortality?" When he finished the sentence, he found he was shaking. His voice, too, betrayed some of his revulsion.

Luke had moved closer to Brother Joseph. Silhouetted in the light of the hallway, the two bore a striking resemblance to an evil Laurel and Hardy. Even though Brother Joseph's face was difficult to see in the dim light, Joe could sense his father's frowning. "I detect a note of protest to this situation, young man. Perhaps you had better rephrase the question."

Joe wiped sweat that had beaded on his forehead. Luke shuffled, coughed, and crossed his arms, as if trying to look important. James, the boy's father, stumbled over to a chair, where a bottle of whiskey was waiting.

"Is this deprivation supposed to help him in any way?" Joe asked carefully. *As if Jamie could take any more abuse,* he thought. *Starved till he's sick, and now this —*

"Perhaps. If the Lord wants to take him, this would be the time to do it. But I think not." Brother Joseph was looking down again at the child in the box, but his eyes were curiously unfocused. "Soon we will have another channeling, and Jamie is again to be the tool. This is, I suppose, a way to make him more receptive to the Holy Fire."

As his father replied, speaking with vague boredom, Joe realized that he had no intentions of letting Jamie out any time soon. *He's doing this because he enjoys it. He likes the fact that Jamie's scared half to death. God didn't tell him to do it, his own insanity did.*

It was going to happen all over again, the same thing that happened to Sarah, though perhaps in a slightly different form. But the end would be the same. A short struggle, then an unmarked grave in the sandy soil. Joe glanced again at Jamie, although he knew the child couldn't see him.

In his mind, their eyes met.

The boy squirmed, as if fighting the restraints. But the movement was so slight, and lacking in energy, that it was barely noticeable. Then he opened his mouth to speak, and what came out was not a whimper of pain but a whisper.

"Help me."

"You'll receive all the help you'll need, little one," Brother Joseph said, with mock gentleness. "Joshua, take him out now. You, son, come with me."

Joe hesitated as he watched the guards moving towards the tank, reaching for the straps on the helmet.

"Come with me now!" Brother Joseph ordered. Joe flinched and followed his father out of the room.

"Luke, you stay with them, make sure Jamie is returned to his new room. Remember, you're still in charge of him. Don't let anyone else near him. That includes our new head of Internal Security."

"Yes, sir," Luke said, snapping off a salute with a toothy, mindless grin. "And thank you, sir. I won't let you down."

"I certainly hope not," Brother Joseph said. The statement, uttered without emotion, had an ominous feel to it.

In shock, Joe followed his father out. After Brother Joseph closed the door behind them, he grabbed Joe by the shoulder and spun him around with surprising force.

"Now you listen to me, you little *shit*, and you listen good," Brother Joseph said, his face only a few inches from his son's. "I will not tolerate this attitude in any of my men, especially from my son! You are of my flesh and blood and you will obey me or suffer. It is clear to me that you disapprove of my treatment of Jamie. Am I right?"

Weakly, Joe shook his head.

His father slapped him once, hard. Joe's face snapped back at the impact. "Don't lie to me! You disapprove and I know it. That's why Luke is in charge of Jamie. You are now in charge of Internal Affairs, and that relieves you of *any* responsibility to the boy, do you understand me? You will have nothing to do with Jamie. You will not even look at Jamie. You will not be permitted at any channeling, and the only Praise Meeting you will be permitted to attend will be one in which *Jamie is somewhere else!* You made the right decisions last night, when we had the fire, but after that little exhibition of insubordination, I wonder if you really had my best interests in mind. If you are caught trying to communicate or assist Jamie in any way, you will be stripped of all rank and the privileges you now enjoy. There is nothing to discuss. My word is final. If you disobey, contradict or embarrass me in any way as a ranking officer of the Favored Ones, you will be court-martialed!"

Joe stared at his father, too numb with shock to feel anything.

"*Do you understand me?*" Brother Joseph shouted, spraying spittle in his son's face.

Joe did not know what to say, what to do, what to think. He felt as if he was frozen in a block of ice; he felt as if he was teetering on the brink of disaster, as if merely breathing would violate some unspoken law. Any answer could easily annoy his father further, so he said nothing. Then, slowly, he reached up and wiped the spit from his cheek.

His father seemed willing to wait forever for an answer. Several long moments passed before Joe summoned the courage to respond.

"Yes, I understand, sir," he said simply.

A faint, sardonic smile creased Brother Joseph's face. He seemed, at last, satisfied. "Good. Then you are dismissed."

Joe turned to leave, and had gone a few steps when his father said, just loud enough to make him jump a little, "Remember, son, you are now in a high profile position. And you represent me, both as my officer and as my son. I keep tabs on all of my officers, in particular the ones recently promoted. This is common knowledge. You will be watched. *Closely.* Do not embarrass me!"

Cindy, Al decided, as Andur crept into his usual spot near the Chosen Ones' hideout, *is beginning to suspect something.*

It had been an uneventful day; for much of it, Cindy had seemed content to watch him, as if by watching she could comprehend him. Coping with the revelation that elves were real, Al had learned from past experience, could take some time. She had spent some time at the pay-phones, calling different law enforcement agencies, using a tattered calling card that looked ready to disintegrate at any moment. Nothing had turned up, and she had returned to the Winnie in a depressed and subdued state, where she scrubbed the countertops again, obviously trying to keep herself occupied. It was all he could do to keep from telling her of his own progress.

It would complicate things, he decided. *As much as I want to ease her mind and tell her what I'm up to, to do so would probably attract attention I just don't want now. This situation is more volatile than anything I've handled before. The last thing I want is for the Salamander to notice us!* He felt a twinge of hurt pride; the Salamander couldn't know such things, could it? He was just flinching from an imagined attack, scared. No way for an elven noble to act. Right?

She was getting wise to him. Earlier today was proof of that. He'd thought he was going to be able to get away from the racetrack in his elvensteed without her seeing. Around the track Andur continued to be a Miata, although there was a chance that by now Cindy had guessed the truth about the beast. After all, there were several hundred other people here at any given time, and there was no point in breaking his cover now just because *one* of them knew what he was! But as he was trying to pull out of the parking lot, Cindy stood in his path, keeping him from leaving.

"You're not going anywhere until you tell me where you're going, buster," she announced sternly, though Al detected a hint of nervousness. "Do you have a harem of elf women somewhere to tickle your ears?"

Al sighed and Andur's motor idled down. "Don't I wish," he replied, trying to keep the mood light.

She continued to block his path.

"You know, you are making quite a scene here," he said conversationally. "People are going to notice."

"Let them notice," Cindy said, coming alongside the Miata and sitting presumptuously on the driver's door, looking down at Al. "They'll just think this is a lover's quarrel. The word all over the track is that we've been seen shacking up in that so-called 'Winnie.'"

"Well, you've got me there," Al said uncertainly, unable to ignore the burning he felt in the tips of his ears.

"I do believe you're getting embarrassed," Cindy noted with a hint of morose humor. "So. These little trips you've been making at night have really piqued my interest. You want to tell me where you're going, or should I *really* start making a scene?"

"Ah, no, don't do that," he said. He looked into her determined face and felt something inside him surrender. "All right. You win."

Cindy smiled in victory, her eyebrows raised in question marks.

"I'm meeting with other elves," he lied smoothly. "It's like I'm going deep, deep, *deep* undercover, meeting other agents, you see? We're following leads. Nothing on Jamie yet. Nothing solid."

"Hmm," she said. She didn't sound convinced. "Why don't they meet you here?"

"Are you kidding?" he replied, slapping his forehead for effect. "With all this metal? You forget what an anomaly I am. Most elves shy away from human settlements, even ones like this that are easy to blend into. There's too much iron and steel around here. Their magic doesn't work. We've got to meet secretly in the woods and have conferences in the shadows of tall oaks." He folded his arms resolutely and glanced stubbornly away. "It's an elven thing."

"I see," she said, but it wasn't really clear that she did. Or that she really believed him. She stood, her expression still suspicious, that tiny touch of humor quite gone. "I don't suppose I'm going to get more out of you than that," she said. "It's better than nothing. You let me know when you find out where Jamie is, okay?"

"I will," Al said, with more confidence. *I'm not lying. I don't know where he is . . . exactly.*

He drove off, but he was aware of her eyes following him until he was out of sight. And he wasn't at all comfortable.

Her determination is disturbing. She's getting desperate, as any mother would. She suspects I'm being less than honest with her —

Well, she's right. I'm hiding things from her. She doesn't trust me. Not that I blame her. Not only am I a stranger, I'm a strange stranger.

Though it was not quite dark yet, he left Andur in his hiding place and started through the woods towards the Chosen Ones. *A thing as evil as the Salamander will be weakest at twilight, when the world of light crosses the world of darkness, and all creatures of the Earth are somewhat befuddled. At least, that's the theory. This Salamander could be one of twilight, in which case my elven behind is nailed but good.*

There weren't many guards this time of night, Al noted with interest as he assumed his position in the boughs of a great oak. His agenda included studying the layout again, analyzing the damage he created the last time he was there, and fishing for clues to Jamie's precise whereabouts.

All this, and without the Salamander seeing me. Tricky stuff. Perhaps if I had to I could disguise my magics as something other than what they are. He remembered the girl-spirit he had seen before, during the Praise Meeting. *The child certainly was busy. If she hadn't been distracted during that out-of-body choreography she might have seen me. Let's see. Is there a meeting tonight?*

He probed the surfaces of the Chosen Ones' buildings, finding a strange absence of activity. *Not much going on. No meeting, that's for certain. The hall they met in is deserted.* He probed further, finding a few guards posted here and there through the complex. He wondered if the entire lot had just vanished, when he traced one of the power lines to the huge dining room where nearly all of the Chosen Ones had congregated. A swift scan of the people failed to turn up Jamie. But then, he remembered, the boy was being kept elsewhere, probably in isolation.

Al pulled back and thought this over. *They seem to have only a skeleton force of security during mealtime, which appears to be around dusk. If we were to go in and get the boy, a time like now would be perfect.* He froze as a guard strolled beneath the tree, and Alinor cursed himself for not throwing up another spell to help conceal him. As soon as the soldier passed, Al replaced the earlier night's spell of unnoticability.

He reached into the complex again, this time probing a bit deeper into the complex of tunnels and rooms, a little surprised to find areas he had missed previously. *This place is enormous,* he thought. *It could hold twice as many as it does now, and with room to spare.*

Al sent his mind following electrical lines down one of the heavily modified areas and suddenly touched a sensitive mind. Now he had eyes and ears! He firmed his contact, and his elven blood chilled when he discovered that the person was one of two walking with Brother Joseph towards one of the huge storage rooms. The other man besides Joseph was overweight and radiated a strong sense of low intelligence, but the one whose mind he had touched was much younger and brighter.

And the younger one was very receptive to his probe. Enough so that Al could ride along in his mind, an unseen, unguessed passenger, eavesdropping on everything.

As he listened to the conversation, he caught the younger one's identity with a shock of surprise.

That's Brother Joseph's son. And he doesn't seem too comfortable here.

They paused before a reinforced door — and when the doors opened up, he could hardly believe what was inside.

If it had been hard for him to keep from flying to Jamie's rescue before, it was doubly hard now. His blood heated with rage, and he bit at the tree limb he clutched like one of the old berserkers, to keep from flinging himself down and taking them all on in single-handed combat. He fought a silent battle with himself just to keep his arms and armor from manifesting, a battle that he came within a hair of losing.

Through Joe's eyes he saw the boy buried in a sensory deprivation tank, a torture so barbaric he could hardly believe the truth of his own senses.

He had to do something. *Now.*

His heart ached as he left Joe's mind and probed the boy's mind for injuries. It was not as bad as he had feared. The child was incredibly resilient; he had suffered no ill-effects from the hallucinations he experienced. Oddly enough, it was the dull gnawing of unrelenting starvation that had helped keep him sane. It was the one constant that the boy could cling to that he knew was real. There was some bruising from beatings — but not as much as he'd feared. Evidently Brother Joseph had come to the conclusion early on that physical punishment would get him nowhere with this child.

I can send a healing to him, Al thought, grimly. *It won't do much for the starvation, but it will help with his other problems.*

The elf reached into the life-web all around him, summoning the power needed to reach the child and heal him, when he became aware of something. Something that flickered like a black fire, stirring from its sleep. At first it was only at the periphery of his powers, emerging from the darkness of its slumber, and he couldn't quite identify it. But then, as it became fully awake, he had no doubt as to what it was.

If I send a healing to the boy, it will light me up like a fireworks display to the Salamander's Sight! he thought in dismay. *Even now, with this simple contact, it might see me. If it attacks me now —*

He withdrew quickly, before the Salamander could sense him — he hoped. If he attracted its attention he could easily become history, of no help to the boy or his mother. Alinor withdrew entirely into himself, letting no betraying spark of Power leak past his shields. He made himself as dark and invisible as the night that had formed around him.

Hiding again. You'd better redeem yourself, Alinor, or your long life will be miserable indeed. . . .

He checked the area — with non-magical senses. A few more guards had taken up positions nearby, but all had the lethargic auras of men who have recently overeaten. *Something else to note. The next shift isn't very alert. Another time a move to liberate Jamie might be most successful.*

He sent a tendril of energy beyond his shields, just enough to see if the Salamander was there, but not enough to give him away. The evil creature was out there, but wasn't directing any energy his way; it seemed more interested in the suffering child — and, oddly enough, the drunken man who was watching him.

But there was something else moving within the confines of the compound, a bright and energetic something that instantly seized his attention. No, not something — someone. And he had seen her before.

The girl.

He turned his attention from the "real" world to the other world: the halfworld. There she was; a glimmer of energy, of spirit, that was quietly, diligently *watching* him. He had no doubts that she had spotted him long before he sensed her, had seen him sitting there in his precarious position in the tree in spite of the "expert" shieldings he had put up.

And she knew when he'd seen her, too.

:Who are you?: she asked, impudently. *:A munchkin?:*

Al didn't respond at once. He wanted to be certain that their conversation was a private one. She drew closer, to the edge of his shields, but no closer.

The nearer you are, he thought, without actually sending the thought, *the less likely that thing will overhear us.*

As if reading his mind, she dropped a portion of her own shields and stepped inside the safety of his.

:Stay away from the monster,: she warned, casting a look in the direction of the Salamander. *:It doesn't see me, and I don't want it to.:*

:I don't either,: Al said, and relaxed. *:Hey, you're pretty smart. What's your name?:*

Although she was only a few feet away, she was still a spirit hovering on the edge of the real world, and her image wavered from translucent to almost solid. She still appeared to be leery of him, a healthy caution.

Then again, to operate as a spirit in such close proximity to the Salamander, and to remain undetected, would require a long habit of caution. *She's been smart and cautious, or she wouldn't be here talking to me. She would already have been consumed, drained to nothing and sent to drift off until someone pulled her across to the Summerlands.*

"Sarah," she said. The reply was closer to speech now than the thought-message she had been sending; with such beings, Al knew, this usually meant a bridge of trust had been established. She looked down now, a little sad, perhaps embarrassed. Al was uncertain what her next move would be as her features became fluid, mistlike. She pointed down towards the Chosen Ones buildings. "I used to live down there."

She's a ghost, and she knows it, Al thought, careful to keep his thoughts to himself. *This is the spirit who was helping Jamie through the channeling. I need to get her to work with me if I can manage it.*

"What are you?" she repeated. "You can see me but

you're sitting there in that tree. You're solid." Her tone became accusatory. "You're alive. But not like most people."

"I'm not," Al supplied. "Remember hearing about elves when you were a . . . well, do you remember hearing stories about elves?"

She stared at him for a long moment. "Naaaw," she finally said. "Those were just fairy tales. You can't be."

"Yes, I am," he said, then glanced down at a guard, who was walking beneath the tree. The Chosen One didn't look up, but his nearness still made Al nervous. Silently, he held a finger to his lips. Why, he wasn't sure; only he could see, or hear, the ghost.

She looked at him with unmistakable derision. "So which one are you? Sneezy, Sleepy, Stupid . . ."

Al shook his head. "Those are *dwarves*, not elves. Anyway, those are make-believe. I'm the real thing." He smiled, feebly. "You can call me Al."

"Huh. An elf named *Al*? Am I s'posed to believe that? What are you doing sitting in the tree? Are you one of *them*?" she continued in an accusatory tone, indicating the guards below.

"No. No, I'm here for another reason," he said, trying to conceal an aching heart from the girl. Just a child. And now —

She said she was from down there. Was she a Chosen One once? She must have been, so how did she die?

Jamie — had she been his predecessor? She knew about the Salamander — had she learned through first-hand experience?

How could he possibly ask her that?

"You a spy?" she suddenly said, and Al could sense a sudden surge of interest. "Like James Bond? Like in the movies?"

Whatever happened to her, the Chosen Ones must be her enemies, he thought, remembering the bizarre Praise Meeting and the careful way she had shielded Jamie from the worst the Salamander could do to him. *She was aiding Jamie during that channeling. She's good, too, because the Salamander didn't move against her. Shall I take a chance with this?*

Do I have a choice?

"Kind of. I'm here to spy on the group down there," he said. "You know, Brother Joseph's church. Did you say you used to belong down there?"

He would have asked her more, but the wash of terror that spread from her to him stopped him cold. "Brother Joseph?" she quavered. "What do you want with him?"

"He took — stole — the son of a friend away from us. I think he's doing something with the little boy, but I'm having a hard time finding out anything." At the unmistakable quickening of interest he felt, he continued. "His mother is here, looking for him. He's from Atlanta, and he came here with his father, but his father is not a nice man. He kidnaped Jamie away from his mother, and I think he gave Jamie to Brother Joseph."

"You're looking for *Jamie?*" she asked, and the question seemed filled with hope. "Jamie's down there. You saw him, didn't you?"

"I saw him." He let his voice harden. "I didn't like what I saw." He took a brief moment to break away from the contact with Sarah to seek Jamie out, worming a tiny tendril of awareness through the complex maze. He was gone; at least he was no longer in the deprivation box.

Al returned his attention to Sarah, a little relieved. "I've got to figure a way to get him out of there. I'm not like you. Their guns can still hurt me." He hesitated. Had he said too much? Did she really *know* what she was? But it was too late to take his words back now. "I can't get through the other things, like fences and doors. But I *can* talk to you, and right now I think we need each other's help if we're going to help Jamie."

He paused and tried to sense if she had been hurt or frightened by his words. "You know — you're not the way you used to be, don't you?"

She shrugged; a ripple in the mist. "It's okay, Al. I know I'm a ghost. Sometimes I don't like it, I want to go on through to the other side, but I feel like I have to help Jamie. Brother Joseph killed me." She solidified for a moment, and there was a look of implacable hatred on her face that turned it into a terrible parody of a little girl's. "I've got to do what I can to keep him from doing it again. That's why I'm still here, helping Jamie."

Then she changed, lightning-like, to an attitude of childlike enthusiasm. "So what do we do now?"

Al considered his options. *From Earthplane to Spirit to . . .*

Hmm . . . well, the next logical step would be Earthplane again, to someone alive and breathing. Perhaps someone who is disgruntled or unhappy. Someone who can physically help us inside the compound. Maybe even some one who could carry Jamie out of there, when the time is right.

"I think I have an idea, Sarah. Here's what I'd like you to do . . ."

:Jamie?: he heard Sarah say from somewhere in the darkness. *:Where are you?:*

His eyes had been closed, but when she spoke the words were like light, breaking through the pain.

He had been dreaming about being tied to a big tree and left there for dead, when a big bony vulture in a pale suit walked in with Joe and just stood there, watching him. Joe didn't do anything to help, and he couldn't understand why, since he had done everything before to make him safe in this horrible world called the "vacation place." He trusted Joe in all things; Joe even brought him food when no one else would. But this must have been a dream, because otherwise Joe would have taken him down out of the tree or at least blown away the vulture with his assault rifle.

Jamie felt hot and knew he must be running a temperature. Otherwise he wouldn't be so sweaty all the time. And he felt so *sick*. He could hardly move, he was so weak. He didn't know where the restroom was, and he couldn't get up anyway, so he just went, like a baby. He didn't like it, and he felt a vague discomfort from somewhere deep in the darkness, but he didn't know what else to do about it.

His whole body had felt funny, heavy and light at the same time, while he was hanging there in the tree, but now it felt like everything was going back to normal. When he tried to open his eyes, it took a minute to realize that he had, since the room had no light.

:Sarah,: Jamie thought, his mind forming the words when his mouth and vocal cords could not. *:What are they doing to me?:*

:Take it easy,: Sarah said, but the words came uneasily, as if she really didn't believe what she was saying. Jamie didn't like that. *:You can go a lot longer like this.:*

:No, I can't!: Jamie protested. *:They're never going to let me see my mom again. They all lied to me. Joe's the only one who told me the truth. They're hiding me from her, Joe said, and they won't let her see me even if she knew I was here.:* He felt tears burning down the side of his face. *:I haven't eaten in I don't know how long. Sometimes the hunger goes away for a while, but it always comes back. Then I have to wet myself and that's something little babies do. What will they do next, put diapers on me?:*

He listened to the silence, knowing somehow that she was still there.

:I'm hungry so much my arms are getting thin. If they don't give me food soon I'm going to just disappear!:

:No, you are not,: Sarah said, sounding like a grownup just then. *:Hold on. Help is on the way.:*

As hope flared, Jamie summoned the strength to sit up precariously on a bony elbow, and looked into the darkness. At first he thought the light that became brighter just then was Sarah, then he saw they were just dizzy-stars.

:Help? Who's coming to help? Joe?:

:Sort of. There will be others. Just hang on a little longer.:

:Sarah? Are you still there?:

The lights faded, and Sarah's presence faded into the darkness.

:Where are you?:

The more Joe thought about it, the more certain he was that the two regular Guard soldiers who were helping him move into his new digs were spies, working directly for his father. They were older than he was by a few years and had been around the Sacred Heart for as long as Joe could remember, and should have been promoted to captain long before now. If there was any resentment in them about Joe's new rank, they didn't show it. They paid the proper respect and sub-servience in his presence, and what little Joe overheard when they weren't directly under his eye did not betray feelings to the contrary.

They performed the tasks set them without a flaw, like robots, or well-oiled cogs in the machine Joe's father had built. Before, he would have been proud of his father's accomplishment. But seeing their lack of emotion, their total implied commitment to Joe and his father, made his skin crawl. If he told them to march into the pond, he had no doubt in his mind that they would do just that.

He began to doubt their facade, however, when he caught them glancing in his direction a few times as if they were trying to make certain whether he was watching them. Then, once, he saw them communicating with some sort of obscure hand signals that he didn't recognize. When he saw that, Joe turned cold. *Spies. For father, and Luke too, no doubt. Figures.*

That he was now head of Internal Security and

should investigate, or at least question, such behavior, was never a consideration. For the time being, anyway, he just didn't care. After seeing Jamie that afternoon, he'd felt numb all over, incapable then of feeling much of anything.

Within the first half-hour of moving into the new apartment, he noticed two tiny microphones, each about the size of a fly, inserted into the ceiling. He wondered if there were miniature video cameras, which would have been the size of a pencil eraser, somewhere in his new place. Until he learned otherwise, he would have to assume there were. And act accordingly. In fact, he wouldn't be at all surprised if a view of his new living room was being presented to the main security station on one of the little monitors on the wall. Perhaps he should wave.

That would only let them know I know, and I don't think I want that yet, he thought, as he made a point of acting as normally as possible. *It's late afternoon now. Dinner will be served soon. I'll most definitely have to put in an appearance there. Even if I'm not very hungry, after what I saw today.*

Jamie. Locked in a box like a lab rat. Already a skeleton from starvation. The haunting memory of the boy's eyes back when he'd tried to get him free — they'd looked at each other for the briefest moment, but that moment was stamped into his memory and wouldn't let him go. It pulled at a place in the middle of his chest, stabbed at his heart with surgical precision. *He trusted me. And now look at what's happened.*

He began to wonder if he had indeed waited too long, that Jamie was doomed even if he acted now to save him. *Sooner or later Father is going to kill him. And why? For what? When Jamie dies, Father is going to lose his precious channeller. It can't have anything to do with reason. My father is simply being sadistic.*

At this, Joe frowned. *Why does that surprise me?* The answer to that was not immediately clear. *Because all along*

I've been denying the truth. When he raised me, he smothered me with deceit that I'm still peeling away, like the plastic wrap on a choice piece of meat. But I have to face facts. My father is doing this because he enjoys seeing others suffer. He likes knowing he has the power of life and death over people. It makes him feel good and serves his own enormous ego.

An ego that will never completely be satisfied. . . .

What a prick.

He looked around at his new place, reluctantly admiring the wealth that surrounded him, and realized that he had been waiting for years to have a place like this. To him*self.* The rank of lieutenant was also something he had dreamed of, but he had thought it would be years away, as there were so many more qualified soldiers in front of him. Now both had been handed to him, by his father, on a silver platter. Although the soldiers who had helped him move in gave no hint that they were jealous, he knew they had to be, on a certain level. *But then, all of Father's wealth has been taken without regard to right or wrong. It's pretty typical for him to hand his son all this stuff, the title, the job, the apartment, without bothering to justify it. He's God's own, right? He doesn't have to justify anything.*

He realized the hour was late and began getting ready for dinner. In the bathroom he regarded the enormous bath with mild curiosity, saw immediately that it was empty. With no obvious means to fill it. Well, it didn't matter.

He stripped and climbed into the shower.

As the hot water washed over his body, he tried to put Jamie out of his mind. But the more he tried, the more solid the memory became. *What did I see in those eyes?* he wondered at the recollection. *He was begging me, but was he accusing me, as well? He might as well have; I'm as guilty as my father.* That he was taking a hot shower in luxury brought on enough guilt; poor Jamie, he knew, was probably lying on a mattress somewhere, too weak to go to the john. *And I can't get food to him. Father made that clear. I'd be drawn, quartered and hung out to dry if I was caught near him. With all the cameras and security in this place, I'll be lucky to be able to use the bathroom without someone watching me.*

At that thought, he glanced up at the ceiling, half-expecting to find a camera staring down at him. *They'd do it, too. Especially Luke. He'd probably have a camera put in here just so he could see me without any clothes.*

Joe put on a clean dress uniform that had just arrived from the laundry and was surprised to find the lieutenant's insignia already attached to it. *Guess Father decided to dispense with the ceremony,* he thought, in a way glad that it had been done this way. The ceremony, at best, would have been awkward. He shrugged and put the uniform on with the new insignia, in spite of the fact he didn't feel he deserved it.

As he donned the uniform, a voice from deep within him reminded him of a poignant fact:

If you don't do anything to help Jamie, the boy will die.

He stopped in the middle of combing his short, blond hair in the mirror and looked himself in the eye. He couldn't remember when he had last performed this simple act of self-searching, and he found it difficult, especially when he was wearing the Chosen Ones' uniform. He felt like a monster. The uniform seemed to be alive; he thought he felt it crawling on his body, like some sort of parasite. He didn't belong in it, and he knew it.

I've got to get out of here, contact the authorities, with or without the evidence. Who knows, maybe there's a missing person's file somewhere with Jamie's name on it. If his mother is looking for him, then there would have to be. But to let anyone know about Jamie, I've got to figure out a way to escape this complex without anyone knowing, at least until I'm well clear. If they come after me, well, I'll just have to spot them before they spot me.

After making his decision, again, he felt a little bit better about himself. In the shiny new uniform, he walked straight, with his head up, strengthened by the knowledge he would soon be ridding himself of it.

Dinner was a strange affair. Rather pointedly, Brother Joseph reminded him that he no longer had to eat with the "grunts," that he could now eat in the senior officers' hall which adjoined the central dining hall. He was still not invited to eat with his father, who dined separately from everyone, but that still suited Joe just fine. *The farther away I am from him, the better. What I'm thinking about here is treason, and my body language will give me away for sure if I don't watch out.*

The senior officers said little after saying grace, just a few bland comments about the quality of the food, which he had to admit was excellent and far superior to what the rest of the Chosen Ones ate. Each of them had been served an individual Cornish game hen, real potatoes au gratin and pasta salad, all delicacies and not at all what he was used to. The meal was served on china, with real silver utensils, and the dining room was furnished plushly, like his own quarters; the contrast between this room and the main dining hall was startling.

He couldn't help noticing as he ate that the atmosphere was definitely strained. No one said much of anything, and Joe had the feeling this was due in part to his presence. The ten officers were men in their forties, and as the meal progressed he felt progressively more and more uneasy. There were five captains, four other lieutenants and General Plunket, Commander of the Guard, who was an old man in his seventies who had actually served in World War II — ancient history to Joe. The general said little as he ate, and became slightly drunk on the carafe of wine as the meal proceeded, which seemed to be typical for dinner, as none of the other men seemed to notice.

"That certainly is a smart outfit you've trained there, sir," one of the lieutenants said, with a suddenness that made Joe jump. The man, Lieutenant Fisher, had been his teacher in a few bomb-making courses. More Junior Guard training, information which he had promptly forgotten. Right now if Fisher had asked him how to make the simplest black-powder pipe bomb, Joe would have had to admit that he couldn't remember. Joe regarded him cautiously, expecting his politeness to be a veil for something sarcastic, but he saw only sincerity in the man's face.

Fisher cleared his throat and continued. "I think you will make a fine addition to the senior staff."

"Thank you, sir," Joe said, almost saluting there at the table. He stopped himself in time. *Looks like I'm gonna have to feel my way around how to treat these guys.* "I'm looking forward to serving as your Internal Security head."

Fisher nodded in agreement but said nothing.

"Damned Nazis, they had the right idea!" Plunket roared from the head of the table, a response to a murmured question from one of the other men. "Train the youths. They had millions of their young 'uns trained to step in at a moment's notice. Had them running the government, the utilities, the post office. We came in through a town of about twelve thousand and all we found were teenagers and old people too feeble to walk, and the kids were running everything! Their fathers had already been conscripted, years before. He had the right idea, Hitler did. Kill the Jew pigs, and make sure the next generation understands why it had to be done!"

He pounded the table for emphasis. Silverware and glasses hopped momentarily. Joe wished he were somewhere, anywhere, else.

"Thank you, sir," he said, because he felt like he had to. "I'm certain the Junior Guard will become true fighting men when they are old enough."

"Here, here," one of the captains murmured. General Plunket muttered something else that was unintelligible. The wine appeared to be catching up to him.

Joe wanted to disappear. *I'm starting to like the compliments,* he realized. *This whole dinner is making me feel proud of them all over again. And I want out!*

One of the officers poured wine, what was left, into Joe's empty glass. "Here, have a drink," he said. Joe accepted without a word, although he didn't like the taste of alcohol, or its effects. *Even Father has a glass now and then. Said it had something to do with making the men feel more comfortable.*

But he had a lot of reasons for not liking what alcohol did to him, and one of them had to do with the walls he had carefully constructed, barriers which he maintained to keep his gift of reading thoughts a secret. *I lose control of it when I drink,* he told himself. Then, *But just one glass shouldn't hurt.* He took a sip and briefly resisted the urge to spit it out. This was a very dry and *bitter* wine, which he didn't care for at all. He would have preferred straight shots of Listerine to this.

"What exactly does your new position entail?" Plunket asked, looking as if he was struggling to get the words out clearly. "'Internal Security.' What does that mean?"

At first Joe was a bit alarmed. *Didn't Father brief him on the new office? Plunket is, after all, in charge of the army. And my superior. Damn him!*

But the one gulp of wine had loosened him up some, and the words came tumbling out.

"Brother Joseph says that it's something we've needed for some time," Joe began. "'Internal Security' is exactly what it says. There are threats from within this organization as well as the obvious ones without. There could be spies. There could be infiltrators. Why, even some of our own trusted men could turn out to be FBI agents or even worse, liberals."

He took another sip of the wine, not quite realizing

until he set the glass down that a deathly silence had fallen over the table. Gone were conversation and the clink of silverware; everyone had frozen in place. A sickening feeling of somehow screwing up came over him; his right hand, still holding a fork, began to shake. They were all staring at him, silently.

"What I mean is, I don't think anyone in the Guard is suspect. New recruits —"

"I think," General Plunket said, with horrible clarity, "that you have said quite enough, young man. I will take this up with our leader. It would appear that you have been misguided in this endeavor."

Joe nodded, not even having the strength to speak. He felt suddenly lightheaded, partially due to the wine, but mostly to his embarrassment.

Why did I have to open my mouth? He wanted to scream. *I should have known all this crap would have been a secret even from the other officers. God, what a fool I am!*

It was then he realized that he was going to throw up. He felt his gorge rising, and uneasiness somewhere deep in his stomach, so he had time to leave to room before it came up. *Get out of here,* he thought. *Before I puke my guts out all over this table.*

He stood and politely excused himself. Amid silent stares, which he could feel burning holes in his back, Joe left the officers' dining hall and began searching desperately for a restroom.

Moments later, after retching none too quietly into a toilet, Joe contemplated flushing himself down the sewer as well. *It would make the perfect end to this day,* he moaned, catching his breath in the stall. *If I were just a little smaller than I feel right now, it would probably work. Good-bye cruel world. Flush.*

In the washbasin he cleaned up some, still a little queasy but feeling better now that the wine was out of his system. He was contemplating a roundabout route back to his new room, so that he wouldn't have to see anybody, when he became aware that he was no longer alone in the bathroom.

He knew immediately that it wasn't someone or something that had been there when he entered, and couldn't see how anyone could have come in without his hearing them. He turned slowly, expecting to find another adult sneering at him. Instead, he saw a little girl, standing in the corner.

She must have already been here, he thought, though he couldn't see how. *What's she doing in the men's room anyway?*

They regarded each other in silence for several moments; Joe still felt dizzy from being ill, and it wasn't until his eyes had focused completely that he thought he had seen her somewhere before.

"What are you doing in here?" he asked, trying not to sound harsh. "This is the men's room. Little girls aren't supposed to be in here."

"I'm not a little girl anymore," she said, and vanished.

A light rose from where she stood, a vague, glowing mist of something that came towards him quickly before he could step back. It touched him; it felt like a child's breath brushing across his face. Then it was gone.

Joe was too stunned to react. *What in God's name was that?* he thought.

But a moment later, he decided that what he had just seen was a hallucination, brought about by the bad wine he'd swallowed at dinner. *Time to go to bed. I'm starting to see things.*

As much as he wanted to put the disturbing vision behind him, he couldn't. On his way back to his new room, he couldn't shake the feeling that he had seen that particular girl before. It wasn't until he reached his front door and turned the key that he knew, with the suddenness of a revelation, who the little girl was. And why she vanished as dramatically as she did.

No, it can't be, he thought, horrified at the prospect of dealing with a ghost. *I am seeing things. I must be.*

He opened his door in a daze of confused shock. And there was his father, Brother Joseph, sitting in an easy chair reading one of his son's books. He looked up as Joe entered and smiled a predatory smile.

"I've been waiting for you," he said calmly. "Please, come in. We have a few things to talk about."

• CHAPTER TEN

"Father," Joe said weakly. "I wasn't expecting you."

Brother Joseph shifted in the chair, holding the book carefully between his two bony hands, as if it were something that might contaminate him. Joe stood frozen in the doorway, afraid to leave or enter.

"That much is obvious," he replied acidly. "Or you would have seen fit to at least conceal this work of the devil. As it is, anyone could have seen this misrepresentation of my ideals. Come. Sit. Let's talk."

Joe cautiously closed the door behind him, expecting a serious explosion to happen at any moment. His father had that sedate look about him that he had come to associate with the calm before the storm. He took a few tentative steps into the room, towards his father, then saw which book he was referring to.

For one moment, relief flooded him. "Father, that's only a novel," he protested, unable to think of anything else to say. He knew it was a mistake, but he had no idea how serious a mistake it was, until his father's face darkened with rage.

"*Only a novel?*" he spat. "Only? My own eyes have seen empires fall on the strength of a novel!"

Joe stood silently, trying hard not to fidget. The book in question, *Interview with the Vampire* by Anne Rice, had been a paperback he'd picked up in Atlanta, before they had even relocated the Church in Oklahoma. At the time he hadn't thought twice about it. Then, later, he realized how unwise it would be to let anyone in the church see it. Vampires meant the occult, the occult meant Satanism, Satanism meant hell and damnation and evil. Even in fiction. Apparently, in the move to his new digs, some of his things had become jostled. At this point, he wasn't even sure if he'd hidden the book before moving, as insignificant it seemed to him. It would appear that the two guardsmen who "helped" him move had seen the book and reported it directly to his father.

"Forgive me, Father," he said, with as much meekness as he could summon. "I intended no insult to the church. It never occurred to me that a book of fiction could be dangerous — that anything in it could be taken seriously. Thank you for correcting me."

"Very well," Brother Joseph said, flinging the book into an unoccupied corner of the room. It flapped like a wounded butterfly. *Paperbacks just aren't aerodynamic.*

The bathroom was beyond his father, and the illuminated doorway framed him with a soft white glow. The lighting in the room itself was subdued, mostly because the furniture hadn't been arranged yet, and many of the lamps were still unplugged. Joe thought he saw something move in the bathroom, but wasn't certain. His father continued, oblivious to everything but the opportunity to make a speech, even though his audience consisted of one.

"Vampires are creatures of the occult. Anything occult is the work of the devil. Novels in general foster mischief. Fiction by definition is a lie — something that isn't real and isn't true. There is no reason to read a lie. I would suggest you limit your reading to the Chosen Ones' Reading List."

"Yes, sir," Joe said humbly. Even sitting in the chair, Brother Joseph still managed to look down on him.

Brother Joseph gazed on him sternly before continuing. "You must understand, Joe, that as my son you represent me. I can't have you reading this fictional garbage, this so-called literature. It weakens the mind and poisons the soul. I suggest that you cull out any unauthorized books from your possession, or I will have it done for you."

Again there was the flicker of movement, this time a little more prolonged, from the bathroom. It was obvious this time that there was something there, that it wasn't just some aftereffect of the wine. Brother Joseph looked away, as if pondering some philosophical concept. When Joe felt it was safe to divert his attention to the motion in the room, he glanced over to the side, to the bright doorway.

The corner of the luxurious hot tub was barely visible. Sitting on the edge of the hot tub was the little girl, the same one that had shown up in the men's room moments before. She watched him, calculatedly, with coldly adult eyes. Joe gulped and found himself steadying his weight against a chair.

"Son, are you feeling ill?" Brother Joseph asked, and Joe was surprised at the level of concern in his voice. "You've become very pale. Why don't you have a seat?"

Gratefully, Joe did as was suggested, sitting uncomfortably on a box.

That can't be who I think it is, Joe thought frantically. *What's she doing here? Why is is she sitting in my bathroom, watching me? How'd she get there?* He felt his world turning cartwheels. *That's not a little girl. She couldn't have gotten in here . . . who am I trying to kid, anyway? That's a ghost. That's Sarah!*

The girl opened her mouth to speak, but when her lips moved he heard her voice in his mind.

:You've got that right,: she said. *:Very clever, Joe. Now, get rid of your father. We've got a few things to talk about.:*

"Plunket said you were acting a bit odd tonight," Brother Joseph continued, unperturbed. "How was the meal?"

Joe thought he was going to faint, or even get ill again, but he had nothing left to throw up.

As if reading his mind, Sarah continued. *:Emptied your stomach already? Now you have an idea what Jamie feels like. Only by now it's much worse for him.:*

He wanted to scream. He wanted to defend himself, tell her that he was doing everything he could to help Jamie, but there were too many obstacles — one of which was in the room with them.

His stomach writhed. If he were to become ill again, he would have to go past Sarah, this ghost, to get to the toilet. *I'd rather choke on it,* he decided.

His father was staring at him, his lips pursed. The concern had changed to something else—calculation. Joe was one of his pawns—but a valuable one. Worth caring for.

"Perhaps you should lie down," he said. "I have to admit, I did become concerned when our general, Plunket, took me aside in the hallway and said you were acting very strange. And asked me about a few things that he felt needed clarifying. Security matters. Most notably, the role of your new office."

Sarah stood up, tossing her head angrily, her little hands on her hips. It was a stance he remembered, when she was defying his father during those last horrible days. She opened her mouth.

:Jamie's going to die!: she shouted into his mind.

He couldn't take any more of it. Telling her that it wasn't his fault became the most important thing to him just then. But he had to do it in a way that wouldn't attract his father's attention. *I'll have to reach down and use that . . . gift,* he thought, but the prospect felt as horrifying as as facing Luke had last night. *I swore I'd never use the gift again. Not since Luke tried to rape me. Never. . . . Jamie, I'm doing my best for him but — oh Lord, please help me through this.*

Then, incredibly, he watched her take a few steps toward them, into the room.

:DON'T COME IN HERE!: he screamed at her, but the words were silent, sent by his mind alone. One

corner of his mouth twitched, that was all his father saw. That, and probably the fact that he went even paler, for he could feel the blood draining from his face.

The power inside him seemed to burst out, like a spotlight, like the sudden bellow of a bullhorn. *:Don't let him see you. You don't know what will happen,:* he continued, closing his eyes and feeling a cold sweat breaking out all over his body. *:Please.:*

She hesitated a moment, as if considering the request. He thought she'd never make up her mind. He hoped she'd take forever. He wished he could die, then and there, and get it over with.

:Oh, all right,: she said, petulantly. *:Just get rid of him. I just wanted you to talk to me, after all.:*

He wiped sweat off his forehead, considering his words carefully. *:It might take a while. Don't rush me.:*

"It wasn't my intention to reveal the exact nature of your new position until later," Brother Joseph continued, ostentatiously ignoring the fact that Joe was staring past his shoulder, into the bathroom. Or maybe he simply interpreted Joe's fixed stare as another symptom of his illness. "Until now it has been a secret, more or less. At least, as far as the senior officers were concerned."

"Huh?" Joe said, knowing he just missed something important. "I'm sorry, Father, you were right, I'm not feeling well tonight. What was that you said?"

His father fixed him with the same fierce glare that a snake would fasten on a mouse it didn't care to eat — yet. "Son, pay attention to me. I don't care if you're sick. You want to know why I don't care? Because the enemy won't care. They could attack us at any moment and it won't matter if you're sick or not. The Jew Commie pigs would probably be glad if we were all sick. You'll have to learn how to do your duty awake or asleep, sick or healthy, and you might as well start right now. Now listen up. This is official business."

Joe sat up and tried to look healthy.

"Do I have your attention?" Brother Joseph did not even try to rein in his sarcasm.

He nodded and tried to sit as straight as he stood on the drill field.

His father snorted. "Good. Show some spine, boy. Show that you come of good blood, *my* blood, that you've inherited a little stamina!"

"Yes, sir," he said, faintly. "Stamina, sir."

His father snorted. "*As* I was saying earlier, your new job as the head of Internal Security was supposed to be cloaked somewhat in secrecy. There are those who think that maybe we don't need an internal office of any kind, that our screening of newcomers is as thorough and efficient as it can be. But it's not enough. You want to know why?"

He blinked and tried to keep his expression attentive and humble. "Why, of course, Father."

Brother Joseph continued, but Joe got the feeling that he would have done so no matter what Joe's response had been. "Good. It's simple. The Evil One works in perverted and mysterious ways. We can't deceive ourselves into thinking that we're immune because of our holiness and purity. He can invade and attack us from within, working on the little hidden weaknesses, the tiny sins people think aren't important enough to confess and do penance for. The Holy Fire keeps this thing away for the most part, but it has told me that the devil is busy at work in our little community. That ruckus a few nights back, the flooding, the electrical problems, none of which were ever explained. That was the devil. That was Satan. And he didn't need permission from nobody to invade our sacred ground!"

Joe took a deep breath, preparing himself, to the best of his ability, for a long sermon. He glanced up to see Sarah had seated herself on top of the counter, patiently waiting for his father to finish whatever non-sense he was spouting.

His father stood up and began rocking back and forth, as if he *was* giving a sermon. "In retrospect, I believe that I'm glad your meeting with Plunket went as it did. I wanted that element of surprise. And believe you me, he was surprised. He's a good, experienced man, and I'm glad he's on our side. But he's one of these who believe that we are immune to Satan. His faith in my abilities to lead, govern and protect isn't misguided. I do these things well, as no other can do them. But I know better than to think that I can't be thwarted. Satan has fouled up my plans more than once. If he gets the chance he'll do it again."

"I understand, Father," Joe said, summoning as much strength as he could, trying to look as attentive as possible. But it wasn't easy.

:*I'm getting tired of waiting,*: Sarah said.

:*I can't rush him,*: he replied in alarm.

:*Well, then maybe I can,*: she said, with just enough mischief in her words to further alarm him.

She came into the room, so swiftly he didn't actually see her move. He froze as she walked past Brother Joseph; his father continued his tirade on the wiles of Satan with a line of reasoning his son wasn't paying any attention to. Sarah took a seat on a box a few feet away from them, crossed her legs in a ladylike fashion and stared at him.

:*Well.*: she said. :*Are you going to do something, or am I?*:

His father, evidently, didn't see a thing. Joe did notice a transparency to her appearance now, which hadn't been obvious when she was in the bathroom. He could see through her, as though she was constructed of an elaborate pattern of faintly colored fog.

:*Surprise. I forgot to tell you,*: Sarah said. :*Right now I'm only visible to you.*:

Joe exhaled a breath he'd been holding in for a

while. Meanwhile, his father continued to rant away, as if he was speaking before a full audience. Maybe he was practicing.

His father frowned down at him, playing the judgmental God instead of the vengeful version. "I just wanted you to know that you handled things, well, I'd say average. You'll have to stand up a little more to the officers than that. Don't disobey. But be firm. And remember who's really in control of the army." He winked and stood up, looking directly at Sarah. Or, at least, where she was sitting. The little girl stuck her tongue out at him. Joe winced, praying for it all to be over.

His father waited for him to say something, and he couldn't bear to. He held his peace, and Brother Joseph watched him in frustration and puzzlement.

Finally, after several moments of silence, he gave up waiting for a response. "I suppose I'll leave you to picking up this room," he said.

He moved towards the door — then sniffed the air with a puzzled expression.

"Do you smell something?" he asked, with one hand on the knob. "Smells like, oh, electricity in the air?"

Joe smelled it, too. He looked at Sarah, who shrugged.

:Make something up,: she said.

"Uh, maybe there's a thunderstorm on the way," he supplied, praying his father would just *go*.

Brother Joseph hesitated at the door. "Perhaps. Maybe I should have someone check out the breakers in this quadrant. It reminds me too much of what happened the other night." He frowned, shaking his head. "There's something else. Like perfume, maybe. Or flowers. Something sweet."

He wrinkled his brow, as if troubled with unvoiced thoughts. His eyes looked odd, as if thinking seemed to be taking greater effort than normal for him this evening. Or as if he almost — but not quite — sensed Sarah's presence, and it bothered him so much he was having trouble concentrating.

Yeah. Like I'm not?

Brother Joseph seemed to be growing more and more uncomfortable as well. Finally he said the words his son had been longing for and dreading all at the same time.

"Good night," his father said, and opened the door quickly, shutting it behind him. His exit seemed — rushed. As if something had alarmed him and he was determined not to show it.

Joe waited until he heard his father's footsteps descend the flight of stairs at the end of the great hallway. Even then, he wasn't able to look at the ghost sitting on his left. Now they were alone.

Alone, with a ghost. Or a hallucination? He only wished he could believe that.

:Okay, Joe, it's time to talk,: she said abruptly. *:Things are going to start shaking up around here real soon. I want your complete attention, as Miss Agatha would say.:*

Joe picked up a book at random and looked up at her covertly over the top of it. From the viewpoint of the spy camera, it would look as if he was reading it. Fortunately it was on the approved list.

Much as he dreaded using it, he was going to have to make use of that gift of his to talk to her. If he were caught talking out loud to empty air — well, his father would surely think him possessed. There was no "insanity" among the Chosen Ones after all — it was either "sane and holy" or "possessed by the devil."

:What kind of things? What do you mean, shaking up?:

:That's not important to you. Jamie needs your help. Remember what he looked like last time you saw him?:

Joe shuddered. He suddenly wished she would just go away. *:You know, I don't need this! I was just fine until you came along. I was going to defect. Squeal to the police. Things* *my father would have me shot for. And probably will, if he has a chance. I can't help the kid by myself; I have to get outside and tell the police what's going on here. It's the only thing that will keep Jamie alive.:*

Her expression remained hard and firm. *:That's not the attitude I was picking up back there at the dinner table,:* she informed him. *:You were starting to feel a little too comfortable, if you ask me. Proud of your "men"! They look more like boys to me. And you trained them to hate as well as fight.:*

Joe could feel himself withering under her gaze. *:Don't remind me,:* he said. *:I know what I did. But I can't help the way I was raised.:*

She had no mercy on him whatsoever. *:Were you raised to kill innocent people?:*

Like Jamie, did she mean? Or — herself? *:No, but —:*

She glared at him, her eyes full of accusation. *:You stood there and watched him kill me. Don't you remember that? What did I ever do? Was I a Communist? Was I even a Jew? Would it have been right even if I was? How old was I? Ten? You've gotten to live eight more years than I did!:*

He flung the book across the room and huddled inside his arms, away from her angry gaze. *:Shut up!:* he screamed inside, resisting the urge to jump to his feet. *:I know what happened! I know what I did and didn't do! I couldn't help it! You can't possibly know what it's like to have him as a father!:*

The words came tumbling out, like rocks cascading down a hill in an avalanche. Then the words ran out, and he buried his face in his arms, sobbing. That he was talking to a ghost no longer mattered to him, and somewhere in the back of his mind was the suspicion that he had gone certifiably crazy. *:You're right, I was going back on my decision to leave, to help Jamie. But how can you know what it's like? For me or for him?:*

She shifted to a place right above him, where he had to look up to see her. *:How do I know? Do you really want an answer to that?:*

Did he? But her attitude demanded an answer, and irked the hell out of him. Who did she think she was, anyway? Who put her in judgment over him? *:Yes, I do. What are you, a mind reader or something?:*

Joe wasn't sure if it was a frown or a smirk that passed across her childish features; at this warped angle, her misty composition made her expression especially difficult to read. It also became difficult to tell if he was really talking to a child, or a very angry adult.

:Okay, smarty-pants,: she said. *:Here's how I know.:*

She drifted across the room before he could make a move to stop her — though he hadn't any idea how he could possibly manage that. Reaching down, she touched him on the forehead.

The room dissolved rapidly around him, burning away in an instant, and all that was left was black space. He felt the space in his mind expand outwards, and he could no longer feel his body. His emotions of grief, confusion and fear all fell from him; broken glass, discarded shards, leaving a neutral vacuum in their place. All was air and non-light; he floated in nothingness. The strangeness of it, of what he understood or couldn't even begin to grasp, triggered the deepest level of fear he had ever experienced. He sensed a loss of bladder control, but his bladder and the plumbing connected to it was nowhere to be seen or felt. He wanted to scream, but couldn't.

Where am I? Where's my body? The thought formed from the purest distillation of fear. *What did she do to me?*

Sarah was invisible in the blackness, but suddenly Joe knew she was nearby, watching, orchestrating this strange dance in the spirit world. Then gradually, the pinpoints of pain from a tormented soul entered his senses, and he felt himself unfolding into a tiny, frail body. A body that wasn't his own.

The pain increased, gnawing at his belly, as if there was a monster trying to eat its way out of his stomach.

He was aware of another being, reminding him the body he was in touch with was not his own but belonging to another. Like a parasite, he saw and felt the torment, but at a distance.

His arms were encased in something soft that held them completely, he felt, as two eyes struggled to open. It felt like a nightmare, but he knew it wasn't. The eyes that weren't tried to see and saw only darkness. Finally, another kind of eye opened and looked *through* his head, seeing people who were standing above him; a man he recognized as Jim Chase, Luke, Brother Joseph, and . . .

. . . himself.

Help me out of here, Jamie was trying to say. *My tummy is hurting. I can't see and I can't hear.* But he just didn't have the strength. The Joe standing above him seemed so capable, so strong, yet so helpless. His objections meant nothing to the ones around him, the ones really in charge. The thoughts blazed through Joe from beyond and burned away all pretenses.

Joe watched himself protest — feebly, it seemed from down here — to his father. He could have easily over-powered all of them right then, and he knew it; from Jamie's perspective, it seemed the only thing to do. Conse-quences didn't seem to matter in this state of starvation and agony; that he was conscious at all was a small miracle.

:No!: Joe screamed, from somewhere beyond himself he couldn't locate just then. *:Sarah, no more of this! Please!:*

:You had to see what Jamie was feeling,: she said without a hint of emotion. *:You had to, for you to understand. You do understand now, don't you? Or do I need to show you what I went through?:*

Joe considered this, wondered briefly what it would be like to be the victim of a strangling. And for a moment, he could actually contemplate the idea in a strangely detached mood, temporarily barren of fear.

But that moment passed.

He felt the tightness around his neck, of his own father's hands crushing his windpipe, of the futile gasps after air, the struggle to get free — felt his lungs burning for air they would never have — his throat collapsing — his eyes bulging —

He wanted to scream and couldn't. She released him before the moment of her death.

He floated in the blackness, numb with overload. *:Too much, too much,:* he heard himself thinking. *:I can't go through any more with her. Sarah, let me out of this place!:*

The silence was maddening. Had she forgotten him? Had she abandoned him to this?

Then — *:When you leave the church,:* she said, *:go to Pawnee and talk to a county sheriff named Frank Casey. He'll help you. And tell him about Jamie!:*

Then Sarah was silent. He sensed that she was gone now, leaving him alone in this place that he could only describe as hell. He was all alone with what his father had done to him, his righteous father who was so convinced that he was right all the time.

He felt Sarah's absence now, though he wasn't certain how he had felt her presence.

He lost it, then, control, sanity, everything — he thrashed wildly against nothing until he was exhausted and consciousness slipped away from him.

Jamie can't hold on much longer, was his last, exhausted thought, *I don't have much time* — Then he slipped into oblivion.

When Joe woke he was laying on his back in the middle of his new living room, spread-eagled like a sacrifice. He sat up suddenly, expecting to see Sarah sitting there, wearing that sly, adult look she had used to wither him.

Sarah was nowhere to be seen. He was completely alone in the new place, and this felt more unsettling than sitting with the ghost.

When he struggled to his feet, the memory of Jamie and his experience in the tank came rushing into him like the wind of a hurricane. The sudden movement, and the recollection, instantly unsettled his stomach, and he had to dash to the toilet, where he heaved into the porcelain god until his stomach and lungs ached.

"Please help me through this," he whispered to no one in particular, as the porcelain cooled his forehead. "Help get me out of this place."

He stripped and got into an icy shower, which helped his queasy stomach. It wasn't until he reached for the soap, dropped it, and had trouble retrieving it, that he realized he was shaking.

I've got to get out of here tonight, he thought, the certainty of it now so absolute that it felt branded on his mind.

Question is, how?

Several plans came to mind, most of which he rejected because they would probably result in several pounds of lead perforating his flesh. He considered just walking out, flashing his new rank if anyone gave him any hassles. But — no, not a good idea. That would be reported right away, and someone would come after him, and he would have nowhere to hide except the forest — that was a dubious haven at best. No, he needed a way out of the place that would not be visible to anyone, or to cameras.

This place is designed to keep people out, not in, he thought frantically. *There has to be a way.*

He toweled himself dry and then thought of one idea that might delay things. He went out into the room and turned off all the lights, as if he was going to bed. Hopefully the tears — and the collapse — would be put down to his sickness. He went to his bureau drawers in the dark, felt for certain textures, then began putting clothes on — street clothes, not the new uniform or the undress "uniforms" of camo-clothing. The jeans were worn, a little too tight, and had holes in the knees, but were clean, as were the plain white t-shirt and old battered combat boots he pulled on. He packed a few essential items, things he couldn't leave without. The small backpack was easily overlooked; if he walked out with a suitcase, however stealthily, he knew he would be asking for trouble.

While he packed, he put together a plan to get out. The trash collector came around three A.M. every morning and emptied three dumpsters the Chosen Ones had leased from the refuse company. The dumpsters were inside the perimeter of the complex, but beyond the buildings, so he wouldn't have to attempt an escape either through the gate or over the fence, both of which were risky propositions. The trucks were rear-loaders, if memory served him correctly. Perhaps he could sneak onto the truck somehow, in that rear compartment, as it pulled away. It was the only way out he could think of that stood a chance of working.

The hour was already late, and the hallway lighting was subdued. No one was in sight as he silently closed the door behind him and made his way down the grand flight of stairs. Instead of going down the well-traveled corridor, which was monitored by cameras, he turned right and entered a maintenance hallway. There were few of these tunnels, because of the expense of blasting the rock, but this section had been dug out of the red Oklahoma dirt. Maintenance tunnels, though they varied in size, all interconnected. And one of them surfaced near the road which would take him to the dumpsters.

The exit was located at the top of a ladder set into the wall. The door opened up, like a storm shelter. He opened it a crack and peeked through the slit, studying the night. A thunderstorm was brewing on the horizon, licking the clouds with snake-tongues of light, giving the air a wet smell.

There should be a guard down — yeah. There he is. If I'm careful, he won't see me. And there are the dumpsters.

The large cubes of metal were very nearby, at the edge of a gravel parking lot, which had a few trucks and earth-moving equipment. When he could see the guard looking the other way, he scurried out of his hole, carefully letting the door close behind him, and sprinted for a large dump truck.

Joe concealed himself in the wheel well of the huge beast and began a long wait.

As the minutes ticked by, he considered his decision and knew it to be a good one. But he was scared, and knew it. He was leaving behind everything he had known for a complete unknown. *They might not even believe me,* he thought. *But what choice do I have? I've gotta go through with this. If Jamie dies, and I don't do anything to help him, I'm just as guilty as my father.*

He wasn't sure if he had dozed off or not. All he knew was that he snapped to attention, his senses sharpened with fear, at the sound of the garbage truck trundling up the way. As it backed up to one of the units, he was dizzily relieved to see only one man working it tonight. It would make it all the easier to hop into the back undetected.

Once the last of the three dumpsters was empty, the refuse man put the truck in gear and began the slow drive to the gate. Joe wondered, fleetingly, if the truck would be searched going out. But this caused only the slightest hesitation; he was already running for the retreating truck, the tag-light giving him a reference.

Like a cat, he hopped into the foul-smelling cavity where the day's garbage had been deposited and pushed into the deeper recess of the truck. He lay down, pulling stray refuse over him for cover. And prayed.

What began as a simple test drive of Cindy's battered Toyota Celica turned into an expedition into Cleveland for supplies.

Cindy commented to Bob after Al left — over microwaved dinners — that her '82 car had been running a little rough, and before she could bat an eye Bob had grabbed a toolbox and had the hood open.

"Eyah, I see the problem here," he commented in the waning daylight, pointing to a thingie that looked obviously loose. "Mind if I have a look to see if anything else is wrong?"

Of course, she didn't mind at all. In fact, she was a bit taken by his offer, which made her blush. One of her fears in buying the car was that she would get all the way out here in God's country and the thing would quit running. When she drove it into Hallet, what seemed like an eternity ago, it sounded ready to do just that. With her limited money, she had little to spare for a mechanic. This offer, like all the help Al and Bob had extended, was a blessing she could ill afford to turn down. Besides, there had been something about Bob's demeanor, which was often cold and icy, that suggested he was thawing a bit.

Was there a hint of, well, softness in his voice? she had wondered, but if there was it was so subtle as to be questionable. Bob was twenty, but a mature twenty, so his age wouldn't necessarily eliminate the possibility of involvement.

But . . . Bob?

It was a concept that almost made her laugh. *It would feel like incest,* she thought. He had seemed like a younger brother in many ways —

Until tonight. Now he was out working on the car. She hated to admit it, but he was reminding her of Jim, before he'd gone bonkers. She couldn't leave him out there on his own — it didn't seem fair. She joined him, holding the light, passing him tools, bringing him rags or something to drink. There was a bond forming between them tonight, reminding her even more of Jim, especially when he started explaining what he was doing.

But it wasn't painful. It was a reminder of the old Jim — a man who might have done something kind, considerate — who would have done something like fix the car of a lady whose resources were wearing thin.

As she watched him, she became aware of a curious current running between them — and her thoughts turned serious. *Would Jamie like this man?* The answer to that was yes, she decided without a moment's hesitation.

When Al returned from his mysterious journey and she turned in that night, Bob was still clanking away under the hood, with a determined, almost robotic tenacity. He looked like an exotic, half-human plant that had sprouted from the car's motor.

"How long does he plan to stay up doing that?" Cindy asked, before retreating to the van.

Al had sighed in response. "As long as it takes," was all he said, and shrugged.

The next morning Bob suggested she take a drive. "Be careful," he warned. "It has a bit more power now than it did."

Then he smiled shyly, handed her the keys as if he was handing her a rose, and ambled off towards the racetrack without saying another word.

Al suggested they go into Cleveland and pick up some odds and ends they all needed. Groceries, toiletries, and the like. Cindy offered to contribute, but Al would have none of that. "Save your money," he ordered as they got into her car. "We've got plenty. Fairgrove's paying for this."

As they drove to Cleveland — strange to see a sign for Cleveland, *Oklahoma* — she couldn't help but notice the new power the car had. She had to consciously drive slower than what she was used to, as the Celica seemed to have a life of its own now.

"Migod — this car can *go*," she commented to Al, who just nodded. "You didn't do anything with your . . . abilities, did you?"

"Oh, no," Al said calmly. "This is all Bob's doing. No elven magic here. Not this time. Just good old mechanical ability. Bob's a natural." He gave her one of those obtuse looks she had trouble reading. "He's not very good with words, but when he likes someone, he tends to do things for them. He'll appreciate it a lot if you tell him how impressed you are with his work."

A natural — something Jamie would admire, she found herself thinking, uncertain why.

But the mention of his elven origins brought back the fears she was trying desperately to deal with, or to at least bury. *Just give it time — sooner or later you'll get used to the whole thing, like being around someone from another country who might seem a little weird at first. Like that guy I met from Iraq, that James used to work with. He didn't change. I guess I did.*

She cast a wary glance at Al, and at the vague outline of the pointed ears in his long, blond hair. *Somehow, with this one, I don't think it will be the same as getting used to an Iraqi. They're human. Al isn't. Though he comes close.*

Remembering the view she had of his sculptured body made her shudder. *Real close.* Somehow, by contrast, Bob seemed more attractive, not less. Al's perfection was *too* much. A reminder of how inhuman he was. Bob on the other hand, was *very* human. Very . . . attractive. . . .

They stopped at the Quic Pic for a badly needed tank of unleaded and proceeded into Cleveland, dropping well below the speed limit in the busy afternoon traffic. "You know, Al, it occurred to me that maybe some of these people have seen Jamie. While we're here, I'd like to show the picture to a few people."

"Sure," Al said pleasantly, but it sounded to Cindy as if he thought the effort would be wasted. *As if he knew exactly where he is, but isn't telling me,* she thought suspiciously. He shifted in his seat when she thought that, raising another uncomfortable question.

Does he know what I'm thinking?

If Al was reading her thoughts, he gave no indication of it. He was gazing absently out the passenger window, apparently with a few thoughts of his own occupying his time.

"Any suggestions on where to stop?" she asked, seeing nothing on the main street that looked even remotely like a supermarket.

"Keep going all the way through Broadway. There'll be a large store on the right, I think." For a moment he lost some of that smug self-assurance, became a little less perfect. "Bob always came along on these trips. He always seemed to know where all the stores were, and what to get."

Cindy suppressed a snicker. *If it weren't for Bob, Al, you wouldn't know how to tie your shoes.* This was a thought she hoped he *could* pick up.

"I hope you have a list," she said, and Al held up a scrap of paper.

Presently they found the Super H discount market on the other side of the business district, as predicted. As they entered the supermarket, Cindy noted that Al blended right in with the crowd. His clothing and demeanor, which was that of a simple mechanic, made him virtually transparent. But as she observed him, there was more than that; she caught a faint glimmer of something surrounding him, something that nobody else noticed. In fact, nobody seemed to notice him at all. Natives walking toward them in the aisles didn't even look up, but smiled warmly at Cindy when she passed. Instead of walking straight into him, however, people walked around him. His movements were fluid, and without any apparent effort he wove through the crowded market, unnoticed. And, she was beginning to speculate, unseen. She'd have to ask him about that later.

Soon the cart was full, stocked with everything from motor oil to Gatorade. Al seemed to know where everything was in this store, so Cindy was content to let him lead the way. Occasionally she dawdled over this or that item, as Al patiently waited for her to come along. In the check-out line she saw a tabloid newsrag with the headlines proudly proclaiming "Phantom Elves Invade White House; Bush Scared." This apparently caught Al's attention, and he winked at her as he dropped a copy into the cart. Cindy rolled her eyes in response.

As they were wheeling the bagged groceries into the parking lot, Cindy looked up to the street, where a line of five cars and trucks were waiting for a Volvo to turn. Something about the sight disturbed her, but nothing really registered as she pulled the cart up next to the car and began handing Al bags.

After the third bag, though, she looked up again. There was the pickup truck, the same one she remembered.

The truck. Their truck.

Jim.

Sure enough, a haggard James Chase was at the wheel. She couldn't quite see his expression at that distance, but his posture suggested exhaustion. Or a hangover?

"Cindy?" she was vaguely aware of Al saying. "What are you looking at?"

"It's him," she said, but it came out a whisper. "Look. Over there. That's our truck! That's Jim!"

Without making any conscious effort, she found her feet moving her in the direction of the truck. *Jamie, where's Jamie? If he's in the truck with Jim, I wouldn't see him unless he sits forward or stands up and looks out the back window like he always does. Please, let him be in that truck!* The Volvo evidently found the gap it was looking for and sped into the parking lot. The truck began edging forward, merging with the traffic.

"*No!*" she heard someone screaming, not knowing

the scream came from herself. "No! Jim, you get *back* here, dammit!"

The truck drove on, with Jim probably unaware of the frantic woman running through the parking lot, trying to catch up with him. "Stop, you sonuvabitch! Where's Jamie? *Where's my son?*"

The next thing she remembered was dropping to her knees on a little strip of grass, a block or so away from the supermarket, sobbing loudly. The truck was nowhere in sight. *He didn't even see me,* she thought, through tears of frustration. *He's going to pay for this!* Cars slowed, and moved on. Nobody seemed willing to get involved.

"Cindy!" Al said from behind her. "What in the seven hells has gotten into you?"

Al's anger seemed to dissolve instantly when their eyes met. "Let's get the car," she said weakly. "Let's go after them." But even as she said the words, she knew it would be futile. The truck was nowhere in sight, and it could have gone in any number of directions.

"After who?" Al asked, helping her. Then realization seemed to dawn on his face. "You mean you saw Jamie?"

"Not Jamie. My husband. He was driving our truck."

They started walking back to the car. Al's expression, however, did not suggest that he was convinced. "Are you sure?"

"Hell, yes, I'm sure!" she said, unleashing all of her frustration and anger on him. "I was there when we *bought* the damn thing. I was *married* to him. We could have gone after him! Where were you, anyway? They could be in Kansas by now!"

Al said nothing. The silence weighed heavier with every passing second, until it became uncomfortable. She began to feel ashamed for her response when Al finally said, "Sorry. I was chasing you."

"I know," she sighed. "I know. Don't be sorry. I'm the one who should be apologizing. It's just that I was so close to confronting that bastard!"

Alinor put the cart into the corral, and they both climbed into the Toyota. He acted like he wanted to say something, then changed his mind.

She prompted him. "What were you about to say?"

Al turned the ignition. She wasn't aware when they had decided he would drive, but somehow it seemed to be the thing to do just then. Her knees were still shaking.

"That might not be such a good idea at this point," Al said as they turned onto Broadway. "To let them know we're in the neighborhood, I mean."

She was about to ask, when she saw why. *They'll just disappear again*, she realized. *Then I may never know where they went.*

"At least we know for certain he's in that crazy place," she observed. "We do. Don't we?"

"We should probably leave this to the sheriff," he replied, without really answering her. "Let's put away the groceries and take a trip out to Pawnee. Let Frank know what we saw."

They drove in silence. Cindy stared out her window, her heart leaping whenever she saw a pickup truck. Then it would turn out to be someone else's, and she would sink back into herself, doing everything she could to keep from bawling.

The last thing Al needs is a crying, hysterical woman to deal with, she thought wretchedly.

But by the time they reached the Cleveland city limits, that's exactly what Al had.

Comforting crying women wasn't one of Alinor's favorite duties, but he seemed to be doing a lot of it lately. And truth to be told, he was beginning to prefer the company of his constructed servants to Cindy. At least they knew how to smile and look pleasant no matter how unpleasant the circumstances. The human seemed to spend most of her time wrapped in gloom or in tears.

Bob was at the RV when they arrived at the track, and when they told him who Cindy had seen in Cleveland, he insisted on going with them to Pawnee to talk to the deputy sheriff, Frank Casey. "Work at the track is done," he said, not expanding on that, in spite of Al's questioning gaze. They were putting away groceries in what Al would later realize to be record time. "This sounds more important, anyway. Did you go after him?"

Al gave him an ugly look. "She only saw Jim Chase, not Jamie. Do you really think that would have been a good idea?"

"I see. So Jamie wasn't with him. No telling what would have happened there." Bob seemed to shrink away from the discussion. "Do you want me to go with you, or would you rather I stay here?"

"No. You come with us," Cindy said resolutely, taking Bob's arm and escorting him out of the RV. "You've been cooped up here long enough."

Al lingered in the RV's kitchen, a bit perplexed. The action of taking Bob by the arm and leading him out as if he were some kind of date was a little confusing. *Cindy and Bob?* Al thought, trying to imagine the two together, and promptly shook his head against the thought. *No way.* Al laughed at himself as he locked up the RV, trying to figure out why something so ridiculous and improbable would annoy him.

Somehow Al ended up sitting in the back, with Bob and Cindy in the front. He hated sitting in rear seats — they never had enough leg room for him — but he kept his complaints to himself. Few words were exchanged between the two, though Al did observe a sort of silent communion. They seemed content to ride in quiet, without the need to fill the void with meaningless talk.

Frank was in the building somewhere, the

receptionist told them when they arrived in the Pawnee County Courthouse. She led them back to his office and told them he would be with them soon.

It was tempting to lean over and study what was on the desk, as intriguing as all the maps and charts were — and how much they excited his curiosity. He would have to content himself to studying the maps at a distance. Not all that difficult, after all. . . .

One of the maps was the same one he had memorized and used to find the Chosen Ones' hideout earlier. The other ones were different, but seemed to represent the same area. He couldn't immediately see what all the lines and diagrams represented, and why they were drawn the way they were. Then he saw it: *he's working up a strategy to raid the Chosen Ones!*

Al held his face expressionless, no mean feat when considering how much this disturbed him. *If they go in it could be a massacre,* he thought. *All those children. It wouldn't be the first time a religious cult had held their people as hostages, and down in those bunkers, they would be in a perfect position to hold out until everyone was dead. It's what they've been training for! All the food and supplies they need are down there.* He frowned as the whole picture, with all its frightening details, clicked into place. It would take no great leap of thinking to turn those people against law enforcement agencies. As it was, they perceived themselves as acting beyond the law anyway. The government of the United States was not truly *their* government. Brother Joseph had the One Answer given to the congregation. What the sheep didn't know was that it was an answer from a hideous monster, through the deteriorating body and soul of a young child. They were beyond the law; they were divine.

They're looking for an imaginary enemy. First opposition to come along will do.

"Hi, folks," Frank said amiably as he entered. His great size still caused Al to look twice. The big deputy toted a coffee cup, tiny in his hand, and yet another map, partially unrolled. "Didn't know you were coming or I would have been here sooner. What's up?"

"I saw James, my ex," Cindy blurted. "In Cleveland this afternoon."

Frank scooped up the maps and diagrams lying on his desk. The only purpose Al saw in this was to conceal the documents from them, confirming his suspicions that the law enforcement agencies involved in this would act secretly and tell them about the results later.

The question is, when *are they going in?*

"Is that so?" Frank said, but he didn't really sound surprised. "We had already concluded that he was with them, but I'm glad we have a sighting. Cleveland, you say?"

"In front of the supermarket. Discount H or something, wasn't it?" she asked, turning to Al.

"That's where we were," Al said, nodding.

She turned away and stared at Frank Casey with accusation in her eyes. "So when are you going to get a search warrant and go in and get him?" Cindy asked. "Don't you have enough evidence now?"

"You saw him in Cleveland, Miss Chase," Frank said, soothingly. "That's a long way from the Sacred Heart property. I doubt I could convince a judge to issue a warrant on the basis of that sighting. Especially this judge. I told you I thought something odd was going on there. To be blunt, the judge doesn't want to help."

"Why not?" Cindy cried, losing her hold on her temper and her emotions. She was shaking in her chair now, wiping away tears. Bob touched her arm; Cindy recoiled from him.

"Am I to understand that you're not making any plans to raid that place?" Al asked, unsure if it was a good idea to show this particular card just yet. "I had the impression, from odds and ends lying around in this office, that you have precisely that in mind."

Frank looked directly at Al, apparently trying to look unruffled and doing a reasonably good job. "Don't know where you got that idea," Frank said. "Such an operation would require information and evidence that Pawnee County doesn't have."

Bob's chin firmed, and it was his turn to turn accusing eyes on the deputy. "But what if the State of Oklahoma has evidence? Or the FBI?"

"Nobody said they were involved," Frank said coolly. "Perhaps you should examine your source of information a bit closer."

Al raised an equally cool eyebrow. "I didn't want to seem nosy, looking closer at what was on your desk. It was difficult not to notice the maps."

Frank sighed. He didn't seem the least bit angry, just tired. Tired and restless, as if something big was going down, and he was running low on the energy needed to bring it off.

"Look," the big man said, leaning forward over his desk. "I'm in a very delicate situation here. Other people have been contacted regarding this cult, individuals we are going to be needing to testify. You are one of these people, Miss Chase. This is a police matter and will be handled by police *only*. I don't want civilians fooling around with this cult. They are lunatics with a cause, and they are all well armed. *All.* I'm not saying that we're going in to get your son, but I am saying that I might not be at liberty to discuss it if we were."

Cindy sniffled and looked at the floor. This was, obviously, not what she wanted to hear.

"Do you understand what I'm saying?" Frank said softly. "I'm trying to juggle ten different things at once here. Please don't make this any harder for me."

"Okay," Cindy said, however reluctantly. "You win. You said other people. What other people? Who are they? Are they parents looking for their children, too? Can I talk to them?"

Frank threw up his arms, his palms outward. "I can't discuss it. Sorry, Miss Chase. Please be more patient. For a little while longer, anyway." Frank got to his feet, a signal which they all followed. "For a few days longer, at least."

A few days, Al thought, alarmed. *Whatever's going to happen will happen in a few days. I need more time!*

From the grim determination he saw on the deputy's face, he saw that he wasn't about to get it.

For the second time that week, Frank Casey watched the sad trio leave his office empty-handed. He wished that he could tell them everything, including the plan to bring in the FBI SWAT teams, and get it over with. Every time he had to dance around the facts like this, he felt disturbed and guilty. Particularly when a mother and child were involved.

But he was under strict orders to keep the operation a secret. Not that the orders were necessary; he understood the wisdom in keeping a lid on any pending raid. When information like that got out in advance, to the public or press, cops died.

A plan as big as this would surely involve casualties. The question was, how many and on whose side.

He wasn't getting enough sleep, and he knew it. It was already noon, and he had spent the entire night on the phone with FBI SWAT leaders, coordinating logistics. Fortunately the bulk of the army they were assembling was going to hole up at a National Guard depot in Tulsa, so as not to alert the Chosen Ones. They would begin moving in under cover of darkness and strike a few hours before dawn, when armies were traditionally the most vulnerable. He hoped the plan would work. But given the apparent luck of the lunatic cult lately, he had his doubts.

If I'm going to be worth a flip during this thing, I'd better get some rest. It will either happen two or three days from now. If

I'm going to sleep, this will be about the last chance I'll have.

Frank was on his way out the door to take care of exactly that when the phone rang.

"I'm not here," he said to the secretary. "I'm going home."

He was halfway to his squad car when he realized he'd left his keys on his desk. When he went back into the office, the secretary frantically waved at him, the phone pressed to her ear.

Frank groaned. *I knew I shouldn't have come back in here. It would have been better to just curl up in the backseat and go to sleep. Better yet, in the trunk. No one could see me there.*

"Who is it?" he asked. "I hope it's important."

"I'm not sure," she hissed. "He says he's from that camp of crazies over there at that church. Chosen Ones, I think he said. You wanna talk to him?"

Frank stared at her. His exhaustion was temporarily forgotten as he went into his office.

"Line four," she said, and he picked up the phone.

"Yes?" Frank said. "This is Deputy Casey."

There was a pause, just long enough for Frank to think it was a crank call after all. He was about to hang the receiver up when a young-sounding male said, in a trembling voice, "Are you Frank Casey?"

"That's me," he replied. "What's on your mind?"

The gulp on the other end of the line was audible. "Everything. I'm an officer of the Sacred Heart of the Chosen Ones. I want to leave the group, but I need your protection."

"Is that right?" Frank said conversationally. *Good Christ, this is a* kid *I'm talking to!* "For what purpose?"

"My father is crazy," the unknown said. "He's going to end up killing someone."

Father? Crazy? Who am I talking to? He broke into a cold sweat, but managed to maintain his casual tone. "Oh? And who is your father?"

"Brother Joseph."

Frank sat up in the chair, rubbed the sleepiness from eyes. *Did I hear that right?* he thought. *Or is the sleep deprivation making me hallucinate?*

"Are you still there?" the boy asked.

He took a deep breath and rubbed sweaty palms on his pants. "Oh, I'm here. I know who you're talking about. You said you need protection. Why?"

The boy sounded desperate enough to be authentic. "Because they'll come after me. They'll come after me and kill me. I'm not joking."

"I don't doubt it," Frank said, not entirely sure he was believing this conversation. "How do I know this isn't some sort of a trick?"

It was the other's turn for a long pause. "Well, I guess you don't know. You'll just have to take my word for it."

"I'm afraid that's not good enough," Frank said evenly. "We can get you the protection," he said, thinking, *Yeah, the jail cell is a pretty safe place. Iron bars. Concrete walls. Reasonable rates.* "What are you willing to give us?"

"Anything you want," the boy said without hesitation. "I know everything there is about the Chosen Ones."

"I suppose you would," Frank said, "if this man is your father." *If this is true, this boy can tell us what to expect. Layout of the bunkers. Who's there.. Or, it could be a trick. Do I take a chance?*

What would it cost me? Another few hours of sleep?

"So tell me," he continued, "what do I call you?"

"Joe," he said. "That's short for Joseph. Junior."

"Of course it is," he replied inanely. "What would you like to do about this, Joe? Could you come down to the station—"

"No!" was the immediate reply. Then, "I mean, they'll be watching for me there. Too risky. I meant it when I said they would try to kill me. They should know by now that I'm gone, and they'll be looking for me. Do you have any extra bulletproof jackets?"

Frank considered this a moment. "Perhaps. Do you really think that's necessary?"

There was no hesitation in the answer. "Yes. I do."

In the silence that followed, Frank decided the boy was serious. *The risk might not be real, but he certainly thinks it is. What I've seen of that bunch, though, it wouldn't surprise me to see them hunt down and kill one of their own. Especially if he's serious about squealing on the whole rat's nest.*

He sighed. "Okay, then. I can't promise a vest because I don't know who has them checked out. There isn't exactly a lot of call for them around here. But I will meet you someplace. You name it."

A moment's pause. "There's a steakhouse out here. Called Granny's something. You know it?"

"Granny's Kitchen?" Frank asked. "Out on Highway 64. Would you like me to pick you up?"

A sigh. Of relief? "No. That's all right. I can see the place from here. Granny's Kitchen it is."

Frank did a quick mental calculation. "I'll be there in ten minutes."

With bells on.

● CHAPTER ELEVEN

In spite of the fact that *he* wasn't sure about taking the kid's paranoia seriously, Frank found himself calling in a few tags, some out of state, on vehicles he didn't immediately recognize. He told himself that he did have to admit he'd seen more strange faces lately. But there were always a certain number of strangers around, especially around race-time down at Hallet. He'd never made any connection with the Chosen Ones — if that was really who they were. What surveillance the PCSO had done indicated this group pretty much stayed on their own land, with only a few of them going out for supplies.

While he'd been trying to dig up information, he'd even questioned the trash collection agency that went out there and turned up nothing. One or two men went in with a single truck at night when the place was dark, passed a guard on the way in and out, and that was it. The guys on the truck never saw anything but a parking lot, the guard and the dumpsters. He'd come to the conclusion a while back that if anything suspicious was going on, it was either kept out of sight of watchers from the edge of the area and from above, or it was happening down below, in the bunkers.

Every tag he called was clean, but that didn't do much to calm his jitters. Shoot, now *he* was getting paranoid! Too much coffee, Frank diagnosed. *Too much coffee and not enough sleep. It's enough to make any man jumpy.*

He pulled in the parking lot of Granny's Kitchen, a

quaint little restaurant he remembered fondly, though he hadn't been there in some time. *I've been with the department now for what, ten years? Where has all the time gone?*

Nothing that he'd ever been through or been trained for had prepared him for what waited for him inside. *What am I walking into here?* Trap — or hoax — or the break he'd prayed for?

The diner was exactly as he remembered it; not a stick of furniture had been moved. The old formica and vinyl booths still lined the walls, each with their own remote-jukebox selector dating back to 1957. The floor was worn through to the concrete foundation in places; the scent was of home-cooking, with an after-taste of Lysol. The cash register sat atop a wood and glass case, which enclosed candy and cheap, locally made trinkets.

The place was oddly silent for the time of day. From the kitchen came the sounds of an ancient Hobart dishwasher, the *tinkle-clank* of glasses and coffee cups being placed in racks, plates being stacked, silverware being sorted.

On duty at the open grill, Old George flipped hamburgers; when he saw Frank he smiled a toothless grin and waved, a greeting that hadn't altered since the deputy was fifteen.

And there was someone else on duty who knew him almost as well as Old George.

"Good God, you look like hell," Peggy said, putting an order pad away in the pocket of an immaculate bleached apron. The waitress looked like she'd walked off the cover of a 1955 issue of *Life*, complete with blond bouffant. Like the diner, she hadn't changed since the fifties.

Frank had dated her briefly in high school, but the romance never advanced past petting, and Peggy had married a real estate agent the same month Frank went into the academy.

She's the kind of girl who can be your best friend, Frank had once observed. *Too damn few of them around*.

She frowned at him, hand on one hip. "Don't you believe in sleep anymore? Or are you too busy catting around at night?"

"Have pity on me, Peggy. It's been one helluva long week," he said awkwardly, glancing around the diner to see who else was there. Two high school girls, one of the locals, named Russ, and a National Guardsman he didn't immediately identify. But no young man. He took a seat at his usual booth. "Coffee, please. For now."

Maybe the kid's waiting outside, he thought, hoping this wasn't a wild-goose chase.

"You looking for someone?" Peggy asked, pouring a cup of coffee, and dropping a plastic-covered menu on the formica table beside him.

He decided to play it cautious. No point in setting himself up to look like a fool to more people than just himself. "Not sure yet. Have you seen a boy — a teenager — hanging around here lately? Not one of the local kids, a stranger." Peggy knew every kid that hung around here — and their parents and home phone numbers. God help them if they acted up when she was on shift. Mom and Dad would hear about it before they cleared the door.

She pursed her lips. "Well, yes I have. Early this morning. Saw him walking along the road. Just thought he was passing through, but he showed up again and made a phone call over at that pay-phone." Peggy pointed to a gas station with a phone booth, across the highway. "He looks kind of like a runaway. That who you're looking for?"

"It likely is," Frank said. *Has to be*. "What did he look like?"

"Blond, looked like a jock. About eighteen, nineteen. Holes in his jeans, wearing a white t-shirt. If it weren't for the military haircut he'd look pretty scruffy. Like you did when you were that age." She grinned. "Or can you remember that far back?"

Old George yelled, "Order up." Peggy winked mischievously and trotted off to the counter, pink uniform skirt swishing.

Military haircut. Could be, though most of those guys were shaved bald. I'll have to ask him about that. If it's him. If he shows.

The door opened, jingling the little bell fixed to it. Frank looked up as he took his first sip of coffee.

Son-of-a-gun. Looks like I've got my chance now.

He came into the restaurant slowly, a predator moving into new territory, feeling his way with all senses alert for trouble. Coolly, professionally, he scanned the patrons sitting at the booths, apparently deciding after a cursory examination that they were not a threat. And that *they* were not who he was looking for.

His eyes alighted on Frank. Frank nodded, warily, and the boy returned the nod. Just as warily.

"You must be Frank," the boy said, walking over to the booth. "I'm Joe. We spoke on the phone just now?"

The boy kept his voice low, just barely audible. Frank followed his example. "Yes, son. Have a seat."

Joe carefully set his pack down on the bench and deposited himself opposite Frank. They regarded each other uncomfortably for a moment before the deputy suggested, "Would you like something to eat? I'm buying."

Indecision passed over the young face, as if the boy was afraid to ask for a handout. "No thanks. I'm not hungry," he replied, in a tone that wasn't very convincing. Then suddenly the boy's stomach growled, loudly; people in the booth next to them gave them a sideways glance.

Frank couldn't suppress a grin of amusement. "Are you *sure*?"

The youngster shifted, uncomfortably. "Well, sir, I am hungry, but I don't want any handouts. I was raised funny that way."

No handouts? If his father really is Brother Joseph, why would that be a problem? That's how the entire circus over there was financed. But then, the boy probably has a pretty distorted viewpoint.

Frank shrugged. "Consider it a loan, then. We can work it out, somehow."

Relief washed over the youngster's face. "Okay then," he said, reaching eagerly for a menu. As Joe studied the selection, Frank was impressed with the boy's fine physique. It took work and dedication to get a body built up that way. Muscles bulged from under the tight shirt, with thick, meaty arms that suggested years of free weight training. Frank's eyebrows raised when he saw the crude swastika tattooed on Joe's forearm, though the boy was deep in the menu and didn't notice. From the symbol's location on the youngster's arm, though, Frank had a shrewd idea that it had been done a few years earlier, before a rapid spurt of growth.

For the rest, Joe was shaving, but just barely. A fine blond stubble was visible on his upper lip and chin, but nowhere else. He was dirty and smelled, and looked like someone on the run, right enough. But this was no teenybopper runaway; for all Joe's apparent youth, this was a full-grown man. And one who, from the dark circles under his eyes, was having a serious crisis.

Peggy appeared with two glasses of ice water, raising an eyebrow at Frank. A silent response from his eyes asked her to save her questions for later. She nodded knowingly and said only, "What will you have, sugar?"

Joe looked up at her and licked his lips, his hunger showing. "How 'bout the chicken fried steak with fries, a hamburger — you got a chef salad? Yeah, I'll take the salad with a side of cole slaw, a large milk. . . ."

"You have quite an appetite," Peggy noted with a grin, continuing the order on another ticket. "How about you, Frank?"

"Just a hamburger and a ginger ale," he replied. "Put it on one ticket. I'll pick it up."

Peggy left with the order. Joe drained his ice water in one gulp. Frank edged his glass over. "Have it. I'm not thirsty. When was the last time you ate, anyway?"

"Yesterday — yesterday morning, actually," Joe replied. "I've been moving ever since this morning around four."

Interesting. Either the Chosen Ones were keeping their folks on short rations, or something had happened to kill the kid's appetite for a while. Maybe the same thing that had caused his defection? "You waited a while before calling the office. You almost missed me."

Joe toyed with the glass of ice water. "I had to lay low today. I knew they were going to be out looking for me as soon as they knew I was gone — by breakfast at the latest. There's always an early Praise Meeting around noon, so I figured now would be the best time to get in touch." He looked up, under eyebrows drawn together in a frown. "I wasn't kidding when I said they were going to kill me."

"Don't worry, you're safe here," Frank said placatingly, still not altogether certain there was anything to really worry about from the Chosen Ones. So far all he had evidence for was an over-active imagination. "Would you like to tell me what this is all about?"

Joe took a deep breath, let it go. "Not sure where to start."

"Why don't we start with your father," Frank urged.

"Yeah. My father." He made a face, as if the words tasted bitter. "It took a while to figure him out."

I bet it did. "So tell me about it. And just for the record, how old are you?"

Joe sighed. "I just turned eighteen. I've been training in paramilitary since I could walk, it seems. Guess what I need to do now is go into the army or something."

Frank nodded, slowly. "Not a lotta call for Pizza Hut delivery guys that handle AK-47s." That was a test, to see by the youngster's response — or lack of it — if what Cindy Chase and her backup band had told him was true.

The kid didn't even flinch, and that made him one very unhappy cop.

"I guess so." He sighed again. "But there are some things I need to take care of first. Will you give me the protection I need?"

"Of course we will," Frank said smoothly. "We've got assault weapons, too."

The deputy let that last statement dangle in the air, like bait. *The question was, would he take it?*

"Yeah I bet you do," Joe replied levelly. "But not as much as what we've got down there."

Frank was now a profoundly unhappy cop. "Would you care to expand on that?"

Joe shook his head, but not in denial. "I guess it's not 'we' anymore. I don't know, its just that a lot of weird stuff has been happening to me lately. Things you wouldn't believe. Things I'm not sure I believe."

"Start from the beginning," Frank advised.

Joe nodded. "As long as I can remember, Daddy was a preacher. He kept talking about the second coming of Christ, the Armageddon, the Sword of God — and this direct phone line he had to God Almighty. Like a Heavenly Hotline or something. Only thing is, he never told me why he could hear God, and I couldn't."

"Well, I'm not too surprised about that," Frank said cautiously. "We gotta lot of guys like that out here in the Bible Belt. Not real big on explanations."

Joe grimaced. "Yeah. I just took it for granted that he was right and I was wrong, as usual, and the only right thing I could possibly do was to obey him and serve whatever church he had created that day. I didn't dare contradict him, even when the contradictions were so obvious that any fool could see he was making this stuff up as he went along. I kinda got to the point where it didn't matter, you know? Like as long as he was handing down the line, I'd swallow it and not even think about it. Then he started the Sacred Heart. Sacred Heart of the Chosen Ones, he called it. God's chosen people. And the only chosen people."

Peggy showed up with a pitcher of water and filled both empty glasses.

Joe emptied his for the third time. "Hot day. Nothing to drink, either," he offered.

Frank let him take his time. It was obvious that this wasn't comfortable for him.

Joe took up the thread again, in a softer voice now. "Funny. From the time I was thirteen I dreamed of being Rambo. I only saw *First Blood* one time, but I remember every line in the movie. I worshipped Rambo, I guess. I kind of felt like I knew where he was at, because I was an outcast, too. But I never told Father that, since I was only allowed to worship two people, him and his Jesus. So when he sent me to a military academy, I was happy. The other kids, they saw the academy as some kind of punishment. Not me. I thought it was great. Like summer camp, training for the Olympics and getting to join the army all in one. I did pretty good, too, until one day they just pulled me out of class and sent me home. Father had a disagreement with the dean over the religious part of our training, wasn't to his liking or something, so I went back to Atlanta."

That much could be checked. Frank nodded, and Joe took that as encouragement to continue.

"I got a big surprise, though. After only six months, the Chosen Ones had grown. There were ten congregations in the south and east, instead of just the one I remembered. And everybody had started wearing guns everywhere." He grinned, disarmingly. "I started thinking that coming back to Atlanta wasn't that bad a deal after all."

"So you could play Rambo?" Frank said cynically. Joe flushed, but nodded.

"Father changed some time while I was gone. He was always crazy and weird anyway, but now it looked like something else was pulling his strings." The kid leaned forward, earnestly. "He would talk to himself when he didn't think anyone could hear him, and he would have these *conversations* with something, only it was like overhearing someone on the phone. You only heard one side of the conversation. He started calling this other thing the 'Holy Fire,' and he said it was telling him the direction the church would go. Like, it told him to begin all the other congregations. It told him to begin the Guard, and then it told him to start training for the war of all wars. Armageddon, with the forces of God toting assault rifles, you know?"

"Excuse me," Frank interrupted. "The Guard? Is that what you call your army?"

"The Guard of the Sacred Heart," Joe supplemented. "Then there's the Junior Guard, which I used to be in charge of."

"Tell me a little more about that," Frank said. "The Guard, the Junior Guard. I'm curious. How many are there? What kind of weapons do you have back there?"

For a moment Frank was afraid pushing for that kind of information might have been premature, but apparently Joe had warmed up enough to be willing to talk. *Poor kid,* Frank found himself thinking. *All these years, and he never really had someone to talk to. Already he feels comfortable enough around me to unload.*

It surprised him to feel pity for the boy. It surprised him more that he wanted to.

Joe frowned, absently, his lips moving a little as if he was adding up numbers in his head. "There's around two hundred fifty foot soldiers. Everyone has an AK-47; Father and General Plunket like them a lot. We have stockpiles of ammo, fourteen thousand rounds per rifle last I counted. Grenades, launchers, AR-15s, M2A2s, six .50-cals."

Frank couldn't help but utter a low whistle. "You're not pulling my leg, are you? That's an army down there."

"You bet it is," Joe replied brightly, but the sudden pride in the Guard seemed to embarrass him. "But — it's bad. I know that now. I don't hold with any of it anymore. Ever since . . ."

The boy looked away, evidently struggling with what he had to say. "Ever since my father killed Sarah. She was just a little girl."

Killed a little girl? Jesus — Frank waited in stunned silence for him to continue. When Joe didn't, he prompted, "What little girl?" *Let him be wrong. Let this be hearsay, God, please. . . .*

Joe swallowed and turned pale. "I — I saw him do it. I helped bury her."

Well, so much for it being hearsay.

"It had to do with that Holy Fire thing. It told him to do it, I think. Her parents were part of the church. They disappeared, and I don't know whatever happened to them."

They're probably dead, too, Frank thought, still in shock, but he didn't say anything. Likely the boy knew it, but was just hoping it wasn't true. *Look, you've dealt with murders before. People die. People kill. It happens. The important thing now is to get the damn evidence that'll put this bastard away.*

Joe shook his head and traced patterns on the formica with the water that had run down the side of his glass. "The church began to center around that Holy Fire thing more and more. It began calling the shots. First we'd train ten men to use a gun, then it would tell us to train fifty. And when that was done we'd get the orders to train a hundred."

Frank didn't like any of this. It sounded like some kind of carnival sideshow — except that people with high-powered firearms were taking it seriously. "And you never actually saw this 'thing,' did you?"

Joe shook his head again, emphatically. "It all came through Father. But then the thing wanted to talk to us directly. The little girl, Sarah. She was used to talk to it at first, and what came out of her would scare anyone. Ugly sounds. Grunts. Then it would talk. Like something out of a movie."

Frank nodded, wondering where reality ended and fantasy began. He had to act as if he was taking it seriously, or he'd lose the boy. He sure thought it was real. *We should be getting this on tape,* he thought. *There's time for depositions later, but I wish I had a recorder going now. This Brother Joseph guy must be one hell of a con artist to convince a little girl to play along with this little parlor show, not to mention the rest of this group. There must be hundreds more down there. And they're all under his thumb.*

Correction. All except his son, now. I've never seen anyone spill their guts like this. He sings like a cage full of canaries. Or like someone with a guilty conscious.

Joe raised his eyes to Frank's again, and the earnestness on his face could not be mistaken. "This wasn't just my father playing like a ventriloquist or something, you've gotta believe me. This *thing,* this Holy Fire, it's the real thing! It ain't — isn't — anything I've ever seen before. But it's real, real as you or me. . . ."

Frank nodded, but his skepticism must have shown a little. The boy frowned.

"I bet you'd like to know where we get our money, right? The Holy Fire, it would give us information on the horse races and the bingo games in Tulsa. And the information *would always be right.* But we couldn't attract attention by scoring big every time we went out there, so the 'luck' was sort of spread around." He swallowed, hard. Frank tensed. Something big was coming. "That wasn't where the real money came from. That was just seed money."

Here we go. Time for the nitty-gritty.

"Drugs. That's where the real money comes from. I

never got involved in the sales, but I knew what they were doing. They used the money from the horse races and stuff to buy coke from the big guys in South America. It got delivered at night about three times a week. Then they would have to move it the next day, out into the street."

Frank cleared his throat. "What kind of large quantities? How much are we talking about here?"

"Oh, three, four hundred kilos a shot," Joe said casually. "Comes in by private plane, mostly. There's a landing strip and camo-nets out on the land. Or when the plane can't make it, they bring it in by truck."

Christ almighty, Frank thought. *All that coke, right under our noses. If what he's saying is true, it's hard to believe that we didn't get a line on any of this. He might be exaggerating the amount. But even if it's one ounce, we can bust them but good.*

Joe caught his attention again. "Now *listen* for a minute. They never got busted, not even once, because of what the Holy Fire would say right before we went out. Like the other night, it told us about the Oaktree Apartments. That there was going to be a bust, and when. *Exactly.*"

Frank squirmed. Which, for a man of his size, was not an action easily concealed. "Oaktree Apartments. In Cleveland?" He had been involved in that stakeout. And the resulting raid had produced zilch.

Every residence on their warrants had been sanitized. Not a shred of evidence, not a dust speck of coke. Nothing. And no explanation. One day before the bust, the place was red-hot. Day of the bust, nothing but empty rooms.

"Cleveland? I guess. But there's more, the reason why nobody ever gets busted. The Holy Fire warned us about the police. There was something about a blue Mustang."

Frank knew about the Mustang; he'd driven it once. The Tulsa County sheriff's office had loaned it to

Pawnee last winter for a drug bust related to one on their turf. *But how in the world did that quack know about it?*

The first thought was that there had to be an informant working from within the department or even the state's attorney's office —

But how could someone cover county cops and Tulsa City stuff? And *state* busts?

Someone who had access to warrant information right across the state? But that was coming out of a dozen different offices — oh, it could be done, but only after the busts were over and the warrants filed —

More than one informant. It was the only explanation.

And it was the least believable. *When a cop goes bad, it's generally an isolated event.* A statewide coordinated effort of counter-informers — run from the sticks? — that was too much to believe.

They knew somehow, he thought in shock. *There's no denying that.* For one moment, he wondered if it was possible this Holy Fire thing was real —

No. It couldn't be. There was some other explanation. Meanwhile, he had to play along, because the kid believed, even if he didn't. . . . "It sounds like this thing needs a medium to talk through," Frank said, thinking quickly. He'd heard of the psychic medium scam, some with a kid hypnotized for good measure.

"A child," Joe corrected. "At least, that's according to my father. That was why Sarah. But Sarah began to resist this medium thing too much, and —"

Frank waited. And waited. "And what?"

"He got angry," Joe said in a soft voice. "He — strangled her. Six months ago or so."

A thin line of ice traveled down Frank's spine. "You did see this?"

Joe nodded, and his haunted eyes begged Frank for forgiveness. "I can show you the grave."

Evidence. "That will help. Is it on Chosen Ones' property?"

"It's hidden, but yeah, it's on our land. Their land." He shook his head. "I'm glad to be out of there, but at the same time I feel sorta lost. Like I don't know where I'm going now."

"Don't worry," Frank assured him. "You're doing the right thing." *Damn bet you are, kid.* "But if the girl was murdered six months ago, then who's he been using for the go-between since?"

Joe stared at the back of his hand. "That's what I'm getting at. This family started showing up at Praise Meetings in Atlanta, before we moved everything out here. There was this little kid — he was kinda like the way I was when I was that age. I think one of the reasons I liked him from the start, now that I look back, is 'cause he wasn't caught up in all that crazy Sacred Heart stuff like everyone else was. And he liked me, I think he kind of thought I was like a big brother. The kid needed someone to look up to, and I just sort of fell into the role, I guess."

Frank was getting an eerie feeling about this, a sense of déjà vu that he couldn't quite shake. *Why does this sound familiar?* he wondered, but saved his questions for later.

The back of his hand seemed to fascinate the boy. "The father, this drunk named Jim, got roped into the Sacred Heart real good. My father convinced him to bring his son to the Praise Meeting. The kid turned out to be better than Sarah."

"The man's name was Jim?" Frank asked, knowing now why this all seemed familiar. And he didn't want it to. "Was his last name Chase?"

Joe frowned. "Might have been. Everyone there is on a first-name basis, but it'd be on record somewhere."

Frank knew he had to ask. "What about the boy? What's he called?"

"Jamie," Joe said. "The boy's name is Jamie."

Oh Lord, Frank thought, keeping his face as bland as

possible. *How do I tell Cindy Chase this?* The answer came to him quickly: *You don't. At least, not yet.*

"He grabbed the kid — actually, he got Jim to grab him and bring him here. He had Jim kidnap the kid out of school, and lie to him, told him that the compound was a summer camp or something. Then they started using Jamie all the time as the medium thing, and they started starving him to keep him quiet, make it easier for the Holy Fire to talk through him. All he gets is juice —" Joe faltered, then picked up the narrative again. "That was when I started to feel bad about my position in the Guard, the whole Sacred Heart thing. Last night — Father made me a lieutenant with a new promotion, head of Internal Security. He must have figured something was wrong, 'cause all of a sudden he started dangling all this stuff in front of me. New apartment, new rank. But — I just can't take it anymore."

"You couldn't take what happened with the little girl?" Frank asked.

Joe shook his head, guiltily. "No, I mean, I know that sounds bad, but I didn't know her. She was kind of a puppet for father, and it was like what was happening wasn't real. No, it's what he's doing to the kid. For weeks they've been starving him, to be a better channel for this Holy Fire, and he keeps getting weaker and thinner — he can't hardly stand anymore. It's torture. I got some food through to him, but it's not enough to save him. I was up against too much in that place. I had to go get help."

Joe shuddered. "Sir, you've got to go in there before it's too late. Father's been putting him in a sensory deprivation tank for some godawful reason, which is just hurting him more. It's something I don't understand at all, it's like he does it just 'cause he *can*. And whatever else happens, Jamie can't go on much longer!"

Joe's eyes were pleading, glistened over with tears not yet ready to fall. "I'm responsible, too. Arrest me if you want to, but go in and save him."

Suddenly all the barriers broke, and Joe put his head down on his arms and sobbed — tiny, strangled sobs that sounded horrible, as if the boy was choking.

Frank was amazed. After all that control, he hadn't expected the boy to break down and cry. The other patrons in the restaurant had already left; now it was just them and Peggy, who turned the front door sign to "Closed," then came over with a box of tissue.

"Sorry," Joe said, after composing himself in the face of a strange female. "I didn't mean to — lose it like that."

"Its okay," Frank told him, feeling a little better now that he knew the kid still had some real emotions. "Cry as much as you want to. We'll figure this mess out somehow."

But the control was back, at least for the moment. After a while, Peggy began bringing their food over. Old George was watching, covertly, his face lined with concern.

"Hope you're still hungry," Frank said. "There's a lot of food here."

Joe's appetite did not seem to be dampened at all by grief; the boy devoured everything in front of him.

"Don't worry, son, we're not going to arrest you," Frank assured him, between mouthfuls of his own hamburger. "For one thing, I don't see evidence yet of any wrongdoing on your part. I doubt any judge in the country would hold you responsible for what happened to the little girl or to the boy, either, as long as you're willing to turn state's evidence. Would you be willing to testify against your father?"

Joe didn't answer right away. He seemed to mull over it, but only briefly. "Yes. I — I know I shouldn't think twice about it, but my father scares me, sir. He has too much power, and what he says goes. If you haven't got a bulletproof jacket lying around, I think maybe you should find one, if you want me alive long enough to testify. Even then it might not make any difference."

"I'll see what I can come up with," Frank said. Now it seemed like a pretty good idea. *Assault weapons. I guess death squads and assassins is a logical next step. After all, this Brother Joseph has killed at least once. . . .*

"Surely he left something behind?" Brother Joseph said carefully.

He had been eating lunch alone in his private dining room, when Luke had interrupted the meal. He didn't like being interrupted at meals. Especially not with news like this.

Joe. Gone. No — not possible.

"No note?" he persisted. "No clues? Nothing at all to tell you about where he went?"

"Nothing," Luke said simply, his eyes staring at the wall over Brother Joseph's head. "He left nothing behind, sir. Some clothing appears to have been taken, but none of the Chosen Ones' uniforms. He vanished, apparently, as a civilian. No one really knows where he is."

The preacher's eyes narrowed at the news. *I knew the boy was up to something,* he thought coldly, a slow rage building. *The devil must have had his claws in him for a long time now. Why else would he turn against me? Haven't I shown him the way? Didn't I give him more than any other father would? I gave him one of the most prestigious honors he could ever hope to achieve. And this is how he repays me? How dare he?*

Then the rage — paused for a moment. *Or — did he? How could he dare?*

"This is simply not acceptable," he said to Luke. "I think that your conclusion that my son has abandoned us and gone to the authorities is premature. He could be testing us, you know. That would be just about his speed." That made more sense. Surely the boy would never dare run off. *He's probably trying to impress me.* He smiled as the logical explanation unrolled before him. "I can see it now, flexing his new muscles as the new Internal Security head, hiding in some corner we've forgotten about, waiting to see what precisely our reaction would be to this. If you think about it, our response would be rather revealing. It would emphasize our ability to handle — or not handle — a defection."

Luke shook his head, stubbornly. "No, Brother Joseph, I just don't think so. Haven't you noticed how peculiar he's been lately? Especially around Jamie. If you ask me, it seems he's had a change of heart about the Cause. The devil's in his heart, and he's not listening to the voice of God anymore."

"Well," Brother Joseph said, smiling thinly. Luke's statement touched a raw nerve, and he tried to conceal it as much as possible. "I'm *not* asking you. Use your head, man! This is my flesh and blood you're talking about! I suggest you organize a thorough search of the complex. If he wants to play this little game with us, we'll show him we can play it better."

"As you wish, sir," Luke said, but it didn't look like he was pleased with the assignment. "We will conduct a thorough search of the complex. Again."

"You do that," the preacher said. "And I suggest you not report back until you find him."

Brother Joseph watched the retreating back, a bit surprised that Luke had actually contradicted him. Nobody in the organization had ever done such a thing.

For that matter, Luke was the only one who could do it and escape serious punishment. His loyalty was unquestioned, and he was totally devoted to his leader and the Cause. But it wasn't like the man to think for himself; usually he just followed blindly, a quality Brother Joseph encouraged in his followers.

But there had always been an unspoken competition between Luke and his son. *Competition and animosity. They've tried to conceal it from me, but I saw it anyway. Interesting that Luke seems eager to declare my son a traitor.*

Never mind. It wasn't going to ruin his day. He had much to look forward to tonight. This particular Praise Meeting was going to be special, he knew. The Holy Fire had been restless lately, an anxiety he could feel in his bones, suggesting that a spectacular channeling was in store for them all tonight.

Alas, it would probably be the last one, at least with Jamie. The boy had been pushed to his limits, though for a good reason, the only reason necessary: *the Holy Fire desired it.* Now the boy was closer to death, which took him closer to God. Brother Joseph had estimated yesterday that the boy had perhaps a week left to him, before starvation and the Holy Fire finished him off. After tonight, he would either be a vegetable or dead, most likely the latter.

The preacher sighed, staring at his unfinished meal. He wished there was some way to do this channeling so that he didn't have to go out and find another host every six months. It was so . . . inconvenient. Jamie in particular had been far better than Sarah, who was, he now saw, a mere container. She had been to Jamie what a hatchback coupe was to an exotic sportscar. The boy was a perfect vehicle, and the only thing that had kept him from disposing of Sarah when she started to resist and substituting the boy immediately had been Jamie's whore of a mother. Cindy had been a nuisance from the very start. It was a good thing she had been left behind in Atlanta.

Why, he wondered now, had Sarah begun to resist? So far Jamie had been quite complacent about the whole thing. Perhaps it had been the girl's age. He noticed that she had begun to mature, a little early, at ten. *That has to be it!* he decided. As soon as girl children began to mature, they took on the attributes of any whore. This womanhood, this *contamination*, must be the evil that made her resist the holy touch.

It was all he needed to formulate a brilliant theory. *If it weren't for men, all women would be spawn of Satan! Why are most preachers men? Didn't Eve succumb to evil, not Adam? And of the church's staff, how many women fulfill any kind of useful role?* The only one that came to mind was Agatha, the retired schoolteacher whom he'd won over years before. And *she* was old, well past menopause. Sterile. Pure. The rest of the women in the place were cattle. *Baby producers. Preferably, boy producers.*

He glanced up at the clock on the wall and frowned when he saw the time. Ten past one. *Looks like my wife isn't going to join me. Wonder what's gotten into her? I'm going to have to check into that. This is the fourth meal in a row that she's taken elsewhere.*

He finished his solitary lunch and went directly to Joe's room. The door was open, evidently left that way since the first search. Frowning, he saw the sinister paperback he'd flung across the room the night before, displeased to see that Joe hadn't destroyed it. *How dare he defy me?* he seethed, poking through the boxes that remained. *When I see him again, I will have to punish him severely for this.*

His pager went off at his waist, and when he checked the number saw that he was being summoned to the central security station. *Ah! Maybe Joe's decided to report in. Mystery solved.*

When he arrived, however, he could see from the expressions on all assembled that this wasn't the case. There were half a dozen security officers there, immaculate in their uniforms, plus Luke. They jumped up from their consoles and saluted as he entered. But nobody seemed willing to meet his eyes, and that alone was enough to stir his wrath.

"Well?" he said impatiently, when no one offered to explain why he had been paged. "What is it?"

Luke was standing in the middle of the cluster of guards. They glanced covertly at the man, deferring the answer to him. He cleared his throat, and with an effort met his leader's eyes.

"One of our people has seen Joe," he began. "In town."

Then he stopped, and the silence was infuriating. "Yes? And?"

Luke coughed. "He was seen talking to a sheriff's deputy. He was not wearing the uniform of the guard. Apparently, they spoke for a long time."

Brother Joseph stared at him, stunned. He didn't know how to respond. *Who saw him? There aren't too many people it could be — only a few of us go out at a time. No one who really knows Joe. . . . It must be a mistake, either that or it's an outright lie!*

"Who says he saw Joe? I want to speak to him personally."

As if on cue, the group parted, revealing a man in the back who looked like he wanted to become invisible. He didn't look well; actually, he was obviously suffering from a hangover. But then, he usually was. Lank blond hair straggled greasily and untidily over his ears; his eyes were so bloodshot you couldn't tell what color they were. His skin was a pasty yellow-white, and his forehead was creased with a frown of pain.

"Jim Chase?" Brother Joseph said. "On your honor, now. Did you see Joe today?"

"Ah, yessir. I sure did," Jim said, though his eyes never quite met the preacher's. He seemed to be studying the wall behind the preacher instead. "Like Luke said, he was talking to this big Indian deputy, there at this diner. I pulled into the parking lot and was going to go in and take a leak, when I saw him through the window with his back turned to me, talking to the cop."

Brother Joseph frowned. "If his back was turned to you how do you know it was him?"

Jim shook, but didn't back down. "I saw his profile a few times, when he looked out the window. It was him."

Brother Joseph stepped closer and examined Jim's disheveled appearance carefully, letting Jim know he was taking note of the state the man was in. He sniffed, once. His nose wrinkled at the reek of bourbon.

"I see," Brother Joseph said, turning away. "You have a strong odor of liquor about you. I've told you before that I don't mind my flock imbibing from time to time. But in your present condition, how can I be certain you weren't, how we say, seeing things?"

Jim didn't seem to have an answer to that. "Sir, I wasn't." He shook his head. "I know your son; you know yourself he's spent a lot of time with my — with Jamie. Besides, I saw his tattoo in the window. The swastika."

Brother Joseph felt himself blanche; he'd always wanted his son to have the blasted thing taken off. It just wasn't politic to be brandishing symbols of something that had failed, no matter how noble their cause had been.

"Seems cut and dried to me," Luke said calmly. "That must have been him, then."

Brother Joseph knew that his tranquil facade would dissolve completely if he stopped to think. And he knew that he'd lose some of the power he had over these men if he didn't take back control; in fact, he could feel the power crumbling now.

Get a grip on yourself. And deal with this. "We must consider Joe a renegade and a traitor," he said, emotionlessly. "He is to be shot on sight, provided it can be done anonymously. Luke, would you kindly dispatch a mechanic to eliminate him?"

"Yes, sir," Luke said. The preacher thought he saw a smirk forming at the corners of the man's mouth.

You would enjoy that, wouldn't you, you little toady? he thought, but retained his own cold smile. It didn't matter. Command had been reestablished. *You see, my followers? The importance of my own flesh and blood pales in comparison to the importance of our mission. I'll sacrifice my own traitorous son without a hint of regret so that we may march on unimpeded!* He nodded, offering tacit approval to Luke to do the job himself. The rest of the guardsmen seemed frozen in shock at Brother Joseph's decision.

Saying no more, Brother Joseph left to visit Jamie in his cell.

After all, didn't God sacrifice his own son?

• CHAPTER TWELVE

These mortals are ineffectual fools, Al thought, during the long ride back from Pawnee. *I can't believe this has gone on for so long without a resolution. Our ways are better.*

It was a judgment he had made a long time ago, but the whole sad situation with Cindy, Jamie, Frank and the Sacred Heart of the Chosen Ones simply reinforced it. After this latest encounter with the sheriff's office, he'd just about decided that unless he intervened, the outcome of this was going to be bleak. *The wheels of justice turn in this county, true, but only slowly. If this were a violation of an elven law, the matter would have been resolved long ago, by spell or swordpoint. If it hadn't been for the Salamander, I'd have found a way to take care of it myself.*

All the way back from the sheriff's office, they were ominously silent. Gone was the hopeful mood during their trip out to Pawnee; Cindy oozed depression. Any moment Alinor figured she was going to break down and cry. It was all he could do to keep his shields up and his mind clear. At this point in the game, he needed everything working in top form.

Keeping Cindy's emotions out, though, wasn't the real problem. His own simmering anger threatened to overwhelm him. *Now I know why I deal so little with the humans' world,* he thought. *I would go mad with all that . . . that . . . red tape!*

Frank had been no help at all. It only confirmed what he suspected all along: that the sheriff's department, though with all the right reasons for their actions, had no intention of including them in any move they might take against the group. That alone rankled him. After all, hadn't he already been in the camp and gotten closer to the situation than any law enforcement officer? *I know more about what's going on in there than they do — or could. They have no concept of the universe beyond their own, immediate physical world. They wouldn't know a ghost if they walked through one!*

He couldn't begin to consider explaining the Salamander to the cop. *He'd probably have me committed or jailed or something,* he thought, shuddering at the possibility of being surrounded by all that cold steel. *They have no idea what they're up against. The Salamander could come in and pulverize anyone's mind without much effort. Great Danaa — it would happily pit all of its followers against the law enforcement people and gorge on the resulting carnage. . . .*

In fact, that was probably what the Salamander had in mind.

What he doesn't know — couldn't know — is that Jamie is being exposed to this thing regularly. If his mind isn't destroyed yet, it will be soon, perhaps even the next time they have their little "Praise Meeting." At the sheriff's rate of progress, Jamie isn't going to last long enough to be rescued.

He considered another nagging possibility. *The Salamander is going to see this raid a mile away. It probably knows about it already. Then what? Is it going to instruct Brother Joseph to fortify the underground complex of bunkers even more? Short of a bombing run with napalm, there would be little chance of getting to the soldiers. And if we did, what would be left? Too risky to the children to even consider it.*

They pulled into Hallet raceway in the late afternoon, and Al reached forward with his mind to make sure the air-conditioning was on in the RV. The temperature was up to at least a hundred now, a county-wide sauna. Heat like that that would only aggravate already touchy tempers. Al would have to be careful lest Cindy blow up in his face; he sighed with the realization that she probably would anyway, regardless of how much caution he exercised around her. *How can I blame her, though? If it were my child — and I'm beginning to feel like it is — I would be frustrated to tears, too.*

Fortunately all at the track had been running perfectly since that last minor fix on the engine, and the team had given them as much time as they needed off. *Thank Danaa,* he thought, wishing that all racing gigs had gone as well mechanically as this one. *If we'd had to deal with a balky engine, I doubt we would have had the time to do as much as we have.*

After they had parked the car, Cindy excused herself. She said she had to go make a call to her bank in Atlanta. Al suspected she just wanted to be alone for a while and didn't say anything. She'd probably go hole up in the ladies' room over by the stands and cry her eyes out.

Bob looked tired and slouched back on the couchbed with a Gatorade and a *Car and Driver* magazine. Not surprising, after being up most of the night working on Cindy's car. Al didn't really want to burden his friend with what was on his mind, but they had made promises to each other that no matter what they would be there for each other. It was a pact encouraged by every one of the Folk who'd joined SERRA, for experience had shown that their kind didn't always do very well going solo in the humans' world.

Especially, Al thought tiredly, *when a Salamander is involved.*

He took a seat across his companion and pretended to study the table top for a moment. "You know, Bob," Al said conversationally. "This, ah, sheriff's office doesn't strike me as being all that efficient in dealing with this mess."

Bob lowered the magazine and gazed steadily at his partner, his eyes narrowed, with a slight frown on his lean features. "Eyah?" he said, but the glint in his eye suggested he already knew what to expect. But he added no more to his comment. Instead, he waited patiently for his friend to continue.

"I mean, look at it. They have all the evidence they need to raid the place, or at least investigate the cult a lot closer. If they did, they'd *find* Jamie, you know they would! But their own laws are preventing them from doing it!" He felt himself snarling and clamped control down on himself. "The laws that were designed to prevent this abuse are indirectly condoning it," he said a little more calmly. "What sense does that make?"

Bob took his time responding, as usual. "I don't pretend to be a part of the humans' world," he replied, slowly. "I know, I am a human, but I don't understand it. I feel like I'm sorta caught between the human and the elven worlds, and to tell you the truth, most of the time Underhill seems a lot more sensible. This is one of those times when it's especially true." He sighed wearily. "I think I know what you're getting at. You want to go in. Like Rambo. Play Lancelot. Do you really think, though, that you can take on this thing by yourself?"

Al bristled at the suggestion, however true it probably was, that this was out of his league. "I don't know if I can or not," he said. "We don't have a choice, and I'm going to have to try. The law enforcement people involved in this deal are blind to the Salamander; they wouldn't believe in it even if we told them about it. How could they hope to combat something they can't even see?"

"Right," Bob said, and shook his head. He knew that no matter what he said, Al was going to go ahead and do what he was planning on doing anyway. And Al knew that he knew. It had never changed anything before, and it wouldn't this time, either. "Had it occurred to you that maybe you should call in some help?"

Al snorted indignantly. The problem was, he had. The

Low Court elves he had contacted — hundreds of miles away, in Dallas — had shown polite interest in the Salamander project, but nothing more. He had explained carefully to them how imperiled the boy was, pushing all the proper elven buttons to rouse their anger. But those he talked to had sadly shaken their heads, telling him that there was nothing *they* could do. There simply was no nexus close enough — even if they had been able to transfer themselves to it in time to do any good. They couldn't operate that far away from the nexus in Dallas. There were no High Court elves there, and while the Low Court was sympathetic to his plight, they were helpless. They simply could not survive more than fifty miles from their grove-anchored power-pole. And he hadn't been able to contact any of the High Court elves of Outremer or Fairgrove. Al checked again, working through his anger — but once again he could touch no one. He released the fine line of communication he sustained and refrained from beating his head against the nearest convenient wall.

"I see," Bob said, as if reading his mind. "No luck, huh?"

"None."

The discovery left him feeling empty, reminding him how different he really was from the other elves. Traveling the world, intersecting with the humans' universe whenever necessary, was for him a way of life. To the rest — except for those in Fairgrove and Outremer, and some rumored few in Misthold — it was an esoteric and dangerous hobby. *They're probably behind shields or Underhill. Damn. Why didn't I tell them about this when I first realized the Salamander was involved?*

"So what do you suggest?" Bob said. "Waltz in there all by yourself, politely inform them you're there for Jamie and then walk out with him?" He sat up, setting the magazine aside, and faced Al. "You really think they're going to go for that?"

"No, no, *no!*" Al said, a bit of his anger slipping past his shields. "Just what kind of a fool do you think I am? I'm going to pull out every trick I can conjure just to get through this one alive. What choice do I have? You know that child hasn't a chance unless I go in after him! Frank Casey is a good man, but he's only one sheriff, and he's the *only* one who knows or cares about Jamie! How much will you wager me that he's the least senior man involved in whatever it is they're doing about the Chosen Ones? I *have* to go in there because no one else will!"

"God," Bob said, wearily. "Listen, Alinor, I'm not blind or deaf. I saw the maps and all, and the way Casey hid them. It's just that you're going to have to go up against that thing, and there is nothing on a magical level I can do to help you. I want you to *think* about what you're doing and not just charge in there like every other macho warrior in Outremer, thinking you can conquer the world just because you can work a few magic tricks. I'm afraid for you, even if you won't be for yourself. This thing scares me."

Al snorted. "Don't think for a minute that it doesn't scare me. I told you, I'm not a fool. Anyone else might act like a 'macho warrior' — but they don't know what they're up against. I do. Believe me, I do."

Near their RV, a barbecue party was in noisy progress. In the distance was the dim roar of race cars, the muted bark of a PA system. Around them the world was functioning normally, while they discussed — what? A raid on a crazed madman and his army — confronting a supernatural monster. Life had progressed way beyond surreal.

But he had a sudden idea. "There is something you can do to help me. Keep a close eye on Cindy when I go in there." Bob flinched at the mention of "there," but Al continued. "Keep her occupied. I don't want her to know what I'm doing."

Bob gave him the Look. "What, exactly, will you be doing? And don't forget the cops. They can still come after us if they find out we're interfering. Remember, the deputy told us to stay out of it."

Al expelled a breath as he gazed at the floor. *What, indeed?* "Here it is. *If* they find out, it'll be after I've gotten in and out. At that point dealing with them will be the easiest part of this whole mess. I play games with Frank's memory, make him forget 'Al,' replace what he knows with memories of some crazy human antiterrorist or something. Let him spin his wheels trying to find someone who never existed. I've done it before. It's the Chosen Ones we need to be concerned with the most."

"No kidding," Bob muttered. "So how are you planning on keeping yourself bullet-hole-free?"

Al shrugged. "I'll go in with James' face, or someone else they'll recognize."

Bob nodded. "Okay. And once you're in, then what?"

Al shrugged. "I wing it, I guess."

Bob groaned.

Jamie came awake in the darkened cell, suddenly aware that someone was sitting in the room with him.

:Sarah?: he sent, but there was no answer, and the presence was solid. It smelled, sweat and dirty clothes and mildew — real.

And another odor that could only mean his father. That smell. Joy juice. *Oh, no, I'm going to get sick again.*

He had barely enough energy to turn over and vomit into a small trash can that had been left there for that reason. A man named Luke had told him to use it if he got sick again, and if he missed it he was going to spank him with a rubber hose. Long welts on his legs and buttocks testified to his poor aim. It was difficult to hit the bucket when you saw two of them.

When he was finished he leaned back on the bed. From the sound his vomit made, he knew he'd hit the bucket, so he knew he wouldn't be beaten this time. But he was still afraid. He looked up through the fog that clouded his vision at the face in front of him he dimly recognized as his father's.

"Daddy," he whispered, since that was all he had the strength for. "What did I do wrong? What am I being spanked for?"

It was always possible that to ask such questions would only solicit more beatings, either from his father or another adult nearby. It didn't matter. It seemed like whatever he did, it was wrong, and it was his fault.

Always my fault.

"Don't talk back to your daddy," Jim said angrily. "Don't you *ever* talk back to me. There's a reason for all this. I know it, you don't have to. Just you wait and see."

Although Jamie heard the words, there wasn't much sense he could extract from them. Another question formed, then slipped past his teeth.

"Where's Mommy?"

Stars exploded in his vision as Jim hit the side of his face. Jamie saw stars and felt his whole face spasming with pain, then aching right down to the bone, his teeth loosening. His head jerked to the side, stayed that way. He had no energy to cry or scream or protest or agree to what was going on. All he could do was to lie there in terror and wait for whoever was inflicting the pain to go away, however temporarily; they would always return, he knew.

"I'll beat the devil out of you yet," Jim said, but his voice sounded like he was further away, though he hadn't heard his footsteps retreating. Jamie heard another voice then, one that sounded like Luke's.

"Tonight's the night," he heard Luke say, further away, beyond the open door where light spilled into the room.

"There's too much of his damn mother in him," Jim

Chase said, as if that was Jamie's fault. "He won't believe in anything! He always has to ask *questions!* It's his damn mother, I tell you —"

He heard footsteps as they left the room. "It don't matter," Luke replied. "Holy Fire can use him now whether he believes or not, and anyway, after tonight it'll be all over with." Luke laughed, nastily. "Until then, we'll let him see what *questions* buy doubters. He gets to see what the darkness of hell is like."

The light went out.

Darkness used to mean terror, now it was welcome. Darkness usually meant the beatings would stop.

:Sarah. Help me.: he called. *:You promised you'd help me.:*

Long moments passed as he waited for his companion. As always she appeared, faithful as ever, this time as a ball of bright white light at the outer periphery of his vision. Her presence, over the last several visits, seemed to be getting stronger. Jamie didn't know what to think about that, except that maybe he was getting closer to becoming a ghost like her.

She hovered there a long while, longer than usual, which made Jamie nervous.

:What's wrong?: he asked.

:I can't stay,: she said, sounding afraid. *:It's getting stronger. If I stay too long it will see me, and I don't know what will happen yet. I came by to tell you . . . .:*

The light flickered, dimmed, threatened to go out. Jamie panicked. *:Sarah! Don't go away.:*

The light brightened. *:. . . to tell you help is on the way. Joe ran away and told the police what was going on. And . . .:*

He waited for her to finish, but he sensed she was struggling against something, like there was a hard wind where she was, blowing her away.

The light surged back one more time, for a brief moment.

:. . . that I love you.:

And the wind blew the light out.

*   *   *

Bob stood in front of the white van with his hands planted on his hips and a frown on his face. Cindy stood beside him, holding his arm tightly, but trying to be so quiet she was holding her breath. "Look," he said — profoundly grateful that it was after sunset and there was no one near enough to see that he was talking to a grill and a pair of headlights. "You know he and Andur went over there with no backup. You *know* he's not up to this! So who's left to do anything? You and me!"

The lights glowed faintly for a moment. Bob wished — not for the first time — that he was one of the human fosterlings with the power to speak mind-to-mind. But then Nineve was probably just as frustrated with this as he was. None of the elvensteeds could speak audibly — and in fact, none could transform up to anything larger or more complicated than a cargo van. Nineve's interior modifications were all due to the same magic Alinor used to modify the Winnie. Otherwise, Bob would have had her shift into a nice solid M-1 tank.

"Here's what I figured," he continued, hoping desperately that what he had *figured* was going to work. "I've been playin' with the scanner Les Huff's got in his trailer; he's got this book on police freqs, and I've been listening every night, tryin' t' see if there was anything goin' down with the cops, okay? Well, just after Al left, there's all *kinda* stuff, radio checks, code-words — sounded like somebody was gearing up for something real big. Well, when we visited that Pawnee County Mounty, he covered up what we thought was plans for a big raid. I figure that big raid's about to happen. And Al's right smack in the middle of it. But — *but* — if you ask the owls where it's all coming from — and then we catch them gearin' up — well, maybe we can force their hand. If we get them to kick off that raid early, while Al's in there, maybe that *thing* he's going up against'll pay attention to them and not him."

Nineve's lights came on and stayed on — and her motor started up abruptly and the driver's-side door popped open. Bob could have wept with relief.

Cindy released his arm and started for the passenger's side as Nineve revved her engine. Bob grabbed her elbow before she had gotten more than a step away. "No," he said, holding her back. "You stay here."

She whirled, balling her fists, her eyes flashing in sudden anger. "No? *No?* What the hell do you mean, *no*? That's my *son* you're talking about —"

"That's the police from a backwater, redneck, prehistoric county we're talking about," Bob replied levelly. "Plus the FBI, the state cops, maybe the DEA for all I know. All good ol' boys *frum roun' ear.*" He imitated the local accent mercilessly. "You're not *frum roun' ear.* You're not military, you're not even male. If you can think of a bigger bunch of macho ass-kickers, I'd like to hear it some time. *Your* son isn't gonna mean squat to them, Cindy. You show up, and if you're lucky, they'll just dismiss everything you tell them as female hysterics and shove you off into a corner to make coffee. If you're *not* lucky, they'll throw you into the county clink to keep you out of their hair!"

She fell silent and stopped resisting his hold. He continued, a little more gently. "Cindy, it's not fair, but that's the way these guys are gonna be, and we've gotta deal with it. I'm a man, I speak their language. I'm a National Guard MP with a security clearance, I know how to handle a gun, I've got grease and oil under my fingernails — if I go in there and find Frank first, I think maybe I can convince him to deputize me and bring me in with them. If I'm deputized, he can *assign* me to find Jamie. And figure I've got a better than average chance of not getting shot in the ass."

He took a deep breath, as Cindy slumped and put her hand to her mouth to keep from crying. "Cindy,

Frank's not a bad guy — he wants to help, but he's got his job to do. He may even be happy to see me. More important, though — if we start a ruckus while Al's in there, we'll be giving him cover. If between us we can't get Jamie out, no one can. But if you go, that's not gonna happen. We'll *both* wind up in the county slammer. You for showing up, me for bringing you."

"All right," Cindy said, in a small voice. "I guess you're right. But — just sitting here, not doing anything —"

"I know it's hard, Cindy," Bob told her earnestly. "It's the hardest thing in the world. I've done my share of waiting, too. Not like this — but I've done a lot of it. Will you stay in the RV and trust me?"

She nodded, shyly — and to his surprise and shocked delight, kissed him, swiftly. Then she turned and ran into the RV.

"Did that mean what I thought it meant?" he asked Nineve. The lights blinked twice, and he touched his lips, a bemused smile starting at the corners of his mouth. "I'll be damned. . . . Well, hell, this isn't catching any fish. Let's get going!"

Bob faced Frank Casey with a stolid, stubborn expression he knew the deputy could read with no mistake. Casey, in his camos and blackout face-paint, looked absolutely terrifying; bigger than usual, and *entirely* like a warrior. If they'd let him wear feathers, he'd probably have one tucked into the cover of his helmet.

Casey was trying to intimidate him with silence and a glower. Bob refused to be intimidated. Casey tried a little longer, then deflated.

"Christ," he muttered, removing his helmet and passing his hand through his hair. "I don't know how you found out about this — but you're here now, and Captain Lawrence says your ID checks out — shit, I can use another hand, I guess." He shook his head. "Consider yourself deputized. Goddamn. At least you got more sense than that hothead buddy of yours with the hair."

Behind Frank, the Air National Guard hangar at the tiny regional airport was as full of feverish activity as a beehive at swarming time; it had been bad *before,* when he first strolled in. But now —

He'd almost been arrested on the spot, until he cited Frank Casey as his contact. Then he'd faced an unfriendly audience of DEA officers, National Guard officers, FBI agents and police. They hadn't liked what he told them about Al.

And I didn't even tell them a quarter of it.

"Yeah, well," Bob coughed. "I couldn't stop him. Tried, but —" He shrugged. "He's real worried about that kid."

"So'm I," Frank said grimly. "But I've got the FBI, the DEA, the County Mounties, the state boys — and half the local National Guard to worry about, too. They made me local coordinator on this thing, they've been letting me call some of the shots. And your buddy may just have blown our raid."

"Maybe," Bob said cautiously. "Maybe not." *How do I play my ace in a way he'll believe? He sure as hell won't believe me about the Salamander. . . .* "Seems to me these guys've got ways of finding out things — like they've been able to screw things up for you before this." The flinch Frank made cheered him immensely. He was on the right track! "So, okay, they may even know about this one. Except you're gonna jump the gun on them. So maybe *now,* 'cause we forced your hand a little, you got a chance of catching 'em off-guard." He cocked his head to one side. "So that's why I asked you to bring me in on this. I know what he looks like; hopefully I can find him before he catches a little 'friendly fire.' *That* sure wouldn't look good on the report."

Frank shook his head slowly. "Man," he drawled, "I haven't heard a line like that since *Moonlighting* got canceled."

Bob almost grinned and stopped himself just in time.

"Right now, the *only* reason your ass isn't in the county jail is because I convinced *my* superiors that *you* are somebody I've worked with before. Your Guard record helped, but basically they're going on my word." Frank looked back over his shoulder at the half-dozen Blackhawk helicopters being loaded at double-time. "Don't push your luck."

"No, sir," Bob replied, with complete seriousness.

"You've got three assignments," Frank said, holding up three fingers, and counting down on them. "Find your buddy. Find the kid. Try not to get ventilated. When you accomplish one and two, get down and *stay* down so you can accomplish three."

"Yes *sir!*" Bob didn't salute, but he snapped to a completely respectful attention. Frank nodded, apparently satisfied.

"Now get your ass over there," he said, nodding at the third chopper in line. "You're with Lieutenant Summer; you can't miss 'em, he's the only black officer in this crowd. He knows you're with his bunch. One of his men turned up sick, so lucky you, you get to ride. And buddy, that's all you got. You manage to liberate a weapon from the enemy, *then* you've got a piece — otherwise, you got nothing."

Bob nodded. He hadn't expected anything else. There wouldn't be any spare weapons on this trip — and even if there had been, there was no one here who'd take responsibility for signing him out on one. If an assault rifle turned up missing after all this was over, and then guys in charge found out an outsider had been brought in at the last minute — there'd be no doubt of where the gun went (whether or not that was the real truth), and the one who'd authorized issuing it to Bob would be in major deep kimchee. And in theory, given his assignments, he wouldn't *need* one. Not having a gun would make him concentrate on those assignments instead of playing Rambo.

Frank looked him up and down one more time. Bob knew what Frank was thinking, given his "nonstandard" clothing. When he'd headed out in this direction, he'd had a small choice of outfits. Instead of going for concealing gear, since he figured he wasn't going to be in the first wave, Bob had chosen to suit up in *real obvious* clothing — his bright red, Nomex coverall. There wasn't a chance in hell that any of the Bad Guys would be wearing something like *that,* which meant that the Good Guys — in theory, anyway — wouldn't mistake him for a lawful target. Al would recognize him if he saw him, even at a distance, even during a firefight. Hopefully Jamie would recognize racetrack gear and trust him. Nomex was fireproof and heat-resistant; he might be able to make a dash into or out of a burning building if he had to.

Of course, this same outfit made him look like a big fat target for the *Bad* Guys —

Frank shook his head. "How come you didn't paint a bulls'-eye on the back while you were at it?"

"Reckoned all they'd see was a red blur goin' about ninety, and figure I was a launched flare," Bob drawled.

Frank's mouth twitched. "Deployable decoy. You're either the bravest bastard I ever met, or the craziest. Get over to that chopper, before I change my mind."

This time Bob *did* salute, and did a quick about-face before Frank got a chance to respond. A huge black man in camos was supervising the loading of his men; as Bob quick-trotted over, he looked up and waved impatiently at him.

Bob broke into a run — hoping he wasn't about to make the biggest mistake of what could turn out to be a very short life. . . .

*   *   *

The gloomy, empty hallway would echo footsteps, if Alinor had been so careless as to make any noise. Wherever the Chosen Ones had gone to, it wasn't *here*, and Al was perfectly happy to have things that way.

But he was going to have to find somewhere to hide for a little, while he got his bearings. There was so much iron and steel around him that his senses were confused; he needed to orient himself — and most of all, he needed to find where the Chosen Ones all were — and where Jamie was.

He slipped inside the door marked "Cleaning Supplies" and closed it behind him. He waited for his eyes to adjust to the darkness, and made out a mop, a bucket, and a sink with two shelves over it, with one gallon jug of cheap disinfectant cleaner on the top shelf. Nothing else.

Not a lot of supplies. I suppose it's easier to punish someone by making them clean the floor with brute force than to buy adequate supplies. Then again, any penny that goes to buy a bottle of cleaner doesn't go to buy bullets — or steak for Brother Joseph. That's the Way of the Holy Profit.

Getting in had been much easier than he had thought it would be. First of all, he'd gone in right after dinner, when the guards were torpid from their meal. He slipped in with Andur's help over the first two sets of fences at some distance from the compound, then he'd walked around to the third checkpoint openly, as if he'd been out for a stroll. He'd altered his face to look like Jim Chase's — then, as he approached the third set of security guards, he'd planted the false memory that they had seen the man going out — supposedly for a walk — about an hour before. They waved him in after no more than a cursory question or two. He continued his stroll towards the main bunker, as the sun splashed vivid reds in fiery swaths across the western sky.

But the next problem confronted him immediately,

in the form of a technological barrier. Illusions weren't going to fool video cameras, and there was one just inside the bunker door. He would *have* to pass it to get inside.

Well, there *had been* one. Technically, there still was one, it just wasn't working right now.

He had paused just out of range, loitering for a moment, as if enjoying a final breath of fresh air before descending into the dank bunker, and had checked out the circuit the camera was operating on. To his delight, he had discovered that they hadn't replaced the wiring of that line after his initial tampering. He had used a fraction of his powers to create an electrical surge that had fried the camera just before he turned to face it. And with the corridor beyond empty it had been child's play to penetrate into the lower level and find this closet to hide in.

Now, as he braced himself carefully against the wooden support-beam and sent his mind ranging along the electrical circuitry, he discovered they hadn't replaced *any* of the wiring, despite all the damage his tampering had been causing. Evidently none of these folk associated the cascading equipment failures they'd been cursed with to an overall failure in the wiring.

Maybe it wouldn't occur to them. They may be the "plug and play" type, using things without understanding them. Al found that kind of attitude impossible to put up with, but most humans seemed to be like that. He had learned that if you asked the average mortal how something he used every day (a light bulb, for instance) worked, most of the time he would not be able to tell you.

Mortals relied on others more than they ever dreamed — even the Chosen Ones, who prided themselves on being self-sufficient. It was a false pride, for without the outside world to support them — in the apocalyptic world they seemed to dream of — their entire way of life would fall apart within weeks.

Never mind that. Just take advantage of it.

He located the shielded security circuits and sent surges along all of them, blowing out every security camera he could find. There was more he could do — he hadn't done much in the way of starting electrical fires yet, except by accident —

Not yet. I might need the distractions to cover me.

The first thing he needed to do was to locate the bulk of the Chosen Ones, using the wires to carry his probes. He found them, as he had expected, still in the communal dining hall. Good; he wasn't likely to run into any stragglers for a while yet.

And now for my enemy. He searched for the Salamander, then, sending his mind cautiously out into the emptier parts of the building complex to look for it. He had a fair idea of where it might be. The room of the Praise Meetings. Hopefully, it would be drowsing.

He recoiled swiftly as he touched it, realizing by the difference in the tension of its aura that it was *not* half aware, as it had been before when there was no meeting. It was awake — but it was preoccupied, as if something else had its attention, and it had little to spare to look about itself.

It was in the Praise Meeting room. In fact, as he examined its energies from a cautious distance, it actually seemed to be *bound* there somehow, as if it had been tied to something that was physically kept within that room. Was that possible? Could a being of spirit and energy be confined like that?

It had been possible during his ill-fated excursion into the world of the humans in the time of the First Crusade. The creatures had been imprisoned within the little copper boxes. They would be freed only if Peter the Hermit actually broke the spell binding them — which he had, so that several of them could travel with other armies than his own. That had been a mistake — as Peter had learned — for once released, there was no controlling them. Even the ones still bound to their containers would seize the opportunity to run amok when released temporarily.

That made another thought occur to him; this creature had actually felt familiar when he'd first encountered it. He had dismissed that feeling as nothing more than the reawakening of old memories. Now he wondered if he really had sensed the presence of an old adversary. Was it possible? Could this creature be one of the Salamanders that had *not* been released, one he knew? Could it still be tied to something physical? If that were true —

That would explain how the damned thing got over here. Most magical creatures cannot just buy a plane ticket, but they can invest themselves in a transportable object, which also gives them the advantage of a physical storage nexus for their power. That could be it. Hmm. The last time I saw those creatures they were spreading violence through the Middle East.

. . . which might partially explain why the Middle East was still, to this very day, a hotbed of violence, if the Salamanders were still there, still spreading their poison. . . .

If this creature has a physical tie, then I can do something about it. I can force it back into its prison, or I can dismiss it from this plane altogether!

He slid his back down along the wooden support-post until he was sitting on the cold concrete floor of the closet, his knees tucked up against his chest. He would have to probe very carefully. He did not dare catch the Salamander's attention; bound or not, it was still dangerous, and he was no match for it in a one-on-one fight.

He still didn't know if it truly *was* bound, either. Even if it was, there would only be a very limited window of opportunity for him to act against it. And he had to know *what* it was bound to.

He allowed his perception to move slowly through the electric lines, extended his probe into the room beyond, testing each object on the room for the peculiar magic resonances that had been on the Hermit's enchanted containers.

Nothing. Nothing again.

But wait. How about something quicker — searching for copper?

Still nothing.

There was nothing there but chairs, a little bit of audio-visual equipment. Nothing that could possible have "held" the Salamander, and certainly nothing that had any feeling of magic about it at all.

Wait a minute — what about on the stage?

He moved his perception to the circuits running the footlights, and "looked" out across the wooden platform. It seemed barren; it held only the podium, a single chair of peculiar construction, a flag —

He recoiled as he touched the Salamander's dark fire. *Blessed Danaa!*

The flag — no, the *flagpole* — radiated the peculiar dark power of the Salamander. There was no doubt, none at all. The creature was bound to the brass, sculptured flagpole.

I don't remember any flagpoles! Copper boxes, certainly, but no flagpoles —

Besides, the pole couldn't be more than a single century old. Two, at the most. And if there had been any human mages capable of imprisoning a Salamander these days, surely he would have heard about them; power like that couldn't be concealed in an age of so relatively few mages and so much communication.

There wasn't even anything of copper, which was the only metal that he recalled the Hermit using for his containers. Copper, not brass —

Brass. But brass is an alloy of copper, isn't it? Maybe it wasn't the shape that mattered, it was the metal. . . .

Blessed Danaa. What if someone found one of the boxes and used it for scrap? That must be it; someone smelted the damned thing down. They smelted it down and made . . . that.

He pulled all of his senses back, quickly, and sat quietly for a moment, calculating his next move. Now would be a very good time to call in an ally.

He closed his eyes again and reached out with his mind, but this time in an entirely different direction.

:Sarah?: he called, hoping he was doing so quietly enough to avoid the attention of the Salamander. *:Sarah? It's time — :*

• CHAPTER THIRTEEN

:Hush!: The little girl literally popped into the tiny closet out of nowhere, surprising Alinor into a start. *:I got Joe to run away. Don't call me like that! It's not listening for us now!:*

:I don't think it'll hear us,: Al replied, after a quick check. *:It's real busy with something.:*

:Jamie,: Sarah said angrily. *:It's getting ready for Jamie. It wants to kill him and take his body, and it can this time! Jamie's real sick — and I can't fight it off now, not when he can't help.:*

Al elected not to ask just how sick Jamie was; he couldn't do anything about it, and there was no point in worrying. If he succeeded in banishing the Salamander, Jamie would be with his mother by dawn. If he didn't, they'd both be beyond help.

:Sarah, what exactly happens when Brother Joseph calls the monster?: he asked. *:Describe it as closely as you can. I think there's going to be a point where you and I can stop this thing, but I have to know exactly what it does, and when.:*

She wasn't an image so much as a hazy shape, but he could tell she was thinking very hard. There was a kind of fuzzy concentration about the way she "looked." *:Well, he has to kind of get everybody all riled up.:*

:Yes, I saw that,: Al agreed. *:Does that anger make the monster stronger?:*

The image of a little girl strengthened as she nodded. *:I think so,:* she said. *:If he doesn't get them riled up enough, it can't come out of the door.:*

:Whoa, wait a minute: Al exclaimed. *:What door? What are you talking about?:*

She faded for a moment, as if he had startled her, but her image strengthened again immediately. :*What? Can't you see the door?*:

He thought quickly. :*Not that I recognize what you're talking about. Look, I'll try to stop interrupting you, and you tell me everything that happens, the way it happens, as if you were describing it to someone who hadn't seen it.*:

:*All right,*: she agreed. :*First he gets everybody all riled up. Then there's a kind of — door. It's kind of in the flagpole. The monster sort of opens the door and comes out, and that's when he's in this kind of world, where I am.*:

She seemed to be waiting for him to say something. :*The halfworld,*: he said, :*That's what elves call it. The place that's half spirit and half material.*: He thought for a minute. :*This door — is it kind of as if you were standing right at a wall, and somebody opened a door, and then the monster kind of unfolds out of it?*:

She brightened with excitement. :*That's it! That's exactly what it looks like!*:

So the Salamander was being confined in the flagpole, much as it had been confined in the copper box. Because there was no summoning spell involved, it required the energy of Brother Joseph's congregation to pry open the "door" of its confinement place.

:*Then what?*: he prompted.

:*Well, then the door goes shut again, and I don't think it can get back in until Brother Joseph lets it go again. So it stays there, and that's when it starts feeding on Brother Joseph. When it feeds enough on him, it can push Jamie out of his body and take over.*:

He chewed on his lip for a moment. He tasted blood and wrinkled his nose, remembering *now* why he'd started carrying packets of cookies around with him. It was a lot less painful to carry around a few cookies than it was to regrow lips and nails.

So, there was a moment, as he had hoped, when the Salamander had to feed before it could take over the boy, a moment when it was in the halfworld. Perhaps because there was no longer anyone who knew the summoning spell it could no longer enter the material world directly. In the spirit world of Underhill, it would be too powerful for him — in fact, it would probably be too powerful for anyone but a major mage, like Keighvin Silverhair or Gundar. In the material world, it would not only have the powers it possessed — fairly formidable ones — but it would have command of all of Brother Joseph's gun-toting ruffians.

But in the halfworld it was vulnerable. In fact, if he could *keep* it in the halfworld, blocked from power, it would probably starve away to a point where he could bottle it back into the flagstaff permanently.

:Sarah, can you protect Jamie from the thing if I keep it away from his body?: he asked. *:I promise I'll keep Jamie strong enough that the thing can't feed on him, but I need you to keep him safe from it.:*

:How?: she asked, promptly. *:I will if I can, but how?:*

Now He hesitated. *:The Salamander — the monster — can't kill you. It can hurt you, but it can't kill you. If you keep between it and Jamie, you can keep him safe —:*

:But it might hurt me?: She tossed her head defiantly. *:Well, maybe I can hurt it, too! And I will if I get the chance! Besides, Jamie hurts a whole lot worse than me.:*

:Sarah —: he hesitated again, deeply moved by her bravery. *:Sarah, you are the best friend anyone could ask for. I think you're pretty terrific.:*

The hazy form flushed a pleased, pale rose color. *:They're gonna start the Praise Meeting pretty soon,:* she warned. *:If you're gonna sneak in there, you'd better do it now.:*

:Thanks, I will.: He uncurled, slowly, flexing his muscles to loosen them. *:See you there?:*

There was a hint of childish giggle, and a cool breath of scent, like baby powder; the glow bent forward and brushed his cheek —

—like a little girl's kiss.

Then she was gone.

The room where the Praise Meeting was held had been constructed rather oddly. There were places, little niches, behind the red velvet curtains covering the back wall where a man could easily stand concealed and no one in the audience (or even on the stage for that matter) would know he was there. Al wasn't quite sure what they were there for. Were they some construction anomaly, an accident of building the place underground?

Probably not, he decided. The niches were too regular and spaced too evenly. They were probably there on purpose, places where helpers could be concealed to aid in stage magic tricks in case the "channeling" ever failed.

Or maybe they were there to hold backup guards in case the loyalty of any of the current guards ever came into question.

Whatever, Al was grateful that they were there, although his hiding place was so near to the Salamander's flagpole that he was nauseated. He managed to slip into place without attracting its attention and concentrated on making himself invisible to the arcane senses, as the first of the Chosen Ones began to trickle into the hall, avid to get good seats in the front row.

He couldn't see much; his hiding place was directly behind the chair he suspected they would use for Jamie, and he didn't want to chance attracting mundane attention by making the curtains move. But his hyper-acute hearing allowed him to pick up good portions of the conversation going on out in the audience, and the gist of it was that something special was supposed to happen at the channeling tonight. Brother Joseph had promised something really spectacular.

And — so one rumor went — the Guard had been placed on special alert. That rumor hinted that a confrontation with secular authorities was about to take place.

"Well, if they want a war, we'll show those ungodly bastards what it means to take on the Lord's Finest!" said one voice loudly, slurred a little with drink.

Al felt a chill of dread settling into the pit of his stomach. *A war —*

"Those godless bastards think they can come in here with the Red Army and march all over us! They think we'll lie right down, or maybe poison ourselves like Jim Jones' losers!" someone answered him, just as belligerently. "Well, they'll find out they haven't got the Lambs of God to deal with, they've got the Lions! When they come in, we'll be ready!"

This could only mean one thing. The Salamander *knew* about the plans to attack the compound, and just as he had feared, it had passed the warning on to Brother Joseph. But did it know when the raid would start? *Blessed Danaa — could it be tonight?*

Before he could even begin to add *that* to his calculations, the noise of a considerable crowd arriving and the sounds of boots marching up to the stage made any other considerations secondary in importance. He sensed the Salamander's rising excitement and knew by that sign that Brother Joseph had arrived to get the evening's spectacle underway.

He tensed and readied his first weapon of the night.

There was the scuffling of feet, and the sounds of two people doing something just in front of his position. He guessed that they were binding Jamie down in the chair, using the canvas straps he'd noted. That was all right; when the time came, those straps might just as well not be there for all that they were going to stop him.

Suddenly lights came on, penetrating even the thick velvet of the curtains, and the crowd noise faded to nothing but a cough or two.

"*My brothers and sisters, I am here tonight to give you news both grave and glorious.*" The voice rang out over the PA system, but from the timbre, Al sensed that even if Brother Joseph had not had the benefit of electronic amplification, his voice would *still* have resonated imposingly over his flock. The man might not be a *trained* speaker, but he was a practiced one.

"*The time the Holy Fire has warned us of is at hand! The time when the evils of all men shall be turned against us is near! Even now, the Forces of Darkness ready their men — and yes, brothers and sisters, I do not speak merely of the demons that have infested even my own son and sent him running to betray us to the ungodly!*"

There was a collective gasp at that, as if the news of Joe's defection came as a surprise to most of Brother Joseph's followers.

"*No, my Chosen Ones, I speak of* men, *men and machines — armed as we are armed with guns and bullets — but they are* not armored *as we are armored, with the strength of the Righteous and the Armor of the Lord! Say Halleluia!*"

A faltering echo of "Halleluia," answered him. Evidently the arrogant, belligerent attitude of those two early arrivals was not shared by the majority of the congregation. But Brother Joseph did not seem in the least disturbed by the lackadaisical response.

"*Yes, they plan to* fall *upon us, like* wolves *upon the sheep!*" he continued. "*But they do not* know *that the Holy Fire has warned us, even as the Virgin was warned to flee into Egypt, even as Lot was warned of the destruction of Sodom and Gomorra! Say Halleluia!*"

This time the chorus took on a little more strength. And it was very nearly time for Al to think about launching his first attack.

"*Yea, and the Holy Fire will tell us all, tonight, the time when the Army of Sin will seek to destroy the Holy! The Holy Fire will do* more *than that, I tell you! Tonight, the Holy Fire will take shape* and *walk among us, even as Christ Jesus took form*

*and walked among His Apostles when He had risen! Say Hal-
leluia!"*

This time the shout of "Halleluia!" was enough to
make the floor vibrate under Al's feet.

"The Holy Fire will lead *us to victory! The Holy Fire will be
our* guide *and our* General! *The form of this* boy *will be*
transformed *into the Chariot of God, the vehicle for the Voice
of God and the Sword of the Almighty! Say Halleluia,* thank
you Jesus!"

Cacophony ensued, and Al sensed that Brother
Joseph was about to turn the energy of the crowd from
positive to negative.

"And who are these Godless Enemies?" Brother Joseph
asked.

The response was a roar in which Alinor picked out
the words "Jew," "Communist," "Liberal," and
"Satanist," as the most frequent.

"And what do we do about them?"

Someone started a chant of "Kill, kill, kill," which was
quickly picked up by the rest, until the entire room —
probably the entire building — resonated with it. The
energy coming from them made Alinor shudder, even
though he was shielded from most of it.

And the Salamander was — literally — eating it up.
Al sensed that the creature was prying open its prison
from within. Like a man forcing a door open against a
heavy spring.

He's forcing it open against the binding spell, Al decided.
He needs the energy of the crowd to do it, as I thought.

He waited, as the Salamander slowly forced its way
out of its prison, opening a doorway into the halfworld,
bit by bit, until it stood free in the halfworld and moved
away from the flagpole —

:Now, Sarah!: Al "shouted," and cast the spell that
permitted him to "step" out of the physical world into
the halfworld. He placed himself squarely between the
Salamander and its home, before the creature was

even aware that he was there. As he got into place and launched a levin-bolt at the creature, Sarah flung herself between the Salamander and Jamie, covering him with her own insubstantial body.

The Salamander saw her just as Al's levin-bolt struck it from behind. It turned — its eyes were pits of fire, and its black body hunched as it snarled with rage and prepared to attack —

And Alinor cast the second spell he had readied. The one that reinforced Sarah's protections, bolstering her powers — sealing Jamie away from its reach.

As the Salamander lunged for him, he cast his third spell — reaching the absolute limits of his ability as a mage — and eluded it by a hair, stepping out of the halfworld and back into his hiding place behind the curtains, with scarcely a ripple in the cloth to mark his movement.

Weakness flooded through him, but he dared not pause, not even for a moment. Timing — that was going to be all of it.

Outside the curtains, Brother Joseph had no idea that anything was going wrong.

He was about to find out differently.

Thank Danaa this isn't spell-casting as such — The thought was fleeting; hardly noted as Al attacked the breaker boxes, fusing everything in sight, so that nothing would protect the lines beyond, and surging every circuit, every wire —

A full lightning strike couldn't have wreaked more havoc. Every bulb in the hall exploded in a shower of sparks — electricity arced from raw sockets and dozens of fires burst into existence as wires shorted out. The Salamander's energy-source fragmented as the crowd itself fragmented into a chaos of screaming, frightened humans, each one clawing for an exit and paying no attention to anything else. Now they showed their true colors, panicking, trampling over each other, ruled only by fear; a selfish fear that cried out from each wizened little soul that *he* was more important than anyone else here, that *he* should be saved—

Brother Joseph screamed at them, howled orders at them, but the sound system had died a fiery death with the first surge, and not even he could shout loud enough to be heard over the screams of his congregation.

Alinor took advantage of the chaos to dash aside the curtains and fling himself at Jamie's chair, pulling out the only physical weapon he'd brought with him, a silver-bladed knife. Jamie's guards had been the first to flee, and Brother Joseph was temporarily paying no attention to anything behind him. Alinor slashed through the straps holding Jamie to the chair; the boy started at the first touch, then stared at his rescuer in numb surprise. Not that Al blamed him; he wasn't wasting any energy on a disguising illusion.

"Sarah sent me," he said in the boy's ear, as he slashed the last of the bonds. He glanced briefly into the halfworld; with no energy-source to help it, with Sarah and Alinor protecting the boy in the halfworld and the physical world, there was only one logical place for the Salamander to go—back into its prison.

And once there, Alinor could see it got no further chance to escape until he delivered it to a greater mage than he; one who could scal it there for all time.

The Salamander had other ideas.

It shrank away from Sarah, the child-spirit incandescent with a cool power far beyond anything that Alinor had sent her, standing between it and its prey like an avenging angel. It didn't even try to confront her— but instead of leaping for the protection of its prison-home, it turned, snarling, and leapt in another direction entirely.

Straight for Jamie's father.

Alinor snatched the boy up and ran with him as the

Salamander made brutal contact and the drunkard's face and body convulsed. Where the Salamander had found the energy to make the leap into an unprepared, unsuitable body, Al didn't know — but he had to get Jamie away, and now, before anything else happened. Once Jamie was safe —

The fires were spreading; one whole corner of the hall was ablaze, giving more than enough light for Al to see his way to the exit with Jamie. He jumped over fallen chairs, kicking others out of the way, as he bullied his way through confused and terrified humans to the door that led to the outside corridor.

But suddenly someone blocked his path, deliberately. A man with a shaven head, in the Chosen Ones' uniform, stood in an attack position and brandished an enormous, unwieldy knife at him, blocking his way.

The man Al cared nothing for. His weapon, however — *Cold Iron* —

Al acted instinctively, without thinking, lashing out with his mind and throwing an illusion of nightmares straight into the man's thoughts, bargaining that he might be marginally sensitive. It worked better than he could have hoped, sending the man screaming to the ground, clutching at his head, howling that his brain was being eaten by serpents.

Alinor kicked him in the side as he passed, to ensure that he did not follow, felt the crunch of broken bones beneath his heel, and ran on.

He shoved his way through the last of the panicked Chosen Ones — old people, mostly, too frightened and bewildered to know where to go — but once he was out in the corridor leading to the bunker entrance he met with a new tide of humans, this time pushing and shoving their way *into* the depths of the underground building.

What —

The answer came with the muffled, staccato *crack* of

automatic weapons' fire just beyond the entrance. He shoved his way into the middle of the corridor just as an explosion blew the doors off the hinges and deafened him.

The people at the farthest end of the tunnel were flung into the air, backlit by the fires outside; they flew at him and hit the ground, in a curious time-dilation slow-motion. Those nearest him cowered away, hiding their faces in their arms. Jamie started and began shaking, but neither cried out nor hid his face.

The raid — great Danaa, they've started the raid —

His ears weren't working right, though he doubted the humans could hear anything at all. Explosions and the sound of gunfire came to him muffled, as if his head was bracket in pillows. He held the boy to his chest and forced his way through the crowd; it thinned quickly as noncombatants fled into the depths of the bunker.

He burst out into a scene straight from a war movie.

Fires roared everywhere; helicopters touched down and disgorged troops wearing SWAT team, DEA and FBI vests, who poured from the hatches and took cover. *They* didn't seem to be firing until they had sure targets; all the random gunfire was coming from sandbagged gun emplacements and the weaponry of the Guard, Junior and Senior.

One of the helicopters hovered overhead, flooding the area with light from a rack of lamps attached on the side. And in the light, Al caught a flash of familiar color — something that didn't belong in this chaos of camouflage and khaki.

A red jumpsuit.

Bob!

The mechanic wasn't that far away, thank the gods. He dashed across the open space between himself and the chopper, praying that the invaders would see he was carrying a child and that he was unarmed, and would hold their fire. Bob recognized him as he was halfway across and ran to meet him. He thrust the child into Bob's arms before the human could get a word out.

"Get him out of here!" Al shouted — and before Bob could grab his arm, he turned and ran back in the direction he had come.

He had unfinished business to attend to.

But the unfinished business was coming to him.

He sensed his enemy's approach before he saw it — then saw, as the Salamander emerged, that his enemies were two, not one. Jamie's father emerged from the mouth of the bunker and beside him was Brother Joseph with something long and sharp in his hands. The drunk's expression had completely changed, his eyes pits of fire, his face no longer remotely human.

So much for James Chase. He was half brain-dead already, from the alcohol; it must have been easy for the Salamander to take him.

The preacher spotted Al first and pointed, his mouth opening in a shout Al couldn't hear. But the Salamander did; its mouth twisted in a snarl, and it made a lashing motion with its arms —

And the razor-wire surrounding the compound came to life, writhing against its supports, trying to reach Alinor. He backpedaled into the temporary safety of a helicopter, but the stuff was still coming, and if it bound him —

A hellish noise right beside him pounded him into the dirt, as the door-gunner in the chopper let loose a barrage against a trio of gunmen that caught Jim Chase and cut him in half. Brother Joseph must have seen the gunner take aim; he hit the dirt in time to save himself, but Jamie's father had only seconds to live —

Seconds were enough for the Salamander.

As another munitions dump exploded on the far side of the compound, light flared and danced around the two men, one dying, one alive — and when it faded, the Salamander glared at Al from out of Brother Joseph's eyes.

The man's eyes swept the space between them and found him, stabbed him. This time Alinor did not run from the challenge. He faced it; walked slowly toward it, oblivious to the gunfire around him, to the explosions as one of the munitions dumps went up in the near distance, a giant blossom of orange flame. None of that could touch him now — not in this moment. There was only one enemy that mattered. The Salamander: ancient as he, perhaps more so — and his enemy since the moment he'd first seen it.

:Al!: Sarah's voice rang inside his head, although he didn't sense her anywhere in the chaos. *:Jamie's safe!:*

That was all he needed. There was one thing he had not yet tried with the beast to defeat it — and it was now, or see the thing loose in the world again, jumping from host to host like any parasite, bringing rage and chaos wherever it went. This fragile world could bear no more of that —

The monster was hanging back for some reason — *Waiting for more power?*

Well, then, he'd give it power. He'd cram power down the damned thing's throat until it choked!

He rushed it; the monster wasn't expecting *that* and tried to elude him, but he grappled with it. It reverted to its old ways and tried to manipulate him as it manipulated the humans, but this time instead of fighting it, Al let it happen. The Salamander infused him with anger, but it could not direct that anger, and in a sudden surge of rage-born strength, Al tore the flagpole from its hands.

And with the pole in his hands — he *knew* what it was. Not just a prison, but a *ground*, a focal point for the Salamander's hold on the physical world.

And any ground could be shorted out.

I've learned *how electricity works, and magic and*

electricity are related in every important way. Only you *don't know that, do you, monster? Come on, give me all you've got, you're getting it back!*

Again, he did not think, he simply acted; linking into every power source available to him, whether the physical fire, the arcing electrical current —

:*Here!*: Sarah cried, and a new source of power surged into him, a power so pure, clean, and strong he did not want to think of what its source might be —

He plunged the staff into the Salamander's chest — and the creature laughed, for how could he expect to harm it with its own ground? He held to his end of the flagpole as the Salamander closed both hands about the other end and opened itself up to drain him of power.

And the moment it opened itself, Alinor leaped back and poured every bit of power he had available *into* it.

The staff shattered as the massed electricity of the compound's power grid arced into it; the Salamander convulsed, its mouth gaping in surprise, and Al loosed the magical power Sarah was channeling into the raw wound.

Its mouth formed the word "No!" but it never got a chance to utter it. Its eyes glared like a fire's last glowing coal, defiant before its death, and between one breath and the next — it vaporized.

Brother Joseph fell to the ground, hardly recognizable as human, a burnt and twisted human cinder. The last charred sliver of the staff dropped beside him.

As Al stood there numbly, a bullet ricocheted off the building nearest him and buzzed past his ear, startling him into life. He glanced around; the Good Guys seemed to be winning, but there was no reason why *he* had to stay around to help —

A hint of movement on the other side of the fence gave him enough warning to ready himself; in the next moment, Andur launched himself over the tangle of wire and slid to a halt beside him. He grabbed a double-handful of mane and hauled himself aboard as another bullet buzzed by, much too close for comfort. He watched a SWAT officer level a pistol at him, then lower it, amazed — then Andur was off like a shadow beneath the moon, leaving the noises and fire far behind. . . .

All Al really wanted to to was get back and into a bed, any bed — but he reached back and touched one mind in all the chaos.

I was never there. You never saw me. Bob ran in and rescued you. It was all Bob. . . .

Then he allowed himself to slump over Andur's neck.

"Hey, Norris!"

Alinor looked up from beneath the hood of the car to see one of the Firestone boys waving at him.

"Yeah?" he said, standing up and wiping his hands on a rag. "What's up?"

"There's a cop here, he's looking for a mech named Al. Big blond guy, says he wears black a lot. Know anybody like that?" The Firestone pitman eyed Al's scarlet Nomex jumpsuit and raven hair with amusement.

"Not around here," Al said truthfully. "The head of Fairgrove looks like that, but he never leaves Savannah." *And that'll teach you for not answering my aid-calls, Keighvin Silverhair.*

"Well, he's with Bob, so I guess it must be something about the raid on those fundie nuts they pulled the other night." His curiosity satisfied, the pitman turned back to his stack of tires, and Al returned to his engine. He was paying only scant attention to it, however; most of his attention was taken up with the four humans heading for the pits.

Frank Casey didn't know it, but the moment he'd passed out of Alinor's sight, Al's appearance and name had been altered. And in the stories he'd told the rest of the crews, the actions that should have been ascribed to Al had mostly been attached to Bob — with the exception of those few that could not logically have been transferred. *Those* Al left alone, taking on a new persona, entirely, of Norris Alison. The story was that Al had gotten into the Chosen Ones' compound and sabotaged their electrical system, giving the impromptu army good cover for their invasion. Then he had somehow slipped past the sentries outside and had vanished.

Bob's *other* partner, the sable-haired "Norris," had shown up the next morning, after Bob supposedly called for extra help on "Al's" disappearance.

Cindy's memories had been altered, though not without much misgiving on Al's part. He hated to do it, but the memory of her discovery of Alinor's species had been temporarily blocked. The not-so-surprising result was that her growing emotional attachments to both Al and Bob had been resolved into a very significant attachment to Bob alone. And now that Bob was the sole rescuer of her child —

Al sighed. *Well, he certainly seems to be enjoying his new status.* His loss was Bob's gain . . . and Cindy *was* mortal; he was her kind. There would be no conflict there.

If anything more permanent ever comes of this, he promised himself, *I'll take the block off her real memories. By then she'll have learned about us all over again, and she'll know why I had to take them.*

Frank Casey wore the look of a very frustrated man as he searched pit row for someone who didn't exist. Finally he gave up and allowed Bob to bring them all over to the Firestone pit for a cold drink.

Al waited while Bob fished soft drinks out of the cooler, watching Jamie out of the corner of his eye. This was the boy's first day out of the hospital, and although he was still painfully thin, he had some of a child's proper liveliness back. When they had all been served, he stood up and sauntered over himself, pulling out a Gatorade before turning to face the others.

"Miz Chase," he said, tugging the brim of his cap. "Well, so this is the little guy, hmm?"

Cindy nodded, and Jamie peered up at him, a little frown line between his eyebrows, as if he was trying to see something and having trouble doing so.

"I don't know if Bob told you, but we're all through here after the race tomorrow. We'll be packing up and heading back. Did you have any plans?" Then, before she could react to what could only be bad news, he added, "You're welcome to come along, of course, if you've nowhere you need to go. We can tow your car, and the boy can sleep or play in the RV. You, well, we could use another driver to switch off with. Our boss, Kevin — well, he might maybe need another hand in the office. If he don't, likely one of the test drivers can dig up a job. Tannim's got a thumb in about everything."

She hesitated for only a moment before saying, with a shy glance at Bob, "If you really don't mind, I think I'd like that. There isn't that much for me in Atlanta except the house —"

"Can always sell it," he suggested.

Then he turned away as if he had lost interest in the conversation, pausing only long enough to drop his race-cap over Jamie's head. The boy lit up with a smile that rivaled the Oklahoma sun and ran to his mother.

The quartet drifted away after a final futile effort to find "Al," and before too very long, the rest of the crew departed in search of dinner and a nap before the long night to come of last-minute race-preps. The only sounds in the pit were those of reggae on a distant radio, cooling metal, an errant breeze —

But suddenly Al had the feeling that he was being watched.

He turned abruptly.

For a moment there was nothing behind him at all — then, there was a stirring in the air, a glimmer — and there was Sarah, watching him with a serious look on her face.

:I've come to say good-bye,: she said solemnly. *:Jamie doesn't need me, and all the Chosen Ones are in jail, so I have to go.:*

He nodded gravely. "I understand," he told her. "You were a very brave fighter out there, you know. A true warrior. I was proud to be on your side."

She looked wistfully at him. *:You're nice,:* she said. *:I wish I could say good-bye right.:*

It might have been that exposure to the Salamander made him more sensitive; it might simply have been that her lonely expression told him everything he needed to know about what she meant by "saying good-bye right."

Well, after all, he *was* one of the Folk.

He triggered the spell and moved into the halfworld with her.

She clapped both her hands to her mouth in surprise and delight. *:Oh!:* she exclaimed — and then she ran to him.

He held out his arms and caught her, holding her, hugging her for a long, timeless moment, trying to make up for all the hugs that she had never gotten. He thought she might be crying; when she pulled away, wiping away tears, he came near to tears himself.

:I have to go,: she said. *:I love you.:*

She faded away, or rather, faded *into* something, into a softer, gentle version of that blinding Power she had been linked with when she protected Jamie and helped him. Alinor wasn't certain he could put a name to that Power. He wasn't certain that he needed to.

"I love you, too, Sarah," he replied, as the last wisp of her melted away.

He waited a moment longer, smiling in the last light

of her passing until he was alone in the halfworld, and finally sighed and triggered the magic to take him back.

With his feet firmly planted on mortal cement, he pulled the windblown hair from his face, packed up his tool kit and headed back to the RV.

After all, there was a race left to run.

Hundreds of children are abducted in this country every year, many by non-custodial parents. We see their faces peering at us from billboards, milk cartons, and on the back of junk-mail ads. The question is: do these pathetic photos work?

The answer is yes. The reason is because of ordinary people, teachers, neighbors, or just passersby, who see something odd in the behavior of a parent and child, and *call*. There are several agencies responsible for helping to find missing children: here are the numbers of two.

CHILD FIND:
1-800-292-9688
MISSING CHILDREN'S HELP CENTER:
1-800-872-5437

Child abuse, whether parental or with parental consent, is *wrong*. Children deserve love, tenderness and reasonable discipline. They do *not* deserve to be beaten, tied up, starved, abandoned, used or misused. There are several groups trying to help children who are mistreated: here is the number of one.

CHILD HELP NATIONAL CHILD ABUSE HOTLINE:
1-800-422-4453

You don't need elves or magic to get a start on helping a child in a desperate situation — you don't even need a quarter. Most pay-phones allow you to call 1-800 numbers completely free of charge, simply by dialing them as written. All you need to start a child back to a decent life is the willingness to get involved.

•

From High Flight and Baen Books

Mercedes Lackey　　　　　*Jim Baen*
Larry Dixon　　　　　*Toni Weisskopf*
Mark Shepherd
Holly Lisle

MERCEDES LACKEY

The Hottest Fantasy Writer Today!

URBAN FANTASY

Knight of Ghosts and Shadows with Ellen Guon

Elves in L.A.? It would explain a lot, wouldn't it? Eric Banyon is a musician with a lot of talent but very little ambition—and his lady just left him lovelorn in a deserted corner of the Renaissance Fairegrounds, singing the blues and playing his flute. He couldn't have known the desperate sadness of his music would free Korendil, a young elven noble, from the magical prison he has been languishing in for centuries. Eric really needed a good cause to get his life in gear—now he's got one. With Korendil he must raise an army to fight against the evil lord who seeks to conquer all of California. And Eric's music will show the way....

Summoned to Tourney with Ellen Guon

Elves in San Francisco? Where else would an elf go when L.A. got too hot? All is well there with our elf-lord, his human companion and the mage who brought them all together—until it turns out that San Francisco is doomed to fall off the face of the continent. Doomed that is, unless our mage can summon the Nightflyers, the soul-devouring shadow creatures from the dreaming world—creatures no one on Earth could possibly control....

Born to Run with Larry Dixon

There are elves out there. And more are coming. But even elves need money to survive in the "real" world. The good elves in South Carolina, intrigued by the thrills of stock car racing, are manufacturing new, light-weight engines (with, incidentally, very little "cold" iron); the bad elves run a kiddie-porn and snuff-film ring, with occasional forays into drugs. *Children in Peril—Elves to the Rescue.* (Part of the SERRAted Edge series.)

HIGH FANTASY
Bardic Voices: The Lark & The Wren
Rune could be one of the greatest bards of her world, but the daughter of a tavern wench can't get much in the way of formal training. So one night she goes up to play for the Ghost of Skull Hill. She'll either fiddle till dawn to prove her skill as a bard—or die trying....

Also by Mercedes Lackey:
Reap the Whirlwind with C.J. Cherryh
Part of the Sword of Knowledge series.

Castle of Deception with Josepha Sherman
Based on the bestselling computer game, *The Bard's Tale*.

The Ship Who Searched with Anne McCaffrey
The Ship Who Sang is not alone!

Wheels of Fire with Mark Shepherd
Book II of the SERRAted Edge series.

To join the Mercedes Lackey national fan club send a self-addressed, stamped, business-size envelope to: Queen's Own, P.O. Box 43143, Upper Montclair, NJ 07043.

Available at your local bookstore. If not, fill out this coupon and send a check or money order for the cover price to Baen Books, Dept. BA, P.O. Box 1403, Riverdale, NY 10471.

KNIGHT OF GHOSTS AND SHADOWS with Ellen Guon •
   69885-0 • $4.99   _____

SUMMONED TO TOURNEY with Ellen Guon •
   72122-4 • $4.99   _____

BORN TO RUN with Larry Dixon • 72110-0 • $4.99   _____

BARDIC VOICES: THE LARK & THE WREN •
   72099-6 • $4.99   _____

REAP THE WHIRLWIND with C.J. Cherryh •
   69846-X • $4.99   _____

CASTLE OF DECEPTION with Josepha Sherman •
   72125-9 • $5.99   _____

THE SHIP WHO SEARCHED with Anne McCaffrey •
   72129-1 • $5.99   _____

WHEELS OF FIRE with Mark Shepherd • 72138-0 • $4.99 _____

NAME: _____

ADDRESS: _____

_____

I have enclosed a check or money order in the amount of $_____

ELIZABETH MOON

THE DEED OF PAKSENARRION

Anne McCaffrey on Elizabeth Moon:

"She's a damn fine writer. The Deed of Paksenarrion is fascinating. I'd use her book for research if I ever need a woman warrior. I know how they train now. We need more like this."

By the Compton Crook Award winning author of the Best First Novel of the Year

Sheepfarmer's Daughter
65416-0 • 512 pages • $3.95 _____

Divided Allegiance
69786-2 • 528 pages • $3.95 _____

Oath of Gold
69798-6 • 512 pages • $3.95 _____

Available at your local bookstore, or send this coupon and the cover price(s) to Baen Books, Dept. BA, P.O. Box 1043, Riverdale, NY 10471.